SKELETON BLUES

SKELETON BLUES

A Quint Dalrymple Mystery

Paul Johnston

This first world edition published 2016
in Great Britain and the USA by
SEVERN HOUSE PUBLISHERS LTD of
19 Cedar Road, Sutton, Surrey, England, SM2 5DA.
Trade paperback edition first published
in Great Britain and the USA 2016 by
SEVERN HOUSE PUBLISHERS LTD

British Library Cataloguing in Publication Data

Johnston, Paul, 1957- author.
  Skeleton blues. – (A Quint Dalrymple mystery)
  1. Dalrymple, Quintilian (Fictitious character)–Fiction.
  2. Murder–Investigation–Fiction. 3. Referendum–
  Scotland–Fiction. 4. Edinburgh (Scotland)–Fiction.
  5. Suspense fiction.
  I. Title II. Series
  823.9'2-dc23

ISBN-13: 978-0-7278-8578-4 (cased)
ISBN-13: 978-1-84751-687-9 (trade paper)
ISBN-13: 978-1-78010-743-1 (e-book)

All Severn House titles are printed on acid-free paper.

Severn House Publishers support the Forest Stewardship Council™ [FSC™],
the leading international forest certification organisation.
All our titles that are printed on FSC certified paper carry the FSC logo.

MIX
Paper from
responsible sources
FSC
www.fsc.org   FSC® C013056

Typeset by Palimpsest Book Production Ltd.,
Falkirk, Stirlingshire, Scotland.
Printed and bound in Great Britain by
TJ International, Padstow, Cornwall.

To Alan,
Shake them boney blues, bro

Acknowledgements

Many thanks to Edwin Buckhalter, Kate Lyall Grant and their excellent team for getting Quint out of his wicker coffin again.

To my superb agent Broo Doherty of the DHH Literary Agency, a large measure of guardian issue single malt.

And boundless gratitude to the family and friends who've kept me going.

Prologue

Edinburgh, February 2034. Winter died early and went to heaven. Spring, descending, gave it the finger. The sky was blue and cloudless, the wind's fangs had been pulled and not even a single haar rolled in from the firth. Last summer the city endured the Big Wet, not that the tourists noticed. The central zone is well equipped with awnings and covered pavements, so they could go from marijuana café to casino to sex show without ruining their hairdos. The locals were used to perma-damp, thanks to the Supply Directorate's absorbent hats, holey hoods and umbrellas that disintegrate in the lightest breeze.

The Council of City Guardians was pleased. The first vote in thirty-one years would benefit from the balmy weather. Campaigning would be easier and the turnout would be high, announced the *Edinburgh Guardian* and the local radio stations. Of course the turnout would be high – voting was compulsory unless you were on your death-bed. Citizens laughed and shook their heads. The auxiliaries who ran the city hid their embarrassment behind regulation stone faces. I just listened to the blues, thankfully no longer banned. Lead Belly's 'The Bourgeois Blues' hit the spot in a city that supposedly doesn't have class distinctions. Then again, so did Big Bill Broonzy's 'Just a Dream' – a dream of democracy . . .

I knew from the start that independent Edinburgh would struggle to rejoin the nation it had left. To be fair, there was no Scotland after 2003, just warring regions and gangs of headbangers. What I didn't know was just how screwed up the city-states and districts that fancied flying the saltire were, Edinburgh included.

I'd have been better off composing the 'Skeleton Blues' on my battered six-string and howling the lyrics in the watches of the night. This here's a protest song.

One

I was in the archives when I got the text message. It read, 'Major case. Where u?' My friend Davie never bothers writing his name and the cheap phone I'd been issued with didn't run to caller ID. I knew it was him, though. He was the City Guard commander in charge of violent crime and he frequently called on me, despite the fact that his boss thought I was a troublemaker. I tried my best.

'Busy on case,' I replied. 'Suck off.' The Council came down hard on swearing, though it claimed not to monitor mobiles. Anyway, it was true. I'd been taken on by the newly constituted Electoral Services Department to help with the voters' roll. A lot of citizens had illicitly left the city in recent months, doubtless convinced the referendum would change nothing.

'Murder,' came the reply. 'Guardian worried.'

That piqued my interest. For an investigator there's nothing like a murder and, for me, an anxious guardian was a bonus. I told Davie where I was and gathered up my papers.

A few minutes later a white 4×4 in City Guard markings pulled up outside what had been the main library when I was young.

'Busy on case,' he scoffed, as I got in. 'Someone lost their canary?' He executed a U-turn on George IV Bridge, scattering citizens on bicycles and getting a dead-eyed stare from a bus driver.

'You'd be surprised how many missing-pets cases I've been getting since the Council reversed the ban on them.'

Davie glanced at me. 'You're joking.'

'No, I'm not. Last week I traced a newt to the pond at—'

'Arsehole.'

'Charming.' I grabbed my seat as he took a hard left on to the Royal Mile, the Guard personnel manning the checkpoint having swiftly raised the barrier. 'So what's this murder?'

'Wait and see,' he said, with a grin.

'Let me guess. Auxiliary?'

'No.'

'Ordinary citizen?'

'No.'

'What, then? Something in the zoo? A peccary?'

'A what? No, much worse.'

'Than a peccary?'

'Piss off, Quint.' Davie pulled up on the esplanade outside the castle and we walked between the statues of Wallace and Bruce that stand guard at the gate.

'Are you really not going to tell me?'

'Can't. The guardian wants to brief you personally.'

'Don't tell me he's signed off on my involvement.'

'He didn't have a choice.'

My stomach somersaulted. 'It's never a tourist.'

'Got it in four.'

He kept his mouth shut till we reached the Governor's House, which had been the public order guardian's quarters for decades.

'Weeks till the referendum and one of the city's precious paying visitors is killed?'

'Try not to look so happy.'

I did what I could.

The public order guardian was in his fifties, but he looked twenty years younger. Then again, he was only appointed eight months ago and the cares of office hadn't got to him yet. Or maybe they just had.

'Ah, Dalrymple.'

'Call me, Quint.' Pause. 'Jim.'

He gave me a cold stare. 'James, if you must.' In theory even guardians could be addressed by their first names these days, but they didn't like it.

'So, you've got a dead tourist on your hands, James.'

The guardian glared at Davie.

'I had to attract his attention somehow,' my friend said defensively.

'Very well. You understand this is confidential, Dalrymple.'

'It's not the first time I've handled a tourist murder.' I cast my mind back. 'Though it's been fourteen years. Usually they're citizens and auxiliaries.'

James Michie, tall and well built though nothing like as solid as Davie, handed me a paper file marked 'Guardian Eyes Only'.

'You're not to take that out of this office.' He sat down and ran a hand over his curly brown hair. 'And spare me your customary suspicions that the city's servants are responsible.'

'You've heard how much I love auxiliaries?' Since he was appointed, there hadn't been a murder in the city – at least one that was deemed worthy of my attention. 'Do you know how many guardians and their subordinates I've found with dirty hands over the years?'

'Do you keep a count?' Michie asked acidly.

'I don't have the time.'

Davie applied his boot to my right calf.

'Never mind about that,' I said, opening the file. I took in the salient details and handed it back.

The guardian looked surprised. 'Is that it?'

'I prefer to view the body and the scene with as few preconceptions as possible.'

'I see. What else do you need?'

'The commander here.'

'Very well.'

'And an authorization enabling me to—'

'Question anyone in the city, including guardians. I know.' He gave me a plastic-covered card.

'The service here is much improved,' I observed.

'I believe you still have a mobile phone,' Michie said. 'Although you should have returned it with your last authorization.'

'Slipped my mind,' I said, looking out the window. I could see across the water to Fife. 'I take it you'll want me to attend the Council meeting this evening.'

'You take it correctly.'

We then took our leave.

'You don't have to be such a smartarse,' Davie said, as we walked down to the esplanade. 'Oh, I forgot. You do.'

'You expect me to kowtow to a prick like Jimmy Michie?'

'He's not a prick. He's good at his job.'

'Uh-huh.'

'You take the piss out of guardians on principle, Quint.'

'Wrong. In this case I was taking the mickey.'

'Ha fucking ha. Someone's been murdered.'

'I haven't forgotten. I'm trying to keep my mind off it till I see what happened.'

We got into the 4×4 and he set off at his usual breakneck speed. The tourist zone didn't look any different from usual, but as soon as we passed the checkpoint on Dundas Street the referendum took centre stage. There were Council posters encouraging people to vote 'yes', and banners and posters from the various parties involved, almost all of them demanding that people vote to join the newly reconstituted Scotland that was supported by almost all the currently independent states – Glasgow, Aberdeen, most of the highlands and islands, Perth, Fife and so on. Our own Council wanted a 'yes' vote to share in the wealth of democratic Glasgow – a world leader in both digital technology and fashion – and in the oil and gas that had been found off the north-west coast. The guardians' aim was to stay in power with minimal changes to what they thought was a benevolent dictatorship, at the same time as benefiting from the union. It wasn't clear how a future Scotland would work, but some kind of federalization was on the board.

Davie took two right turns and stopped in a cul-de-sac.

'Eyre Terrace,' I said. 'How did a tourist end up here?'

'I thought you were keeping an open mind.'

'Just thinking aloud, guardsman.'

'Commander.'

'Jackass.'

There were two more Guard 4×4s in the street.

'Subtle,' I said.

'I told the buggers to keep a low profile.' Davie stormed over to a guardswoman who was leaning against the nearest vehicle.

'Second floor,' I said, when he came back.

'I know, dung for brains.'

'What was her excuse?'

'Didn't you recognize the 4×4? The medical guardian's here.'

I might have known that Sophia, my supposedly secret lover, wouldn't have been able to keep away.

We found the scene-of-crime team packing up when we got to the second-floor flat.

'Afternoon, citizen,' said the man in charge. I'd run into him often at sites of violent death. 'We're finished. The medical guardian's people will take the body to the infirmary.'

'You still won't call me Quint, will you, Andy?'

He narrowed his eyes. 'Raeburn 297 to you, citizen. You were demoted.'

Some Guard personnel have never got over that, even though I left the Guard in 2015 on my request and demotions have been forgiven – one of the Council's many attempts to make the 'perfect' city more user-friendly.

'Anything you have a burning desire to tell me?' I asked, knowing what the reply would be.

'My report will be in before the Council meeting.'

'Wonderful.' I wanted to see things for myself, but scene-of-crimes people can speed the process up – though they can also mislead, intentionally or otherwise.

'The body's in the bedroom,' Raeburn 297 said. 'Quint.'

I laughed, then looked around the living room. It was a standard two-bedroom citizen's place, though the curtains – some kind of red plush – were unusual and definitely not from the Supply Directorate. The sofa and armchair were newer and more comfortable than mine, though that wasn't difficult.

'The named resident is one Clarinda Towart,' Davie said.

'Did she find the body?'

'No, she hasn't been seen today, either here or at her work. I've distributed her photo and description to all barracks.'

'Let's have a look.' He handed me his file. The unusually named Clarinda was blonde, thirty-four and very attractive. 'She's in the Prostitution Services Department.'

'Aye. Normally to be found in the Waverley Hotel.' That was the city's most expensive tourist establishment.

'What was she doing bringing a client home?'

'If that's what happened. Good question.'

'Thanks, sidekick. We'll follow it up after we view the body. Who reported it, then?'

'Anonymous phone call to the command centre at 11.58 a.m. Male voice, muffled.'

I heard footsteps in the other room.

'What are you waiting for?' said Sophia McIlvanney.

'Medical guardian,' Davie said respectfully.

'Are you coming in or not?' she said, eyeing us impatiently. 'I do have other duties.'

I resisted the temptation to call her 'darling'. Just.

'Good afternoon to you, too.' I'd last seen her two nights ago. She had been tender then, but that wasn't her default mode when she was working.

We followed her into the bedroom. There was a strong smell of excrement. An oriental man with light brown skin was lying face up on the floor. He was naked, his arms and legs open wide. It was hard to judge his age as he was completely bald.

'Cause of death was strangulation,' Sophia said, pointing to the deep red furrow on his throat. 'Ligature, thin strip of leather half an inch wide – the technicians have it. Time of death between two and four last night, I'm estimating. The post-mortem may narrow that down.'

I kneeled down beside the dead man. 'No watch.'

'Stolen, probably. His clothes are gone too.'

I waited for her to continue. She wasn't fond of interruptions.

'No evidence of sexual activity – no condom either. There's no obvious marking on the body apart from—'

'The bruise on his sternum, suggesting that the killer held him down by one or both knees.'

'Correct,' she said tartly. 'Of course, it's easier to garotte from behind.'

'Maybe this killer likes looking in his victim's eyes,' said Davie.

'A pleasant thought.' I looked back at Sophia. 'Did you find any ID?'

'Yes,' she confirmed. 'Raeburn 297 has it. I didn't catch his name, but the victim's Malaysian.'

'Chung Keng Quee,' Davie supplied. 'I've got a guardswoman checking what the Tourism Directorate knows about him.'

I looked around the bedroom. The walls had been painted scarlet and the bedclothes were a similar colour and silk, as far as I could tell.

Sophia was watching me. 'Yes, silk. This has the characteristics of a bawdy house.'

That made me laugh. 'Have you been reading historical novels?'

Spots of red appeared on her cheeks. 'I suppose you'd call it a knocking shop.'

'Whatever it is, it shouldn't be for tourists.' I turned to Davie. 'We'll need to ask the checkpoints, not just the nearest one, if anyone of the victim's description was let through.'

He nodded and went into the living room to make calls.

'Well, this is nice,' I said, moving closer to Sophia.

She stepped away. 'You do know that Malaysia is a major player in the Far East and one of the city's best sources of high-paying tourists?'

'Actually, yes. Presumably that's why Michie's got me on the job. When will you have the p-m results?' She recently started doing autopsies again to keep her eyes and hands in; previously she'd concentrated on directorate administration and policy.

'Before the Council meeting.'

'Can you brief me first? I don't want to go in there with just my dick in my hand.'

She slapped my face, not very hard. 'You know I don't like that kind of language.'

'It's a quote,' I said, keeping my distance. 'Well, a paraphrase. From *The Godfather*.'

She looked at me blankly.

'Seminal 1970s gangster film.' The Council had allowed citizens to see many previously banned movies as part of its 'look how good we are to you' drive a few years ago. That didn't mean its own members watched them.

Sophia shook her head. 'Popular culture is a waste of time.'

'Not of mine.'

She pressed buttons on her mobile and ordered paramedics to pick the body up.

'I'll see you later, Quint,' she said.

'If you're lucky.'

She raised her hand, but then gave me a sweet smile.

Victory.

'Getting anywhere?' I asked Davie.

'The night squads from all the north-side checkpoints have been told to go to the castle. If they don't have anything, I'll get all the others up.'

'Taxis?'

'They aren't allowed outside the central zone with tourists.' He scowled.

'Unless—'

'Extra money changed hands. I doubt you'll get anyone to own up to that.'

'Their numbers will have been registered at the checkpoints, even if the passenger managed to . . .' He broke off when he realized that Guard personnel could have been bribed too. 'Shit!'

'Quite. Any news on the unusually named Clarinda Towart?'

'No.'

'Hasn't anyone noticed that the victim's missing from the Waverley?'

'The maid reported that the "Do Not Disturb" sign was on the handle. I've got a man on the door.'

'We'd better get up there, then.'

We headed out.

'Anyone spoken to the neighbours?'

'The guardian told me not to.'

I sighed. We'd been down this road often in the past. The Council was very keen on discretion. As if the locals wouldn't have noticed the Guard vehicles in the street.

'He didn't tell *me* though,' I said, stepping across the landing.

The scuffed black door opened a second after I knocked.

'City Guard,' I said, allowing Davie to lour over the short thin man in a grey singlet. 'Can we come in, please?'

'Ah ken you,' the citizen said, blinking. 'You're Dalrymple, that detective guy.'

'But Ah don't ken you,' I said, smiling to put him at his ease.

'Charlie Dixon,' he said, stepping back and ushering us in. 'You'll have tae excuse the mess. Since ma wife died . . .' The words trailed away.

'Sorry to hear that,' I said. 'Recently?'

'Aye, last month. They cut aff both her breasts, but it wus too late.'

'I'm very sorry, Charlie,' I said, motioning to Davie to keep his distance.

The living room was in a hell of a state, clothes hanging off the furniture and dirty plates on the table, chairs and floor.

'You should be able to get help from the Social Services Department.'

'Och, Ah cannae be bothered.'

'Davie, will you call them?' If the commander was irritated by the request, he didn't show it.

Charlie cleared a space for me on a less than pristine chair. He sat down opposite, failing to notice that he was crushing a copy of the *Edinburgh Guardian*. Best thing for it.

'Can you tell me anything about the woman opposite?'

He looked up at me blearily. I'd noticed several empty bottles of citizen-issue whisky around the place.

'Lady Clarinda?' he said bitterly, scratching his stubble with long fingernails. 'Thinks she walks on water, that yin does. She always treated Linda like durt. Ah dinnae speak tae her.'

'Do you know what she does?'

'Obvious, isn't it? She's a fancy woman. One o' they that whores themselves for the city.'

I shared his disgust. The Council should have stopped providing prostitutes of both sexes to tourists years ago, but they were a major source of income.

'Have you ever seen her with a client, Charlie?'

His eyes widened. 'Whit, doon here? She's in one ae the big hotels. Besides, tourists arenae allowed oot o' the zone, and you wouldnae see her wi' an ordinary citizen.' He caught my eye. 'Here, whit's happened? What are they Guard cars doin' in the road? There hasnae been a murdur?'

'What makes you say that?'

'Only . . . Ah heard a right racket last night. Shoutin' and screamin', mustae been aboot two in the mornin'.'

'Clarinda?'

Charlie thought about that.

'Dinnae ken. Didnae sound like her. One o' the voices was pretty shrill though.'

'And she's shrill?'

'Oh aye. Break yer eardrums easy. Linda used tae tell her tae shut up, but that just made her wurse.' He sobbed suddenly. 'Ach, Linda.'

I got up. 'You didn't hear a taxi in the street last night? Or any other vehicle?'

He stayed where he was. 'Naw, son. I was drinkin' the pish the Supply Directorate calls whisky. The yellin' woke me up then I passed oot again.'

I turned away and saw Davie nod.

'Social Services will be down to help, citizen,' he said.

Charlie didn't answer. He was too deep in his grief.

Before we headed for the hotel, we checked with the other neighbours. None of them had a good word for Clarinda, but none had heard anything – or they weren't saying; so we didn't tell them about the body. The Council would be impressed by our discretion.

Two

I flashed my authorization at the grey-haired manager of the Waverley, not that it was necessary. She knew me of old.

'You'll be wanting Mr Chung's keycard, citizen.'

'I will, Muriel.'

'Try not to scare the guests,' she said, glancing at Davie. 'It's room 435.'

I took the card. 'Anything about Mr Chung attract attention?'

'I've asked my people. He's been here for a week. Seems to have been a quiet type.'

'Any special services provided?'

She knew what I meant. 'No, there's no record.'

That was a surprise. 'Is Clarinda Towart around?'

Muriel laughed. 'At this time of day? She doesn't come on till mid-evening.'

'Anyone see her last night?'

'I'll check while you're up there.'

We headed for the stairs. As usual, Davie beat me.

'You're a physical wreck,' he said.

'I could have taken the lift.'

He looked at my donkey jacket and crumpled jeans. 'They wouldn't have let you in.'

A black couple in colourful robes came down the corridor. We stood aside. The fourth floor was reserved for important – read stinking rich – tourists. This pair may have been royalty. The man nodded at us graciously.

'So,' I said, as we headed towards 435, 'we know that the victim was well off.'

Davie stopped at the door, on which the Do Not Disturb sign was still in place. 'Shouldn't we have a scene-of-crime squad here?'

'Not yet. I've got to report to the Council in a few hours. I'm not waiting for another report.' I slid the card into the slot and pushed open the door, having slipped on a pair of the latex gloves I always carried. 'Take your boots off.'

We entered in our socks. The room was a suite, furnished in an over-the-top antique style. Queen Victoria would have felt at home in the dark wood and velvet. There was a painting of a stag at bay over the fireplace.

'Delightful,' I said, taking a roundabout route to the desk in the far corner. There was nothing on it but the standard hotel folder and advertisements for the city's attractions. The drawer was empty.

'Seems to have liked his drink,' Davie said, holding up an almost empty bottle of top-grade island malt whisky.

'No dirty glass?' I said, taking in the well-stocked booze table.

'Not that I can see.'

We couldn't check for DNA on the bottle as that technology wasn't provided by the Public Order Directorate – far too expensive.

I moved into the bedroom. The bed was made up. In the ornate wardrobe I found a couple of flash suits and four silk shirts. The rest of his clothes were in the drawers. I opened the bedside table.

'Weird.'

'What is?' said Davie, at the door.

'Mr Chung was presumably some kind of high-flyer, but there's no laptop or mobile phone.'

'Maybe they were stolen at Eyre Terrace.'

'Or not. Call Raeburn 297 and ask if he retrieved either or both, will you?'

While he did that, I raised the mattress, with some difficulty. There was nothing under it, or the bed itself. A pair of hotel slippers was neatly lined up alongside.

'No,' Davie said. 'No computer or phone at the murder scene.'

I got the feeling that someone had been in here before us. I also knew that sharp operators like Chung would have had backup. I looked around the room. Where would he have hidden something small like a memory stick or diskette? Anywhere was the answer and I didn't want to wait for the scene-of-crime team to take everything to pieces. This called for creative thinking.

I went into the bathroom, all black and white tiles and a free-standing copper bath with dragon's feet. The wide shelf behind the sink was strewn with the dead man's shaving gear, electric toothbrush and paste, and numerous unguents. I emptied out his toilet bag. Interesting. There was a tube of toothpaste identical to the one on the shelf, even though the latter was almost full. I held the second tube up to the light. There was a faint line above the crimped end. I pulled gently and it came away.

'Bingo,' I said.

'What is it?' Davie said, from the door.

I held up a black memory stick wrapped in clear film. We don't use sticks in the city, having got no further than diskettes in most directorates' limited technology, but I'd seen the odd one in the past.

'They missed this.'

Davie frowned. 'Who?'

'The person or people who took his computer and phone. Don't tell anyone, not even your boss. I want to see what's on it first.'

After poking around for another quarter of an hour without finding anything else of note, I gave up.

'All right, call in the techies.' The toothpaste tube and its non-minty contents were in my pocket. 'Let's see what Muriel has come up with on the mysterious Clarinda.'

The answer was not much. No one had seen her the previous evening, though she'd been with an overweight Swede two nights ago; he was still in one undamaged piece.

'The only thing I can tell you about Mr Chung is that he went on the Captain Porteous Trail yesterday morning.'

'Oh aye?'

'We've got a copy of the booking.'

'Right.' I leaned closer. 'Em, Muriel, did you give Chung's keycard to anyone else? Tell me now and I won't have you sent to a city farm.'

Her eyes sprang open. 'Anyone else? No.'

'No undercover operatives?' You can usually spot auxiliaries in plain clothes several miles off.

'No, citizen, I swear.'

'How easy is it to get a master keycard?'

She laughed sharply. 'Come on, citizen. You know how the city works.'

I did indeed. The only people who could have got hold of such a thing were senior auxiliaries. How reassuring – a conspiracy was already in the offing.

* * *

'I'll see what's on that stick on a secure computer later,' I said, as Davie drove up the North Bridge. Even though the afternoon was almost over, the sun was still shining brightly and I could see beyond the stumps of the long destroyed chimneys of Cockenzie power station; the city has relied on numerous smaller generating stations since the drugs wars.

The Tourism Directorate is a grey building on George IV Bridge, adjoining the High Street. Davie parked outside and headed for the pretty young guardswoman who was waiting on the steps.

'Hello, Cullen 542,' I said, keeping things formal because I knew Davie and she had had a thing a year ago.

'Call me Kirstie,' she said, stealing my gambit with a smile.

'Call me Citizen Dalrymple,' I replied lamely. 'What have you got for us?'

'Chung Keng Quee wasn't an average tourist,' she said, looking at her notepad.

'Meaning?'

'The directorate has him marked as a Class One visitor, his accommodation, meals and excursions covered by the city.'

That was interesting, though not entirely unexpected.

'Who's his handler?'

'The Finance Directorate's special adviser, executive.'

Davie and I exchanged looks.

'Well done, Kirstie,' I said. 'Anything else?'

'I overheard the tourism guardian talking to the Malaysian consul in the hall earlier. He wasn't pleased.'

'Excellent,' I said, 'you'll go far. Overhearing is an important part of Public Order Directorate work.'

Davie gave me the eye.

'Good work,' he reiterated. 'Full debriefing in the command centre at six p.m.'

Kirstie saluted and went on her way.

'No,' Davie said in a low voice. 'No comments about debriefing.'

'You were the one who raised it, so to speak.' I led him to the entrance, holding up my authorization.

'The finance guardian's SPADE,' Davie said, when he caught up. 'That slimeball Billy Geddes.'

'Let's give him the benefit of the doubt. For the time being.'

Davie scoffed. 'Just because you were at school with him . . .'

I started on the stairs. The Prostitution Services Department was on the second top floor, below the guardian's office. That showed how important it was.

'Wouldn't it be an idea to tell the guardian we're here?' Davie asked.

'It would be a courtesy,' I said, 'but you know what my manners are like.'

I was panting by the time we got there, which seemed appropriate. A balding middle-aged male auxiliary was manning the outer office. I showed him my authorization and took in his name badge.

'Right, Colin – you don't mind if I call you Colin? – here's how this goes. You do exactly what I tell you and you contact no one, including the guardian. Either now or later.' I glanced at Davie. 'If you do, the commander here will trample you underfoot.'

It would have been a long time since Colin did his stint on the city line as a trainee auxiliary, and he wasn't up for an argument. He gulped and nodded.

'Good. I want the file on Clarinda Towart.'

'Um . . .'

I leaned over his desk. 'Um what, Colin?'

'Um . . . it isn't here.'

Davie stepped up. 'See this boot?' he said, raising his right leg. 'It's a very effective enema.'

'No . . . I'm telling the truth. The . . . the guardian asked for it this morning.'

'Did she now?' I motioned to Davie to lower his leg. 'Never mind. What can you tell us about Clarinda? Off the record, of course.'

Colin looked as if a great white shark had just appeared in front of him; with climate change they've been spotted in the North Sea, soon to be renamed the Scottish Sea. 'Off the record?' he asked feebly.

'Yes,' Davie said, raising his leg again.

'Well . . . I've never had much to do with her . . . personally.'

It was common knowledge that Prostitution Services Department auxiliaries sampled the goods.

'But some of your pals must have,' I said.

'Em . . . yes. Do I have to give you names?'

'Not at this stage. I'm trying to get an idea of what kind of person she is.'

'Well . . . I'd say not very nice.'

Davie swallowed a guffaw.

'Explain,' I said with a smile.

Colin fiddled with his pencil. 'Clarinda Towart is . . . the most unpopular operative in the directorate.'

That was interesting.

'Why?' Davie demanded.

Colin avoided his eyes. 'She . . . she's rude, overbearing, probably an alcoholic and has seventeen inappropriate behaviour reports on . . . on record.'

'Why's she still in the PSD?' I said.

The auxiliary shook his head. 'I have no idea. You'd have to ask the guardian.'

I intended to, but not now.

We left the Tourism Directorate and headed to the castle in the 4×4.

'What do you think?' Davie asked.

'Too many loose ends as yet.' I took in the poster on a lamp post. A grinning skeleton danced above the words, 'Edinburgh Skeletons – The Ultimate Thrill!'

'The Council's really lost its marbles this time,' I said. 'Who wants to tramp around the streets and end up staring at a glass-encased skeleton?'

'The dead Malaysian for a start,' Davie said. 'He went on the Porteous Trail.'

'We'll have to check that.'

'There's also William Burke and a new one about Thomas De Quincey, whoever he was.'

'The ignorance,' I groaned. 'Hugely well-known author of *Confessions of an English Opium-Eater*, died in Edinburgh in the 1850s.'

'Fascinating.' Davie drove on to the esplanade.

'He also wrote several essays on murder as one of the fine arts.'

Davie opened his door. 'Sounds like he ate too much of that opium.'

'Nothing very aesthetically pleasing about Mr Chung's passing, certainly.'

'Though I've seen much worse.'

'Or better, as De Quincey would have it.'

We walked between the statues of Wallace and Bruce, thankfully not in skeletal form. On the way to the command centre my phone rang.

'Quint.'

'Sophia.'

'Mr Chung.'

'What did you find?'

'There was a lot of whisky in him. He would have been drunk, very drunk.'

'That figures,' I said, recalling the whisky bottle in his suite. 'Garotting him wouldn't have been difficult.'

'No. Did you see any whisky in Eyre Terrace?'

I racked my memory. 'I don't think so. The techies' report will confirm that.'

'Hm. Time of death remains between two and four. Have you found anything?'

'Nothing concrete. See you at the Council meeting.'

The public order guardian was in his chair in the command centre. He rose to greet us, which surprised me. Had I suddenly become his golden boy?

'What news, Dalrymple?'

'Not much, Michie.' I filled him in, omitting the memory stick. He looked bilious.

'Are your nuts in a vice?' Guardians loved it when you talked dirty. Not.

'Get a grip, man,' he said, leading me away from the bank of outmoded screens and keyboards.

'My point is, the victim was a Class One visitor.'

'I'm aware of that.'

'Who's squeezing you? Jack MacLean?'

'The finance guardian has . . . been in touch.'

That figured. He was Billy Geddes's boss. I kept Billy's involvement to myself.

A skinny young male auxiliary approached us tentatively.

'What is it?' the guardian barked.

'The scene-of-crimes team report on Eyre Terrace,' the weed said, handing over a file and scuttling off.

Michie opened it. I read what I could from beside him. No computer, mobile phone, watch, money or credit cards found – the victim's wallet contained only his passport. Fingerprints still being checked against records – that would take some time given the paucity of the digital archives – but both Clarinda Towart's and Mr Chung's had been located, the latter's only on the bedstead. No alcohol in the flat, only Clarinda's prints on the glasses. Fabric and other trace analysis under way, but nothing particularly suggestive. What was interesting was the lack of prints on the ligature.

The guardian handed me the file. 'Why would this prostitute murder her client?'

'Whoah,' I said. 'Who says she killed him?'

'She's gone missing, hasn't she?'

'Maybe someone's after her.'

James Michie snorted. 'Why make things more complicated?'

'See you in the Council chamber,' I said, giving him back the file.

I needed to get my ducks in order – before I shot them down.

* * *

'Citizen Dalrymple,' said Fergus Calder, the senior guardian, in his usual
smooth manner. He should have stood down at the end of his year-long
term, but it had been agreed he would stay in place to provide continuity
in the lead-up to the referendum. 'Here we are again.'

I looked around the semicircle of guardians above me. We were in what
had been the Scottish parliament before Scotland fell apart in 2003, along
with most other states. The guardians were hopeful that Edinburgh would
become the capital of the reconstituted nation if the referendum result was
positive.

'What can you tell us about this unfortunate business?' Calder asked.
He was also in charge of the Supply Directorate and had somehow survived
a major scandal there last summer. He was easy-going on the surface but
there was steel beneath his skin.

I ran through the scene at the flat, handed over to Sophia for the post-
mortem results, then went on to what we'd found at the suite in the Waverley
– apart from the memory stick. Then I turned to the tourism guardian.
Mary Parlane was in her late fifties and had taken to wearing her grey hair
in a bun. She'd been in post for over a decade and was generally regarded
as competent and incorruptible, a rare combination.

'Perhaps you could tell us about Clarinda Towart, the occupant of the
flat where Mr Chung was found. After all, you have her file.'

She looked down at me through thick lenses in mock-tortoiseshell frames.

'Of course I have her file, Quintilian.' She was one of few people in
the city who used my full name. She knew it irritated me. 'She works
for the PSD. Works, I might add, extremely well.'

'Despite her seventeen citations for inappropriate behaviour and her
alcoholism.'

That didn't have the effect I hoped for. The guardian continued without
a blink.

'It's true that she has a drink problem and that she can get out of control.
But her clients . . . well, I won't say they love her, but she's extremely
popular. Men and women come back every year to meet up with her.'

'Class One visitors like Mr Chung?'

She looked at the file. 'Yes, but not exclusively.'

'Where is this Clarinda Towart?' put in the public order guardian.

'We can't find her,' I said.

'Try harder,' said Jack MacLean, the finance guardian, resplendent in
one of the hand-tailored suits he favoured – they were made in Glasgow.

James Michie glared at him, but kept quiet. He hadn't been a Council
member long enough to take on one of its biggest hitters.

'I was wondering if your special adviser, executive might know,' I said.
'Billy Geddes was the dead man's handler.'

Jack MacLean grinned, never a good sign. 'I've spoken to my SPADE. He had dinner with Mr Chung last night and left him at the Waverley at eleven fifteen. He has no knowledge of the prostitute.'

I'd be checking that. Billy had knowledge, carnal and other, of many female PSD operatives. And he had a habit of inserting his fingers into mucky financial pies.

'So what are we saying, citizen?' Fergus Calder asked. 'That Citizen Towart is the killer?'

'She may be, but her fingerprints aren't on the ligature.'

I raised a hand.

'Obviously she could have been wearing gloves. Tourism Guardian, do you know Clarinda Towart personally?'

'Of course. She's been in the department for years.'

'Does she strike you as someone who could put her knee on a possibly comatose man and throttle him?'

Mary Parlane thought about that. 'No, Quintilian, she doesn't. She gets drunk and she can be disruptive, but deep down – like many people in the PSD – she's a caring soul.'

I wasn't buying the generalization – I'd seen some city prostitutes who were as hard-hearted as Tamburlaine the Great – but I accepted the guardian's specific character reference.

I turned back to Jack MacLean. 'Care to tell us what Mr Chung was doing in Edinburgh? Or should I ask Billy Geddes?'

'Leave him out if it,' the finance guardian said. 'Chung was a businessman. Light engineering. That's all I know.'

I didn't believe for a second that he was so innocent. Maybe I would ask Billy after all.

'Citizen?' the senior guardian said. 'You have been frank with us?'

I brazened it out.

'Because there are always places for suitable candidates in the mines.'

That was when I knew for sure there was dirt to be dug.

'One last thing,' I said. 'Why was there an anonymous call about the dead man?'

I left them to ponder that. It wasn't as if I knew the answer.

Three

'What now?' Davie asked.

We were in the canteen in the castle. He was working his way through the first of three bowls of stew, while I was eating haggis. The Guard version was a lot better than the one ordinary citizens got.

'Clarinda Towart.'

'I've put a pair of guardswomen in her flat.'

'That's a start. The tourism guardian's giving Michie a copy of her file. We need to chase up her close friends.' Every citizen had to declare five names annually. 'And her parents.'

'They're dead. I checked while you were in the Council meeting. The father when she was twelve and the mother a couple of years ago – cancer, both of them. And no siblings.'

'Shit.'

'What about the victim? Shouldn't we talk to the Malaysian consul?'

'Let's leave that for now. I'd rather find out more first. Besides, the guardians might object to me being undiplomatic to a diplomat.'

'That wouldn't usually stop you.'

I raised the stump of my right forefinger. 'Moving on. The memory stick. I'll see if I can get into it.' I looked around. 'Not here, though.'

Davie grinned. 'Off to the medical guardian?'

'Later, yes.'

'Does she know you're . . . coming?'

Up went the finger again.

'And then there's your manure-gobbling pal Billy Geddes.'

'True. But he'll have been forewarned by Jack MacLean. Again, I want to find out more first. Billy's always best approached from a position of strength.'

'I can do that.'

'Jesus, Davie, the man's a cripple.'

He had finished bowl number two. 'So what? He's a poisonous little fucker who's screwed the city dozens of times.'

'Right enough, but let me handle him.'

The commander grunted, then looked over my shoulder.

'Guardian incoming.'

James Michie sat down on the bench and put Clarinda Towart's file between us.

'Not eating?' I said, as I cleared my plate.

'Food is the last thing on my mind.'

'Or stomach. Don't worry, we'll nail the bastards behind this.'

'That's what I'm afraid of, Quint.'

I ran my eyes over him. He was finally looking his age.

'You think there's Council involvement, don't you?' he said.

I raised my shoulders. 'Even if Billy Geddes is up to his elbows in the mire, that doesn't mean his boss is. As for the tourism guardian, she's one of the few of her rank that I trust.'

He stared at me.

'Present company excluded.' Not that I had full confidence in the guardian – I didn't know him well enough.

'Care to tell me what you're prioritizing?'

'The curiously named Clarinda,' I said, examining a piece of pineapple. It didn't seem to come from a can. Another Supply Directorate deal with a distant country? I wondered if Malaysia exported them. 'Thanks for the file.'

'Relatives, close friends?'

At least he knew something about public order procedure, even though he'd spent much of his career in the directorate's accounts department.

Davie had finished bowl three. There were four bananas on his tray, but he could take them with him.

'Duty calls,' I said, standing up.

'Keep me informed,' the guardian said plaintively.

I promised I would, even though I was already hiding things from him.

I followed Davie to his office off the command centre and closed the door behind me.

'Let's have a look, then.'

I opened the file. 'Clarinda Morag Towart, born September 6th 2000, attended Primary School 12 and Senior School 14.'

'They're in Leith,' Davie interjected.

I looked further down. 'There's no record of gang activity.' Edinburgh had been plagued by criminal outfits in recent years, one of the most vicious being the Leith Lancers. They were finally overcome last summer, though inevitably some members would have slipped through the net.

'I bloody hope not.'

'Joined the PSD at twenty-one after service on City Farm 9, two years of it voluntary.' I turned pages. 'Her early reports are glowing.'

Davie threw a banana skin in the bin. 'I wonder why she became a prostitute.'

'According to her application, "I want to help the city in any way I can". It's a bit old-fashioned, but she seems to have been committed. Many citizens were, when there was still faith in the Enlightenment.'

'Now they just do it for the extra food and clothing vouchers, and the superior housing. No way a single citizen would get a flat the size of hers otherwise.'

I nodded. 'Don't forget the tips. They're allowed to keep them now. Often they build up savings in foreign currencies.'

'The joys of free enterprise.' Davie wasn't a fan of the Council's loosening of the regulation that allowed citizens to start their own businesses. 'Anyway, she went off the rails often enough.'

I was looking at the citations. Some of them were pretty serious – abusing auxiliaries in clubs and restaurants, throwing food at other diners, vomiting in front of tourists in Rose Street. Members of the PSD were supposed to act like cultivated escorts rather than delinquents. Which led me to her alcoholism.

'Three separate months in Rehabilitation Centre Number 2, the first in May 2031. According to the doctors she made good progress, though none of them was able to ascertain why she turned to drink.'

Davie was halfway through his last banana. 'Does there have to be a reason?'

I shrugged. 'A trigger, perhaps.'

'Father died when she was wee.'

'Wouldn't necessarily explain why she hit the bottle in her late twenties.'

'Was he a boozer? Was her mother?'

'Neither seems to have been, at least excessively.' Citizen-issue beer and whisky weren't good for you, even under the controlled rationing system.

'What about her friends?'

'She's only given three. There's a note from the head of the PSD saying that this is frequently the case with prostitutes.' That chimed with my own experience of questioning them during cases. 'They keep themselves to themselves when they're not working.'

Davie took out his notebook. 'Names?'

'Alice Lennox, registered nurse. She lives on Henderson Row, down the road from Eyre Terrace. They met during Clarinda's first detox.'

'Friend whose shoulder she can lean on.'

'Maybe. Then there's Rory Campbell, carpenter and theatre director.'

'What?'

'Theatre director? Yes, it is unusual. Then again, the Council did license a few venues outside the central zone a couple of years ago.'

Davie looked unimpressed. 'Have you been?'

'Aye. They mostly stage amateurish attempts to take the piss out of the system – *Nineteen Eighty-Four* in 2034, that kind of thing.'

'Don't they get censored?'

'Not officially.' I caught his eye. 'But I bet arms are twisted if anything too obviously critical of the Council appears.'

'Typical Quint. Always look on the shite side of life.'

'As good a proverb as any, guardsman.'

'And the third friend?'

I looked at the file. 'Duncan Denoon, zookeeper.'

Davie laughed. 'Clarinda and the weird bunch.'

'She was at school with him.'

The zoo was a major tourist attraction before the last election and the Council had gradually built it up again. There were no elephants or bears any more, but they'd managed to get hold of a lioness and a tiger. I wondered if Billy Geddes's business expertise had been involved in those deals.

'So?' Davie asked.

I thought about it. Hauling in Clarinda Towart's friends might be counter-productive, especially if one or more of them was helping her.

'Put discreet surveillance on them tonight and we'll make contact tomorrow.' I stood up.

'Off to the medical guardian's?' Davie said, with a wink.

'Only computer I can trust.'

'Among other things.'

'Thank you and goodnight. You'll pull the files on the friends?'

'Yes, sir, yes, sir––'

'No bags full yet.'

I left the castle, but I never got to Sophia's place that night.

My phone rang before I got to the esplanade.

'Quint, it's Alison.'

She was the nursing auxiliary at my old man's retirement home. My heart and stomach started to tango.

'What is it?'

'Hector's collapsed. There's an ambulance on the way.'

'What happened?'

'I'm not sure. He's been morose the last few days, but nothing out of the ordinary. I'm so sorry, I must have missed something.'

'Don't worry. He's good at hiding things. I'll go straight to the infirmary.'

I rang off and called Sophia. She said she'd come as soon as she got Maisie, her daughter, to bed. As a pathologist, there wasn't much she could do – at least I hoped not – but she would gee the appropriate team up.

I jumped into a Guard 4×4 and told the driver to take me to the hospital. She was one of Davie's many friends, a sweet young woman called Drew. I told her what was going on.

'I'm very sorry, citizen,' she said.

'Call me Quint.'

'Wasn't your father one of the original guardians?'

I nodded. Auxiliaries have to study the history of the modern Edinburgh Enlightenment. 'He was information guardian.'

'But he resigned over Council policy.'

I wondered how the textbook explained that. He felt the Council was taking too much power for itself and that corruption was inevitable. He got that right.

'I resigned from the Public Order Directorate, you know.'

'You were demoted, supposedly because you lost your nerve after your lover was killed on a raid.'

I rubbed the faded DM tattoo on the back of my right hand. 'Thanks for the "supposedly".'

'I've heard plenty about you, citizen . . . I mean, Quint. You're no coward.'

I nodded my thanks as she pulled into the infirmary, the city's original house of healing. The newer version in the southern suburbs was blown to pieces in the drugs wars. The old building's Gothic towers and crumbling grey stone were lit up minimally and the asphalt in the yard was pitted. Tourists were treated in a clinic in the central zone.

The nurse at reception directed me to a room on the second floor. The door was open, a white-coated doctor leaning against the frame.

'Citizen Dalrymple,' he said, when he saw me. I didn't know him from Hippocrates. 'Your father's . . . comfortable.'

I followed him into the room. It was one of the few singles. Sophia must have laid down the law.

The old man was lying propped up by pillows, lines from bags of clear fluid running into his fleshless arms. He was sweating and his face was worryingly pale, parchment skin stretched over prominent bones. He looked like an only marginally living skeleton.

'I heard he collapsed,' I said.

The doctor, Simpson 527 or Ranald Stewart according to his ID badges, opened a file. 'To be honest, we're not sure. His blood pressure's low. Has he had problems with bowel and/or bladder incontinence?'

'Not that I've heard.' I'd seen him less than a week ago and Alison would have told me. Then again, the old bugger might have been cleaning up after himself. He'd always been terrified of hospitals.

'Any sign of him being in pain?'

I considered that. 'I see him once a week, so if it came on gradually I might not have noticed. He'd hide it, you can be sure of that. He's the opposite of a hypochondriac.'

'An egosyntonic.'

'I'll take your word for it. People of his generation, the ones who were involved in the early Enlightenment and came through the drugs wars, are hard as crucifixion nails.'

Ranald Stewart wrinkled his nose. 'A delightful analogy, not least in an atheist state. Anyway, we'll be running tests on him.'

Sophia bustled in and took the file from him. After perusing it, she took my arm. 'If you'll excuse us, Doctor,' she said imperiously.

'What's wrong with the old man?'

She looked into my eyes. 'It may be his system shutting down, Quint. What age is he now?'

'Eighty.'

She squeezed my arm. 'We'll take the best care of him.'

'Thanks for arranging the room,' I said, looking around and blinking back tears.

'He *is* an ex-guardian.'

'Resigned.'

'Doesn't matter. Come on, let's go back to my place.'

'I should stay here.'

'They'll call me as soon as he comes round.'

I looked at the shrunken relic on the bed. He'd been six feet four in his prime, but he'd been shrinking for years.

I touched his cheek. There wasn't much warmth to it. 'Will he survive the night?'

Sophia raised her shoulders. 'I honestly don't know. But you've always said he's a bonnie fighter.'

I nodded. To my shame, the memory stick came to mind. I could try to open it at Sophia's. On the other hand, I could use her computer in the infirmary. I went for the latter. For a change, she didn't demur. She let me into her office and left the keys.

I spent the next two hours shuttling between the old man's room and the computer. His condition didn't change and neither did that of the stick – I couldn't get past the password demand.

Frustrated, I went out into the yard and breathed in air that didn't smell of disinfectant and unwashed patients, many of whom were still in reception.

The window of a luxurious car hummed down.

'How is he, Quint?'

'Billy? What the fuck are you doing here?'

'What does it sound like? Asking about your old man.'

I stared at the crumpled face in the back seat. 'Why do you care? He thinks you're a tick on the body politic.'

'You and I were once friends, Quint.'

'Once being the operative word.'

'Forget it, then.'

I relented. 'He's out for the count. They're going to run tests.'

'I'm sure Sophia's looking out for him.'

I left that unanswered. The temptation to lay into him about the dead Malaysian was irresistible because I hadn't been able to get anything from the stick.

'You weren't expecting to find Chung Keng Quee here, were you?'

He shook his head. 'He's no use to me in the morgue. Will you ever give up trying to nail me, Quint? Haven't you heard that I saw him to the Waverley after dinner last night?'

'Which means nothing. You could easily have gone back or arranged for him to be taken to the Eyre Terrace flat. I suppose you know Clarinda Towart.'

He shrugged his uneven shoulders. 'I might be a cripple thanks to you, but I can still get it up.' I had chased him in front of the horses at the racetrack in Princes Street Gardens back in 2020.

'You get it up with PSD operatives?' I said sanctimoniously. 'That's against regulations.'

'Oh, fuck off, Quint. Anyway, I haven't seen her for months.'

I pressed on, knowing I was on a hiding to nada. 'What was the nature of the dead man's business in the city?'

'He's an entrepreneur.'

'Light engineering?'

He peered out at me. 'I don't think so. Who told you that?'

I didn't answer. Jack MacLean was either out of the loop or had tried to mislead me at the Council meeting. Whatever the case, Billy didn't need to know.

'I'm going back inside. If you're involved in the murder, I'm going to find out.'

'I'm not,' he said, his voice harsh.

I raised an eyebrow and left him to his flash car. It was probably a present – read bribe – from some hyper-rich slimebag who wanted a piece of Edinburgh. I hoped the brakes failed on Forrest Road.

I spent the rest of the night in a back-stabbing chair by my father's bedside. I woke up when I heard him groan.

'Morning, old man,' I said, smiling as best I could. The pale light of dawn was visible between the tattered curtains.

'Failure,' he said, his voice cracking. 'Where . . . am I?'

'In the infirmary.'

'Fuuuuck.'

'You'll be lucky.' I put my hand over his. 'You know, you collapsed last night.'

'Did . . . I?' He winced.

'You're in pain.'

'It's . . . nothing.'

'Yes, it is. I'm calling the doctor.'

'Noooo.'

I pressed the call bell.

'Where does it hurt?' I said, leaning forward.

'None . . . of your business.' The last words came out in a rush, as if he wasn't sure he had the breath for them.

Ranald Stewart arrived with a couple of nurses and shooed me out.

I could hear the old man's gasps and groans from the corridor.

Four

Sophia arrived and took me to her office. She called Dr Stewart and got an update, such as it was. Hector was in pain and numerous tests would be done. His vital signs were reasonable and there was no reason to think he was at death's dark and dreary door. Yet.

'Go and get some sleep, Quint.'

'I've had a few hours.'

'In an infirmary chair? I'll have to admit *you* next.' She smiled and moved closer. 'I'm serious. You're no use to your father in tatters. Go to bed.' After taking my hands, she kissed me on the lips. That helped.

'All right,' I lied. I was awake and there were things to do.

I walked up to the castle to clear my head and found Davie in the command centre.

'I'm really sorry, Quint,' he said, putting his arm round me. 'How is he?'

'Hanging on. They're checking him out.'

'Can't be too bad if you're here.'

I let him think that, trying to suppress the sounds of agony I'd heard.

'Any news, big man?'

'Nothing earth-shattering.'

'That's a relief.'

He led me to his office. 'Here are the files on Clarinda Towart's friends.'

'No sign of her?'

He shook his head. 'Nothing from the twenty barracks, the tourist zone facilities or the city line towers.' He paused. 'Do you think she's alive?'

'No idea. We're light on data.' That reminded me. I handed him the memory stick. 'Give this to your best techie. Ask him to keep it to himself.'

'He's a she.'

'Good for her.'

I flicked through the files while he was gone. He was right. Nothing stuck out like a narwhal's horn. The surveillance reports that had been recently added showed that the nurse, Alice Lennox, who worked at the tourist clinic in what had been St Mary's Roman Catholic Cathedral, had returned home at 10.23 p.m. and was still there. Her registered partner, Christopher Fleming, had gone to work at the same clinic at 7.09 a.m. Davie had asked for his file too so he'd be checked. As for the animal keeper, Duncan Denoon, he lived in an accommodation block at the zoo, which was three miles west of the centre. The access road, though well protected during daytime when the tourists visit, was less than safe at night. The report said that he went to bed at midnight, having watched a film about climate change with his colleagues. He was feeding the pygmy hippopotami at 8.05 a.m.

That left the carpenter and theatre director Rory Campbell. He was easily the most interesting of the three. He'd been an auxiliary for five years, serving in the Labour Directorate after his basic training and year in the guard. Then he'd got himself demoted for striking an officer. He retrained as a carpenter, working on building sites, and during that time he developed an interest in drama. After acting in several underground productions, which the Guard knew about but turned a blind eye to, he started directing. His first effort was a musical version of *Macbeth* and the second a version of *Waiting for Godot* in Edinburgh dialect – both after the ban on drama had been lifted. His file photo showed a shaven-haired individual with piercing eyes.

Davie came back with a tray of croissants and coffee.

'Thought you might have missed breakfast.'

'Bet *you* didn't.'

'I'll scrape up the leftovers.'

I couldn't help laughing. There were seven croissants.

'This Rory Campbell. He was at the Theatre of Life in Clerk Street till 1.23 a.m. What about the midnight curfew?'

'He's got an exemption with some of his people because they have to clear up after shows.'

'The Theatre of Life. That's the old Odeon cinema – the number of great movies I saw there when I was a kid. Concerts too.'

'Before my time,' Davie said. 'Substantially.'

'What show's playing now?'

'Something called . . .' He hesitated. '*Spar/Tak/Us*.'

I looked at the paper he was holding. 'Spartacus was a gladiator who led a slave rebellion against the Romans.'

'Even I know that.'

'I think I saw the film at the Odeon. What's the title getting at? Spartacus take us what? Out of here?'

'Edinburgh citizens are slaves who need saving?' Davie pondered. 'How did that get past the Recreation Directorate censor?'

'Good question. Not that there's supposed to be a censor for citizen plays.'

'Uh-huh. Let's take in the show tonight and nail this Campbell afterwards.'

There was a knock on the door and a grizzled guardsman appeared. 'You'll be interested in this, commander,' he said, handing a file to Davie.

He ran an eye over the contents. 'Ya wee beauty! We've got the taxi driver who picked up Clarinda Towart on Tuesday night. And guess what – they went through the Nicolson Street checkpoint ten minutes after midnight.'

'Nicolson Street that becomes Clerk Street, where sits the Theatre of Life.'

Davie gave me a curious look. 'Correct.'

'Are they bringing the driver in?'

'He'll be here any minute. Let's go and wait for him in the main interrogation room.'

'Why not use one that isn't wired for sound? You never know who might be listening.'

'The guardian?' he mouthed.

I raised my shoulders. 'Or someone looking out for him,' I whispered. 'Better safe than shat on.'

He nodded and we headed for the smallest and dingiest of the interrogation rooms. James Michie wasn't in the command centre so we got clean away.

Five minutes later the door opened and a slim citizen in his thirties was marched in and pushed on to the chair opposite us. Davie had pulled his file so we knew about him. That didn't mean he wasn't going to be questioned.

'Name?' demanded Davie, in full bull-in-a-souvenir-shop mode.

'Bruce Kilgour,' the driver said, smiling at us defiantly. 'Citizen number 3—'

'Never mind that!' Davie roared. He wasn't good with self-assured citizens. 'What were you doing on Nicolson Street on Tuesday night?'

'As I'm sure the file tells you, I was driving a female citizen. City Regulations permit us to take citizens who work for the PSD if there are no tourists in the vicinity.'

Davie ignored that. 'Was she alone?'

Kilgour paused, which gave him away.

I put a hand on Davie's arm. 'Bruce, if you come clean, you won't have your licence permanently revoked. Or be sent down the mines.'

Davie glowered at me and then the citizen. 'Answer the fucking question!'

'I . . . yes, I mean, no . . . I mean . . . there was a tourist, a Chinese-looking guy with the blonde. He got down on the floor when I stopped at the checkpoint.'

'Good,' I said, playing very nice cop. 'So where did you take them? The Theatre of Life?'

He accepted the cue with alacrity. 'Aye. They went in and I waited for about twenty minutes.'

'See anyone else?'

He shook his head.

'Then where did you go? I presume it was still just the woman and the tourist.'

'Aye. Round by Craigmillar and Willowbrae, then over to Eyre Terrace. Do you know it? We didn't stop anywhere else.'

Kilgour had got his nerve back. Either he was telling the truth – and the final destination suggested he was, at least in part – or he thought he was in the clear.

'Right-oh, Bruce,' I said. 'Did she choose the route or did you?'

'Em, I did. She told me to keep clear of the checkpoints.'

Davie leaned across the table. 'You should have fucking reported that!' he yelled, spraying the driver's face with saliva.

'Aye . . . I suppose I should have.'

'Did you go inside with the woman and the tourist at Eyre Terrace?' I asked.

He shook his head. 'No way. She was pissed. Told me to get tae fuck. At least she paid up.'

'With vouchers or foreign currency?' I smiled. 'Don't lie. There are Guard personnel in your flat as we speak.'

'Something foreign. Malaysian, I think she said. We exchange it at the Finance Directorate.'

'I know,' I said, with an encouraging smile. 'Anything else?'

He thought about that. 'Aye. Even though she was a tart, she was really cold with her customer. Kept pushing him off and telling him to keep his hands to himself. Didn't stop him haring after her into the tenement, mind.'

I sat back.

'Can I go now?' Kilgour asked.

'No, Bruce,' I said. 'You'll be held here till we've finished our checks.'

'Aw, come on.'

Davie raised his fist and there was no more complaining.

Outside I made sure Davie knew what he was to do: a background check on Bruce Kilgour, his clothing – both what he was wearing and what was in his flat – to be examined by the techies for matches with fabric traces found in Clarinda's place, a fingerprint comparison and all the other basics. He knew, of course, and threatened to belt me for demeaning him.

'What are *you* going to do now, smartarse?'

'See how my old man's getting on.'

'Shit. Sorry.'

'Forget it. We can't both be distracted. Then I'm off to the zoo.'

'Citizen Denoon?'

'The very one.'

'Watch out for the penguins. They bite your ankles.'

I erected a finger, this time the full-length middle one.

On the way down to the esplanade I called Sophia.

'He's having a bone scan, Quint,' she said.

'That doesn't sound good.'

'We'll see.'

'Anything else?'

She paused. 'His spinal CT shows abnormal masses.'

'CT? What's that?'

'Computerized tomography. It's a hi-tech machine that takes multiple images of the bones and internal organs.'

'The city has that kind of equipment?'

'We got it recently – from Glasgow, of course. I've involved our best oncologist in the field.'

Bitter liquid raced up my throat. I had an image of Clarinda's neighbour, Charlie Dixon, whose wife had died of breast . . .

'Cancer? Is it cancer?'

Again, Sophia didn't immediately reply. 'It looks like it. But George Allison is very good. There'll be therapies, options . . .' Her voice trailed away.

'I'm coming over.'

'Don't, Quint. He's in the cancer centre at Pollock, I'm not sure for how long. I'll let you know. Keep yourself busy, dearest. Everything's in hand.'

I sat down on the wall and looked to the south. Arthur's Seat and the crags stood proud in the clear air, surrounded by what had been renamed the Enlightenment Park decades ago. To the west lay the cancer centre. It had taken over some of the buildings that had been student residences back when the university was a large international institution rather than the much smaller community college it had become. I was tempted to go despite what Sophia said because the centre had a bad reputation, though maybe that was undeserved – resources were limited. Local people viewed a transfer there as a sentence of death. There were few chemotherapy drugs available so radical surgery was the preferred treatment. I doubted that would be an option for Hector.

Then I had a thought. After Clarinda Towart's taxi stopped at the Theatre of Life, it would have been only a five-minute drive to the cancer centre. Did she and/or Mr Chung have a connection with it?

I called Davie and asked him to find out from Bruce Kilgour if he'd omitted to mention stopping there; and for the number of the techie who had the memory stick. I put in a call.

'Napier 406,' came a crisp female voice.

I identified myself and asked about the stick.

'I'm afraid I'm having a hard time, citizen,' she replied. 'I've managed to open some of the files, but they're in an ideogrammatic language.'

'You mean one with symbols rather than letters?'

'Yes, I think it may be some form of Chinese, citizen. There are standard numbers too.'

'Any idea what kind of texts they might be?'

'Hard to tell.'

'Contracts?'

'I can't say.'

'All right, keep at it. I'll ask the commander to find someone who can read Chinese.'

The guardswoman laughed. 'Good luck, citizen.'

I called Davie.

'Chinese? You're kidding, Quint.'

'Try the Tourism Directorate. There should be guides from when we had Chinese tourists.' China's economic miracle went to hell in a rickshaw a few years back and now we rarely saw visitors from what had been the world's biggest economy since the USA broke up in 2005.

'Guides speak. They don't have to read.'

'Just try, will you?'

'Yes, sir. Any news about Hector?'

'He's at the cancer centre having tests.'

'Fuck.'

'Quite.'

'That wanker of a taxi driver says he didn't go down Dalkeith Road.' Meaning he wouldn't have passed Pollock.

I rang off and got into the nearest Guard 4×4.

'Citizen Dalrymple.'

The guardsman at the wheel was young and built like a bison.

'Call me Quint.' I peered at his badge. 'Hamish.'

'It's an honour. We studied *Public Order in Practice*. Great manual.'

I'd written it before I left the Guard. 'It could do with an update.'

'The instructors have added notes.'

'Cheeky bastards.'

He laughed, then looked around.

'Don't worry, I'm currently persona grata.' I showed him my authorization. 'Take me to the zoo, please.'

Hamish gave me a dubious look.

'Yes, they've lost a poisonous snake.'

His big brown eyes opened wide. 'Really?'

'What do you think?'

'Oh, I get it.' He started the engine. 'Your sense of humour is well known.'

'Is that right? Drive before I lose it.'

He did so. He seemed a decent type. It was a shame the Guard had got its claws into him. By the time he was thirty he'd either be a tartar or a burn-out. Then again, maybe the Guard would be reformed after the referendum. Yeah, right.

Once we were out of the central zone and heading for Haymarket, there were campaign posters galore. Citizens had been allowed to start their own parties, one of which, to my amazement, was called Enlightenment Edinburgh Forever. Its poster showed the castle, home of the widely despised Guard. Maybe the party was funded by the Public Order Directorate.

'What do you think of all this?' I asked the guardsman.

He glanced at me. 'I'm voting "yes", if that's what you mean, citizen.'

'Call me Quint.' I waited.

'Quint.'

I smiled. 'Good, Hamish. Are you a yes-man because you believe a reconstituted Scotland will be good for the city or because you've been told to be one?'

'We're encouraged to think independently.' He grinned. 'On this issue alone.'

'So why would we better off with the Glaswegians, the Aberdonians and the other states having a say in our future?'

He accelerated past a tourist bus with lions and tigers all over it. Another Guard 4×4 was escorting it. No chances were taken with Edinburgh's precious visitors.

'As I understand it, all the cities and regions will discuss major issues on a democratic basis, while each will retain its own system of government.'

'That sounds like the party line. Anyway, you know what the Council's beloved Plato thought about democracy. Why should it work in Scotland after decades of violence and mob rule?'

Hamish stopped to let an elderly female citizen cross the road. She looked surprised.

'As I understand, the other states are better organized now.'

'None of them has a Council like ours.' I thought of a noxious individual who'd been in the city last summer. 'Though the Lord of the Isles has set himself up as a tin-pot king, so maybe we're not the worst.'

That got to him. 'The worst? Edinburgh under the Enlightenment is the perfect city.'

'Aye, right.' I looked at the dilapidated houses on both sides of the road.

At least there weren't the usual potholes, this being the route both to the zoo and the airport.

Hamish had taken the huff. I hoped I'd sown at least one seed of resistance. If not, he'd be reporting me to the public order guardian.

He pulled up outside the zoo. 'Do you want me to wait?' He gave me a big smile. 'Quint.'

'If you've nothing better to do.'

'I'll watch out for terrorists,' he said, putting his hand on the butt of his Hyper-Stun.

'I'd be scared.'

I headed through the ticket office, showing my authorization twice.

'This is a Council investigation,' I said to the middle-aged female auxiliary at the turnstile. 'Tell no one, including your superiors.'

She looked suitably impressed. Maybe she was one of my few fans.

I walked up the hill through the crowds of lightly dressed tourists. I could have found out where Duncan Denoon was, but I didn't want to land him in the shit. Besides, I knew he was in charge of the pygmy hippos.

When I found them, I looked at the pair of animals through the wire enclosure. They were less ugly than the full-sized version. According to the sign, they were mother and son – Kimba and Jumba. There was no sign of a keeper, so I walked over to the rhinoceros. He was called Derek, which seemed less than he deserved. Then again, American visitors might not have gone for Big Horn.

'A fine creature,' said a voice behind me. 'Citizen Dalrymple.'

I turned and found a skinny man in his thirties in the green uniform that keepers wear. His brown hair was twisted into dreadlocks – those have been seen in the city since the Council repealed the regulation on short hair.

'Hullo, Duncan,' I said, taking in his name badge. 'Just the man I'm after.'

'A fine creature,' he repeated, gazing at Derek.

'Pity about the name.'

'It was ma father's.'

'Ah. Sorry.'

'Nae bother. We get to choose the animals' names after we've been here ten years.'

I took his arm and led him away from a crowd of French children, back towards the pygmy hippos.

'Were you expecting me?' I asked.

Duncan Denoon shook his head. 'Should I have been? I know you from the paper. Where would the city be without you?'

Amazingly, he wasn't being ironic. The answer was, even more screwed up.

'I want to ask you about Clarinda Towart.'

'Oh aye?' He didn't seem concerned. 'I haven't seen her for . . . let's see . . . a month or so.'

'How was she?'

That got his attention.

'What's this about? Is she all right?'

I looked out to the Pentland Hills beyond the city line – bandit country, even though wind turbines had been placed along the ridges in the last two years.

'To be honest, I don't know, Duncan. She hasn't been seen since Tuesday night.'

He laughed. 'I wouldn't worry about that. She'll be off on a bender or recovering from one.'

'Does she often do that?'

'Aye.' He shook his head. 'It's a shame, but she cannae beat the booze. I've been trying to help her for years.'

He was about as far as it was possible to be from what I imagined was the glamorous Clarinda's type. A simple soul, soft-spoken and touchingly ridiculous with his hairdo, he was clearly into animals more than humans.

'When you last saw her, did she say—'

All of a sudden the bushes at the far end of the enclosure erupted and there was a loud boom. I hit the ground as a rain of earth, branches and diced hippopotamus came down.

Five

Longstanding Guard experience and a couple of explosions last summer meant that I clapped my hands over my ears instantly. They were ringing as I stumbled to my feet, but I could still hear screams from tourists and from closer to hand. Duncan Denoon was on his knees beside me, his hairdo in tatters, staring in horror at the scene of devastation in the enclosure and wailing like a lost soul. The skin and flesh had been stripped from one of the hippos, leaving it a blood-drenched skeleton. The other was on its back, wounds all over its body.

Other keepers arrived, along with some of the on-site paramedics. I allowed myself to be led to the ambulance and cleaned up. I had a couple of minor scalp wounds, but nothing much else. The fence had stopped much of the detritus from hitting me and Duncan. He refused to leave the scene, and was still screaming and pushing away helping hands. My heart went out to him.

As they were trained to do, the zoo personnel concentrated on the tourists, moving them away while comforting them. None seemed to have been injured. After ten minutes an elderly male auxiliary in a suit approached me.

He said something I didn't catch.

I cupped my ear.

'Cullen 103,' he shouted. 'Zoo director.'

'I'm not deaf,' I responded. 'Just suffering from what I hope is temporary tinnitus.'

'Why are you here, Citizen Dalrymple?'

I showed him my authorization.

'And?' he persisted.

'And nothing. Any thoughts as to why poor Duncan's hippos were blown up?'

'I was going to ask you the same question.'

'No break-ins or other disruptions recently?'

He shook his head.

'That means it was an inside job.'

His eyes shot open. 'Hold on. None of my people would do this. They – we – all love the animals. Besides, Guard personnel patrol at night and there are plenty of staff about during daylight hours.'

'I rest my case. Does anyone have a grudge against Duncan?'

'Not at all. He's one of the most popular keepers. He leads sing-songs every night.'

We watched as the inconsolable keeper finally allowed the paramedics to take him away from the scene.

My phone rang.

'Where are you, Quint?' Davie said anxiously. 'There's been an explosion at—'

'The zoo. I know, big man. I was twenty yards from it.'

'Are you all right?'

'Hearing's a bit shafted, but yes. I was talking to Denoon when it blew.'

'Bloody hell. Do you think you were targeted?'

'Don't know. You'd better get over . . . no, it's OK. The guardsman who brought me here will drive me back. I presume the techies are on their way.'

'Confirmed.'

Hamish had arrived panting, his face red. 'Sorry, I was in the canteen.' Another Guard gannet.

'What happened?' he asked.

I let the auxiliary fill him in.

As he was finishing, the paramedics started moving rapidly. They lifted the suddenly unresisting Duncan on to a stretcher and slid it into their vehicle. I ran over. They were ventilating him with a bag valve mask. One of them prepared a syringe with a long needle, then ripped open the clothing on his chest, ran a finger down his ribs and inserted the needle skilfully. Adrenaline, I guessed. Several minutes passed before the medics stopped what they were doing. Fuck.

'Cardiac episode?' I asked.

One of them shrugged. 'Probably. The post-mortem will show.'

I couldn't help thinking that Duncan Denoon, having lost his beloved animals, had died of a broken heart.

'Where to?' said a shocked Hamish.

'Head for the castle.'

I called Davie and asked about the locations of Clarinda Towart's other two friends.

He called me back. 'Alice Lennox is at the clinic and Rory Campbell's in his flat in Dumbiedykes. Late riser by the looks of it.'

'A night owl. At least he isn't far from his place of work.'

'True. Are you thinking they might be targets?'

'It's got to be a possibility, though I haven't a clue why anyone would blow up those wee hippos, never mind Duncan Denoon. He's dead, you know.'

'Bugger. I'll dig into his background.'

'Do that. And have Guard teams standing by in the vicinities of Lennox and Campbell.'

'Right. The taxi driver Kilgour's clean, by the way. No matches to fabric and other traces.'

'OK, let him go. But have him watched.'

'Done. Oh, we're having a problem finding anyone who can read Chinese.'

That was bad news. Knowing what was on the memory stick could be a big help.

'Keep looking. Try the senior auxiliary retirement homes. There might be some old professor.'

'Will do. What are you up to?'

'Going to have my ears tested.'

I cut the connection and rang Sophia. She was alarmed when I told her about the explosion.

'You should come in for a check-up.'

'Is Hector back?'

'No, he's still at the cancer centre.'

'I'll go over there. What was the name of that oncologist?'

'George Allison. Shall I tell him to expect you?'

'No, thanks. Taking people by surprise is my speciality.'

'I've noticed,' she said. 'But I still love you.' She terminated the call.

Typical Sophia – she could go from soul mate to automaton or vice-versa in a split second.

I turned to Hamish. 'Change of plans. The cancer centre.'

He glanced at me. 'Can I ask why?'

'You just did.'

He drove past the rusting rugby stadium at Murrayfield. It was covered in 'yes' banners.

'All right,' I said. 'It's my father. He's having tests.'

'I'm very sorry, citi—, Quint.'

'We don't know the whole of it yet. I'll take a taxi if you need to get back to work.'

'I am working,' he said proudly. 'For the city's chief investigator.'

The innocence of youth. I hoped he'd never lose it like I had. The perfect city did that to you.

'Go down to the South Bridge,' I said, as we approached the High Street. I wanted to have a look at the Theatre of Life further down.

The old art deco cinema with its Doric columns was a dirty grey colour, but the exterior was still striking, largely because of the huge, almost naked figure of a man wielding a sword that had been hung above the entrance. When I was a kid there had been late-night screenings of *Braveheart*. My mother threatened to disown me if I went to see the Hollywood clown with the saltire painted on his face. I went seven times, most of them with Billy Geddes. The audience was drunk on booze and patriotism, cheering as the English were massacred and booing – even crying – when Wallace was hung, drawn and quartered. A few years later Scotland and England no longer existed.

'What's that all about?' Hamish asked.

'*Spar/Tak/Us*? According to the sign, it's a theatrical, musical and choreographic extravaganza. Of course, auxiliaries can't go to citizen productions.'

'Doesn't mean they don't.'

Well, well. The guardsman wasn't as innocent as he looked.

'I'll let you know. I'm going tonight.'

'Can I come?'

'No. You'll stick out several miles.'

'I've got off-duty clothes.'

'Which are better quality than citizen-issue.'

That shut him up. Soon he turned left and approached what used to be the Commonwealth swimming pool. It had been refurbished and opened for citizens a couple of years ago – one of the Recreation Directorate's better efforts. Hamish went left on to Enlightenment Park Road and then right into the cancer centre. The complex of buildings used to be student residences before the last election in 2003. Many were damaged during the drugs wars. Five years ago the Medical Directorate managed to obtain funds for redevelopment. There are fine views over the leonine Arthur's Seat, but they wouldn't be much comfort to the patients; few who went in came out alive and those who did only lasted weeks. That wasn't at all reassuring. It didn't help that the place was out of the city centre and walled in like a lazaretto.

Hamish parked in front of a nineteenth-century building in the Scottish baronial style. It had a four-storey tower, from the top of which hung a large 'yes' banner. I wondered what that meant to the patients. A sign above the entrance said it was Administration.

'I'll wait for you,' Hamish said. 'Em, good luck.'

'Thanks.'

I went in and asked the red-faced and unusually plump female nursing auxiliary behind the desk for George Allison.

'Dr Allison. I take it you have an appointment?'

'I don't need one,' I said, showing my authorization. 'Marion.'

As I'd hoped, she wasn't impressed by my using her first name. 'Wait,' she said.

'Please, Simpson 174.' I took out my notebook and wrote her barracks number in it. That made her scowl – one of the old school.

Shortly afterwards I heard footsteps on the elaborate wooden staircase. The man in the white coat was tall, dark brown-haired and strikingly handsome.

'Citizen Dalrymple?' he said, offering his hand. 'Sorry to keep you.'

'You didn't. Sorry not to phone ahead.'

He smiled. 'Are you?'

I let that go. He was obviously a smart one.

'How is my father?' I said as we went up the stairs.

'I'll tell you in a moment. You have quite a reputation, citizen.'

'Call me Quint.'

He ran his eye over me. 'I don't think so.'

'No problem, George.'

We walked down a corridor that was gruesome in the extreme. I looked from side to side, then stopped at a particularly disturbing display case.

'Metastatic cancer,' Allison said. 'See the damage to the sternum and ribs.'

I did. 'Is it necessary to have all these skeletons on display?'

'Of course. They're a teaching aid.'

'But this is a child.'

He smiled, then pointed to the pelvis. 'No, it isn't. It's a dwarf. A female aged thirty-nine with achondroplasia. She died six years ago.'

I walked on, trying to keep my eyes off the succession of skeletons with growths and extrusions on different bones.

'My speciality is bone cancer,' the oncologist said, catching up with me and opening a door on the left. 'Which is why your father was referred to me.'

My stomach did a succession of somersaults.

'Take a seat,' he said, waving me into a red-leather armchair. 'You arrived in good time. I'm finishing the report.'

I managed to get a grip on my breathing. 'The old man has bone cancer?'

He looked across the wide desk at me.

'It's hard to be sure. He certainly has cancer in his spine. Whether it originated there or has metastasized from another organ or organs is yet to be clarified.' He passed a file over.

I opened it.

'That's the former guardian's lower spine. The dark patches are tumours.'

There were several – seven according to the report that was attached to the images.

'Is he in pain?'

'He would have been in considerable pain, but we have him on morphine now.'

That almost made me smile. Hector's hatred of opiates, born and nurtured during the drugs wars, was long-standing.

'What else can you do?'

Allison held my gaze. 'Very little, I'm afraid. Palliative care is the only option.'

I swallowed hard. 'How . . . how long has he got?'

He stood up and came round to the armchair. 'It's hard to estimate, citizen. A week, a month. He seems to be a fighter.'

'He is that,' I said hoarsely.

'We'll keep him here until we've run more tests.'

'Can I see him?'

He shook his head. 'Better not today.'

I gave him my mobile number so he could keep me up to date, then took the hand he offered.

'I'm very sorry, citizen. It's an advanced case, but nothing could have been done even if he'd presented earlier. He's too frail for surgery. We have limited resources and radiotherapy is only offered to younger patients with reasonable prognoses.'

I saw red. 'You discriminate against the old.'

'In your father's case, no. As I explained, there's nothing we can do except ease his passing.' He dropped his gaze. 'As for the others, we have to work with the funding we're allocated.'

I stood up and walked away, urgently in need of talking to Sophia.

I sent Hamish off to the castle after he dropped me at the infirmary. He had seen how upset I was and refrained from talking, for which I was grateful.

Sophia was in her outer office, leaning over an assistant's desk. The moment she saw me, she straightened up and led me into her private domain, closing the door. She embraced me.

'I'm so sorry, Quint. George Allison phoned.'

I couldn't speak. She sat me down and wiped my tears, whispering how much she loved me and the old man. He'd initially been suspicious of her, but he liked Maisie and in the last six months he had often been to Sophia's residence for Sunday lunch. He once told her he was happy I'd found someone who cared for me, immediately qualifying that with the usual comment about how much of a failure I was.

I choked back a laugh.

She was sitting on the arm of the chair, holding my head to her chest.

'What's funny?' she asked.

'He . . . I don't know . . . how I'll cope without . . . him.'

Her mouth was close to my ear. 'Don't think about that now. Concentrate on making the most of the time he has left.'

'He'll be out of it, won't he?'

'Not completely.'

'I want you to bring him back here.'

Sophia nodded. 'I already mentioned that to Allison. He doesn't have any objection unless Hector's condition worsens. They have specialist pallia-tive care personnel there.'

I tried to forget my problems. 'You never told me cancer care was rationed.'

She moved back and looked down at me.

'That's not how I'd put it.'

'Of course it isn't. You need to work with the funding you're allocated.'

She flushed. 'That's a rather bald way of stating it. The issues are complex.'

'Yeah, yeah.' I got up.

'Quint!' she said sharply. 'We're doing all we can for your father.'

'Good for you,' I replied, giving her a glare she didn't deserve. 'But he's not the only patient in the city.' I walked out of her office.

She caught up with me in the corridor.

'I understand how you feel, Quint. Don't think I haven't fought for better resources.'

'I'm sure you have,' I said, brushing her away. Then I stopped. 'Duncan Denoon. Has the p-m been done?'

'Not yet.' She took my arm, ignoring the junior doctor who passed. She usually didn't like our relationship to manifest itself in public. 'Do you think you should be working?'

'Why not? I've got to keep my mind occupied.'

'I suppose you have,' she said, letting me go. 'I'll let you know what we find.'

I raised a hand.

'And Quint?'

I stopped.

'I love you.'

I turned, my face drenched with tears again.

'I love you too.'

But at that moment it wasn't enough.

To my surprise I saw Hamish in the Guard 4×4 in the yard.

'Hume 253 sent me back,' he said, his eyes off my damp and no doubt red eyes.

Typical Davie.

'I'm to take you to the castle. Is that all right?'

I got in the front seat and nodded.

Hamish kept quiet on the short drive. I squeezed his arm when we pulled up on the esplanade.

'Thanks, guardsman,' I managed.

Davie was in the command centre. Hamish had obviously told him about the cancer centre and how I'd been.

'What's happening, Quint?' the big man asked, putting his arm round me.

I waited till we got to his office and I'd taken several deep breaths. Then I told him.

'Fucking shit,' he said under his breath. 'I'm really sorry. Poor Hector.'

I communed with my thin Supply Directorate handkerchief till it was soaked.

'Look, Davie . . . I've got to keep working. I can't deal with this otherwise.'

'Are you sure?'

I nodded. 'I'm not being callous. Or maybe I am. But that's the way it is.'

'You'll make time when you have to,' Davie said. 'I know you will.'

He was right and his saying it made me feel better. I'd been a bastard to Sophia. She wouldn't mind, but I did. It had been the other way round when I first knew her – she was known as the Ice Queen. I was probably the only person in the city apart from Maisie who knew how loving Sophia could be. I was privileged and I had no doubt we would survive whatever was ahead for Hector.

'Want to bring me up to date?' I said.

He nodded. 'The explosives experts have found the remains of a pretty sophisticated detonator at the zoo. The bomb was Remtex.'

'The improved version of Semtex? You can get anything on the black market these days.'

'We're checking where it might have come from.'

'Any sightings of people who shouldn't have been in the zoo?'

'The dead man's workmates are being questioned, as are the Guard personnel who were on duty overnight.'

'Maybe a tourist planted it,' I said. The suggestion surprised me as much as it did him. My overwrought subconscious was asserting itself.

'We can hardly interrogate them. Anyway, there have been hundreds at the zoo since it opened this morning.'

'And what would the motive be?'

Davie rocked back in his chair. 'Friend of Mr Chung?'

I thought about that. 'A hypothesis based on zero evidence.'

'True. Ditto an enemy of Mr Chung. Still no reports of Clarinda Towart, by the way. The squads watching the nurse and the theatre director haven't reported anything out of the ordinary.'

'That's a relief. There's been too much of out of the ordinary recently.'

'Aye. We're still digging into the zookeeper's background. He seems to have been an animal-lover in a big way, and popular with his colleagues. His parents disappeared in 2031, suspected runaways to Fife. He was questioned back then, but said he didn't really get on with them. Preferred his hippos.'

'And eccentric hairdo.'

'I saw that on his ID photo. What the hell?'

'Poor sod.'

'Apparently he was hetero, though strangely he didn't have a close companion.'

I laughed despite myself.

'As for a Chinese speaker, we've tracked one down. The problem is, she's ninety-two. She used to be a professor. I spoke to her on the phone. She sounds compos mentis.'

'All right. I still want to keep the stick's existence secret. Is she in a retirement home?'

'Amazingly she isn't. She's got a flat in Great Stuart Street.'

'I'll go and see her tomorrow.'

'Why not now?'

'There's the Council meeting, then I'm going to see *Spar/Tak/Us.*'

'Can I come? To the play, I mean.'

'No. You'll stick out like a giant redwood.'

'A what?'

'It's a tree, dolt. The largest and oldest living things in the world, native to California. At least they were. Maybe they've chopped them all down for firewood now.'

'Thanks for the dendrology lesson.'

'What?'

'Dendrology, the study of—'

'I know what it is. How do you?'

He grinned. 'We had a lecture in barracks when I was a less giant redwood.'

I laughed, then felt my heart contract as I remembered my father.

At least the Council meeting would be a temporary source of amnesia.

Six

I sat on the seat that had been placed in the middle of the Council chamber and looked around the guardians. There was an atmosphere of suppressed panic, but Fergus Calder put on his best don't-worry-I'm-in-control manner.

'First, Quint, let me say on behalf of the guardians how sorry we were to hear about your father's health problems.'

So much for amnesia. I glanced at Sophia. She shook her head. Who had talked? George Allison? There was supposed to be doctor–patient confidentiality, even in Enlightenment Edinburgh.

'Thank you,' I said brusquely. 'Shall I begin? The bomb at the zoo.'

'What on earth is going on?' said Mary Parlane, the tourism guardian. Her hair had made a concerted effort to escape from the bun. 'It's a miracle no visitors were injured.'

'Or citizens, apart from the unfortunate Duncan Denoon.'

'Quite so,' the guardian said, reddening.

'The bomb was located at the rear of the pygmy hippopotamus enclosure,' I said. 'I don't think the person or persons responsible wanted injuries or fatalities.'

'Tell that to the hippos,' said Jack MacLean, with a hollow laugh. I'd be dealing with him shortly.

'What are you suggesting, citizen?' asked Mary Parlane. 'That there are citizens who hate hippopotami?'

I shook my head. 'Somebody was sending a message to the keeper.' I looked up at Sophia again. 'I don't think they meant to kill him.'

'The citizen died of an acute myocardial infarction,' she said. 'The post-mortem showed some minor coronary artery disease, which was probably asymptomatic. As he was conscious after the explosion, it's likely that the extreme stress of seeing what had happened to the animals he cared for brought on the attack.'

'Thank you, guardian,' Calder said. 'Well, citizen?'

'We're looking into Denoon's background. Nothing suggestive yet – apart from the already known fact that he was a close friend of Clarinda Towart. He said he hadn't seen her for a month. She, before you ask, is still missing. The Guard's keeping a close eye on her other two friends.'

James Michie glared at me. 'Why haven't you briefed me, Dalrymple?'

I held his gaze. 'I assumed Hume 253 was doing that.'

'Not his job. If I find you're concealing things, I'll—'

'That'll do,' the senior guardian said firmly. 'Quint?' His continued use of my first name made clear he was on my side. For the time being, at least.

'We're making minimal progress with the Chung Keng Quee murder.'

'That's irritating,' Calder said. 'The Malaysian consul has been chasing me all day.'

'We do know that a taxi driver by the name of Bruce Kilgour took Clarinda Towart and the victim through the checkpoint on Nicolson Street shortly after midnight on Tuesday – or rather, early Wednesday.' I decided not to mention the stop at the Theatre of Life until I'd checked it out.

'What?' exclaimed Jack MacLean. 'He's not supposed to take tourists out of the central zone.'

I nodded. 'A violation of City Regulations he'll no doubt be punished for – though we've let him go under surveillance in case he's involved more than he's saying.'

'But . . . but . . .' said the finance guardian, outraged.

It was time to prick his balloon. 'You told me the dead man was in light engineering, guardian. Are you sure about that?'

His eyes widened. 'Em, no.'

'But you don't deny he was in the city on business? Your SPADE told me so.'

'I . . . no, why should I deny that? There are many outsiders in Edinburgh on business. I don't get involved with them all.'

I let him squirm for a while, then moved on. 'There has to be a possibility of more attacks,' I said, looking at James Michie again. 'I suggest the Guard goes on full alert.'

'Don't be ridiculous,' the public order guardian retorted. 'Mary, what have you put out about the bombing?'

'That it was a gas main.'

I laughed. Enlightenment Edinburgh didn't have piped gas.

'Our visitors don't know any better,' the tourism guardian said defensively.

'Um, this may be a stupid question.'

All eyes turned on Kate Revie, the recently appointed education guardian. She was in her late thirties, red-haired and as thin as a flagpole.

'Could the murder, the explosion and the missing woman have anything to do with the referendum?' she asked.

Not a stupid question at all. I hadn't raised it because there was no evidence to suggest a link, but anything was possible.

Fergus Calder had turned as white as the ghost of David Hume. The same couldn't be said for Jack MacLean. His face was salmon pink.

'Kindly explain your reasoning,' he said to the education guardian, as if he were a professor and she a floundering first-year.

'I don't have any,' Revie said, looking down. 'It was only a passing thought.'

'I for one don't mourn its passing,' MacLean said, smiling viciously.

'Hold on,' I said, unimpressed by his bullying. 'Nothing can be ruled out. You're in charge of the city's business dealings with other Scottish states – and with countries further afield like Malaysia. Can you be sure someone from outside isn't trying to muscle in?'

He was too hard-nosed to show discomfort, but he declined to answer.

Shortly afterwards I was sent packing. As I turned, I saw Sophia shake her head and Kate Revie smile at me. One out of two wasn't bad.

'I'll walk to the theatre,' I said to Davie, who was waiting outside the Council chamber.

'Shame. I was planning on giving you an escort with fifteen Guard vehicles.'

'Ha. Any news?'

'You were only in there twenty minutes.'

'Plenty of time for a body to turn up.'

'Thankfully, no.'

'I have a feeling it won't be long. The bastard who blew up the hippos isn't going to stop there.'

'Not the penguins?'

I sighed and set off for the Theatre of Life.

There was a queue outside the former cinema, citizens showing more excitement than was usual in Enlightenment Edinburgh.

'Ma Johnny told me it's great,' said a young woman with a beehive hairdo.

Her friend, who had a plait that reached her backside, was equally keen. 'Them gladiators. They dinnae wear a thing in one scene.'

Great. Naked males. Right up my boulevard. The queue started to move and I handed over the ticket an undercover operative had procured for me. I didn't recognize any, but there was bound to be at least one in the audience.

I went into the auditorium and got several surprises. First, it was a lot smaller than it had been. I remembered that the Housing Directorate had built a block of flats for privileged citizens – read informers – to the rear. Second, there were no seats. Audience as mob was presumably what the director was after. Third, at least fifty of the spectators were wearing helmets and armour, and carrying swords. Either the costume and properties departments had been slaving to produce replica gear or they'd found a hoard of Roman relics. Surely the blades weren't metal.

When the auditorium was packed, the lights went down. Fortunately the woman with the beehive wasn't in front of me. Trumpets blared and the curtain rose on an enclosed space with high railings on three sides. Immediately gladiators wearing very little went after each other with swords, spears and axes. The dings and clangs were very convincing – except that I doubted they'd have practised with real weapons. A fat man in a toga stood outside the enclosure, a swollen purse in one hand. It looked very like a Guard ammunition pouch. The director was taking the piss. Good for him. Then the scene changed to the interior of the villa. Topless female slaves served wine and fruit to more toga-wearing slobs and their other halves. A naked gladiator with his hands in chains was shown in by heavily armed soldiers.

'Look upon the terror of the Republic!' said toga number one. 'Feast your eyes on the Thracian, Spartacus!'

The Roman women, who were showing only slightly less breast than the slaves, started gaping and gasping. One was in a robe cut from fabric that looked suspiciously like the Council tartan. Another went over and cupped the gladiator's balls. So far, so soft porn.

Then the stage lights dimmed and a spot was directed on to Spartacus. It was only then that I recognized Rory Campbell. His hair had grown out and reached his shoulders and he wasn't just the director. He broke into a speech about injustice and the awfulness of the conditions he and his comrades suffered – terrible food (a sympathetic roar from the audience), brutality from the guards (same again) and life without hope (even louder approbation).

'I will break these chains,' he said, raising his hands above his head and then dashing them downwards. 'I will lead all who value freedom, all who hate slavery to a better life. Death to the Romans! Death to all who rob people of their liberty!'

There was pandemonium in the audience. I did enough to show I was enthused. It wasn't difficult but as my mother, a former senior guardian, used to say, 'Fine words won't feed a mouse.' Unfortunately there had been plenty of guardians who confined themselves to the former and left the rodents – the citizens – to their undeserved lot.

The action progressed, with the gladiators breaking out – cue much running-through, hacking and fake blood – and gathering enough slaves to form an army. Rory Campbell knew what he was doing. The men and women in helmets started to move through the auditorium, touching audience members on the shoulder to make them part of the rebellion. The noise level increased even more.

Then Spartacus started to sing. Campbell had a fine tenor voice and was accompanied by a gladiator incongruously playing an acoustic guitar. The chorus was quickly picked up by the audience – 'Deliver us from slavery, destroy the ruling class' – and I found myself joining in. Fergus Calder would have been appalled, though maybe not surprised.

After that there were battles with impressive choreography and buckets of tomato sauce, more songs, a stylized duel between Spartacus and a Roman commander and even a love story – in those scenes both the leading man and his dusky female companion kept some of their clothes on. Then Rory Campbell got even smarter. Crixus, a gladiator from Gaul, criticized Spartacus's tactics and mocked him for a lovesick boy. That led to a split in the rebels' forces. The audience was taken aback, especially when the two men separated without bitterness. Spartacus then spent the night alone, looking out over his horde. He delivered a moving soliloquy about the difficulties of leadership and the need for sacrifice, but defended his decision to let Crixus go. The freedom to choose had to be given to every man and woman. The audience cheered him to the rafters.

The climax came with a tumultuous battle against the Roman general Crassus, who was portrayed as a jumped-up City Guard commander – Davie would have hit the said rafters. Now came another neat if risky move by the director/star. Extras in Roman uniforms – wearing name and barracks badges to ensure everyone made the connection with the Guard – entered the auditorium and mingled with the crowd. Shadow fighting broke out to mimic the action on the stage. Finally the rebels were hacked down and Spartacus was left alone. He broke into song again, this time glorying in the courage of the former slaves and swearing that their sacrifice would ring down the ages – as indeed it did. Then, the second he was struck from behind by a short and panting legionary, a red curtain came down. Then there was a series of clatters as skeletons fell on to the front of the stage.

The crowd was silent for a few moments, then started cheering louder than I'd ever heard at any rugby or football match – but it wasn't the end. A white sheet with lyrics in large print was dropped in front of the blood-red background and the cast lined up below, leading the audience in the *Spar/Tak/Us Hymn*, as it was called:

> 'O take us, Spartacus the brave,
> From slavery to joy,
> Clean Rome's rotten body
> And strike away all fear.

> So we can live in liberty
> With power in every soul
> And joy in daily labour
> That each has chosen free . . .'

There was more, making the similarities between Republican Rome and contemporary Edinburgh as clear as the spring day that had just passed. How the show hadn't been closed down, I had no idea. Maybe the swords were real after all – not that the City Guard with its Hyper-Stuns would have been bothered.

The audience dispersed slowly, embracing the fighters, both rebel and Roman. Rory Campbell obviously had the measure of his fellow citizens. They took part but didn't get carried away. That, I had the feeling, was the point. After twenty minutes there were only stagehands and cleaners left. I headed for the stage.

'Ye cannae go up there, pal,' said a burly man in grey overalls. He was holding a claw hammer.

I showed him my authorization, saying, 'I want to see Spartacus.'

He raised a lip and let me climb up, then patted me down before leading me backstage. There was a row of cubicles, most of the doors open. I glimpsed actors changing into citizen-issue clothes, along with discarded costumes and armour. The atmosphere was full of greasepaint and sweat.

'This clown wants tae see ye, boss,' said Claw Hammer.

Rory Campbell was still in his skimpy loincloth, cleaning off his make-up. Although he wasn't tall, he was a fine figure of a man. The city's gyms – public or private – were no doubt responsible.

'Quintilian Dalrymple,' he said, grinning. 'I've seen your picture often enough in the *Guardian*.'

'Call me Quint.'

'All right. But you're still a fucking Roman.'

'Oh aye, Dalrymple's a famous Roman name. Gaius Julius Dalrymple, Quintus Horatius Dalrymple . . .'

Campbell laughed. 'I've read Caesar's *Civil War* and Horace's *Odes*. Not in the original, unfortunately.'

'I'd have thought the former would be more to your taste.'

'Was that what you got from the show?'

'Just a bit.'

'Are you here to shut us down?'

'No. I agree with a lot of what was said.'

This time his laugh was sharp. 'Sure you do. I know what your function is, citizen – you clean up the Council's shit but pretend you're still one of us. They'd make you public order guardian in a minute if you let them.'

'Not my kind of thing. I got myself demoted nearly twenty years ago.'

Campbell pulled on a crumpled grey shirt. 'Aye, you're a real maverick.

Till the Council comes calling, then it's "Yes, guardian," "Certainly, guardian," "Is my tongue high enough up yer erse, guardian?".'

I picked up a helmet that was heavier than I'd imagined and sat on the room's only chair. 'I don't like a lot of what the Council's done, Rory, but anarchy wouldn't be good for anyone except the gangs.'

'That old justification. Come on, man. We aren't in the drugs wars now. We don't need a dictatorship, even one that thinks it's benign.'

'You might be right. But inciting rebellion doesn't strike me as very smart, especially when there's a referendum in a few weeks.'

He shook his head. 'As if that'll change anything. The Council will stay put. Maybe things will get worse if they get a cut of the outsiders' cash. More surveillance equipment, more Guard personnel, more guns.'

I shrugged. 'Depends on the vote. It's free, after all.'

'Are you that stupid, Quint? The guardians are playing a clever game, supporting a new Scotland. You think it's because they're planning on improving citizens' lives?'

I thought back to the semicircle of figures in the Council chamber. 'Some of them, yes.'

'Fergus Calder?'

'Not sure.'

'Jack MacLean.'

I smiled. 'I doubt it.'

'You know what we're up against.'

'You'd better be careful, Spartacus. The Council will have found out what you're doing here.'

'Of course they have, you daft cunt. The Recreation Directorate sees this as a feel-good play that sends people home with a skip in their step and is instantly forgotten.'

I thought about that. The recreation guardian was a recent appointee, a man in his fifties who had taught theatre studies. Maybe he knew what he was doing.

Rory Campbell handed me a glass of island whisky.

'Where did you get that?'

'The Lord of the Isles. He said he hadn't enjoyed himself so much in years.'

'Not counting the last time he hanged some crofters.'

'Maybe.'

'Definitely,' I said, taking a sip. It was nectar. 'Do you often get outsiders in the audience?'

'Not so often. The senior guardian comes with his counterparts from other Scottish states from time to time.'

I felt the floor move beneath me.

'Do you use a different script then?'

He shook his head as he pulled on a pair of finely tooled brown cowboy boots.

'No. And before you ask, I got these from the first minister of Glasgow.'

'Andrew Duart? He's been here as well?'

'Aye, with a rather formidable police chief called Hel—'

'Hyslop.'

'I might have known you'd be a pal of hers.'

'The opposite. But I bet she enjoyed the crowd scenes.'

He smiled. 'She did look a bit concerned. Then again, she was carrying a rather large pistol.'

So the Council knew all about the Theatre of Life. I wondered if any of the guardians had the information I was about to ask for.

'Clarinda Towart,' I said, watching Campbell's face closely.

'Ah, Clarinda. Wonderful name, wonderful woman.' He sounded plausible.

'She was here for twenty minutes on early Wednesday morning.'

The actor-director caught my eye. 'She was. So?'

'So why?'

'Why not?' he replied casually.

'Do you want to spend the night in the castle?'

He smiled mockingly. 'See? You think you're a private eye, but the minute someone talks back you fall back on good old Guard methods.'

He had me there; it was time I regained the initiative. 'Chung Keng Quee was here too.'

That got to him, though he disguised his surprise quickly.

'I don't know who or what that is.'

'Right. I'm not joking about the castle.'

This time he took me seriously. 'Look, Clarinda can be a handful. She always has been. She drinks and then she does stupid things. She got it into her head that the tourist she'd picked up had to meet me, I've no idea why. Why should an Asian care about a citizen actor? I gave them a drink from the bottle you're sampling and sent them on their way. I mean, representatives from other Scottish states are one thing, but I'd lose my licence if anyone found out a tourist was here.'

'I *have* found out.'

He eyed me cautiously. 'So you have. I wonder how – and why you're so interested.'

I ignored those points. 'What did you talk about with them?'

'The play, what else? I gave the Chinese—'

'Malaysian.'

'Really? I gave him a quick tour of the set and let him handle a helmet and some weapons.'

'And what did he think of that?'

'He was pleased, kept laughing in a weird high voice. He was pissed too.'

I went for broke. 'Later that night he was murdered – garotted to be precise – in Clarinda Towart's flat.'

'What?' He was a professional dissembler, but the shock looked genuine.

'And since then there's been no sign of your close friend Clarinda.'

That disturbed him even more. He gulped whisky.

'What . . . what do you think has happened to her?'

'Turn that question on yourself.'

'I've no idea. Honest.'

I believed him, but I called Davie and we took Spartacus to the castle to mak siccar.

Seven

On the way I called Sophia.

'Your father's stable, Quint,' she said. 'They have him sedated.'

I wondered why George Allison hadn't called me with an update as he'd promised. Then again it seemed there wasn't much to tell.

'Where are you?' she asked.

'Working.'

'Still? You need rest.'

'So you don't want me to come down to your place when I finish.'

'You're always welcome.'

That got to me. Spartacus's activities had kept me occupied for the evening, but now I was face to face with the nightmare of my old man's approaching end, and I was struggling.

'Quint?'

'I'm all right,' I said unconvincingly.

'Cut short what you're doing and come to me.'

I said I would, but it was a lie. Even with Sophia, sleep – whatever preceded it – would come slowly. Could you be haunted by someone who was still alive?

Davie glanced at me after I'd cut the connection.

'Are you seriously going to interrogate this citizen now?'

I looked back at him. 'Why not?'

'For fuck's sake.' He drove to the esplanade in silence and parked. 'Out,' he said to me.

'What?'

'You heard me. Guardsman? Take this sorry citizen to Moray Place.'

'You're getting above yourself, big man.'

'No, I'm not. Go to bed.'

I finally saw sense. 'OK, but take Citizen Campbell back to his place in Dumbiedykes.'

Davie stepped closer. 'Are you serious? He could be over the city line by dawn.'

'You've got him under surveillance, haven't you?'

'Ah.'

'Ah as in, "Sorry, Quint, I'm being a dolt"?'

He manhandled me into the waiting 4×4. As I was driven away, I caught sight of the actor-director's face. He looked concerned, but I didn't know what about. Surely it couldn't be me.

The second I lay down on Sophia's bed, I fell into a sleep deeper than the Marianas Trench, into which, Billy Geddes once told me, the vengeful Japanese had sunk the entire Chinese fleet of warships after the country's economic crash.

I was woken by a high-pitched voice singing, 'Come on, man with the silliest name in Edinburgh, breakfast's getting cold.'

I grabbed the seven-year-old, receiving two plaits in succession, one in each eye.

'Ow! Ah!'

'That will teach you,' Maisie said seriously. 'Look but don't touch.'

Sophia had to be responsible for instilling that command, probably because her daughter was often to be found in the infirmary. The rate she was going, she'd be the youngest doctor in history.

I was able to change my clothes after taking a shower because Sophia had finally allowed me to keep some in her residence. Ordinary citizens weren't supposed to spend the night in the circular street's fine Georgian houses and she used to restrict my visits. These days I spent more nights with her than in my dump in Gilmore Place – though I needed to go back there to listen to the blues. Sophia preferred chamber music. So did Maisie.

The cook had produced the full Scottish for me. Sophia was eating toast and low-sugar strawberry jam.

'You snored,' she said.

'Sorry. I'll get a plumber to clean my pipes.'

Maisie finished her orange juice and stared at me. 'I've seen plumbers' rods,' she said. 'They're far too big for your external and anterior nares.'

I looked at Sophia hopelessly.

'She's right. You've got very delicate nostrils.'

The driver arrived to take Maisie to school.

'Good day, Quint man,' she said, allowing me to kiss her cheek.

'She's been reading Dickens,' Sophia explained. 'Keeps correcting his grammar.'

'I got off lightly, then.'

'I'm very pleased you slept well.'

'I'm not pleased that I failed to take advantage of you.'

She smiled. 'What you don't know is that I took advantage of you.'

I raised an eyebrow.

'I called George Allison before you came down. Your father should be back in the infirmary by early evening.'

'That's good.'

We embraced and nuzzled each other tenderly.

Shortly afterwards we headed for the High Street in her 4×4, where I got out and walked up to the castle. Not even a peck on the cheek was allowed in open view.

'When do you want that Campbell tosser in?' Davie asked, in his office off the command centre.

'How about eleven o'clock?' I looked around, but there was no sign of James Michie. 'I'm going to give the memory stick to the Chinese professor. What's her name?'

'Hang on.' He shuffled files on his desk. 'Here it is. Margo Paterson, 12e Great Stuart Street.' He handed me the file.

'What do I need to know about her?'

He shrugged. 'I told you, she's ninety-two. She used to be a professor of Mandarin – in the USA before it fell apart.'

'That'll do. Hope the stuff in the stick's Mandarin.'

'Don't tell me – there are different versions of Chinese?'

'Remember that restaurant we stuffed our faces in?'

He grinned. 'How could I forget?'

'There were several types of dish – Szechuan, Cantonese and so on.

Something similar goes for the languages. I think there are at least seven main ones.'

'And you know this how?'

'Hector was professor of rhetoric, remember? He was forever going on about how people used language to get what they wanted. Chairman Mao was one of his favourite examples.'

'Chairman Who?'

I left, shaking my head. Then again, ignorance of the old tyrant was a kind of bliss.

Great Stuart Street in the New Town was in two sections, divided by the oval Ainslie Place. The professor's residence was on the southern bit. The cobbled street was lined with elegant four-storey buildings that had once been family houses, but were split into small flats both before and after the Enlightenment came to power. 12e turned out to be the basement. I knocked on a door that had seen better centuries.

'Who are you?' said the short, square old woman who opened up. She was wearing glasses with thick lenses and her white hair was topped by a red woollen hat like a tea cosy.

'Quint Dalrymple,' I said, offering my authorization.

Professor Paterson held it close to her glasses.

'Any relation to Hector Dalrymple?' she said, handing it back.

'I'm his son,' I said, the words catching in my throat.

'What's the matter?'

'He's not well.'

'I'm sorry to hear that. Come in, come in.'

I followed her into a realm of dust, books, piles of paper and cats. One hissed at me as my boot narrowly missed its tail.

'I knew Hector before things went to pot. He organized a conference at the university here. I gave a keynote speech on the rhetoric of Mao Zedong. He was very interested.' She cleared books from a tattered armchair and pointed me to it. 'Is he dying?'

I was taken aback by her directness. 'I . . . yes, it seems so.'

'I could hear it in your voice,' she said, sitting behind a desk piled with folders and adorned by a large and venerable typewriter.

'But I'm not here about my father.'

'Of course not. What can I do for you, young man? I hope it isn't anything to do with the Tourism Directorate. I've done enough unpaid work for them over the years. It's not as if I haven't enough of my own. I'm translating a little-known novel from the Cultural Revolution. It was smuggled to France in a consignment of bamboo shoots and only recently came to light.' She put her hand on the typewriter. 'Well, spit it out.'

I stifled a laugh and took out the stick and a Guard laptop.

'Could you have a look at some digital files?'

'What?'

'On the computer.'

'You'll have to show me how it works. When I was at Penn State, I refused to have anything to do with the monstrous machines. The brain is connected to the hand by nerves, not wires.'

I'm no digital expert, but I managed to open the file index and select one.

The professor leaned forward, her eyes only a couple of inches from the screen.

'Oh, this is easy. Standard Mandarin, in which I happen to be fluent. Where did you get it?' She laughed gruffly. 'You can't say, of course. Well, what do you want to do? Shall I dictate?'

'If you could give me the gist . . .'

'Very well. "Agreement between Malaysia Company State 245/12 and Edinburgh Council of Guardians, ref. Tourism Directorate.'

I was engrossed and scribbling fast.

'There are a lot of details I won't bother you with. Addresses, that sort of thing.'

'Any names?' I showed her how to scroll down.

'Names of people? No. Shall I go on?'

'Please.'

'Five thousand Malaysian tourists per year to be accommodated in Edinburgh at the best hotels. The sum involved is ten million ringgit.'

'What's that in Edinburgh pounds?'

'I've no idea.'

'There are a lot of clauses outlining what the city is to provide. Everything of the best quality. Malaysia must have a booming economy.'

Billy Geddes would know about that.

'Let's open some other files.'

I did so.

'This one's with the Housing Directorate,' said Professor Paterson. 'Seven million ringgit for the provision of wood and other building materials, and two million for furniture.'

'Shame we chopped down all our forests,' I said.

'Quite. This one's with the Finance Directorate.'

Surprise, surprise.

'A hundred million ringgit for the provision of . . . weapons.' She peered at me. 'That can't be right.'

I hoped it wasn't.

'But it is,' the professor said. 'Five thousand Stun-Rifles – whatever they are – ten thousand twenty-shot-magazine semi-automatic pistols, twenty thousand grenades and . . . Good God! Two main battle tanks.'

I finished my notes.

'This is extraordinary,' she said.

'Professor Paterson, it's also very dangerous information. I'm going to send Guard personnel down here to look out for you.'

'Do call me Margo, Quintilian. And no, thank you. I don't want people cluttering up my home.'

I looked around. There wasn't room for another cat, let alone the most sylphlike guardswoman.

'All the same. I also need someone to take the dictation you mentioned earlier – initially a précis of all nineteen files and then the full texts.' I hated to imagine what else would turn up. I could have stayed myself, but I needed to think how to proceed.

'I'll tell you something funny,' Margo said. 'I left Pennsylvania in 2000 because public order had broken down. I was born and grew up in Edinburgh, and I was here for the last election and then the drugs wars. I didn't expect we'd be going back into battle when I was still alive.'

'You'll be safe here,' I said glibly.

'You misunderstand. Obviously you haven't read my file. If the city's to be defended, I'll be on the front line. Even when my eyesight began to fail I was able to act as a rifle loader.' She looked up at me. 'The question is, who will the Council be fighting this time?'

She'd nailed it. I had a nasty feeling the enemy would be its own citizens.

Before I left, I called Davie and asked him to select a guardswoman and man with both secretarial and advanced combat skills. There was no shortage of those, but they also had to be people he could trust. He promised to find the appropriate personnel.

'Good luck to you, Quintilian,' Margo said, as she showed me to the door, banging into me three times.

'And to you. I hope it isn't necessary.'

She laughed softly. 'But you think it will be.'

She was right.

I walked towards the west end of Princes Street, my mind a maelstrom. I could go to Billy Geddes and present him with what I'd found, but that could lead to me being put out of action, maybe terminally. Going to Jack MacLean would almost certainly have the same result. What the hell was the Council doing? I didn't believe that Sophia knew anything about it, though the Medical Directorate might be involved – I had to wait for the full list of contracts. Also, the fact that they were in Chinese perhaps meant they were only drafts. Negotiations might still be ongoing, with only a few people involved – Billy, MacLean, Fergus Calder. The Tourism Directorate didn't seem to be doing anything wrong and the same went for the Housing Directorate, at least so far as I was aware. The weapons were the problem. They were enough to start a revolution. Or put one down. I remembered how Rory Campbell had described *Spar/Tak/Us* – was it really just a sop to citizens?

Davie called. 'Citizen Campbell's here.'

I'd forgotten about the interview. Davie could do it.

'Give him the second degree – to clarify, that's the one that doesn't involve physical injury.'

'I'm aware of that.'

'Press him on his show. He claims it isn't anti-Council. I'm not so sure.'

'Where are you going?'

'There's something I want to check.'

'Go all secretive then,' he said, cutting the connection.

It was a long shot, but I didn't fancy being indoors for an hour or two.

The Porteous Trail that Chung Keng Quee had been on started in Greyfriars Kirkyard, off the southern end of George IV Bridge. It was outside the tourist zone, which no doubt gave the trippers a thrill, not that there was anything of citizen Edinburgh about the area – the Tourism Directorate had made sure of that. The presence of the Museum of Edinburgh – once, and perhaps to be so again, that of Scotland as a whole – nearby made it feel like the city centre. In truth the checkpoint was to keep citizens out, except on Sundays, rather than tourists in, at least in this vicinity.

I tailed a group of French, African and Asian tourists. One of the guides, female auxiliaries in plaid skirts, spoke English and the other French. Leaflets in other languages were handed out. I kept an eye on the three Asians, though none of them looked like Chung Keng Quee. If they acted suspiciously, I could get their names from the guides later. The group stood around John Porteous's now-vacated grave and looked at the stone. I knew his story, not least because the man had been in charge of the City Guard in 1736. I'd used him in my public order manual as an example of how not to handle a crowd.

'John Porteous was not a popular man,' said the English-speaking guide. 'He was overbearing and arrogant, particularly hated by Edinburgh citizens of the lower class.' She broke off and smiled. 'Our own City Guard is, of course, widely loved and respected.'

I almost choked and burst out coughing. So much for keeping a low profile.

'He was also one of the earliest Scottish golfers, which also shows how egotistical he was.' The Asians looked askance, unaware that the first Council had outlawed golf as a game that expressed individual rather than collective endeavour. All the city's courses had been turned into auxiliary training grounds and citizen parks.

The group was led out of the old churchyard, turning left down the hill towards the Grassmarket. Suddenly a man in rags, his wrists chained, was marched out of an alley by men in red eighteenth-century guard uniforms and black tricorne hats.

'Three smugglers were condemned to death,' announced the guide. 'This one, Andrew Wilson, was the only one to suffer the ultimate punishment, as his companion William Hall was transported for life and the third man, George Robertson, escaped from prison by pulling apart the bars of his cell window.'

By now we were approaching the great bulk of the New Tolbooth, a replica of the prison cum meeting house that used to stand on the High Street. Executions were carried out at the original building, and the same happened at its modern counterpart, only they were fake.

'On April 14th 1736, Andrew Wilson was hanged here in the Grassmarket.'

An executioner in black clothes attached a rope to the frame under the actor's shirt and he was hoisted up a gibbet extending from the wall above a nightclub. He kicked for a while and then croaked, literally. The crowd cheered. I'd blame Hollywood for the levels of violence that people are used to globally, but Los Angeles disappeared into a gaping fault line that opened ten years ago.

'However, the crowd was unhappy,' continued the guide, 'and a riot ensued. Captain Porteous was instructed to call out the Guard. When the crowd turned on them, the commander ordered his men to open fire. Six people were killed and many more wounded.'

By now we were in the shade of the New Tolbooth's rear wall. Shots rang out from speakers on the wall along with roars and screams. The men in red raised their muskets and puffs of smoke issued from the muzzles. The bangs were less than impressive, but the tourists still clapped.

'John Porteous was tried and condemned to death for the killings,' said the guide. 'He was imprisoned in the Tolbooth here.'

He was actually held in the original building on the High Street, but I allowed a modicum of artistic licence.

'The Edinburgh crowd heard rumours that Porteous was to be reprieved. Although he was due to hang on September 8th, the people didn't wait.'

We were then led up Victoria Street and on to the High Street. Near St Giles' Cathedral, the group stood around the cobblestone heart that marks where the Old Tolbooth stood. More men in red uniforms appeared, then about a dozen men and women in ordinary eighteenth-century dress. The man playing Porteous stood in a nightgown and open shirt, his feet in open-backed slippers. The make-believe mob grabbed him, pushed the soldiers to the ground and dragged him up the road.

The tourists were excited now, following the actors as if they themselves were members of the mob. The guides shouted to be heard. Everyone started running and in a few minutes we were back in the Grassmarket. This time we stopped under a dark red pole that stuck out above a shop. Men from the mob got a rope round Porteous's neck – I hoped they managed to attach it to the frame – and he was unceremoniously lynched, abuse at full volume coming from both actors and tourists.

'But then,' the guide yelled, 'things took a turn for the worse.'

That made me smile. I'd forgotten the details – how could the unfortunate commander's situation have deteriorated? Easily, it turned out.

'He was pulled down and his clothes stripped from him, the shirt wrapped around his head.'

This was duly done, though the actor kept on a vest and long johns.

'Then he was pulled up again, though the mob had not bound his hands. Captain Porteous struggled free. The citizenry broke his arm and shoulder, and tried to incinerate him.'

All this took place before me. I was glad to see that the actor's foot didn't catch fire.

'Again he was pulled up, after being savagely beaten, and at last the murderer died.'

Mob and tourists broke into loud cheers as Porteous swung motionless above them. It was a vile but compulsive sight.

The guides led us into the premises below the makeshift gibbet. I'd thought it was a shop and so it was in part, but the main attraction was the horizontal display case showing Porteous's skeleton. The bones were dark brown, stained by the earth that would have covered them after the coffin lid rotted. The breaks to arm and shoulder were clear, and several ribs were shattered. The City Guard commander's lower jaw was separated from the rest of his facial bones. It looked like he'd screamed so hard that he'd dislocated it.

The tourists were busy buying souvenirs, which included models of the hanged man and framed pieces of supposedly original City Guard uniforms. At least the Tourism Directorate had made an effort to make the red more faded than the uniforms worn by the actors. There were also copies of Walter Scott's *The Heart of Midlothian* and other novels, including *The Black Dwarf*, in various languages. The former described the Porteous lynching in detail, as stickers made clear.

I was about to head out when I saw what might have attracted Chung Keng Quee. At the rear was a door with a bronze nameplate. The words on it were 'C. T. Enterprises'. Above them was engraved the profile of a reclining female figure with a very pronounced bosom.

I called Davie and asked him to bring Rory Campbell with him. Along with a battering ram.

Eight

The crowd had dispersed by the time Davie arrived. I got into the 4×4.

'Ever been in there?' I asked the actor-director.

'No. Why would I go to a tourist shop?'

'Do you know the name of the company in charge?'

'The Tourism Directorate,' he said, with a wry smile.

'Come on, you know citizens have been given licences to operate in the central zone.'

'A few, yes.'

Davie turned to glare at him. 'The interview isn't over, shithead.' He looked at me. 'Citizen Campbell hasn't been very cooperative. We need to squeeze his nuts.'

I smiled coldly. 'Whatever it takes.'

'Fucker,' said Rory. 'I knew you were a Guard bully at heart.'

I let that go. 'So you've never heard of C. T. Enterprises?'

'Why should . . .' He looked at me. 'Is it something to do with Clarinda?'

'That's what we're going to find out.' I raised a hand. 'Not you.' I opened the door and waved to a guardsman, who came over.

'Citizen,' he said stiffly.

'Sit with this specimen, will you?'

Davie gave him the nod, then went to the back of the 4×4. He opened the top-hinged door and took out a one-man ram.

The female citizen at the till opened her mouth but didn't say anything. She knew better than to question the Guard.

'Hello, Grizel,' I said, reading her badge. 'Nice old Scots name. What can you tell me about C. T. Enterprises?'

She was young and slim, with unusually well-styled black hair. 'Nothing much,' she replied. 'I only see Clarinda every evening when she checks the takings.'

'How long have you been working here?'

'About six weeks.'

I pointed at Rory Campbell.

'Ever seen him?'

She shook her head. 'What's this about?'

'Wait outside, Grizel. You won't make a run for it, will you?'

'Why should I?'

I didn't think she was involved in whatever Clarinda Towart was, but I waved to the guardsman and inclined my head towards the young woman. Davie had cuffed Campbell to the rail along the back of the front seat, so he wasn't going anywhere.

'Have you got a key for that door?' I asked, as she was putting on her coat.

'No.'

'All right, thanks.'

She gave me a shy smile.

'Shall I smash it in?' Davie asked.

'We could always knock first.'

He did so, loudly.

I turned the handle. The door didn't budge.

Davie swung the ram at the lock. The wood around it splintered but the door didn't open.

'Mortice lock,' he grunted.

I shouted my name several times. There was no answer.

Davie applied himself to the door frame in the vicinity of the lock.

'Doesn't smell too healthy.'

'No, big man, it doesn't. Strange that Grizel didn't notice.' I glanced over my shoulder. She was in the Guard 4×4, eating a sandwich.

'The door's a tight fit,' Davie said, putting his shoulder to it.

When he got it open, the reek of rotting human being washed over us.

'Fuck,' he said, raising his arm to his face.

I was breathing through my mouth, but that only meant I could taste the corruption.

'That's not Clarinda Towart,' Davie said, leaning in.

'No, it's a male.'

'Well spotted.'

The body on the desk was naked and swollen, the lengthy sideboards clear on the face that was turned towards us. His mouth was open almost as wide as Captain Porteous's.

I called Sophia, then the scene-of-crimes team.

My very-much-not-fan Raeburn 297 eyed me dubiously. 'Another suspicious death, citizen.'

'Don't blame me.'

The techie was pulling on plastic coveralls. 'Oh, but I do. If you hadn't got yourself demoted the city would be a much safer place.'

He might have had a point – except that if I'd stayed in the Guard I'd either have self-destructed or been quietly disposed of by a Council member who didn't like where I was sticking my snout.

Sophia arrived a few minutes later and suited up. She looked tired, her face even paler than usual.

'Everything OK?' I asked.

'As you see,' she said, pointing into the shop, 'it's not the missing citizen.'

'Unless she was a transsexual, no.'

I let her get on with her job, though she could have delegated it. That was one of the reasons for her exhaustion.

'Come with me,' I said to Grizel, after opening the door of the 4×4. I led her to the rear of the New Tolbooth.

'What's happened?' she asked nervously.

'I was wondering if you could tell me.'

'I don't understand.' She genuinely looked at a loss.

'There's a dead man in the back office.'

'What?' she shrieked. 'Who is he?'

'No idea.' I raised a hand. 'Don't worry, you don't have to look at him. Yet.'

'I . . .'

'You?'

'I don't know what to say.'

'You never saw anyone go into the office apart from Clarinda?'

She shook her head.

'What did you think when she didn't show up the last two evenings?'

'Nothing. It often happens. I put the takings in the safe in the floor.'

'What's the combination?'

Grizel gave me a dubious look. 'I can't tell you that.'

'It's a murder case. You have to tell me everything.'

She thought about that and then nodded. '19-10-26. There's a panel under the chair at the sales desk.'

'Thank you.' I caught her eye. 'Anything else you want to say? You'll be taken to the castle to make a statement, but you might be able to save us valuable time by talking now.'

She looked down. 'Clarinda's been different the last couple of weeks. More . . . decisive. I think she's stopped drinking.'

That would explain the absence of booze in her flat. Perhaps she'd been putting on an act with the taxi driver and others.

'And?' I could see she hadn't finished.

'Well . . . I don't like to say this, but she was rude to some customers.'

That sounded like the old Clarinda.

'Who were they?'

'First there was a French couple. They were complaining about the prices and she told them to . . . get to fuck.' Grizel looked offended. 'Tourism Directorate protocol strictly forbids bad language.'

The young woman seemed to be an ideal citizen.

'And then there was a Chinese man. She told him to leave her alone. To fucking leave her alone.'

That *was* interesting. We'd have to show her a photo of Chung Keng Quee.

'When was this?'

'Monday, just before closing time. That's 8 p.m.'

'All right.' I beckoned to Davie and got him to arrange things.

'Don't worry, Grizel. When you're finished up there you'll have the rest of the day off.'

'Will I have to go back on the directorate labour rota?'

I shrugged. 'Why? Do you like working here?'

'Yes,' she said simply.

'I don't know when the shop will reopen, but I'll tell the tourism guardian how helpful you've been.' I glanced at her badge again. 'Grizel Monzie.'

She smiled sweetly.

A guardswoman took her off to another 4×4.

'Let's have a chat with Rory Campbell.'

'The tosser's gone to sleep.'

'Not surprised. He works his arse off on stage and goes home late.'

'What was the play like?'

'I'll tell you later.'

I got into the Guard vehicle and nudged Campbell.

'What's going on?' he said, blinking.

'There's a dead man in Clarinda's office.'

'What?'

His shock was convincing.

'Where's Clarinda?'

'You tell me.'

No reply.

'Let's show him the corpse's face.'

Rory Campbell's jaw dropped. 'Look, I really have to get to the theatre, there's a new cast member to—'

'It won't take a minute,' I said. 'Wait here.'

I went over to the shop. The guardsman at the door handed me over-shoes and gloves. I stepped around the markers on the floor and made it to the back office. Sophia was making notes, while Raeburn 297 was on his knees beside the desk.

'What have you got?' I asked my lover.

'Caucasian male, forties, five foot ten, approximately twelve stone, close-cut brown hair, brown eyes, circumcised. Manual strangulation, with clear marks of both thumbs on the throat. He's been dead for at least forty-eight hours, note the lividity and the absence of rigor.'

'Knee on his chest,' I asked, leaning forward.

'I'd say so.'

I turned to tech-team leader. 'Any ID?'

'None. No clothes or footwear either. I've found a footprint, though – a size eight.'

'Fingerprints?'

'Taken and sent to the castle for comparison with citizen records.'

That would take time if they weren't Clarinda Towart's.

Sophia went out and I followed. Guard tape had been wrapped around tree trunks and lamp posts. Behind it stood many a tourist. That wouldn't impress the Council. At least none of them looked like Chung Keng Quee.

'I'll have the preliminary p-m results by the evening, Quint.'

'Obviously you'll be checking if he consumed a large amount of alcohol.'

'Obviously. That would explain how Clarinda Towart is able to strangle and garotte men who are bigger than her.'

'Who says she's the killer?'

Sophia shook her head, though she managed a smile. 'Typical. Discount the obvious and dream up a ludicrous conspiracy.'

I smiled. 'That's your beloved Quint.'

She held my gaze. 'Your beloved Hector's almost finished his tests. He'll be back in the infirmary soon.'

'What are the tests showing?'

'Nothing you don't know already.' She squeezed my arm. '*Courage, mon brave.*'

'*Merci,*' I said, despite the sudden dryness of my mouth.

Then the medical guardian kissed me on the lips. I could hear the rapid intake of breath from nearby Guard personnel.

Davie and I went into the shop with Rory Campbell. He looked like he was going to be sick when he saw the dead man, but he managed to hold it in. Outside again, he said he'd never seen him before. I was convinced.

In the shop Davie located the floor panel and pulled it up. Then I input the numbers on the unusually hi-tech display. The door sprang open. There were neatly separated bundles of foreign currency, most of which I didn't recognize. Some of it was Malaysian ringgits. At least I knew what the enemy looked like now.

Raeburn 297 came by.

'Can you check for fingerprints on this, please?' I asked.

He nodded. 'I'm not getting many traces in the office, dirt, fabric or the like. I think our killer's cleaning up after him or herself.'

'Interesting,' I said. 'He or she must also have had keys for both the back room and the main door. The sales girl didn't say anything about the latter being open. Of course, she has keys.'

Davie looked puzzled. 'Surely it's Clarinda Towart.'

I exchanged glances with the senior techie.

'I wouldn't go making assumptions like that, commander,' said Raeburn 297. 'There's no proof yet.'

I smiled at him, but he stayed glum. In his book I was irredeemable.

'We should talk to the neighbours,' Davie said, trying to reassert himself.

'You'd better check with the guardian,' I said. 'Discretion is the better part of etc.'

He went outside to make the call. I saw the tourism guardian arrive, her hair loose. Her people started ushering onlookers away, handing them vouchers.

'Free casino chips?' I asked, joining her.

'Among other things. What on earth's going on, Quintilian? We have to find Clarinda.'

'Are you sure there's nothing more you can tell me about her, Mary?' She shook her head. 'We didn't even know about her involvement in the shop. I've just been told that she filed her company with the Finance Directorate three months ago as required, but they failed to notify us.'

That was interesting. I'd be asking Jack MacLean for an explanation. In the meantime I had a tricky job to do.

'Do you think you could have a look at the dead man?'

Mary Parlane blanched, then steeled herself. 'Very well.'

I took her in, waving at the paramedics to stand back.

'Bloody hell,' the guardian muttered, hand over her nose. 'It's a long time since I saw a corpse.' She looked at the swollen face. 'No, I'm sorry. Never seen him before.'

I led her out and told the paramedics to take the body away. Raeburn 297 glared at me.

'Sorry,' I said, flushing. 'Are you finished?'

'As it happens, citizen, I am – at least in the immediate vicinity of the deceased.' He smirked at me. I deserved that.

Mary Parlane went back to her auxiliaries, while I got into the 4×4.

'Right, Rory,' I said to the drowsy actor-director. 'It's time we had a proper chat.'

Davie grinned as he gunned the engine and headed for his home ground.

I looked through Campbell's file after he'd been put in the smallest interrogation room. Davie was collating reports.

Then the door opened without a knock and James Michie walked in.

'Guardian,' Davie said, getting to his feet.

I stayed on my backside, which didn't go unnoticed.

'Progress report,' the guardian demanded.

'Minimal,' I said, unimpressed that he'd vetoed canvassing Grassmarket locals until the Council meeting. 'I'm waiting for the post-mortem report.'

'How about doing something off your own bat?' Michie said waspishly.

'We're about to interview one of Clarinda Towart's two surviving friends,' Davie said.

'Ah.'

'The surveillance team on the other, Alice Lennox, reports that she's at work and has had no suspicious encounters.'

'Good.' The guardian sat down. 'What news of your father?' he said to me emolliently.

I told him.

'I hope he'll be comfortable in the infirmary,' he said, looking away.

There was a knock on the door and a middle-aged guardswoman poked the top half of her body round. 'Oh, I'm sorry, guardian, I didn't realize you were here.'

'Never mind. What's in that file?'

'I . . .'

Uh-oh. Davie's wide eyes told me that she was one of the pair sent to Professor Paterson.

'Em, it's not important, guardian,' she said, pulling away.

'Anything that concerns the serious crime commander concerns me,' said Michie. 'Hand it over.'

'It's just a surveillance report,' Davie said desperately. 'On—'

'Hand it over.'

The guardswoman did as she was told.

'You can go,' Davie said.

'No, she can't,' countermanded the guardian. '"Synopsis of Files on Memory Stick CKQ16"?' He looked at Davie and then me. 'Explain.'

I shrugged and Davie started to talk rubbish.

Michie put a hand up. 'Guardswoman, what was your assignment?'

She swallowed hard and told him. He sent her on her way.

'What's the meaning of this?' he demanded. 'Why wasn't I told about the stick? I take it the reference is to the dead Malaysian?'

'Correct,' I said, trying to take command of the situation. 'I wanted to see if the data was relevant before bothering you with it.'

'It would appear that it is,' he said drily.

'Could I see it?' I asked.

'No, you fucking can't see it! Give me your authorization, now!'

I shook my head. 'It was issued by the Council, not you, James.'

'Don't you "James" me! I'll have you down a coal mine in half an hour.'

I took a deep breath. 'Look at contract reference Fin Dir 4.' That was the one covering the large weapons shipment.

He turned pages and then read, his eyeballs protruding. 'This . . . this is impossible,' he stammered.

I took the file from his slack fingers and ran an eye over the pages. There were three more contracts with the Finance Directorate, relating to the supply of narcotics, the construction and delivery of two armed launches and the provision of hi-tech medical equipment. Other directorates were involved in less sensitive merchandise.

'What's Jack MacLean doing ordering weapons?' Michie said. 'They come under my directorate's control. And main battle tanks? What would I do with those?'

Trust a guardian to take it personally.

'Narcotics are in your purview too,' I pointed out. Drugs for the city's visitors are delivered to the Tourism Directorate from a City Guard store.

Michie had his phone out and was pressing buttons. I grabbed it.

'How dare—'

'Think about it, James,' I said. 'We need to find out what MacLean — and maybe the senior guardian — are doing before we go in boots first. These contracts may only be drafts. They're translations from Chinese. Chung Keng Quee was Chinese Malaysian.'

Michie got his breathing under control. 'There must have already been substantial negotiations for things to have got so far.'

I nodded. 'But that doesn't necessarily mean the deals will take place.'

'I still don't understand why I wasn't involved even at the planning stage. What would the Finance Directorate want with so much weaponry?'

'I suggest we investigate further, guardian.' I handed him his phone.

'I can see the sense in that.' He looked at Davie. 'Commander, tell me why I shouldn't reduce you to the ranks with immediate effect?'

'Because you're going to need me,' Davie said.

'He's right,' I put in.

'You're going to need Quint too.'

Michie stood up. 'Quite the mutual admiration society. Very well, both of you stay in position. For the time being.'

'I'd advise that you don't talk about this to anyone, especially Council members.'

'I'll think about it, citizen,' he said pompously.

It was obvious he was going to keep quiet. Getting into a fight with Calder and MacLean would do him no good at all.

'You will, however, keep me fully up to date with the investigations,' he said, heading for the door. He'd left the file with me.

Davie and I said 'yes' several times before the door closed behind the guardian. Then we breathed deep sighs of relief.

'All right, Rory,' I said, after the interrogation had got nowhere, 'we'll let you get back to work.'

Davie demonstrated his disapproval audibly.

'Just one thing. Did you get the impression the last time you saw Clarinda that she was off the drink?'

The actor-director laughed. 'You're joking. When she brought that Asian guy to the theatre she was steaming.'

'Could she have been putting it on?'

He scratched his head. 'I don't think so. In my business you get to be able to spot people who're taking the piss. Especially when they're *on* the piss.'

'There's nothing in Clarinda's file about her having acting experience.'

'Naw, I told your bull here. I've been friends with her since we met on compulsory harvest duty when we were in our early twenties. She's a free spirit. That why I kept up with her.'

'She's a whore,' Davie said brutally.

Rory Campbell smiled. 'And what are you?'

I put my hand on Davie's arm.

'Give tonight's crowd a rousing show, Spartacus,' I said, as we took him down the corridor.

'Always do.'

'I'll be seeing you again, ballet dancer,' Davie muttered, brow furrowed.

I was sure he was right.

Nine

I met Sophia outside the Council chamber.

'Hector's on his way to the infirmary,' she said, after kissing me.

'How is he?'

'Sedated. We'll see if we can bring him round later. There's a pain-management nurse with him.'

I felt guilty. What was I doing chasing my tail with bastards like Jack MacLean when I should be at my father's bedside? On the other hand, that would be exactly what MacLean and his bent friends wanted.

The meeting began.

'We have another body, citizen,' Fergus Calder said, as if it was my fault.

I told the guardians about the discovery in the shop that contained Porteous's skeleton. Most of them had already heard on the Council grapevine. I wouldn't have liked to drink the vintage made from that. Grizel Monzie had been shown a photo of Chung Keng Quee and didn't recognize him – though she went on to say that she couldn't distinguish between Asians.

She'd also been taken to the morgue to view the dead man. She threw up and denied all knowledge.

Then I told the Council about C. T. Enterprises. I'd got a copy of the business's registration department from a savvy guardswoman who knew how to navigate the Finance Directorate's complex digital archive.

Holding it up, I said, 'The company was registered on November 4th last year and hasn't yet been required to file an earnings report. Its activities are described as "tourism business".' I looked at the relevant guardian.

'That's strange,' Mary Parlane said, staring at Jack MacLean, 'because there's no record of it my directorate's files.'

The finance guardian feigned indifference, or at least that's how it struck me.

'Jack?' Mary prompted.

'What? Oh, it'll be a clerical error. Won't be the first time something is lost between my state of the art directorate and those that still use ink and paper.'

'Perhaps you could provide funds for the rest of us to become part of the digital world,' the tourism guardian said icily.

'We're working on that, Mary,' said Fergus Calder, 'as you know. Citizen Dalrymple, where is Clarinda Towart?'

'Still in the balmy spring wind.'

'Her photo and description have been distributed to all barracks and border points,' said James Michie. 'It seems she's gone to ground.'

'Foxy lady,' said MacLean, with a self-satisfied smile.

I frowned at the public order guardian and he managed to keep his cool.

'And the new body?' asked the senior guardian.

'Male, as yet unidentified,' I said, looking at Sophia.

She gave details of the post-mortem. Considerable force had been applied to the throat, cracking the hyoid bone and crushing the trachea. Could a woman have done that? In this city of highly trained Guard personnel, hundreds were in the frame apart from Clarinda Towart.

'Like the Malaysian,' Sophia added, 'this victim had consumed a large amount of non-citizen-issue whisky – by non-citizen-issue I mean a considerably higher-quality brand. The toxicologists may be able to identify it in time. The dead man's liver is also seriously compromised by cirrhosis.' She paused. 'There's something else. The subject has a T2b tumour in his bladder.'

'Would he have known about it?' I asked.

'Possibly. I've sent his file to the cancer centre. If he's been treated, we'll be able to ID him.'

'And if not?' asked Kate Revie.

Michie took his chance. 'I've been in discussion with the medical guardian. She has people working on an image that will recapture the dead man's appearance before decomposition set in. It'll be distributed around the barracks and all directorate departments.'

'I'm hoping someone in the cancer centre will recognize him from the photo of him in his current condition,' Sophia said. 'He isn't greatly changed.'

'In the absence of clothing we can't even tell if he was a citizen,' I said.

James Michie dived in again. 'I have Guard personnel following up missing-persons reports.'

'And we're checking the hotels in case he's a tourist,' said Mary Parlane.

'What about motive?' Fergus Calder asked.

'Don't know,' I said. 'The fact that he was in the back room suggests he went willingly. It would be difficult to drag him in there without attracting attention. Perhaps he said the wrong thing.'

'Is that supposed to be a joke?' the senior guardian said.

I shrugged. 'Not necessarily.'

'If it's not necessary, remove it from your thoughts.'

Easy for him to say. I decided to insert my middle digit into Jack MacLean's fundament.

'Finance Guardian, both deaths have links to your directorate.'

That got me a sharp look.

'Clarinda Towart has a company that only your directorate knew about, while Chung Keng Quee was taken under Billy Geddes's wing.'

'So what?' said MacLean.

Fergus Calder looked down at me. 'I tend to agree.'

'In that case,' I said, 'you won't mind me questioning your SPADE.'

The finance guardian shrugged. He'd be on the phone to Billy as soon as the Council meeting was over. I didn't care about that. I had a hold over my former friend now. Leaving him alone when he was expecting otherwise might make him careless.

'You might also want to consider this,' I said. 'Why did Clarinda Towart set up a company? What exactly were her enterprises?'

Silence.

'Your view?' the senior guardian asked.

'I haven't formulated one yet.'

I was dismissed shortly afterwards. Davie wasn't waiting for me as he'd gone to interview Alice Lennox, the last of Clarinda Towart's friends. I decided to walk to the infirmary. To keep my mind off seeing Hector in his reduced state, I thought about the people in the investigation. I didn't trust Rory Campbell, not least because he was known to the senior guardian and the leaders of outsider states. He needed further probing, even though he'd handled himself credibly – after all, he was an actor. But the strangest character of all was Clarinda's friend Duncan Denoon. Had the pygmy hippos been targeted at random or was someone sending a message – either to the unexpectedly dead keeper or someone else in a shared loop? The question nagged at me up the Royal Mile and down George IV Bridge, then it sank into my subconscious. There was no way of telling when or if it would resurface.

The old man was ensconced in his single room by the time I arrived. He was festooned with drips and his breathing was ragged, despite the oxygen tube in his nostrils. A young black-haired nurse I didn't know stood up.

'Simpson 520, citizen,' she said. 'Dr Allison assigned me to your father.'

'Call me Quint.' I looked at her badge. 'Fiona. What's to be done?'

'I've reduced the morphine supply. It's better if he spends some of the time even partly conscious.'

'The tests?'

'Confirmed that there are tumours on his spine. And others in his liver and lungs. We aren't sure which is the primary.'

I sat down beside the bed and touched Hector's shrivelled arm. He seemed to have shrunk even more in the short time since I'd seen him and the skin on his face was stretched tighter.

'You can speak to him,' Fiona said. 'It might help bring him round. I'll wait outside.'

'Wake up, you old bugger,' I said, blinking away tears. 'I want to talk to you.'

His eyelids stayed shut.

'What am I supposed to say, eh? That I need you, that I don't want you to go . . . that I love you? There, what do you think of that?'

Nothing, apparently.

'The city's going to hell in a main battle tank and you're lying here in a dwam. What's the good of that? I need you to tell me to keep going. I need you to rip the shit out of the Council and its functionaries.' I sobbed. 'Come on, old man, wake up.'

In his normal contrary fashion, he didn't.

'Keep at it, Quint,' came a soft voice.

I turned and saw Sophia at the end of the bed.

'Sorry. Simpson 520 left the door open. Regulations require it when there are no medical personnel present.' She came over and put her arms round my shoulders. 'Tell him everything you haven't been able to. Even if we can't be sure what he hears, it'll be good for you.'

'I don't care about me.'

'But I do.'

We stayed in that position. After a while I started to speak again. I told Hector what a great father he'd been when I was a kid, encouraging me in most things I did – though he wasn't keen when I started collecting slugs. I talked about the holidays we'd been on before the Enlightenment took power: a driving tour round northern France when I was twelve – he slipping me sips of wine when my mother was buried in her papers; a trip to the Cyclades when I was fourteen – the first time I ate octopus, with disastrous results; and an amazing voyage on a chartered cabin cruiser down Loch Ness in 2001 – when I was at the wheel I managed to get a rope tangled round the propeller shaft and the old man stripped off and dived in to clear it. My mother disapproved, not least since he was a poor swimmer, but he was my hero.

Sophia handed me a rough paper tissue.

'That's beautiful,' she said, squeezing my arm. 'Go on.'

So I talked about the forming of the Enlightenment Party, which both my parents were involved in – so was I, in the youth wing. As professors they fitted in, but none of the others could speak like Hector. He was a brilliant orator, persuading crowds of frightened and disenchanted citizens that independence was the only way. After Edinburgh had achieved that, he kept morale high during the drugs wars, when food and power were in short supply. Without him, I wasn't sure the Council would have lasted more than a year or two. I told him that I knew how proud he was of my work in the Public Order Directorate, even though he regarded it as at best a necessary evil. Without his understated support I wouldn't have stayed in the Guard as long as I did.

I stopped to wipe my eyes.

Sophia brought me a glass of water.

'It's all been for nothing,' I said to her.

'What has?'

'The Enlightenment, independence, the original ideals of the Council. Look at the city now. In a month people will vote to join a new Scotland. Have the sacrifices that citizens have made for thirty years been worth it? I don't think so.'

'You're overwrought,' she said. 'Don't think about the city. Talk to Hector.'

I did, for another hour, but I didn't seem to be getting through to him. Fiona came in and reduced the morphine drip. He remained comatose.

There was a knock on the door. Sophia went over and let Davie in. He looked down sadly at the old man and touched my hand.

'What's going on?' I said.

'I wouldn't bother you, but . . .'

'What is it?'

'Alice Lennox, Clarinda Towart's friend. She's . . . being difficult.'

I leaned close to Hector's head.

'It's Quintilian. Can you hear me?'

Nothing.

I was drained. I knew Sophia would keep me up to date. I stood up and kissed her.

'All right,' I said to Davie. 'Let's go.'

'I've got her and her boyfriend in the castle, in different rooms,' he said, when we were in the corridor.

'Why?'

'She pulled a knife on one of the surveillance team. Or rather, a scalpel.'

'Is that right?'

Suddenly I felt reinvigorated.

'What about her man?' I said, as Davie drove out of the infirmary gates.

'Christopher Fleming? He came quietly. Just as well. He was runner-up in the city heavyweight boxing championship last year. I thought I knew the name.'

'So what happened?'

'My guardswoman Watt 362, aka Wonderful Wendy—'

'Jesus, Davie, is there any female auxiliary you haven't bedded?'

'Em, the medical guardian.'

'Hilarious. Go on.'

He waved at the Guard personnel at the checkpoint. 'Wendy was under-cover as a nurse in that clinic for tourists. Citizen Lennox must have suspected something. If one of the doctors hadn't grabbed her, it could have been bad. They said Lennox has got a black belt in karate.'

'I wouldn't like to be in the flat below when that pair get down to it.'

Davie laughed.

'The interesting point,' I continued, 'is why did she react like that?'

'Obviously she's afraid someone's after her.'

'Exactly. The person who did for the Malaysian and the latest victim?'

'Or maybe Clarinda's turned against her. Wendy was wearing a blonde wig.'

He pulled up on the esplanade and we headed up the cobbles.

'Might be an idea to tell the guardian about this,' I said. 'Make him feel wanted.'

'He already knows. The call about the attack came through the command centre. He's waiting for us.'

Ten minutes later we were outside the holding cell containing Alice Lennox.

'How's your father?' asked James Michie.

'No better, but thanks for asking.'

'You'll be pleased to hear that the Council has approved door-to-door in the vicinity of the shop in the Grassmarket. I've got a squad on it.'

'Good,' I said. 'Guardian, are you thinking of taking part in this interrogation?'

'I've got the citizen's file,' he said, brandishing the cardboard folder.

I took it from him and had a quick look.

'Do you have much experience of questioning citizens?' I asked.

'Well . . . I thought I could learn from the experts.'

Davie was staring at his boots.

I smiled. 'As long as you don't intervene. Whatever happens.'

He nodded avidly.

We went in. Alice Lennox was still in her pale-blue nurse's uniform, her auburn hair loose. She had freckled cheeks and full lips, and her eye-catching body was trim. Her wrists had been cuffed and attached to a ring on the table. She looked at us with contempt.

'I'm Quint—'

'I know who you are,' the female citizen said sharply. 'And the other two.'

The guardian was about to speak – no doubt to demand respect – but Davie nudged him.

'What's this about, Alice?' I said, sitting opposite her.

'Don't call me that.'

I shrugged. 'Attacking a member of the City Guard with a lethal weapon earns you five years on the farms. Surely you don't fancy that.'

'If that's what I have to do . . .' the nurse said nonchalantly.

Handbrake turn. 'When did you last see Clarinda Towart?' I watched her carefully and picked up no intimation of fear.

'Clarinda? What's she got to do with anything?'

'Good question.' I glanced at the guardian. 'A murdered tourist was found in her flat on Wednesday.'

'What?' Her surprise seemed genuine.

'It's true,' said the guardian solemnly.

I could accept that level of involvement. 'So when did you last see Clarinda?'

Alice Lennox twitched her head. 'Em, last weekend. She came to lunch on Sunday.'

'How was she?'

'Fine,' she said, raising her shoulders. 'Fun.'

'Drunk?'

She stared at me. 'Not particularly.'

'Did you help her with that? I know you have in the past.'

'No. She . . . she's getting her life together.'

'Have you ever heard of C.T. Enterprises?'

'No.' She gave that some thought. 'Is it something to do with Clarinda? She never mentioned it.'

'We'll be talking to Christopher,' Davie warned.

'Christo,' Alice corrected. She didn't seem concerned.

'What do you think of Clarinda's job?' I asked.

'It's a disgrace,' she said, glaring at Michie. 'A city that forces its own citizens to service tourists has no heart.'

'Prostitution Services Department personnel are all volunteers,' the guardian said primly.

'Fuck off! Most of them have no option.'

Davie walked behind her and put heavy hands on her shoulders. 'That's not how citizens talk to guardians.'

'Fuck you too!'

'Or to senior auxiliaries.' Davie lowered his head till it was level with the prisoner's. 'As a rule I don't hit women, but I wouldn't mind beating the shit out of your fancy man.'

'He'd knock your head off,' she scoffed.

'You think? His wrists are cuffed like yours. And I've got big boots.'

James Michie looked uncomfortable. I gave him the eye and he behaved.

'None of this is necessary, Alice,' I said. This time she didn't bite my lips off. 'Tell us why you attacked the guardswoman.'

She tried to shake off Davie's hands. I nodded and he stepped back.

'I . . . I knew she was wrong. It wouldn't be the first time a tourist has been attacked in the clinic.'

'Really?' said the guardian. His innocence was worrying.

'No, it wouldn't,' Davie said. 'Last year an Indonesian was slashed by a rival gang member after he'd been taken to the tourist clinic with broken fingers.'

Alice nodded. 'See? I was taking precautions.'

'But you've got a black belt in karate,' I said. 'Why grab the scalpel?'

She didn't answer immediately. 'I saw it on the trolley.'

Now she was lying. She was also nervous, her fingers trembling.

'Who did you think the guardswoman was, Alice?' I said, my voice low as if I was excluding the guardian and Davie.

'I . . . I . . .' Suddenly she dashed her forehead against the handcuffs. In seconds there was blood all over the table.

Michie blanched and left to get help. Davie took a field dressing from his back pocket and held it against the wound. A few minutes later paramedics led her away, conscious but dazed.

'That went well,' said Davie.

'It certainly did not,' James Michie said, his cheeks blazing. 'You drove her to that, citizen. She was going to talk.'

'No, she wasn't,' I said. 'But what we do know is that she's terrified of someone, so terrified that she didn't rely on her karate when she mistook the guardswoman for someone else.'

'Clarinda Towart,' Davie said.

'Maybe, but she wasn't worried when we talked about her.'

'Who else?' asked the guardian.

'Don't ask me,' I replied. 'But I'm going to ask Christo. I think it'd be better if you left us to it.'

Michie complied.

The man three doors down was big, almost as big as Davie. His biceps bulged under the sleeves of his nurse's top. His dark hair was cut very short, making a feature of his thick black eyebrows.

'Why am I here?' he demanded, in an implausibly high voice.

'He doesn't know what his girlfriend did,' Davie whispered, helpfully late.

I introduced myself.

'I said, why am I here?'

'I heard you, Christo.'

'How do you know . . . Is Alice here?'

I looked around the room. 'Don't see any Alice. Do you, Davie?'

The commander checked under the table. 'No Alices.'

'Where's Clarinda Towart?' I asked.

'What?'

'You heard me.'

'I don't know. Have you tried her flat?'

'Oh yes.'

'And?'

I decided to change tack. 'Do you like Clarinda?'

'She's all right. Bit of a pisshead.'

'The term's alcoholic.'

He shrugged. 'She's my partner Alice's friend. Where is Alice?'

'Do you know about Clarinda's business?'

'I know she goes with tourists. So what?'

'Ever heard of a company called C. T. Enterprises?'

'No.' He made the connection. 'Clarinda's got a business? I'd never have expected that.'

'Are you frightened of Clarinda?'

He looked at me as if I was mad. 'You're joking. She's a pussy cat.'

That was a lie, if other people who knew her were to be believed.

'Are you frightened of anyone else?'

'I'm a heavyweight—'

'Answer the question.'

'No.' Christo grinned. 'Certainly not you and your toy boy.'

Davie managed to restrain himself.

'OK, here's what Alice did.' I told him. 'She's fucking terrified, man. Who of?'

That got under his skin. 'I . . .'

'Right then,' said Davie. He stepped over and put his arm round the prisoner's neck.

'Boxing's a strange hobby for a nurse,' I said.

'I grew up . . . in Muirhouse,' Christo gasped. That was one of the city's most dangerous areas. 'Let . . . go.'

Davie maintained pressure.

'Who's Alice scared of?'

He opened his mouth wider and I raised a finger. Davie slackened his grip lightly.

'Alice . . .' Christo said. 'Promise she won't get punished.'

'It's possible,' I conceded, with a show of reluctance.

'She . . . she met this guy . . . near the clinic . . . a couple of weeks ago . . . a tourist . . .'

'Let go, commander.'

Davie obliged.

Christo Fleming coughed and then spat on the floor. 'Bastard,' he said, glowering at Davie.

'A tourist,' I prompted.

'Aye, a tourist. I never saw him. He's a big guy from somewhere in

Eastern Europe. He . . . he followed her when she left the clinic, said he wanted her to work for him. He said Clarinda had recommended her.'

'What kind of work?' I asked.

'Not sure. Smuggling, something like that. Definitely against regulations.'

'She should have reported the approach,' Davie said, shaking his head.

'But she didn't do anything. She told him to get lost. That's when he dragged her into a backstreet, pulled a knife on her, threatened to gut her.'

'She didn't use her karate skills?'

'You don't get it. This guy's a monster, built like a house.'

'Shouldn't be hard to find him if he's still in the city,' I said. 'What's his name?'

'Don't know.'

I could see he was lying. I nodded to Davie.

'No . . . for fuck's sake . . . I don't think it's his real name . . .'

I sat back. 'Let's have it.'

He swallowed. 'Goliath.'

Davie laughed, then stopped when he saw the prisoner was serious.

'Better get your sling ready,' I said. 'David.'

Ten

I found Alice Lennox in the castle's small sickroom. Her forehead had been stitched and she was lying on the only bed, one wrist cuffed to the frame.

'What do you want?' she said, turning away.

'Goliath.'

Her body tensed.

I moved closer. 'Tell me about him or you'll never see Christo again.'

'Idiot,' she said bitterly. 'He shouldn't have told you.'

'He didn't have much choice.'

She moved her head towards me, hatred in her eyes. 'If you've hurt him . . .' Now she looked like an avenging angel. There was a lot of anger in this citizen.

'Is it true that Goliath is an Eastern European headbanger?'

'Yes,' she hissed. 'Or so he said.'

'Why didn't you report him?'

'You people are so fucking spineless. You don't protect ordinary citizens, you only care about the tourists.'

'I can assure you I'd have paid attention.'

'He's not alone, you bastard. Even if you catch him, his pals will get away. It'll only take one to cut me to pieces.'

'Even with big Christo to look after you?'

'He's good with his fists, but he wouldn't stand a chance against a trained killer.'

I stood there studying her, which made her turn away again.

'Describe Goliath.'

'About six foot six, at least eighteen stone – most of it muscle, shaved head, big hands, broken nose.'

'There can't be many tourists like him. We'll find him.'

She gave me a twisted smile. 'No, you fucking won't. He's got friends here, friends you can't touch.'

'Such as?'

'I don't know names, but he told me some of the city's leaders were looking after him.'

What a surprise. 'Where did you meet him?'

'Both times he grabbed me on my way home and dragged me into the alley behind the Portrait Gallery.' That was on Queen Street, not far from the tourist clinic. 'It was dark. I don't think he comes out in daytime.'

This was all very interesting, but something about it didn't add up. If Goliath was under the protection of local big shots – and Jack MacLean sprang to mind – why was he going after a citizen nurse?

'I still don't get why you attacked the guardswoman with that scalpel. She isn't six foot six.'

Alice Lennox glared at me. 'Are you deaf? I told you he's got people with him. I haven't met any, but I know one of them's a woman. He told me . . . she'd be turned on if he raped me.'

'How about Clarinda Towart? Could she be involved with the big man?'

She closed her eyes. 'Maybe. With her anything is possible.'

I left her to her sore head. I was pretty sure it would turn out to be catching.

James Michie was in the command centre, looking over a guardsman's shoulder.

I took him aside and told him what Alice and Christo had said.

'Some of the Council looking after a foreign gangster? That sounds unlikely, Quint.'

Davie came up, which saved me contradicting Michie.

'Commander, do we know anything about a group of Eastern European criminals?'

'No, guardian, but I'll have a look. If we don't, I'll get on to the Tourism Directorate.' He went over to a terminal and started hammering at the keyboard.

'Something's certainly scaring her.'

'Come on, man, it's obvious,' said Michie. 'She thought the guardswoman with the blonde wig was Clarinda Towart.'

'That did cross my mind. But since we can't locate her . . .'

I walked away and called Sophia.

'Hector's still in a dream world, Quint.'

'Lucky him. I'll be over later.'

'Hold on, I've just heard from the cancer centre. They've identified the dead man from the shop.'

'Call Michie, will you? He wants to be involved. And get a copy of the file sent to the infirmary pronto.'

'Right.'

I waited while the guardian's mobile rang and he scribbled notes. He turned to me, ecstatic.

'Positive ID on the dead man,' he crowed, waving away the guardswoman at the nearest desk. By the time I'd got there, a file was on screen.

'Rollo, Mungo,' Michie said. 'Born 15/3/1996, address 14 Craigour Drive, Moredun, labourer in the Roads Department. Father Angus, bus driver, died 1/9/2011, mother Marjory, cleaner, died 12/2/2003. Brother John, born 9/6/1999, auxiliary in the Supply Directorate.'

'Well, well,' I said. That organization is a den of thievery and corruption. 'Come on, James, spit it out. The only reason you've got him on your system is because he's got a record.'

'Indeed,' he nodded enthusiastically. 'A long one. Assaulted a citizen when drunk, 2016 – a year down the mines; assaulted a citizen when drunk, 2018 – eighteen months down the mines; assaulted a—'

'Anything apart from alcohol-fuelled violence?'

'Oh yes.' The guardian licked his thin lips. 'Robbery of Supply Directorate delivery truck, 2029. Caught with accomplices after siege in Bruntsfield.'

I vaguely remembered that. 'A guardsman was killed.'

'Correct. The gang had obtained rifles and pistols. Three of them were killed, but Rollo survived. He was sentenced to life down the mines, but pardoned after the regulations were changed in 2032.'

That was when the Council decided to pretend it was the citizens' friend, releasing prisoners and putting its faith in rehabilitation.

'Since then?'

'Nothing.'

'You need to pull his file from the main archive. Among other things, I want to know what he's been doing and the identities of his close companions. And sexual partner, if there is one.' Often citizens didn't disclose the latter since the regs had been relaxed.

He sent the hovering guardswoman off to do that.

'What do you think?' Michie said. 'Did he have dealings with Clarinda Towart?'

'It's a reasonable assumption. He was killed in her office.'

'But you think there's more to it.'

'We need evidence. I'm going to check Rollo's medical file.'

Davie waved as I went. He was shaking his head. Obviously he had nothing on Goliath and his sidekicks yet.

I went into Hector's room when I arrived at the infirmary. Fiona, the nurse, smiled at me.

'We've reduced the morphine. The pain doesn't seem to be worse.'

'How can you tell?'

She looked at the still figure on the bed. 'To be brutally honest, he'd be writhing about and screaming.'

I sat down and touched the old man's arm.

'This is your son,' I said. 'Wake up, will you? I want to talk to you about Juvenal's sixth satire.'

Nothing. He was an expert on the Roman writer and never missed an opportunity to jaw about him.

'Give him time,' Fiona said. 'Rest is good.'

I appreciated her support and rewarded her with the best smile I could manage. Visiting Hector was getting difficult. I'd begun to wonder if he would come round and, if he did, whether he'd know me.

I went to Sophia's office. She had a pile of files in front of her.

'The top one,' she said, pointing. 'I gather Hector's still out for the count.'

'Is that a medical term?' I leant over the desk and kissed her.

'No, but labia oris is.'

'Don't get lippy.'

She groaned.

I removed files from the seat opposite her and opened Rollo's. His first appointment had been last December.

'What's transitional cell carcinoma?' I asked, after getting halfway down the first page.

'Tumour in the epithelium, the tissue that lines the bladder.'

'Do you know this Dr Kevin Jones?'

Sophia nodded. 'He's good, but deeply in love with himself. George Allison thinks highly of him.'

'So Jones stuck a tube with a camera on it up the dead man's penis. Lovely.'

'Cystoscopy is a standard diagnostic tool.'

'I thought hacking people apart was the cancer centre's default mode.'

'Is that what happened to Hector?' she asked angrily.

'No, but he's a lost cause. Shouldn't Rollo have had an operation?'

'Read on.'

I did as I was told. 'Surgery was set for May 14th.'

Sophia shook her head. 'I know, the waiting time is awful. We don't have the personnel or resources.'

'Would he have made it if he hadn't been killed?'

'You mean survived until the operation? Probably.'

'And what about the operation itself?'

'The tumour was well into the outer part of the muscle. It would have grown in the next three months. He might have ended up with a permanent catheter. We don't do bladder reconstruction.'

'What about chemotherapy?'

'For this kind of cancer, we don't have the drugs. In any case, his liver would have failed in the next few years.'

'So Rollo was in profound shit. Did he know? Jones's notes are pretty sparse.'

'I doubt it. We tend not to scare people.'

'You prefer to let them die in ignorance.'

Sophia stood up, her cheeks red. 'I do what I can with what the Council allots me, Quint.'

'Well, you'll be pleased that the Finance Directorate's working on a consignment of hi-tech medical equipment.'

'What?'

'You don't know about it?'

'Not a thing. I draw up a list of this directorate's requirements and present it to the Council. Most of it goes on drugs, though the cancer centre has received some recent machines, especially for scanning.' She stared at me. 'What's going on?'

I told her about the dead Malaysian's files, including the one that covered weapons and tanks.

'This is insane. What's the Finance Directorate doing?'

'You know Jack MacLean. What puzzles me is where the money's coming from. It's possible the deals haven't been made yet. Still, there's not much income and a hell of a lot of expenditure.'

Sophia sat down heavily.

'You need to get to bed.'

'Thanks, Dr Dalrymple. Who else knows about this?'

'The people who translated and collated the texts – they're reliable – and Davie and the public order guardian.'

'James? Why hasn't he raised it in Council?'

'Because I asked him not to.'

'What on earth for?'

'You know how I work. I want to be sure before we go for broke. These are the city's big beasts we're after. Fergus Calder is probably aware. As is someone I'm going to tighten the vice on.'

'Billy Geddes.'

'Correct.'

'Would you like to borrow a scalpel or six?'

'It's a thought. No, I'm going back to the castle to get the files.'

'You realize Geddes will tell MacLean immediately.'

'No, he won't.'

'Why not?'

I put the stump of my right forefinger to my lips. 'I'm keeping my labia oris closed and so should you. After this.'

We kissed and fondled, then parted.

'Come to my place when you're finished,' Sophia said, straightening her clothes.

I managed not to respond with a double entendre.

Back in the command centre I told Davie and Michie what I'd discovered about Mungo Rollo, which wasn't much. They'd been more successful.

'The dead man was working as a rubbish collector in the tourist zone till two weeks ago,' said the guardian. 'Then he dropped out of sight. I've got people heading for his address now.'

Davie held up a file. 'Rollo was rehabilitated a year back November. He's been thrown out of citizen pubs twenty-three times since then. At least he seems to have given up on violence. As for his friends, two are made-up names and the other died in 2028. Rollo was hetero and didn't declare a sexual partner.'

'Shit. What about his brother?'

'On his way,' said Michie.

I decided to leave Billy till later, but I asked the guardian for the full files. He wanted to know what I was going to do with them.

'Geddes?' he said, as if he'd swallowed a bullfrog. 'He'll go straight to MacLean.'

I sighed. 'No, he won't.'

'What the——' Davie had moved to the bank of screens and was watching one in the top corner. It was from a camera at the bottom of the High Street, about a hundred yards from the ruins of Holyrood Palace.

I joined him. The picture wasn't great, the street lights being dimmed in the late evening. A Guard 4×4 was sitting in the middle of the road, the driver's door open. A figure in a grey auxiliary suit was lying on the asphalt, one foot still in the vehicle.

'Go back in slow motion!' Davie ordered.

The operator complied and we watched as a tall figure in a long black coat and a woollen hat pulled down low walked up to the 4×4 as it waited at the traffic lights. He – the gender wasn't obvious apart from the figure's substantially above-average height – pulled out a black semi-automatic pistol and fired three shots at the driver from close range.

'Send out an all-barracks alert!' said the guardian to anyone who was listening. 'Circulate the shooter's description!'

Davie and I ran out and sprinted to the esplanade. It was only a few minutes' drive to the scene. Tourists leaped to the sides of the road, though there weren't many of them in this area so late – they'd be eating in the venues around Rose Street, drinking in the George Street bars or throwing their money away in one of the many casinos.

Another Guard vehicle had arrived before us. Davie leapt out and took charge.

'Commander,' called a young guardsman, 'he's still alive.'

We ran over. John Rollo's name badge was spattered with blood, as was his barracks number, Napier 311. He'd taken two shots to the chest and another to the head. He was struggling to breathe, his mouth spattered with dark red foam.

'He's trying to say something,' said the paramedic who'd shouldered her way in.

I leant closer, hands on the wet tarmac. The stricken auxiliary coughed and my face was splashed with the warm discharge from his lungs.

'Guh . . . Guh . . . Go . . . Go . . .'

I put my ear closer to the dying man's mouth, but all I heard was the final rattle.

'Shit,' I said, under my breath.

'What did he say?' Davie asked.

I told him.

'Goliath?' he whispered.

No wonder Alice Lennox was frightened.

After the scene – and my face – was cleared, we went back to the castle. The guardian had been busy in our absence.

'The senior guardian and his directorate's head of personnel are on their way.'

I gave the Malaysian's files to Davie and told him to hide them away.

'Also,' said Michie, 'teams on foot and in vehicles are searching the surrounding area.'

'Are they banging on every door?' I asked.

He nodded.

'Have you called in extra bodies?'

He didn't nod.

'You need to. Wake up ten Guard day-shift personnel from every barracks.' That would give us two hundred more people on the ground, though Goliath might be miles away by now if he had transport near the scene. There are no cameras south of the Royal Mile that far down.

There was a commotion as Fergus Calder and a female auxiliary I recognized came into the command centre. The senior guardian's bodyguards stomped in behind him.

James Michie went over to brief him. I nodded to the head of personnel, a fine-looking woman with the unusual name of Yolanda. I'd caught her *in flagrante delicto* with the former deputy supply guardian last year, as her crimson face demonstrated.

'What do you think of this, Quint?' Calder asked, in a loud voice.

I walked closer and told them what I'd heard John Rollo say. That took their breaths away.

'Who knew Rollo was on his way to the castle?' I said.

The senior guardian looked at Yolanda.

'I . . . I haven't been able to establish that yet,' she said. 'My people are working on it.'

I doubted they'd find a smoking telephone.

'Next question,' I said. 'What did Rollo know that led to him being killed?'

'I'll check that,' Calder said, giving his head of personnel a disparaging look.

Again, I didn't think he'd find anything sending up smoke signals. Anyway, I'd be making my own enquiries. I had a source in the Supply Directorate; and I could twist Yolanda's arm.

Davie came up. 'Preliminary reports from the door-to-door in the Grassmarket. No one saw Mungo Rollo enter the shop. They didn't see any big bald men either.'

'He's shown us he can obscure the top of his head,' I pointed out.

Fergus Calder smiled crookedly. 'But I rather doubt he can remove the bottom parts of his legs.'

Typical guardian wanting the last word.

'Anything on the firearm?'

Davie called forward a techie, who showed us an enhanced image of the big man's right hand and its contents.

'I'm pretty sure that's a Jarilo .45 calibre semi-automatic,' the guardsman said. 'It has a nineteen-shot clip.'

'Oh, great,' I said. 'Where's it manufactured?'

'Somewhere called Bor. Used to be in Serbia before the region turned into Mob Central.'

So there we were: Eastern Europe.

Shitski.

Eleven

'Come on, Quint,' Davie said, a few minutes after Calder and his crew had left. 'A body's been found at Mungo Rollo's place.'

A few minutes later we were roaring southwards, two more Guard vehicles behind us.

I called Sophia and told her. 'Don't bother coming yourself. You need to dele—'

'See you there,' she said, then terminated the call.

We went past the Theatre of Life, Spartacus thrusting his sword skywards on the building's facade. I thought about Rory Campbell. He was convincing, overly so. He needed closer attention, but developments in this case were coming faster than tourist planes.

'I hope we're in time,' Davie said, foot on the floor. 'The guardswoman I spoke to said the locals were taking an interest.'

'You really need more than a Hyper-Stun in the badlands.'

'I've told the guardian that more than once,' he said, shaking his head.

We were in the outer suburbs now, the lighting on the streets sparse. Not many citizens chose to live this far out as there was little security. The

Guard concentrated its personnel and resources on the tourists and the city line. We went past the ruins of what had been the new infirmary. Moredun was half a mile further on.

'Anyone living out here's got to be a smuggler,' Davie said, turning into Craigour Drive. Two teenage males moving towards the parked Guard vehicle ahead were caught in the headlights. They turned and ran, but not before aiming catapults at us. There were a couple of heavy thunks on the bodywork.

'At least they didn't have firearms,' I said, my heart racing.

Davie grunted. 'Give them time.' He drew up behind the other 4×4 and got out. 'Commander on scene,' he shouted.

The door of number 14 opened and a young guardsman appeared, Hyper-Stun in hand. 'Good to see you, Hume 253,' he said, relief written on his face.

Davie turned to the vehicles that had been following us. The Guard personnel had fanned out and taken defensive positions.

'Everything's all right now, laddie. What have you got?'

I followed them in. The stars shone down, but the moon wasn't in evidence. There was a reek of sewage cut with burnt rubber. No lights shone in any of the surrounding houses.

'Lovely,' Davie said, from a room at the back.

It turned out to be the kitchen. A man was seated at the narrow table, his head touching the bloody and brain-spattered surface.

'Execution-style,' Davie said.

I nodded. 'Shot in the back of the head, maybe more than once.'

'Let me see,' said Sophia, bustling in. Behind her was Raeburn 297.

'You people should be suited up,' he said disapprovingly.

Sophia already was.

Davie and I went outside.

'Did you check the rest of the rooms?' he said to the guardsman.

'Yes, commander. There's no one else here, dead or alive. And no weapons.'

'I'll be judge of that,' Davie said, pulling on overshoes and gloves and going back in.

'What struck your eye, Gavin?' I asked, after taking in his name tag. The young man seemed sharp.

'The place is a wreck,' he said. 'The furniture's decrepit and filthy, there's shit on the bathroom walls and the only bed's been pissed in.'

'Do you think anyone was living here?'

His brow furrowed. 'Maybe using it as a dosshouse. I can't imagine even a gang member staying in this shithole.'

'Quint!' Davie shouted, from upstairs.

I thanked the guardsman and navigated the half-broken stairs.

'You have to know where to look,' he said triumphantly. He'd knocked through the board over the old fireplace.

'Is that what I think it is?'

'What do you think it is?' Davie asked, holding up a package wrapped in clear film.

'Remtex.' I'd seen the brown plastic explosive often enough.

'Correct. I'd say there's at least two pounds of it.'

'Detonators?'

'Not here.'

So Rollo or his friends had another hideout – unless they were carrying it or them around.

'What did Mungo Rollo have against pygmy hippos?' I said.

'You think he set those charges?'

'The techies can match the traces in the zoo, but it's definitely a possibility.'

'Quint?' Sophia called.

'See what else you can find, Sherlock.'

'Yes, Watson.'

In the kitchen Raeburn 297 and his people were on their knees marking and measuring footprints. The floor was covered in grime so their job was easy. Sophia was writing notes on the victim, who was wearing a black-leather blouson and blue jeans.

'Shot once in the base of the skull with a large-calibre weapon. The bullet shattered his lower jaw as it exited. Keep an eye out for it, Raeburn 297.'

I could see pieces of bone and tooth on the table.

'Any ID on him?' I said to the head techie.

'None,' he replied. 'But he's not a local.'

'How do you make that out?'

Sophia pointed to the dead man's undamaged upper face. I was reminded of Chung Keng Quee.

'Fuck. Another Asian – maybe Malaysian – tourist.'

She nodded. 'This is going from bad to worse.'

'I hate to imagine what worst might be.'

Davie thundered down the stairs. 'Look at this,' he said, a black plastic bag in his left hand. He held it open so we could look.

It was full of bones.

'These are human,' Sophia said, after examining some.

Another dead tourist, a lump of high explosive and a bag of human remains – a smart investigator would hand back his authorization. Then again, the Council wouldn't accept it.

'Come back with me?' Sophia asked, after the body and bones had been taken to the infirmary.

'What, to the morgue?'

'No, idiot. I'm not doing the p-m till morning.'

'I suppose I could squeeze in a few hours of sleep, after I find out how the old man's doing.'

'I just did that. He's comfortable but still not awake.'

'So how does Fiona know he's comfortable?'

'Calm down, Quint. She's very experienced.'

Sophia drove her 4×4 back to the city centre. 'What is it, Quint?' she said. 'You look like you're wrestling with a proposition from Wittgenstein.'

'I should be so lucky.' I turned towards her. The green dashboard light gave her a fey look and her ice-blonde hair was tied back, emphasizing her cheekbones. 'I'm trying to work out why I'm on this case.'

She glanced at me. 'Because you're the only person in the city who can make sense of it.'

'The city or the case?'

'You know what I mean.'

'The translated contracts make it clear that Jack MacLean's up to no good, probably Fergus Calder too. So why have I been taken on?'

Sophia was driving up Dalkeith Road. The cancer centre was a couple of hundred yards ahead.

'Maybe you're seeing a conspiracy where there isn't one,' she said. 'It wouldn't be the first time.'

'What, you think the dead Malaysian raised the contracts on the off-chance the various directorates would sign them? Don't forget, Billy Geddes was looking after him.'

'And wherever Geddes goes, trouble follows.'

'That's a pretty good rule of thumb and missing first finger.'

We came to a temporary checkpoint, part of the Guard's effort to track down the man who'd killed John Rollo.

'Any luck?'

'No, citizen,' said a middle-aged guardswoman. 'He's either made it to the city line or he's gone to ground.'

I nodded. 'Keep at it.'

Sophia drove past the raised barrier. 'All right – MacLean, Geddes and maybe Calder have been negotiating with the Malaysians.'

'And one more Asian, perhaps Malaysian, is on the way to the morgue.'

'Though we don't know that he was in league with the first victim. Obviously the Council needs to catch the killer or killers, not just of the latest victim and Chung—' She broke off.

'Keng Quee.'

'Thank you, but of Mungo Rollo and his brother.'

'Not sure anyone cares much about the former but the latter, yes. No one kills an auxiliary and gets away with it.' That was the general rule, but the porous nature of the city line and the border further out meant several murderers had escaped punishment.

Sophia reached the Canongate and turned left up the High Street. 'Are you sure we shouldn't come clean about the contracts?'

'Are you?'

She pursed her lips. 'Unlike you, Quint, I actually trust my fellow guardians.'

I laughed. 'Jack MacLean? I wouldn't buy a pack of condoms from him.'

'You don't need to,' she said, smiling. 'I keep us well supplied.'

'True, though stealing from Medical Directorate stores is highly unethical.'

'Stealing!' She almost drove into a lamp post. 'How dare you? I'm entitled to as many as I need, like every other citizen.'

'That's doing wonders for the birth rate.'

Sophia's jaw jutted. 'You're right, it's becoming a major problem. And it doesn't help that people keep slipping out of the city.'

'Don't worry, everything will be fine when we join with the other states.'

She gave me a sharp look. 'We'll get more drugs and equipment to treat ailing citizens.'

I thought about that. If she was right, why was the Finance Directorate potentially ordering medical supplies from Malaysia? Could MacLean be playing a double game? Or were he and the senior guardian doing what they could to maintain – or even increase – the Council's grip on the city?

We had crossed the central zone and turned on to Heriot Row. Billy's flat was on the elegant street. I considered getting Sophia to stop. Waking my former friend would shake him up. For about three seconds. No, I needed more, not least since the discovery of the executed Malaysians.

I followed Sophia up the steps to her residence. What happened next stays between her and me.

Sophia and Maisie had gone when I clattered downstairs in the morning. The housekeeper, who regarded me as an interloper of the worst kind, reluctantly allowed me to eat the croissants that were still on the table.

I called Davie. 'News.'

'Morning to you too, Quint.'

'Morning news.'

'Dick. Right, Raeburn 297 and his people are still out at Rollo's house. Get this, under the sink they found a Jarilo .45 semi-automatic with fifteen rounds in the mag.'

'So four shots had been fired.'

'Well remembered.'

'One into the Asian in the kitchen and three into John Rollo, aka Napier 311.'

'Could be, though the bullet hasn't been found.'

'But why leave the pistol there?'

'Search me. Raeburn 297 says there are no fingerprints on it, but there's blood spray around the muzzle, suggesting it was used on the latest victim.'

'Close-range shots, yes. Sophia will be able to remove gunshot residue for comparison with that on Rollo.'

'Where are you, Quint? The guardian's looking for you.'

'Tell him I'm following a lead.'

'Want to tell me what?'

'John Rollo.'

'Right. Oh, there's been no sign of Goliath.'

'I'd scale down the search if I were you.'

'Thanks for the advice,' Davie said gruffly.

'You're welcome.' I broke the connection.

There was a Guard 4×4 outside the checkpoint on Darnaway Street. I asked the grizzled guardsman at the wheel to give me a lift. He complied immediately, waving away my authorization.

'On the job, citizen?' he asked, as we headed down Heriot Row.

'Being messed around.'

He grinned. 'You don't remember me, do you?'

I took a closer look. 'Actually I do. You were in the Guard squad at my mother's residence.'

He nodded. 'Long time ago.' He glanced at me. 'Sorry for your loss.'

Something in his tone made me open up. 'My father's in the infirmary, prognosis hellish.'

'I'm even sorrier to hear that. He was a fine guardian – so was your mother, of course, but I always liked the information guardian. He kept us going during the hard times.'

'We all have to go eventually,' I said, embarrassed by the cliché but unable to come up with anything more profound.

'He'll be a decent age now.'

'Eighty.'

'Keep your spirits up, son,' he said. 'That's what he'll be wanting.'

I blinked back tears.

He gave me time to compose myself. 'You'll be looking into the Supply Directorate auxiliary who was murdered,' he said, turning on to Princes Street.

'Napier 311, aye. Did you know him?'

'I was on a border post with him for six months ten years ago. Solid kind of guy. He had one failing, though.'

I kept quiet. Auxiliaries often clammed up about colleagues and pressing them was the worst approach. The great roof of the Supply Directorate warehouse, which had been Waverley Station before independence, was on our left now.

'He had a fuckwit of a brother who was in and out of the mines. John was forever sending him food parcels against regs.'

I frowned. 'Doesn't sound like a major failing to me.'

The driver laughed. 'You think? The thing was, John hid razor blades and screwdrivers in the bread and cake. At least three guardsmen were injured and a lot more citizens. But he wouldn't stop. He really loved his brother.'

I was tempted to let slip how Mungo Rollo had ended up, but managed to hold back.

The Supply Directorate is based in an ugly grey concrete building across the road from the former rail station. I remembered where the head of personnel's office was on the sixth floor. I took the stairs and arrived panting, but I got my breath back before knocking on her door.

'Come,' she called.

I swallowed a laugh. The last time I entered, she'd been in the process of doing exactly that.

'Oh, citizen,' Moray 402 said, getting to her feet. At least she was on her own, her clothing where and how it should have been.

'Oh, Yolanda,' was my riposte.

Her cheeks went on fire. She was a good-looking woman, but I wasn't paying attention to that. Sophia would amputate my balls without anaesthetic.

'Napier 311,' I said. 'The late John Rollo. I need his file.'

'I have it here.'

'Good. Did you know him?'

'Of course. I make it my business to meet all auxiliaries above Grade 3.' She handed me the file.

I took the cardboard folder but didn't open it. 'Give me your impressions of him.'

Yolanda didn't like that. 'In personnel we try to avoid subjectivity, citizen.'

'Call me Quint,' I said, knowing that would get to her. 'Go on.'

'I . . . why don't you read the file?'

'Because the longer you take to answer, the more I'll suspect you're hiding something.'

She looked like I'd let loose a black mamba. 'I . . . I'm hiding nothing.'

'Do you want to hook up with your friend Joe?' That was the former deputy guardian who'd performed cunnilingus on her in this very room. 'It won't be so bad in the miners' huts with this glorious spring we're having.'

Moray 402 put her hands to her forehead. 'I'm not hiding anything, citizen,' she said, with feeling.

That convinced me she was. 'Did you know Rollo's brother, Mungo?'

She shook her head, but her eyes were all over the place.

'You knew him all right. What did John ask you to do?'

She was shaking like a puppet whose strings had got badly twisted. 'I . . . John and I . . . were lovers.'

I bet that wasn't in his file. Senior auxiliaries like Yolanda, especially those in charge of personnel, weren't supposed to get involved with subordinates.

'Since when?'

'About a year ago. He was promoted to head of warehouse personnel, so we saw a lot of each other. Things developed . . .'

I caught her eye. 'You don't exactly seem devastated by his murder.'

'How do you know what I'm feeling?' she said sharply. 'Besides, John wasn't my only lover.'

'I know,' I said, touching her desk. 'Your backside was about here when—'

'That's enough. You may have an authorization but you can't treat me like a PSD operative.'

That was an interesting link. I ran with it. 'Do you know Clarinda Towart?'

'Who? No. I'd remember that unusual name.'

This time I was persuaded. I went back to the Rollos.

'What did you do for Mungo?'

'I . . . John told me how much of a liability his brother was. He was an alcoholic. I . . . does this have to come out, citizen?' She shot me a sultry look.

'How can I tell?'

She dropped her gaze. 'I arranged for John to have access to incoming medical stores. There's a drug that helps with alcoholism.'

'First I've heard of it.'

'It only started coming in last December.'

'Why did John need your help? He was in charge of warehouse personnel.'

'Only four senior auxiliaries in the directorate have access to medical deliveries before they're dispatched to the infirmary.'

'And you were the one he fell for? Had already fallen for.'

Moray 402 glared at me. 'What do you mean?'

'He seems like the calculating type. Did you obtain access for him elsewhere in the warehouse in the last year?'

'I . . . oh God . . . yes, there was more.'

I waited patiently.

'Citizen, I'll do anything to keep this between us.' The come-hither look was back and she'd stuck her chest even further out.

'What else did you do for him?' I said.

'What can I do for you?' she asked, running her tongue round her lips.

'Not going to happen, Yolanda. Answer the question.'

'Narcotics,' she said, almost whispering. 'Tourist whisky.'

'And?'

There were tears coursing down her cheeks.

'Remtex.'

'When?'

'Last November, I think.'

I sat back. Mungo Rollo was out of rehab by then. Had he set the bomb that led to Duncan Denoon's death at the zoo? If so, why had he waited three months to go after him?

'Why was John shot to death in the street?' I asked.

'I don't . . . I . . .'

'Someone knew he left the directorate heading for the castle. That individual tipped off his killer.'

Moray 402 looked aghast. 'It wasn't me, I swear.'

'You never heard of Goliath until last night?'

She shook her head vigorously.

'Who else could have been in touch with the killer?'

'I don't know. A member of John's staff?' She put her hand on the phone. 'I'll round them up.'

'No, you won't.' I got up and went over to her. 'Give me your mobile.' I then called Davie on the desk phone and told him to send a vehicle down.

'It wasn't me,' Yolanda repeated forlornly.

'I know,' I said.

After she'd been led away, I went down the stairs and crossed the road to the warehouse entrance. The guardsman on duty checked my authorization and asked if there was someone he could call.

I declined his offer. I knew exactly where I was going.

Twelve

Jimmy Taggart was in the drugs squad's mess-room. He was eating a plate of smoked salmon.

'Testing it for the tourists, Knox 31?'

'That'll be right,' the white-haired guardsman said, getting to his feet. 'How are you doing, sir?'

'Up to my eyes in it. You?'

'Glad to set my eyes on you. Do you want some of this?'

I shook my head.

'The fridge is full of other exotic stuff that fell off the back of a directorate lorry.'

'Uh-huh. I should report you to the public order guardian.'

'I doubt he knows this unit exists.'

'You could be right there.' I took in the elderly man with the scarred face.

He'd been in the tactical operations squad I commanded during the drugs wars and had also joined me in a firefight in the warehouse last summer. 'Fancy a job?'

Jimmy looked at me impassively. 'I'm going to finish my service here next year and spend my retirement fishing.'

'Don't worry, the job's in the warehouse and won't distract you from your current duties.'

'Oh aye?'

'Did you know John Rollo?'

He nodded. 'I heard what happened. I never liked him. He fancied himself in a big way.'

'But good at his job?'

'Never heard otherwise. He wasn't in charge of us.'

'So you're the perfect investigator – one foot in and one foot out.' The drugs squad was nominally part of the Public Order Directorate.

'What?'

I told him about the Remtex, the drugs and the alcohol.

'Explosives and drugs – medical and narcotics – are only kept here temporarily until they're delivered to the final consignee. Tourist whisky goes to the stores in the Tourism Directorate basement.'

'I know, but Rollo couldn't have got into the secure sections here without help.'

'True. He'd have to change the manifests too. There's no shortage of clerks who'd do that for a fee.'

'Right. I want you to extend feelers. We know Rollo was dirty, but we don't know how much. Who was he working for? I also think he was ratted on when he got the summons from the castle yesterday evening. See if you can find out who did that.'

'Just a wee job, then,' Jimmy said, grinning.

'You know how this place works better than anyone else. Plus you have a Hyper-Stun.'

'True. That usually keeps the fuckers at bay.'

'I'll call you later,' I said, gripping his shoulder on my way out.

As I walked towards the Mound, three thoughts struck me. The first was that John Rollo could have been sold out by someone in the castle. I didn't trust James Michie enough to put him on to that. The second was that no one had owned up to seeing Mungo Rollo go into the shop in the Grassmarket. Was it likely he'd sneaked in there unnoticed, even at night? At least one member of the Guard patrols might be in on the murder. And the third was that Jimmy Taggart had been present when my lover Caro was killed in 2015. That made me think of my father. He was one of the few people still alive who knew her well. How many breaks with the past was I going to have to cope with?

Davie was in the command centre, talking to the guardian. I nodded to them.

'Progress?' Michie asked.

'Not yet. You?'

'No sign of Goliath or of Clarinda Towart,' he replied, shaking his head. 'I'm not convinced about this Eastern European stuff. We're checking if Goliath's photo, even the small bit of face that it shows, is that of an Edinburgh citizen, but that'll take some time to complete. No match yet.'

'Have you told the senior guardian about the dead Asian?'

'No,' he said, looking at his boots. 'I'm waiting for more information.'

'I'll see what I can do. Have you got Raeburn 297's report?'

'Preliminary only.' He handed me a file. 'There are photos.'

I took a look. The dead man's lower face was a mess and it would be hard to identify him.

'Right,' I said, 'I'm off to the Tourism Directorate and then the infirmary.'

Davie handed me another file, that of John Rollo. 'You might want to cast an eye over this – note the folded corners.'

The guardian nodded, clearly pleased to be in possession of knowledge that I wasn't. I didn't tell him what I'd discovered.

I went into Davie's room and opened Rollo's file. It was the standard auxiliary model, his date of death already noted on the front. Being a contrary soul, I went to the end, ignoring the pages Davie had told me to check. I've never liked being handed information on a plate, especially a rough-edged one from the castle canteen.

Rollo had grown up in a tower block in Little France, slightly nearer the centre than his brother's house. He was a smart kid, doing well in primary school after the last election and going through senior school when the drugs wars were at their worst. He'd been a member of the City Youth, a paramilitary organization that was used as backup troops during weekend operations, and had received a citation for bravery. After that he went through auxiliary training with excellent reports, got another bravery citation on the border and was shot in the shoulder during a stint on the city line in 2024. Subsequently he'd been invalided out of the Guard and assigned to the Supply Directorate. He was hetero, had no long-term partner – there was no mention of Yolanda – and was highly regarded by Fergus Calder, who was personally responsible for his last promotion. That was interesting.

Davie came in. 'What do you think? Am I right?'

I raised a hand. 'Give me a minute.'

He started muttering to himself about how I never gave his work its due, blah blah.

I grinned at him. 'Did you notice that one of his close companions at senior school was Paul Towart, Clarinda's brother?'

His face fell.

'And that he was in the same Guard tower on the city line as Duncan Denoon?'

'What?'

'In 2023. The zookeeper was a citizen recruit working in the kitchen.'

'You think that's significant.'

'I don't do coincidences.'

'All right, but look at what I found.'

I sighed and found the marked pages. 'June 2031, suspended for a month after a spot check revealed six scallops in his pocket.' I raised an eyebrow.

'He was dirty.'

'Slightly off.'

'Go on,' Davie said eagerly.

I turned to the next page with its corner down. 'September 2032, reprimanded for taking a directorate vehicle without approval from his superior. This guy was a criminal mastermind.'

Davie glared at me. 'And the last one.'

'December 2033, suspected of involvement in the robbery of a delivery van containing tourist provisions and alcohol. Cleared after internal directorate inquiry.'

'I tell you, he was dirty.'

'I agree. This is between you and me.' I told him what I'd learned from Yolanda. 'In addition to that, he knew Clarinda's brother and Duncan Denoon. Where does that leave us?'

Davie was at his desktop computer. 'As regards Paul Towart, in a hole in the ground – or rather, a heap of crematorium ash. He was killed in a directorate raid in Leith in 2026. Suspected member of the Leith Lancers.'

We had wiped most of them out last year. 'I wonder if John Rollo knew him then,' I said, flicking through his file. 'Nothing in here, but there wouldn't be.'

'And the zookeeper. Do you think Mungo knew him too? And together they blew up his beloved hippos? Why?'

'I've no idea, guardsman.' I got to my feet. 'Yet.' I headed for the door. 'Oh, and Davie? Good work.'

I could hear the expletives as I went from one end of the command centre to the other. Fortunately James Michie had absented himself. He'd have been horrified.

I went up the stairs in the Tourism Directorate and knocked on the guardian's door, despite the attentions of her skinny grey-suited male secretary, who looked like he'd only recently finished auxiliary training.

'What is it?' she called. 'I told you I wasn't to be disturbed, Ross.'

'Not his fault,' I said, after I'd let myself in and closed the door.

'Quintilian,' she said, irritated. 'I'm very busy.'

'I can imagine, Mary. I'm about to make you busier.'

She sat back in her chair and sighed. Her grey hair was tied in a loose knot and her face was pale. 'Go on, then.'

'You heard about the dead Asian in Moredun?'

'Just what we need. Fergus told me to keep quiet about it.'

'Which doesn't mean you can't help me identify him.' I pushed the file over her desk.

'For the love of Plato,' she said, after taking in the photos of the dead man. 'Get an auxiliary you trust to compare them with recent arrivals to the city.' All visitors are photographed at the airport.

She pressed a button and her secretary came in. She explained what she wanted him to do and he left with the photos.

'He's very young,' I remarked. 'Are you sure he's reliable?'

'Ross is my son,' Mary Parlane said, giving me a stern look.

It was rare for guardians to give family members jobs, but not contrary to the new regulations.

'Are there many Malaysian tourists?' I asked, wondering if she knew about the contract referring to five thousand a year.

'A few hundred. I gather the country's an economic powerhouse.'

'So you're hoping for more.'

'Hoping, but not expecting. They find us expensive.'

That suggested she was in the dark. I considered telling her about the contract, but decided against it. I could trust her more than most guardians, but I didn't want to put her in danger. The fact that I'd done so with Sophia didn't make me feel good. James Michie could take his chances, as long as he kept his mouth shut.

'I gather you've been sent stills from the CCTV at the bottom of the Royal Mile,' I said.

'Yes, but again there isn't much to go on – not much of the killer's face is visible.'

'But he's at least six foot six.'

'The only tourist that tall is a twenty-three-year-old from New York. He has a solid alibi for yesterday evening. He was on the Old Town Ghost Tour and the guide remembers he was there all the time. She could hardly miss him.'

'What about Eastern Europeans in general? Goliath is supposed to have sidekicks, one of whom is a woman.'

'None of whom has been caught on camera. We don't have anyone from Eastern Europe in the city and haven't had for decades. As far as I know, the area's gone back to the *salade macédoine* of old – warlords, brigands and gangs, with no organized states.'

That was what I'd heard too.

'John Rollo,' I said, watching her face closely. I didn't see any suggestive reaction. 'Did you know him?'

'I met him at the Supply Directorate's last New Year party. He was one of Fergus's golden boys.'

I nodded. 'Did you ever see him here?'

'In the directorate? No. Why should he have been here?'

I told her about the thefts of alcohol, even though they probably took place in the warehouse. 'Can you ask your staff?'

'I'll send out a general request for information.' She frowned. 'Though I doubt it'll do much good. Auxiliaries don't like talking about their own, especially the dead.'

I was aware of that but it was worth a chance. I got up to go.

'Mary, this case is getting out of hand. Is there anything you can think of that we might be missing?'

The tourism guardian rubbed her eyes and put her glasses back on. 'I wish I could do more, Quintilian, but I'm as much in the murk as you are.'

That was a great help.

I walked to the infirmary. It was a curious day – no rain, but the sun obscured by grey-blue clouds. It was still unseasonably warm. From not having enough evidence, we now had too much. The problem was tying it together. What was Clarinda Towart's involvement? I was pretty sure she wasn't just a drunken prostitute – the fact that she'd started a company suggested otherwise, though its purpose was still a mystery. Could she be in with the Finance Directorate? With MacLean and Billy Geddes? The Rollos had been up to no good, that was uncontestable, but I had the feeling they – especially John – weren't working for themselves. As for the mysterious Goliath, was he really an Eastern European? Apart from Alice Lennox's testimony, the unusual pistol was the only thing that suggested he was. We still had her and Christo Fleming in custody. Maybe it was time to let them go. Or set Davie loose on the former. I wasn't convinced Alice thought the undercover guardswoman was a female sidekick of Goliath. And I was still puzzled about the bomb at the zoo. We needed to look deeper into the dead keeper's background now we knew that he and John Rollo had served in the same Guard tower. Then there was the latest dead Asian. Perhaps Sophia would be able to cast some light on them after the post-mortem, but I wasn't holding my breath. As for the bag of bones, what the hell?

I managed to distract myself with those thoughts until I walked between the infirmary gates. Then I took a deep breath and prepared to visit my father. Would he have shrunk further overnight?

The answer was that he had. The nurse, Fiona, gave me a sweet smile but I wasn't buying it. His face looked like that of an unwrapped mummy.

Then his eyes opened and I froze. They fixed on me as I moved towards him.

'He came round half an hour ago,' Fiona said.

'Can he see me?'

'Probably, but there's no way of telling how much his brain is processing. He's still on a large morphine dose.'

'Hello, old man,' I said, putting my hand on his. It was cold.

His eyes were still on me, but otherwise the only visible movements were the slow rise and fall of his chest.

'I'm going to assume you can hear me,' I said.

Nothing changed.

'Blink if you understand.'

Nothing.

'Never mind, you're as stoned as the castle. Lucky you.'

As if in agreement, Hector's eyes closed.

I kept on talking, reminding him of shared experiences, assuring him he'd soon be better, describing the weather like a typical tongue-tied Edinburgh native.

'Hello, Quint.'

I turned and saw Sophia at the door.

'I'm trying to entertain him,' I said, 'but I don't think I'm getting through.'

She came over and checked. 'I just spoke to Fiona. She'll reduce the morphine a bit more. Maybe then you'll get a response.' She put her hand on my shoulder. 'Maybe.'

I nodded and tried impersonation. 'Hector Dalrymple, this is Plato, son of Ariston. Wake up and listen to what I think about Juvenal.'

Nothing. I stood up.

'I thought Juvenal lived centuries after Plato,' said Sophia.

'He did, but everyone exists in the same time in the afterlife, don't you think?' I bit my lip and blinked. The thought of the old man departing this world was still agonizing. And I didn't believe in any kind of life after death.

'Come on, Fiona will keep me advised of Hector's progress.'

We went to her office.

'Are you up to working?' Sophia asked, eyeing me cautiously.

'What else am I going to do?'

She gave me a sympathetic smile and slid three files over her desk. 'P-m on the Asian. I'm no biological anthropologist but he seems to have Chinese upper-facial characteristics. He was in his late twenties or early thirties, well nourished and exercised. His hands bear the marks of manual labour. He has a six-inch-long tattoo on the back of his right shoulder.'

I looked at the photograph. 'A purple snake. Chung Keng Quee didn't have that or any other tattoos. But he had similar facial characteristics, so this guy may have been Malaysian Chinese.'

'It's a good possibility.'

'But maybe they weren't associates. Tattooing smacks of gang membership.'

'Great,' Sophia sighed. 'As regards cause of death, you know that. Time of death, not more than four hours before he was found, maybe an hour less.'

I made the calculation. 'So after John Rollo was shot, but not long. His killer – if it was the same individual – must have gone straight to the house in Moredun.'

'According to Raeburn 297, a Jarilo .45 was used, but the powder residue is different. But there's another factor to take into account with the Asian – he was shot at point-blank range.'

'John Rollo was shot close up too.'

'Not so close.'

That made me think. 'The Asian wasn't constrained.'

'Exactly. No marks on wrists, ankles or anywhere else. No alcohol in his system and no puncture marks. He could have been poisoned, but the toxicology tests will take time.'

'Maybe the shooter – he or she, alone or in company – managed to scare the victim enough to sit with his back to the gun. Or the opposite – he wasn't scared at all.'

'Quint, are you sure you want to stay on the case? You realize that Hector's system might cease to operate at any time.'

That hit me like a hammer blow. I knew she was right but I couldn't sit next to him, waiting for the death rattle. I didn't want the sight of him enfeebled and helpless to be imprinted on my memory. His passing would last a second, but he could – and probably would – fight long and hard.

'I should be with him, shouldn't I? It's my duty.'

Sophia came over and put her arms around me. 'It isn't a question of duty, Quint. You have to do what's best for you as well as for him. I don't think he recognizes you and, in any case, he's slipping deeper into oblivion. And he won't be alone.'

I clutched at that get-out clause like a greedy auxiliary on the take. My self-esteem was minimal, but I couldn't face hours, maybe days, in the drab room, waiting for the end.

'Besides, he'd want you to solve this, especially since the finger's pointing at guardians.'

She was right there. The old man hated corruption and power-grabbing like the plague. Which, in the peculiar ways of my mind, brought something to the surface.

'Have you heard of a drug that cures alcoholics?'

'What?'

I told her what John Rollo had stolen for his brother – Alceteron, according to the Supply Directorate manifest.

'I don't know it. There are drugs that reduce cravings and cause aversion to alcohol. Not that we have them.'

'This is supposed to be a cure. It came from Canada.'

'You say John Rollo took it for his brother. It didn't work in his case, did it? His stomach was full of whisky.'

I nodded. 'Is Mungo's body still here?'

'You know I don't release murder victims until cases are closed.'

'You could take samples to see if there are any traces of this Alceteron.'

'Toxicology will sign up anything unusual.' She squeezed my arm. 'But how do you expect us to find traces of a compound whose elements we don't know?'

'Good point,' I said, with a rueful smile. 'What about the bag of bones Davie found?'

'Extraordinary. I'm about to start work on them. Preliminary inspection suggested that they come from one individual.'

'George Allison's an expert on bones,' I said.

'Do you want me to involve him?'

I considered that. Could we trust the oncologist? 'See how it goes without him.'

'Fine by me. I can't stand the man.'

My phone rang.

'Quint, Davie. We've located Goliath.'

My heart did a somersault.

'Where?'

'Second-floor flat, 36 Rankeillor Street, alive.'

'On my way.'

'Not even a kiss,' Sophia said, as I bolted for the door.

I blew her one. And another in the old man's direction as I ran out of the infirmary.

Thirteen

It was only as the female driver of the Guard 4×4 that I'd commandeered turned on to the South Bridge that I made a connection. Rankeillor Street was between the Theatre of Life and *Spar/Tak/Us* star-director Rory

Campbell's flat in Dumbiedykes. There had been some pretty monstrous gladiators in the show. Was Goliath one of them?

'Shots fired!' came a voice over the radio. 'Take cover!'

'My kind of operation,' the middle-aged driver said, licking her lips.

There were still a few Guard members who'd been through the drugs wars and not moved to safer directorates. She was obviously one.

We arrived and the driver got out at speed, looking for an assignment on the front line.

The street was filled with Guard vehicles. To my surprise, Fergus Calder was there, as far out of range as he could manage. I ignored him and made my way forward, bending low behind the 4×4s. I saw Davie and went over to him.

'What happened, commander?'

'A guardsman saw a tall man in a black coat and woollen hat coming back from the corner shop. After we got here I sent three of my people up the stairs.' He shook his head. 'Three shots were fired, probably from a pistol. We haven't heard from them since.'

'They only had Hyper-Stuns, I suppose.'

He nodded. 'I should have waited for armed backup, considering what the fucker did to John Rollo.'

There was a burst of static on his communications unit.

'Senior guardian here. Commander in charge, respond.'

Davie did so.

'This man murdered an auxiliary,' Fergus Calder said.

'Four now,' said Davie.

'For the love of Socrates. I want him dead, do you understand?'

I took the device from Davie and spoke into it. 'Dalrymple here. I want to question him.'

'This isn't your decision, citizen. I'm deploying an armed unit. Out.'

I looked at Davie. 'I'm going up there.'

'Are you out of your mind?'

'Probably. Get me a vest and helmet.'

A minute later I was as armoured as was possible for anyone not in the special team that was kitting up at the end of the street.

'Take this,' Davie said, handing me his Hyper-Stun.

'No, thanks. Carrying those didn't do your people any good.'

He glared at me. 'I'm coming with you.'

I laughed. 'Goliath versus slightly shorter Goliath? I don't think so. I'll have your comms unit though, but it'll be switched off. I'm going to gain his trust.'

'You really are a lunatic, Quint,' Davie said desperately.

'Don't worry, I've got several cards up my combinations.'

He was shaking his head as I stood up and walked to the door, my arms raised. I made it to the street door and then to the first-floor landing. From there I saw the bodies of the Guard personnel – two men and a woman – sprawled on the next flight of steps. Each had been shot in the middle of the forehead. Goliath could handle his gun.

I stepped over the victims, but couldn't avoid getting blood and other matter on my boots. Then I heard the door to the right on the next landing open and saw the muzzle of a large pistol. I raised my arms again.

'I only want to talk,' I said. 'I'm not armed.'

No answer.

'And I'm not a member of the City Guard. I'm a . . . negotiator.' I was making a fool of myself if Goliath was an Eastern European with zero or minimal English, but I didn't know any Serb, Croat, Bulgarian, Albanian or whatever. I had a feeling, though, that the shooter could speak English as well as I could.

I made it on to the landing, my armpits drenched. The pistol was still pointed at me.

'There's no way out of here, you know. And the senior guardian wants you dead. I'm your only chance.'

Nothing for nearly a minute and then the door opened a bit more.

'Come forward,' said a deep voice. Goliath was Scottish, but I couldn't place his light accent. A Highlander? Why had Alice Lennox said he was Eastern European? Or was there another giant at large?

When I reached the door, I was grabbed and slammed against the wall front first. Heavy hands patted me down, relieving me of the comms unit and tearing off my helmet and bulletproof vest.

'In,' he said, giving me a shove that sent me headfirst into the main room. It was furnished with standard citizen-issue furniture.

As I got to my feet, I saw three people tied together in the corner, a late-middle-aged man and woman, and a teenage girl. They were all gagged.

'My uncle, aunt and cousin Lorna,' Goliath said, like a vicar at a tea party.

I turned and looked at the man. 'That's why the search didn't find you.' He'd taken off his hat, revealing a shaven head.

'Aye, Uncle Peter managed to distract them from where I was.'

'We haven't got much time,' I said. 'Armed specialists will be up here any minute.' I was hoping that Davie would have stalled the senior guardian but, even if he had, we needed to move quickly. 'Let them go,' I said.

'Fuck off.' Goliath had bright blue eyes. 'Who are you, anyway?'

I told him.

'Quint Dalrymple? I've heard of you. Hel Hyslop thinks you're a sneaky bastard.'

He was on speaking terms with the chief of Glasgow police. That was interesting, but also a source of concern. Hyslop was a Tasmanian devil in woman's clothing.

'I can only help you if you help me.'

'Sweet,' he mocked. 'You want to be my friend.'

'No,' I said. 'You killed John Rollo and an Asian, among others.'

He looked aggrieved. 'An Asian? I did not. And what do you mean "among others"?'

'Chung Keng Quee, Mungo Rollo, Clarinda Towart?'

'Fuck off. I've never heard of any of them.'

I didn't believe that, but I wasn't in a position to argue.

'So you got your orders from Hyslop?'

He grinned. 'You havnae a clue, pal.'

'Who else do you know in the city?'

A windowpane smashed and a bullet thudded into the rear wall. Goliath and I hit the floor and crawled under the windows. So much for Fergus Calder paying heed to Davie.

The captives were making frantic noises, their eyes wide. They were in the line of fire and I couldn't do anything about it.

'Dalrymple!' came the senior guardian's voice through a megaphone. 'Get out of there!'

Easier said than done. Goliath was pointing his Jarilo .45 at me.

'Why did you shoot John Rollo?'

'Fuck off.'

'Boring. Who told you to?'

'Screw you,' he said, with a harsh laugh.

'You're going to die if you don't give me something.'

He shrugged. 'Everybody dies.'

'Not during my investigations,' I said, directing a kick at his jaw. To my surprise it made good contact. I grabbed for the gun, but he pushed me away.

More shots came through the windows, one hitting Uncle Peter in the left knee. He gave a muffled squeal.

I threw myself on Goliath from a crouch. He tried to give me a Glasgow kiss, but I pulled my head back in time. Good idea, though. I brought my own forehead forward at speed and heard his nose crunch. His grip loosened and I managed to seize the gun. I put it against the side of his head.

'Talk, you bastard!'

'Get . . . tae . . . fu—'

I'd grabbed his balls with my free hand.

'Who gives you your orders?'

A fresh burst of rifle fire came through the windows. None of the hostages was hit this time.

Goliath's face was red, his eyelids squashed together. Tears ran down his unshaven cheeks.

'The Lord . . .' he said, in a high voice.

At first I thought he was singing a hymn. Then I got it.

'The Lord of the Isles?'

He nodded. I released the pressure on his scrotum. Bad idea. With a surge of strength he pushed me away. Before I could react he was standing at the window.

'Here I am, fuckers!' he yelled. 'Here I—'

A volley sent him flying backwards and filled the air with a red mist. Lorna let out a muffled scream, then slumped forward. Her mother's eyes were wide open in horror.

I crawled over to Goliath – no way was I getting up, in case Calder had told the marksman to dispose of me too. The big man had taken several shots to his chest and one to the side of his head, but he was still breathing.

'Who's your contact in the city?' I asked, mouth to his ear.

He coughed up dark blood.

'Clarinda?' I asked.

Goliath stared at me, then gurgled his life away without saying another syllable.

Davie was first into the flat, arriving while I was untying the hostages. Lorna had come round, and I took her and her mother into a bedroom. We'd interview them later. Uncle Peter was taken down to an ambulance, while Goliath was left for Sophia and the scene-of-crime team.

'Sorry,' Davie said, after he'd taken me aside. 'I managed to delay the senior guardian, but—'

'He was very keen on ending Goliath's life.'

'The bastard did kill auxiliaries.'

'Quiet,' I said, turning away as Fergus Calder came in, bodyguards in front of and behind him. I handed the Jarilo to Davie.

'Glad to see you're in one piece, citizen,' the senior guardian said.

'Are you?' I said, stepping closer. 'I could easily have been hit like the harmless hostage.'

Calder gave me a questioning look. 'I'd never describe you as harmless. Did the target say anything?'

'Fuck off.'

The bodyguards moved towards me.

'He said "Fuck off" to me several times,' I clarified.

'Nothing else?'

'Screw you. And get tae fuck.' I smiled. 'His exact words.' Well, almost.

Fergus Calder looked around. 'Well, we have our killer.'

'You think Goliath garotted Chung Keng Quee and Mungo Rollo?'

'Obviously.'

'And shot the Asian?'

'What's the matter with you, Dalrymple? Of course he did.'

'And that's why you were so keen to have him killed.'

He raised his thin shoulders. 'As well as Napier 311, he killed three Guard personnel and took three innocent citizens hostage. As you know, we spare no effort to hunt down those who murder auxiliaries.'

'Well, he denied everything except John Rollo's murder.'

Sophia arrived. 'You're all right, Quint,' she said, relief flooding her face. 'I couldn't make sense of what I heard on the radio.' Guardians could access the Public Order Directorate communication channels.

'Fergus here did his best to turn me into a colander,' I said, giving the senior guardian the eye.

He shook his head at Sophia and left.

'Did you have to come up here on your own?' she said. 'Have you got a death wish?'

I thought of Hector lying in the infirmary. Maybe I had.

Davie came after me when I left.

'Where are you going?' he asked, putting a hand on my shoulder.

'A place where Fergus fucking Calder won't set his assassins on me.'

'Come on, Quint.'

'I don't know how clean the senior guardian is.' I put my mouth close to his ear. 'Besides, the dead man told me he took his orders from the Lord of the Isles.'

'What?'

'And that pompous old slimeball was taken to see *Spar/Tak/Us*, despite the fact that no outsider visits have been reported in the *Edinburgh Guardian* for months.'

'You think the senior guardian tried to have Goliath killed before he talked?'

I nodded. 'He didn't have time to tell me who his contact in Edinburgh was.'

'It's obvious,' Davie said. 'Clarinda Towart, the invisible woman. You realize she's probably crossed the city line?'

'She could have, but my gut tells me she's still in Edinburgh. It's less clear if she's still alive.' I watched as James Michie got out of his 4×4 at the end of the street. 'Don't tell your boss where I've gone – or about this conversation.'

'Bugger off then, smartarse.'

I raised a finger behind my back then obscured myself among the emergency vehicles and personnel. The actor-director lived in Oakland Place, only a few minutes away. It was the third in a row of terraced houses that dated from the 1970s. They were dilapidated, the window frames rotten and the front doors in serious need of replacement. As I stood outside the street door of number 14, I wondered about his neighbours. There was no name on the button for the ground-floor flat. I pressed the bell next to a grubby card with his name handwritten in green. After several minutes I heard footsteps on the stairs inside.

'Citizen Dalrymple,' he said, rubbing his eyes. He was wearing a torn T-shirt and grey pyjama bottoms. 'This had better be good.' He turned and headed back upstairs, leaving me to close the door.

The place smelled of rancid bacon fat. I gagged as I went up. After I'd closed Campbell's door, the olfactory assault was much more pleasant. It was a long time since I'd smelled joss sticks. I was sure they hadn't come from the Supply Directorate.

'Tea?'

'No, thanks, Rory. I woke you up.'

'You know I work late.'

'This is urgent. Come clean with me and I'll keep you out of the castle.'

He sat down at a pristine antique table. I drew out the chair opposite him and ran a hand over the tabletop.

'Where did you get this?'

'Friend found it for me.'

'Not an outsider, by any chance?'

His eyes opened wide.

'Rory, do you know a big guy, well over six feet, built like an outside lavvy, shaved head?' I raised a hand. 'Do not talk bollocks.'

He shrugged. 'I can think of several in the play who match that description.'

'Any not turn up for the show last night?'

'No, they were all there.'

'When did you last see or communicate with Clarinda Towart?'

He looked away. 'I told you. Tuesday night.' I was close to buying that.

Normally if someone I'm questioning avoids my eyes I get suspicious, but this guy was an actor and a good one, so all bets were off.

'Did you know Duncan Denoon?'

Campbell met my gaze. 'The zookeeper? Aye, he was often at Clarinda's, cleaning up after her. Nice guy but a bit dim – animals meant more to him than humans. He came to the show maybe three weeks ago. Dropped in afterwards and we had a drink.'

'What did you talk about?'

'His pygmy hippos. I was thinking about putting them in the show.' He laughed. 'I don't even know if the Romans had them.'

'You mentioned that the senior guardian brought the Lord of the Isles to *Spar/Tak/Us*. Are you sure about that?'

'As sure as eggs are eggs.'

'Which, given the vagaries of the Supply Directorate, means you aren't certain at all.'

He smiled. 'I was using the expression in its original sense.'

'All right.' I got up and looked around the room. It was furnished and decorated a lot more individualistically – not to say eccentrically – than standard citizen abodes. Dyed sheets hung from the ceiling and most of the furniture was handmade. I remembered Campbell was a trained woodworker.

'Yes, they're mine,' he said, pre-empting my question. 'I did them before the theatre took over my life.'

'Do you know Alice Lennox?'

He shook his head.

'Christo Fleming?'

'No. Who are they?'

'Alice is another friend of Clarinda.'

'Oh, the nurse. Clarie did talk about her a few times. She helped her in rehab, didn't she?'

'Yes.' I fixed my gaze on him.

'What?' he said, a lot longer after most citizens would have cracked.

'I'm weighing up whether to take you back to the castle.'

For the first time I got to him, making him stand up and pound his hand on the table.

'What is it you want from me?' he roared, Spartacus in full flow.

Good question. I didn't have anything on him or anything to ask that wouldn't tell him more than I wanted him to know.

'Thanks for your time,' I said, getting up and heading for the door. 'Oh, by the way, who are your neighbours?'

'Downstairs? I don't know. They only moved in a few days ago.'

I was pleased. The surveillance team hadn't made him suspicious. They'd be carrying out a search of his flat when he was at the Theatre of Life tonight.

As I walked back to Rankeillor Street, I remembered the purple snake on the dead Asian's shoulder. I knew for a fact that Rory Campbell didn't have one as his upper body was often naked in the play. Duncan Denoon didn't have one either.

It would be interesting to see if Alice Lennox and Christo Fleming had been tattooed.

And why she had claimed Goliath was an Eastern European.

I commandeered a 4×4 and directed the driver to the castle.

Fourteen

James Michie was in his chair in the command centre.

'Quint,' he called, as I tried to make it to Davie's office unnoticed. 'Where did you dash off to?'

'I'm fine, thanks for asking.'

He stared at me. 'Oh. Yes, it must have been a terrifying experience. I'm glad you weren't hit.'

'Are you also glad that Goliath committed suicide by firearms squad? Then again, the senior guardian was set on his death. Did he ask you to provide specialist personnel?'

Michie looked down. 'No, he didn't. But he's entitled to give direct commands to any auxiliary.'

It was obvious he was annoyed. I set off again, but he was quick to follow me. We sat in Davie's office. The commander was on the phone.

'That was Nasmyth 01, the last of the barracks commanders to report,' he said. 'Goliath definitely wasn't an auxiliary.'

'I don't think he was a citizen either,' I said, 'though the archive search should continue.'

The guardian had turned to me. 'Why not a citizen?'

I needed to be careful. 'He had an accent I couldn't place – Scottish but I don't know where from. Maybe the far north. Definitely not Eastern European.'

'What did he say to you?' Michie asked avidly.

I gave him a selection of the dead man's abuse.

'Anything else?'

I put on my best poker face, not that I've ever played it – the original Council banned all card games in its anti-gambling drive. That only applied to citizens and auxiliaries, of course. Tourists were encouraged to bet their shirts and all other garments in the casinos and at the hippodrome in Princes Street Gardens.

'Nothing?' the guardian said, in frustration. 'You didn't question him?'

'I tried, believe me. And I would have gone on trying if Fergus Calder hadn't let the snipers loose.'

Davie diverted the discussion. 'We've started canvassing the residents in Rankeillor Street. Maybe Goliath was spotted with someone else.'

Michie opened the thick file he'd brought with him. 'Do we believe that this Peter Dobie was his uncle?'

'I'm waiting on the archive files,' Davie said.

'When can we interview them?'

'Dobie's in the infirmary with a serious wound to his knee. His wife, Mavis, is also there, in shock. They're not sure when she'll come out of it.'

'That leaves Lorna,' I said. 'She's with them, I presume.'

Davie nodded. 'Under guard.'

'Tell them to give her some space.'

'Why?' demanded the guardian.

I sighed. 'So she's less stressed when I question her.'

He accepted that grudgingly.

There was a knock at the door and a young guardswoman carried a pile of paper to Davie's desk.

'The Dobie files,' she said.

I laughed. 'Sounds like the title of a pre-Enlightenment spy novel.'

'The Dobie Memorandum.'

I almost fell off my seat. James Michie had hidden depths – and maybe even a sense of humour.

'Peter Ian Dobie,' read Davie, 'born 12/9/1970, bus driver. Married Mavis Elisabeth Dobie, née Melville, born 30/3/1987, cleaner. Lorna Melville Dobie born 2/8/2018, pupil at High School Number 7.'

I extended a hand. 'Give me Peter's and the guardian the wife's. You take Lorna's.'

For a while we read and made notes.

'Right,' I said. 'Peter Dobie has only average reports but no infractions either of the Transport Department code of practice or of the City

Regulations. He plays chess weekly, has an allotment in the Enlightenment Park, doesn't drink alcohol and cleans the pavement on Rankeillor Street.' Citizens were expected to take on such civic duties, but these days few did.

'A model, run-of-the-mill citizen, then,' said Michie. 'The same goes for his wife.'

I looked at Davie.

'Lorna seems to be a good kid, decent but not striking school reports, keen on sewing and reading. No boyfriend, a couple of girlfriends from her class. Not sexual, obviously.' The Council allowed hetero- and homosexual relations from sixteen. Lorna had six months to go.

'The interesting thing is Peter Dobie's siblings,' I said.

'Mavis had none,' said the guardian.

'Well, Peter had two brothers. The eldest, Joseph, was killed in the drug wars in 2013. Unlike many, the body was positively identified – by Peter himself.'

'And the other,' Michie said impatiently.

'The other, Martin, disappeared in May 2032.' I raised my eyes. 'He was a guardsman.'

'What?' they said in unison.

'Ferguson 169. Know him?'

They shook their heads.

'Get his file,' I said to Davie. He battered away at his keyboard.

'Yes,' he said. 'Ferguson 169, born Martin Alexander Dobie, 1/2/82, trained as a bricklayer, accepted for auxiliary training January 2005, joined Guard after border duty, stayed in border and city line units for nearly twenty years, reports excellent.' Davie looked up. 'He must have liked shooting at people. Oh. He was shot in the abdomen in October 2027 and took a year to recover. Subsequently took up managerial post at the Tourism Directorate.' He stopped. 'In the Prostitution Services Department.'

The wraith of Clarinda Towart rose before me, but I batted it away.

'Children?' I asked.

Davie scrolled down. 'Yes, a son. Born 24/6/2004, before his father was in the Guard?' His face fell. 'Shit. Ronald Douglas Dobie, died of influenza in April 2006.'

'The mother?' said Michie.

'No record,' Davie said. 'And there's no cremation report.'

The guardian was appalled.

'Remember, it wasn't uncommon for mothers to withhold their identities back then,' I said. 'The first Council required only one parent to register. The aim was to get women out of traditional roles if they wanted that.'

'Who was looking after the child when it died?' asked Michie.

'He,' I corrected.

'Martin and Peter Dobie's mother, Miriam. She died in 2007 in a drugs gang battle.'

I stood up.

'Where are you going?' said Davie.

'The infirmary.'

'But what happened?' the guardian insisted. 'Was the dead baby's identity given to another boy?'

'The one we know as Goliath?' I said. 'It's possible. Or perhaps he didn't die. In either case, his accent suggests he was out of the city for a long time.'

'Where did he get that unusual pistol?' Michie said.

'If he was out of the city, there are plenty of places he could have bought it.' I paused. 'Or been issued with it.' I headed for the door.

'What do you mean by that?' the guardian called.

I left him to work it out.

My phone rang as I was on the way down the cobbles.

'Citizen Dalrymple, it's Cramond 537,' came a high male voice.

'Who?'

'Ross Parlane.'

Son and secretary of the Tourism Directorate. 'Call me Quint, Ross.'

'Em, yes. You asked for certain information.'

'I did.'

'The dead Asian,' he said warily, as if photos of the deceased had affected his intestinal tract badly. 'He didn't enter the city by air or sea.'

So he'd crossed the border illicitly. Not many tourists did that, though people from other Scottish states did – none of them on legitimate business. It was the first time I'd heard of a person from the Far East coming in that way.

'As regards Napier 311, no Tourism Directorate staff recognized him or had other than bureaucratic dealings.'

John Rollo had either done his thieving at the Supply Directorate warehouse or his contacts in tourism were keeping their heads down. No surprises there.

'All right, Ross, thank you.'

'Citizen,' he said hurriedly. 'My mother – the guardian – asked me to say that she'd appreciate your keeping the directorate out of the limelight.' He cut the connection.

That struck me as the kind of thing Mary Parlane would never have said. The pressure was obviously getting to her.

*   *   *

My phone rang again as I was halfway to the infirmary.

'Quint, where are you?' It was Sophia and she sounded tense.

I told her. 'What's going on?'

'Your . . . Hector.' Her voice was suddenly hoarse. 'He's raving. Fiona thinks he's . . . he's near the end.'

I started running, my head filled with images of my father in the bony arms of death. I had a stitch by the time I passed the museum, but kept going. I stumbled in the infirmary gates and slowed my pace, trying to catch my breath by the time I got to Hector's room. I could hear his voice, uncommonly loud, from outside.

Fiona was on the far side of the bed, while Sophia was holding my father's right hand and talking to him. I went close and she stepped back.

'What's all this, old man?' I said, putting my hand on his. 'You'll wake the dea—the other patients.'

He carried on shouting, his voice cracking and straining. I could only make out odd words – 'thieves', 'traitors' and 'motherfuckers' being the most repeated. I'd never heard him use that term of abuse before. He must have been reading Elmore Leonard. Or updating his translation of Juvenal.

Then the volume dropped and he turned his face to me.

'Fai . . . failure?' he said, his eyes filling with tears.

'Yes, it's me, old man.' I blinked back tears of my own. 'Calm down.'

He twitched his head. 'No . . . no time. He . . . he was . . . there.'

I glanced at Sophia. She waved Fiona away.

'Deep breaths,' I said, as if I had a clue. 'Who was where?'

'At the . . . the cancer centre. The . . . motherfucker.'

'Who?' I said, wiping his eyes.

'The thief . . . of the . . . century.'

I patted his hand. 'Don't upset yourself.'

He glared at me. 'Billy . . . fucking Geddes. I saw him . . . with . . . George . . . Allison.' The breath caught in his throat and he started to blink rapidly.

Sophia pushed me aside and put a manual air balloon over his nose and mouth, then called for Fiona.

I watched as they worked on my father. After what seemed like an age his breathing returned to something approaching normal, at least for a man in his condition, and his eyes closed.

'Is he in pain?' I asked.

'Possibly,' Fiona said, 'but if I increase the morphine drip, he may slip away.'

I shook my head and looked at Sophia.

'We've stabilized him, Quint. That's all we can do.'

I spent the next three hours at Hector's bedside. He was sleeping calmly, his breathing gradually becoming less rough.

Fiona took his hand. 'His pulse is stronger,' she said. 'I think he's rallying.' I wasn't surprised. He'd set his mind on getting his message to me and, although he'd exhausted himself doing so, he was holding on. He'd probably ask for kippers and croissants when he woke up. No, I was kidding myself.

I resisted the temptation to leave the infirmary and go after Billy. Instead I went to Sophia's office. She'd have done the p-m on Goliath by now.

After I told her how the old man was doing, I asked about Peter Dobie.

'I knew you'd be interested in him,' Sophia replied. 'He needs the kind of knee reconstruction we can't provide. He was sedated, but he's conscious now – if pretty woozy.'

'And the big man?'

'You saw what happened to him.'

I nodded. 'They didn't have to shoot him. Fergus Calder wanted him dead.'

'You think he didn't want Goliath to talk?'

'Goliath's real name was Ronald Douglas Dobie, I suspect. Someone, maybe his mother, identity unknown, got him out of the city when he was two. It was during the drugs wars and that wouldn't have been difficult. Did he have a purple snake tattoo?'

'Like the Asian? Yes, in the same place. What does it mean?'

I shrugged. 'Search me. Anything else interesting?'

'He was very fit, significant muscle development all over his body. And there was gunshot residue on his hands, as you'd expect. It matches that on the auxiliary he shot.'

'*Quelle surprise.* Is Mavis Dobie stable?'

'Stabilized, i.e. sedated.'

'Shit. What about the daughter?'

'She's only fifteen, Quint. It was a terrible experience for her.'

'I know.' I got up. 'Which ward?'

Sophia shook her head. 'I'll take you.'

'You don't have to.'

'I do. I'm playing mother hen. The second you upset her, I'll have you thrown out.'

'Cluck,' I said.

That earned me a stare so withering that Heathcliff would have been proud. Then I remembered my father and what he'd said. These were no laughing matters.

*　　*　　*

On the way to visit Lorna Dobie, Sophia leaned closer and said, 'There's an elephant in this hospital.'

'I hope it doesn't get blown up.'

'You know what, or rather who, I mean.'

Of course I did. 'Billy Geddes.'

'Yes. Shouldn't you be stitching his backside to his wheelchair?'

I'd been thinking about that. 'Not yet. I need to tie things together more. Besides, he'll just tell me to piss off and get Jack MacLean to send his gorillas round.'

'Very zoological, this conversation.'

I didn't have time to reply. She steamed into the ward in full imperious mode, taking the files a quick-thinking nurse handed to her. There was a curtained area at the end. Outside it, she ran her eye over the charts.

'Peter Dobie's still less than compos mentis, as is his wife. The daughter's sitting here with her mother.'

I tried to force my way in first. Sophia could be terrifying to ordinary citizens. To my surprise on this occasion her bedside manner was superb. She put her arm round Lorna's thin shoulders and comforted her, saying that her parents would be fine. Then the girl spotted me.

'Hello, Lorna,' I said, with a tentative smile.

She wasn't exactly over Venus to see me, her forehead immediately furrowing and her eyes wide.

'I'll come with you,' Sophia said. 'Citizen Dalrymple's a good dog really.'

I decided against biting her head off. For the time being.

In Sophia's office, I made tea and demanded biscuits.

'I ate them all,' the guardian said.

I shook my head. 'This is what we're up against, Lorna. Council corr—'

'—ectness,' supplied Sophia rapidly, giving me the eye. 'My next ration isn't till tomorrow.'

Aye, right. Since when did guardians have rations? Lorna seemed impressed though.

'I'm very sorry you had to go through that ordeal,' I said.

'Wasn't your fault,' she said, eyes down, then suddenly up. 'Or was it?'

'No,' I said, truthfully but still guiltily. Bastard Fergus Calder. 'He was your cousin, yes?'

'Dougie? So Dad said. He seemed nice enough.' She bowed her head. 'Until he tied us up this morning and shot the Guard people.'

'When did he arrive?'

'Just after seven thirty. We'd started supper.'

Goliath, definitely Ronald Douglas Dobie in my book, must have hidden somewhere after shooting John Rollo – or gone round the houses to shake off the Guard personnel who had flooded the area.

'A guardsman rang the bell later, but my Dad had already hidden Dougie under the big bed. Not that there was much of a search.'

Black mark, James Michie and Davie – though with thousands of properties to check, I would let their people off.

'Did you hear your parents talking to your cousin?'

'A little. He said he liked it in Skye. Where's that?'

I gave her a blank look. The Education Directorate pays no attention to Scottish geography, concentrating on Edinburgh. I was interested because Skye was part of the Lord of the Isles' fiefdom. It looked like Goliath had told me the truth about who gave him his orders – or was he the kind of shithead who lied to the very end?

'I tried to talk to him,' Lorna said, 'but Mum and Dad wouldn't let me, so I went to my room.'

'Did you hear anyone leave the flat?'

'No, citizen.'

'Call me Quint.'

'No, Quint,' she said, her cheeks reddening. 'My room's next to the front door and I'm a light sleeper, so I'd have heard.'

'And then?'

'We had breakfast and I was about to go to school when Dougie turned nasty. He held that horrible pistol on Dad and made him tie us up, then roped Dad to us. The gag was the worst thing. That and needing the toilet.'

'Did Dougie say anything after that?'

'No, he just stared at us with fierce eyes.' She paused. 'Hang on, he made a call from the house phone.'

I pricked my ears up but didn't speak – now wasn't the time to be pushy.

'"I've been spotted," he said. "Tell her."'

Her? Who could that be? Clarinda? Hel Hyslop? Some female operative working for the Lord of the Isles?

'He didn't say a name, Lorna?'

She shook her head.

The Guard would check the number called.

'Was there anything else that struck you?' I asked.

Lorna burst into tears. 'Why . . . why did they have to . . . shoot him?'

I wasn't going to get the senior guardian out of that one, even though Dougie/Goliath had killed at least four auxiliaries. And if he hadn't shot the Asian – which seemed to be the case – we were after another killer.

Or was it the same one who had throttled Chung Keng Quee? I wondered how many Jarilo .45s there were in Edinburgh, apart from Goliath's and the one in Mungo Rollo's house.

Fifteen

I looked in on Hector. He was out for the count again, his mouth twisted as he breathed lightly. Fiona told me that she would reduce the morphine in the evening if he came round. I asked her to call Sophia the instant he woke up. If the old man started talking again, I wanted someone reliable to take notes. Then again, Sophia and I would be at the Council meeting later. I'd have to arrange cover.

I rang Davie from outside the infirmary and asked him to meet me at the museum. I'd remembered that there was a display of animal skeletons, from blue whale to mouse. I didn't know why I wanted a look, but I'd learned to let my subconscious do its thing.

After taking in the spectacular blue whale, which had been found over two hundred years ago at the mouth of the Forth, I found myself in a small room with snake skeletons. They were remarkable, dozens of rounded ribs coming off skeletons that had been deliberately posed in striking shapes such as whorls and curls. Several had their jaws wide apart, the fangs still in place. The tattoos on the Asian man and Goliath were heavily stylized, the heads larger than the bodies. In the next room were the skeletons of pygmy animals – no hippos, thankfully, but owls, a marmoset, a tapir and a goat. Pygmy animals. We were still no further on with the explosion at the zoo.

I mentioned that to Davie when I got into the 4×4.

'What the hell do you want me to do?' he replied, frustrated.

'Calm down, sweetie. Alice Lennox is a potential lead. We'll talk to her and her boyfriend later.'

'If we can find them.'

'What?'

'Michie let them go – said they'd been in the castle long enough.'

I took a deep breath. 'And did the all-knowing public order guardian ascertain whether they had purple snake tattoos on them?'

'No,' Davie said, with a grin. 'But I did. Well, I turned a guardswoman loose on Lennox, but I checked Christo Fleming myself. Nothing on either of them.'

'Hm.' I wasn't sure if that was good news or not.

We arrived in Rankeillor Street in less than five minutes. The emergency vehicles were long gone – even the crime-scene team – and a solitary Guard 4×4 was parked outside the Dobie place. Davie went over to the Guard personnel and then came back.

'The door-to-door's finished. The only person who saw Goliath was an old man opposite. He called it in. The guardian's personally checked him out. Besides, he's lost both his legs to diabetes. Not exactly Professor Moriarty.'

'I'll be the judge of that,' I said, hoping I'd remember to check Michie's work, not least because as far as I knew the call had been anonymous.

'Don't you want to call Raeburn 297?' he asked, as he went up the stairs.

'And try to get blood from a stone? No, thanks. His report will go to Michie and he can present it at the Council meeting.'

'Why are you being so offhand about what the techies might have found, Quint?'

I tapped the side of my nose.

'What does that . . . oh, I get it. You reckon you can lay hands on something they've missed.'

'It wouldn't be the first time.'

He muttered something as he lifted the Guard tape that crisscrossed the door.

'Pardon?'

'How's Hector?'

'Ah. He's out for the count.' I told him what the old man had said about Billy Geddes.

'Well, knock me down with a pig's pizzle.' There had been a time when the Supply Directorate provided those for human consumption. Davie was probably a fan.

'Why aren't we stomping around his luxury flat with him attached to our boots?'

I explained that I wanted to build more of a case and also to see if Billy panicked.

'You went to school and university with him, Quint, and the fucker gets away with—'

'Murder? I rather doubt it, at least not directly. You take the main room – don't bother about the bullet holes – and look everywhere, under what passes for a carpet too.' There was a large bloodstain where Dougie/Goliath had expired and a smaller one where Peter Dobie had been sitting.

'Yes, sir. Meanwhile you're—'

'Doing the bedrooms.'

There were only two such rooms in the oddly laid-out flat – Lorna's by the main door and her parents' beyond the living room, looking out over the street. The Housing Directorate had split the original flat in two back in the days when citizens got cramped housing and liked it. They were more mollycoddled now, but perhaps the Dobies liked the location. Close to the Theatre of Life and the cancer centre – was either of those significant? Or both?

'There are a couple of bottles of Laphroaig at the back of the cupboard,' Davie called.

'That's from Islay, isn't it?'

'So it says.'

Islay was the historical centre of the Lordship of the Isles, something I'd found out when I researched the title after I'd met its less than savoury current holder last summer. More evidence, admittedly circumstantial, that Dougie/Goliath was one of the Lord's men.

I walked around Peter and Mavis's bedroom. There wasn't much room, even with the less than enormous Supply Directorate double bed. Goliath could only just have fitted under it. There was a chipped dressing table with a mirror cracked from top to bottom – bad luck for somebody, maybe Dougie. I pulled open all the drawers, but there was nothing out of the ordinary. Then I lay on the bed and bounced up and down. The mattress was predictably hard, but not to the extent of there being something hidden in it. I got off and pushed the bed to the window. There was a lot of dust on the ancient linoleum, but that wasn't all. I made out recent scratches near the wall. The lino came away easily. A panel about two foot square had been cut into the floorboards. I felt for a depressed section, got my fingers into it and pulled up the wood. The space below was empty. Apart from a Scene of Crime squad note, upon which had been scribbled the words, 'Nothing here, citizen.' Bloody Raeburn 297. That made me even more determined to put one over him.

'Here, Quint,' said Davie.

I went into the bathroom to find him standing on the toilet seat, his head in a gap in the low ceiling above.

He sneezed. 'Some kind of storage space.'

'Any bodies?'

'It's about a yard high and one and a half square.'

'Small bodies?'

'Bugger off. There are three bags in here. The techies have checked them, there's fingerprint powder all over the place.'

'What's in them?'

'One's got women's clothing, out of fashion even for Edinburgh. Another's empty and . . . the third's full of *Edinburgh Guardian* cuttings. Here.' He handed it down.

I looked at the sheaves of discoloured newsprint. There was no obvious pattern – a rugby match report from 2018, a citizen bring-and-swap fair from 2023, a photo of a man with an enormous leek . . . Someone would have to go through all this, but that person wasn't going to be me.

'I wonder why the techies didn't take—' I broke off when I saw the handwritten note on the inside of the lid: 'Not really our kind of thing, citizen, but well done on finding it.' Right, this was war.

I went into Lorna's room. Like the bathroom it didn't have a window, only a glass rectangle above the door. It must have been seriously sweaty when the temperature was high, as it often was in climate-change-afflicted Edinburgh.

There was a single bed, covered with a shocking pink blanket, a small desk and a wardrobe. I could see boot prints on the lino, Guard boots – the techies had done their job. I looked around. The mirror, this one undamaged, had photos stuck around it – girls, boys, sometimes including Lorna. The first Council banned personal photography on the grounds that it encouraged egoistic thought, but the relaxing of the City Regulations had made old-fashioned, non-digital cameras available to citizens who could be bothered to wait for shipments to arrive from Mongolia.

There was no one apart from Lorna's parents that I recognized in the photos. It surprised me that Raeburn 297 hadn't taken them and I looked without success for a sarcastic note. He must have filmed them. Ha, something to nail him over.

Then I saw it – a small picture, cut down from a larger one half-covered at the bottom. It showed only the face and hair of a female, but I knew exactly who it was: Clarinda Towart, looking neither drunk nor made up like a Prostitution Services Department operative.

I called Sophia and asked her to put a discreet guard on Lorna Dobie.

Davie was standing in the doorway with a Scene of Crime note in his hand.

'This was in the fridge. Says they took the food for analysis.'

'Read consumption.' I showed him the photo. 'Raeburn 297's in deep shit.'

We went down the stairs. It struck me that there was nothing apart from the whisky that was Dougie's. If Alice Lennox was telling the truth about having been approached by him some time ago, he must have been staying elsewhere.

One step forward and one back – par for the case.

Davie dropped me at the infirmary. Hector was still doing his impression of a mummy with the sorest throat since the Old Kingdom. Fiona was off duty. Her replacement was older and more down in the mouth. She'd got the message about calling Sophia if the old man started to talk.

I decided to talk to Lorna on my own and sent the attending guardswoman on her way. I wasn't proud of myself, but pressure had to be applied. I hadn't been able to think of any reason why she should have Clarinda's photo – then again, Dougie had told me the latter was his Edinburgh contact.

Mavis Dobie was still sedated. I smiled at Lorna and asked her if she was hungry. We ended up in the canteen. At least they had biscuits, though they were for people with strong teeth.

'Who's this?' I said, slipping the photo across the surface of the table.

Lorna froze, a biscuit halfway to her lips.

'Where . . . Is that mine?'

'Yes. Answer the question.'

'But . . . it's mine. You can't take it.'

'Believe me, I can. I have.' I turned nasty. 'Would you like to continue this conversation in the castle?'

That scared her. I felt bad, but it was necessary.

'It's . . . it's Clarrie.'

'Clarrie?'

'Yes, Clarrie.' Lorna looked unabashed now, as if she'd got over the shock of having her personal property taken – she was a child of the newer, user-friendly Council.

'What does Clarrie stand for?' I asked, playing dumb.

'Clarinda,' she said, with a sweet smile. 'Lovely name, isn't it?'

'It is.' I decided against saying it was the cover name the poet Robert Burns had used for Agnes Maclehose, with whom he had a rare unconsummated affair – that might have distracted her. 'Is Clarrie a friend of the family?'

Lorna was taken aback. 'No, no.' She clammed up.

'It's important,' I said, my voice harsh.

'What's her surname?'

'Towart,' she said reluctantly.

So the missing woman had been using her real name.

'Where did you meet her?'

'I . . . she . . . she was assigned to me.'

The coin dropped. 'You applied to join the Prostitution Services Department.'

She nodded. 'It didn't go down well with my parents.'

I made no comment about that. 'You're fifteen, so you can't have known her long.' Although teenagers could apply to the department at fifteen, they weren't accepted until they were sixteen – and then only rarely. Applicants were given a mentor, whose job was to put off people who didn't know what they were getting into as much as to encourage them.

'I met her seven times,' Lorna said, eyes down. 'A week back Wednesday was the last time.'

Well before Chung Keng Quee's murder, let alone the subsequent deaths. 'Where?'

'She has a shop in the Grassmarket.'

So that was what Clarinda did in C.T. Enterprises – no, I wasn't buying it. 'You look uncomfortable, Lorna,' I said. 'Why?'

She stopped biting a hangnail and glared at me. 'I'm in love with her, all right? You nosy, dirty old man . . .'

Nosy I could live with, dirty too, but old? I managed to restrain myself.

'And you're lovers?' I said, in a low voice. People were staring at us.

'Yes,' she said, blinking. 'But I'm not sure Clarrie really loves me.'

It isn't uncommon for mentors to get involved with applicants, even though it was against regulations. Clarinda had shown before that she didn't care about those.

'When's your next appointment, Lorna?'

'To . . . tomorrow, at four in the afternoon.' She looked at me in alarm. 'What are you going to do?'

'Nothing,' I lied, passing her the last biscuit.

Would we finally manage to lay hands on the phantom Clarinda at her place of business? I didn't like the odds, but there wasn't another game in town.

By the time of the Council meeting I hadn't made much progress. I met the public order guardian outside the former parliament building.

'Quint,' he said, nodding.

Screw first names. 'Guardian, why the hell did you let Alice Lennox and Christo Fleming go? They've disappeared off the radar.'

His face fell. 'Oh. I'm sure they'll turn up soon enough.'

'Are you? Alice is one of Clarinda Towart's two surviving friends. It would have been good to keep eyes on her.' I didn't mention that I'd been planning on releasing her myself, but in that case she'd have been under surveillance from the second they walked out of the castle gate.

'I hope you're not going to embarrass me in front of my colleagues,' Michie said.

I shook my head. 'You know too much. You haven't been tempted to come clean about the Malaysian contracts, I hope.'

'I'm in a difficult position. We really must get this sorted out.'

I let that go, but it wasn't as if 'this' was a straightforward case.

Fergus Calder came past, secretary and bodyguards in tow, and Michie went after him like a good little doggie.

I was called to report immediately. I told the Council where we were on most fronts.

'So this Goliath was an Edinburgh citizen?' said Kate Revie.

'In his early years. The question is, why did he come back?' I looked at the senior guardian. 'And who was giving him orders?' I kept Dougie/ Goliath's fingering of the Lord of the Isles to myself for the time being.

Neither Calder nor Jack MacLean reacted to that, but then guardians can do stone-face with extreme competence.

'These newspaper cuttings you recovered from the Dobie flat,' MacLean said. 'Anything interesting?'

I wanted to ask him if there was anything interesting about his SPADE Billy Geddes's presence in the cancer centre, but held back. Ditto with Lorna's photo of Clarinda.

'An experienced Guard team is going through them,' James Michie said pompously.

Jack MacLean looked unimpressed, but didn't say more.

'Senior guardian,' I said, 'I'd like to ask a question.'

There was a flash of concern in his eyes.

'Fire away, Quint.'

'Thank you, Fergus.' I gave him a tight smile. 'Have you received representations from the Malaysian consul about the dead man in Moredun?'

That shut him and everyone else up, though not for long.

'It's my impression,' said the senior guardian, 'that the man's identity has not been established.' He looked at James Michie, who looked at me.

'That . . . er, that is correct,' confirmed the public order guardian.

'So you haven't told the consul,' I said. 'And he hasn't asked about a missing Malaysian?'

'Quintilian,' said Mary Parlane, 'may I remind you that the Tourism Directorate has no record of the man. He did not officially arrive in the city.'

So what was he doing here, I wondered. Maybe he wasn't Malaysian at all. We were up a dead end, at least temporarily.

'And this Goliath?' Calder said, changing the subject adeptly.

Sophia ran through the results of the p-m, mentioning the purple snake tattoo that linked him to the dead Asian.

'Yet he was a Scot,' MacLean said.

'Sounded like one to me, plus he has relatives in the city.'

'What are they saying about him?' Calder asked.

'The parents are still sedated,' I said, catching his gaze. 'I imagine they'll want to know why Dougie, as they knew him, had to be shot to pieces.'

The senior guardian frowned. 'The man killed four auxiliaries, let alone the Asian.' I let him go on thinking the latter. 'Plus, he'd taken three citizens hostage. I hardly think Hyper-Stunning him and putting him through a rehabilitation programme would have been appropriate.'

I went into full assault mode. 'Except that's what City Regulations require, even for those who kill auxiliaries.' The first Council abolished the courts and assigned the Public Order Directorate to assess guilt and punish offenders. During the drugs wars that meant the city's enemies were put against a wall, if they were lucky. Things were much less severe now, but the regs were still sacrosanct. Which didn't stop the Council changing them and omitting to tell ordinary citizens.

Fergus Calder gave me a twisted smile. 'I took the decision to terminate this Goliath's life because of the serious nature of his crimes. You know that as senior guardian, I have the power.'

'Fine,' I said. 'But he took a lot of potentially valuable information with him to oblivion.'

'I gather Goliath made a phone call from the Dobie's flat around ten p.m. yesterday,' said Jack MacLean. I wondered why he was interested in that detail from my report.

'Correct,' James Michie put in. 'The number dialled was 274-9003. It's a street phone in Oxgangs. My people have canvassed the area, but no one saw who answered.'

'No one talks to the Guard out there,' I said. Oxgangs wasn't far from the city line and was sparsely populated. Like Moredun, people who chose to live there were more often than not up to no good.

The finance guardian didn't seem unduly distressed by the negative response. Maybe he was relieved. I didn't trust him further than I could throw him, a form of exercise I'd be very happy to undertake.

I looked at Sophia. We'd discussed the anti-alcoholism drug Alceteron, before deciding against raising it. She wanted me to nail Billy too, but he was slippery as a purple snake and I hadn't yet been able to find out what he was doing in the cancer centre. Maybe Hector had been seeing things, though his decades-old dislike of Billy seemed alive and well even at this late juncture.

Fergus Calder gave me a dismissive smile. 'You really aren't getting very far with the case, citizen. We're still where we were days ago. Find Clarinda Towart.'

I hadn't told Michie about the photo of the missing woman. Davie and I would set up Lorna's meeting with Clarinda tomorrow afternoon. If we caught her, the smirk would be on my face.

Sixteen

'Time for a feed,' Davie said, as we arrived at the castle.

He was right. He ate numerous mutton chops while I had just the one battered haddock. Since European Union quotas in the early century and the sinking of many fishing fleets in the maritime version of the drugs wars, the sea had been teeming with fish.

'Now what?' he said, breaking a toothpick on one of his molars.

'Peter and Mavis Dobie. I'll have them regain consciousness forcibly if I have to.'

He nodded. 'And *moi*?'

I laughed. '*Tu* can check something I've been remiss about. The zookeeper, Duncan Denoon. We should have looked into his accommodation block.'

'I did,' Davie said smugly. 'He slept in a dormitory with seven other male keepers and had next to no personal possessions.'

'Very good, commander. And did you check his leave requests?'

Citizens living in directorate facilities have to fill in forms when they want to visit relatives or friends. The times and destinations are recorded in a ledger.

'Erm, no,' mumbled Davie.

'Get to it, then,' I said, standing up. 'You can drop me at the infirmary on your way.'

'Now I'm a fucking taxi driver.'

Which made me think.

'Bruce Kilgour.'

'The guy who took Clarinda and Chung Keng whatever to the theatre and the long way round to her flat?'

'The very one. Have you got his file?'

'He's been checked,' Davie said, looking through the heap of paperwork on his desk. 'Here it is.'

I opened it and took in the notes that had been added by the Guard personnel who had visited his flat and followed up on his friends. There were no names I recognized. Still, Kilgour was interesting because he was one of the few Edinburgh citizens with his own transport; not that he owned the taxi, he rented it from the Labour Directorate, which had subsumed the former Transportation Directorate in 2024 – it had become obvious the city didn't need a fully blown directorate to run the buses, citizen and tourist, and lorries and vans.

Bruce Kilgour lived in Goldenacre, in the north of the city and under a mile from Clarinda Towart's flat. Significant? He was fifty-two, had worked as a Supply Directorate delivery driver for twenty-three years before winning one of the monthly ballots for a taxi three years ago. His record was spotless – no infractions of City Regulations, no suspicious activities, a wife, Moira, who'd been with him since 2014 and an eighteen-year-old daughter called Debra. Who had applied to the Prostitution Services Department a little over a year ago. I immediately thought of Lorna Dobie – did the girls know each other?

Mary Parlane sighed as I identified myself on the phone. 'What now, Quintilian?'

'Debra Kilgour.'

Silence.

'Mary?'

'What? The name means nothing to me.'

'Get Ross to look her up in the directorate's system.'

'I can do that myself.'

I waited, hearing clicks on her keyboard.

'Got her. Oh.'

'Tell me she's being mentored by Clarinda Towart.'

'She isn't.'

I thought of Debra's age. 'She *was* mentored by CT?'

'Correct. Finished 30/11/33.'

Three months ago. 'Where has she been assigned?'

'The Lucky Strike Casino.'

'On Rose Street.'

'That's right. She seems to be popular with the customers. What's this about?'

'Better you don't know, Mary, at least for now. Please don't alert her in any way.'

'Of course not, Quintilian.'

I cut the connection.

'Fancy going to the Lucky Strike later?' I said to Davie.

'I don't like gambling.'

'It pays for the Enlightenment's existence.' Again, I was struck by the Malaysian contracts – how would the city be able to pay what were presumably very large amounts of money for the tanks and so on?

I told him what I'd discovered. A guardsman was dispatched to the Tourism Directorate to pull Debra's file. We'd learn more about her before visiting.

Davie dropped me at the infirmary. 'Give my best to Hector if he's . . .'

'Compos mentis? All – or even partly – there? In his right mind?'

'Cool it, Quint,' Davie said, abashed.

I squeezed his arm. 'Sorry, my friend. I've managed to concentrate on other things but now I have to face him. It's . . . not easy.'

'I know.'

We sat there in silence, then I opened the door and waved him away.

Fiona was back with Hector. She smiled and inclined her head to him. The old curmudgeon was awake. As I came closer, his dry lips cracked into a smile that would have scared children miles away. Me, I was crying.

'Fail . . . ure,' he said, as I sat next to the bed and took his hand.

'Old man,' I replied, looking into his pale eyes. 'Don't tell me you're getting better. I couldn't bear it.'

He croaked out a laugh. 'No . . . I'm for the chop . . . this time.'

Hector had always been strong on self-awareness. Fiona's irritated twitch of her head showed that she hadn't told him about his condition.

'Rubbish, you'll be out of here in days,' I said.

'Out in . . . a wicker box,' he said, smiling terrifyingly again. 'No wood to be . . . burned on my account,' he added. 'It's in my will.'

'My, this is an uplifting conversation. I think I'll go back to the castle and talk to the gangbangers on Death Row.'

The old man stared at me. 'Have they brought back . . . Death Row?'

'Of course not.' Then I thought of Goliath flying backwards with his chest punctured. I nodded to Fiona and she withdrew.

'Nice girl,' Hector said.

'Keep your shrivelled fingers to yourself.'

He was affronted. 'I would . . . never . . .'

That was true. Hector Dalrymple, unlike his son, was a comprehensively decent man.

'Billy Geddes,' I said. 'Don't go all red and have a heart attack.'

'He was in . . . the cancer centre, Quintilian, believe me.'

'I do.'

'With the doctor who was treating me—?'

'Jones,' I said, dredging my memory. 'Kevin Jones.'

'And the . . . high . . . heid yin.'

'George Allison.'

'That's . . . him. I couldn't . . . decide . . . which was the . . . slimiest . . .'

'I don't suppose you heard what they were saying?'

The old man glared at me. 'I'm not . . . senile . . . you know.'

'Could have fooled me. Come on, out with it.'

He took several deep breaths.

'They . . . they're expecting a big . . . delivery this week. Drugs . . . machinery . . . surgical supplies . . .'

Sophia would be interested to hear that.

Fiona came back in. 'He's tired out, citizen,' she said. 'Have you been upsetting him?'

'No. Have you noticed how he always does exactly what he wants?'

'It has come to my attention, yes.'

'Put the fear of Plato into him,' I said, releasing the old man's arm. 'On second thoughts, don't bother. He'll argue for hours.'

'I like a bit of philosophy,' said Fiona, auxiliary to the core.

'Me too,' I said on my way out. 'Particularly Kant.'

She gave me a sharp look that was entirely merited.

'What should we do?' Sophia asked, after I'd relayed Hector's words.

'I'll talk to Davie. We need at least basic surveillance of the cancer centre. Anything more will attract Michie's attention.'

'But he knows about the Malaysian contracts.'

'Doesn't mean he won't crack.' I shook my head. 'Anyway, that isn't the main problem. If goods are coming in – and bypassing the Supply Directorate, Fergus Calder's personal power base – it suggests the contracts have been signed. Maybe what we saw were only drafts, but final versions may have been enacted.'

Sophia's mouth was open. 'All those weapons. The tanks . . .'

'Exactly.'

'What's going on, Quint?'

'Maybe Jack MacLean is in charge of things and Calder's just a puppet.'

'That wouldn't surprise me, but to what purpose?'

I sat down opposite her. 'What's the one thing you can always expect the Council to do?'

She stared at me, fully aware of what I meant but unwilling to say the word.

I shrugged. 'Survive. No matter what happens in the referendum, the ruling body will retain power, even if Edinburgh joins a new Scotland. Don't tell me you haven't had discussions about the future.'

Sophia frowned. 'Of course we have, but nothing's been said about imports from Malaysia. Anyway, what's that got to do with the murders?'

'Everything,' I said, 'but I don't know how yet. Which is why I need to question Peter and Mavis Dobie. I hope they're awake.'

She nodded. 'The woman's been traumatized, though. Why don't you start with her husband?'

'All right. I presume there's still a guard on the daughter.'

Sophia picked up the phone and spoke brusquely. 'She's in the infirmary library, which is always staffed.'

'Thanks.'

'Quint, I'm worried.'

I wasn't surprised, given that her mind was sharper than a fresh scalpel. 'You think there'll be changes in the Council and Allison will get your job?'

'It's Maisie I'm frightened for. You know how it goes with former guardians. They're excluded from everything. That's not what I want for my daughter.'

I leaned over and grabbed her shoulders. 'Don't worry, I'm in your corner. Though putting on your gloves would be a good idea.'

Sophia's jaw jutted out. 'I'll fight barehanded if I have to.'

I left her office at speed. George Allison and his backers didn't know what was waiting for them.

Peter Dobie had been moved to a single room, a guardswoman on the door. She knew me and opened up immediately.

The wounded man's knee was in traction, the wires and weights making my eyes water. He wasn't looking too happy either.

'Citizen,' he said weakly. 'You look all right.'

'Hello, Peter,' I said, nodding. 'Sorry about your injuries.'

'The bastard bullet broke ma thigh bone as well as ma knee.'

I sat beside him. 'Ronald Douglas Dobie. Tell me his story.'

'Ach, Dougie,' he said, biting his lip. 'He should never have come back tae Embra.'

'When did you find out what happened when he was a boy?'

'My aunt told me before she died. I never expected tae see him.'

'When did you first see him?'

He stretched for a glass of water and I helped him drink from it.

'It must have been last October. He wus waiting for me outside the street door, told me who he wus.'

I was watching him closely but there were no signs of untruthfulness. 'What made you believe him?'

'He showed me a copy of his birth certificate. There were some photos of my auntie too.' He twitched his head. 'Besides, ye know who's family.'

I let that dubious statement go. 'So he stayed with you last October, did he?'

'For a couple of nights, aye. I . . . I don't know what he wus doing. He wus oot late at night.'

I frowned. Lorna hadn't been straight with me. 'You must have suspected he was up to no good.'

'I didnae suspect anything. He's . . . he wus family.'

For all the Council's three-decade-long attempt to minimize the importance of the family, people – especially ordinary citizens – still stuck to it.

'Did you ever see Dougie with anyone?'

He shook his head.

'Or with anything suspicious in his possession?'

More shaking.

'How about a pistol like the one he used yesterday?'

'Not until he pulled it ootae his coat.'

'So you had no idea he murdered an auxiliary with it?'

'Naw.'

I changed tack.

'Did Gol—Dougie tell you about where he grew up?'

'Oh aye. He wus on Skye, still is.' Peter Dobie broke off and wiped his eyes with the back of his pyjama sleeve. His nephew's death had definitely got to him.

'Did he tell you what work he did?'

'He said he wus a facilitator. I had tae ask him what that wus.'

It sounded like Finance Directorate-speak, the kind of thing Billy Geddes would be keen on. Maybe he'd been advising the Lord of the Isles. I asked if Dougie had mentioned his leader.

'They've got a lord?' Dobie said, surprised. 'Who would want tae go back tae that wicked system?'

Who indeed, particularly with Angus MacDonald in the ermine seat? It was handbrake-turn time and it wouldn't be pretty.

'Clarinda Towart,' I said.

Dobie's eyelids sprang open, but he didn't speak.

'I can see you know her. What do you feel about your daughter applying to the Prostitution Services Department?'

He glared at me, cheeks red. 'What d'ye think? She's not joining, I'll tell ye that.'

I raised my shoulders. 'None of my business. But you know the Council's keen on young people making their own choices. On the other hand, if you tell me about Clarinda, I might be able to keep Lorna . . . unsullied.'

'Could ye do that, citizen?'

By trading information with Mary Parlane – perhaps to minimize the disgrace Clarinda Towart had brought on the Tourism Directorate – I probably could. I showed him my authorization.

'See? This gives me the right to question even guardians. Tell me what you know and I'll do what I can.'

Dobie looked at me dubiously. Like most citizens, he wasn't used to the city's servants being on his side. Then again, I was an unusual kind of city servant.

'This Clarrie – that's what she calls herself – Lorna brought her home in . . . must hae been November. I had tae sign a paper saying she'd explained tae us what would be required of Lorna before she finished school.'

'Mentoring sessions every fortnight, a two-week camp in the summer, several Saturday mornings in the PSD offices.'

'Aye, all that.' He lowered his gaze. 'It's bloody disgusting what they have tae do when they finally join that fuckin' department. What are we doing letting our daughters prostitute themselves tae tourists for the good of the city?'

Sons were taken on too, though fewer of them. He was right, of course. Back in the day, when the drugs wars had recently finished and the city was desperate to re-establish itself as a global tourist destination, offering official sexual services was widely accepted. That was probably because the weekly sex session with a partner chosen for you had hardened people who were already as tough as old Supply Directorate boots. With the relaxation of the regulations, opposition to the PSD had increased and fewer applications were being made. That made it even more surprising that a seemingly naive girl like Lorna would have gone down that path. Was she really in love with Clarinda?

'So you were surprised when Lorna applied?'

'Fuckin' stunned. Mavis took it really bad, cried for weeks. I talked tae Lorna, but she wus determined tae do it. Not that she told me why. I dinnae understand females.'

I didn't count myself an expert on that subject, but I'd see what I could get from Lorna later.

'What did you think of Clarinda, then?'

Peter Dobie curled his lip. 'A tart frae top tae bottom – face plastered with make-up and a skirt that didnae leave anything tae the imagination.'

'Someone else's daughter,' I murmured.

He ignored that. 'And she stank of booze. Wouldn't surprise me if she's an alkie. Loud-mouthed cow an' all. Treated us like muck.'

That squared with what her neighbour, Charlie Dixon, and people in the Tourism Directorate had told me.

'Was Dougie ever with you when Clarinda came?'

Dobie stared at me. 'Dougie? No, I don't think so.'

'Did you know he had a purple snake tattoo?'

'Aye, on his shoulder. Told me he got it somewhere up north – I cannae mind the name. Apparently it's originally frae some country in the Far East.'

My ears pricked up. 'Malaysia?'

'That's it. There's quite a few o' they folk there . . . what's the name of the place?'

I didn't want to prompt him again.

'Kishorn, that's it. The Malaysian guys are building a port.'

Were they now? It sounded like the Lord of the Isles was looking towards distant horizons as well as Edinburgh.

I checked on Hector. He was dozing, apparently not in pain. I left him to Fiona's tender ministrations. Sophia's secretary told me she was in the morgue. I called her.

'Quint,' she said, breathless. 'Come over.'

I did what I was told without enthusiasm. Morgues, I can leave rather than take. Breathing through my mouth was no good – then I tasted the corruption, which was even worse.

A male nursing auxiliary pointed me to a pair of wellies and handed me surgical gloves.

'At the far end,' he said.

Great. I walked past three corpses that were being worked on, finally reaching the steel trolley beside Sophia. The bones from the bag found in Mungo Rollo's house had been laid out on it. The skull was intact and most of the other bones were present.

'This is fascinating,' Sophia said.

I looked at the interrupted rib and skeletal structures. In total they were only about four feet long.

'A child?' I asked, as a wave of sadness dashed over me. Having your remains bundled up in a bag was bad enough for anyone, but it was even more poignant for someone who hadn't reached maturity.

'On the face of it, a girl of about nine, judging by an estimated height of forty-seven inches,' Sophia said. 'But when I was looking at the pubic bones I noticed these linear and circular grooves.'

I followed her fingers and made out the markings.

Sophia looked up at me. 'These mean that she'd given birth. Quite likely more than once.'

I blinked. 'At nine years old?'

'It's not unheard of, though very rare.'

'The girl was under four foot,' I said.

Sophia gave a conspiratorial smile. 'But she isn't a girl. The cartilage epiphyses have been replaced by bone.'

'I see.'

'No, you don't. That only happens when bone growth has been completed, which doesn't happen until you're between seventeen and twenty-five. So this is a—'

'Dwarf. An adult one.'

'Took you long enough.'

'You weren't playing fair. Sorry, I'm in a rush. What about how old the bones are?'

'That needs more work. The complete absence of flesh and other tissue could mean several things, though they weren't left in the open for carrion creatures as there are no marks on the bones.'

'Long-term decomposition?'

'They'd be deep brown, not this creamy colour.'

'Acid bath?'

'Maybe. Or boiling.'

I had a flash of cannibals crouching round a fire in the badlands outside the city line. Or inside the line, considering where the bones had been found.

'I'm having difficulty with the cause of death. Obviously some bones are missing, but so far I've found no signs of injury.'

'The victim could have been shot or stabbed only in soft tissue.'

She nodded. 'An alternative is poison. I'll need to take bone-marrow samples.'

'Sophia, how many dwarfs are there in the city?'

'Hardly a question for me,' she said, with a smile. 'There can't be many. I've never seen one in the infirmary.'

I looked at my watch. I needed to get Lorna Dobie prepared for her scheduled meeting with Clarinda Towart.

'Keep me up to date,' I said.

'Please.'

I sighed. 'Thank you.'

'Child.'

I gave a hop and a skip. After I'd given back my wellies and binned my gloves, I called Davie.

'You know Goliath?'

'Yes,' he said warily.

'Well, we've got a female David.'

'Explain.'

I did, then asked him to pull the files of all the city's dwarfs. It struck me that might not be the approved term. What else could they be called? Midgets? That sounded even worse. Little people? We weren't in Ireland before it went back to the Dark Ages. Or in a fairy tale.

Though maybe we were; one written by the Brothers Grimm at their most brutal.

Seventeen

Hamish, the young guardsman, was waiting in the infirmary yard when I came out with Lorna Dobie. He beamed at us both.

'The commander asked me to take special care of you,' he said, bowing like the chauffeurs who ferry outsider dignitaries around.

That didn't sound like Davie.

'Have you taken a fancy to me?' I asked, after Hamish had ushered Lorna into the back seat.

'No, citizen,' he said, unabashed. 'I want to learn from you.'

That made me feel worse. Unattractive to young men, in my fiftieth year and a role model to Guard recruits – things had to get better.

We had a couple of hours till Lorna's meeting. I led her up to the castle, after giving Hamish a sad smile, and handed her over to a matronly guardswoman.

Fortunately James Michie wasn't in the command centre, so I made it to Davie's office without being diverted. What would the guardian have made of the dwarf issue?

'There are three dwarfs in the city,' Davie said, brandishing files. 'Another five, all members of the Caw family, disappeared, presumed to have crossed the line just over two years ago. The other three make up another family, the MacFarlanes.'

I looked through the documentation.

There was a knock on the door. One of Davie's reliable guardsmen looked in.

'Speak,' Davie said.

The guardsman grimaced. 'Having a bit of trouble with the dwarfs, commander.'

'I said, speak!'

'Right. All three are registered at a tenement in Newington, but no one's seen them for quite a time. At least six months. Apparently they kept themselves to themselves and no one noticed for weeks.'

I looked at the files. 'Father, Raoul – there's a name you don't often see in citizen files – aged sixty-eight, a painter of the artistic kind. Retired two years ago, having worked for the Tourism Directorate.' I glanced at Davie. 'Apparently his Edinburgh panoramas are all over the tourist hotels. Wife, Magda, twenty years younger than him, also employed by the Tourism Directorate in the – get this – Prostitution Services Department. As an exotic dancer.'

Davie was taken aback.

'Quite. And a son, Cezar.'

'He'll be the only one with that name too,' interjected Davie.

'Though he wasn't employed by the PSD. He was in the Education Directorate, writing senior-school textbooks.' I looked at his and his parents' close companions. None of the names were familiar.

'All right,' I said to the guardsman, 'get over to the MacFarlanes' place – don't go inside – and talk to the neighbours.' I turned to Davie. 'Is Clarinda's shop operating again?'

He nodded. 'Seemed like a good idea to let that happen. I had the door to C. T. Enterprises fixed.'

'We need to set up plainclothes people in the vicinity.'

'Already done.'

'Smartarse.'

'Somebody has to be.'

'Get a scene-of-crime squad round to the MacFarlanes' – you'd better put Raeburn 297 on to it. Without my compliments.'

I got to my feet as he picked up the phone, set on finding Lorna Dobie. He waved at me to stay put.

'Two things,' he said, when he'd finished giving orders. 'The news cuttings from the Dobie house – no obvious leads or patterns have turned up yet.'

I wondered what would constitute 'obvious' in this situation. We didn't have a clue what we were looking for.

'Hold on. Tell them to check for anything to do with dwarfs by the name of MacFarlane.' Then I had another thought. 'And ask the Tourism Directorate if there are dwarf tourists, now or in the past.'

'Will do. The other thing is Duncan Denoon.'

'The zookeeper.'

'Yes. He usually went to the citizen cinema in Murrayfield on his nights off.'

That was unlikely to get us anywhere.

'Apart from three times in the last six weeks, when he went to Rose Street. According to his barracks mates, he liked a drink.'

Citizens were allowed into the tourist zone on Sundays, although the casinos were out of bounds and there were two citizen-only bars, in the back lanes.

'Take his photo with you. We'll check if they knew him tonight.'

Davie raised a hand. 'You're losing your touch.'

'You think? You're wondering why the Tourism Directorate didn't report Magda MacFarlane's sustained absence from work to the Guard, and why I'm not asking them. Also, why I'm not asking the Education Directorate about its failure to report the absence of Cezar?' I smiled tightly. 'Because I'm going to do that later. Now we're going to catch Clarinda.'

By a quarter to four all was ready in the Grassmarket. Undercover Guard personnel were mingling with the tourists, while uniformed counterparts patrolled in the normal way. Davie and I had separated. He was on the north side, twenty yards from the shop that contained Clarinda's office, while I was in a café opposite it to the south. I could see Grizel Monzie working the till, smiling at customers. Shit, Grizel. I hadn't checked her out. Maybe she was another of Clarinda's lovers, though that wouldn't necessarily feature in any file. Or maybe she was in on Clarinda's activities – whatever they might be.

I emptied my cup of coffee and went outside after Lorna Dobie made her way through the crowds towards the shop. I bent my head to one side so I wasn't too obvious to Grizel. Who, it struck me, would know Lorna – and hadn't bothered to mention her visits or those of anyone else to C. T. Enterprises. I turned away and called Davie.

'Make sure the girl in the shop is taken into custody, big man.'

'Check, medium-siz—'

Dickhead. I walked on, my eyes fixed on Lorna's brown coat. I'd drummed into her to act normally, but she looked all around before going in. I kept behind an over-sized tourist, waiting till Grizel saw her. Which duly happened. They exchanged smiles and the shop girl pointed to the rear, Lorna nodding.

Action. I pushed myself past people and barrelled into the shop. I knew Davie would have his teams seal off the area outside in seconds.

Grizel's eyebrows leapt for her hair-line as I went past. The door at the back was closing but I slid forward and managed to get a foot in the way. Then frame and door made a sandwich out of my boot. I yelled and lowered my shoulder. There was a crash as a heavy figure appeared beside me and we ended up on the floor.

'Here come the cavalry,' Davie said, getting to his feet. 'Stay where you are!'

I got up, flexing my foot. It hurt but I could bear it.

'You!' I said, glaring at the figure in front of Lorna.

The city's second-best heavyweight boxer grinned at me. 'Citizen, this *is* a surprise!'

'Christo Fleming,' said Davie, chest out. 'What were you going to do to that wee girl?'

'Hey,' said Lorna, 'I'm not so wee.'

'You are compared with him,' I said. 'Who told you to come here, Christo?'

The boxer shrugged. 'No one. I often pop by when I'm on my break.'

'Grizel?' I called. She came in, cuffed to a guardswoman.

'Have you ever seen him before?'

'Aye,' she said sullenly.

'You know who he is?'

'Of course. I like the boxing.'

'What about Lorna here?'

'I . . . yes, she's been here a few times to meet Clarinda.'

'Pity you didn't mention that before,' Davie said.

'You didn't ask,' she said, standing her ground.

'Were you supposed to take Lorna somewhere?' I asked the boxer.

'What's that?' he said, banging the side of his head. 'I don't hear too well.' He laughed. 'And there's the head trauma. Sometimes I can't understand what people are saying. Or remember things.'

A likely story or two. Then again, the Recreation Directorate's decision to ban padded headgear was lamentable. Of course, the crowds loved it.

Grizel and Fleming were led away. I stayed with Lorna.

'You haven't been honest,' I said.

She gave me a blank look. 'What do you mean?'

'You told me you only met Dougie the evening before he was killed. According to your father, he first came to the flat in November.'

She was a cool one, staring at me and then shrugging. 'I was confused . . . after the shooting. Still am.'

'Fair enough. Grizel Monzie – is she being mentored by Clarinda too?'

'I don't know.'

'Yes, you do.'

'She used to be.' Lorna's gaze dropped. 'The PSD didn't take her. I told you. I love Clarrie. I hate the thought of that bitch Grizel being with her.'

Mentoring wasn't supposed to be a hands-on job, but Clarinda Towart did what she wanted.

'Your old man doesn't think much of Clarrie,' I observed, as I led her out of the shop.

'That's what you think,' she said bitterly. 'They had it off in my bed after she briefed him and Mum.'

I stared at her. 'How did your mother take that?'

Lorna smiled bitterly. 'She was pleased they didn't use the big bed.'

Clarinda moved in mysterious ways her worrying works to perform.

Back at the castle, we got hold of Grizel Monzie's file. There was nothing in it that caught the eye, apart from her application to join the Prostitution Services Department, dated 21/4/33, ten months ago. She was already eighteen then, a late starter. More interesting was the Tourism Directorate document attached. Grizel had been failed for 'a general lack of inter-personal skills' last August and assigned to the directorate citizen labour rota. It couldn't be a coincidence that she'd ended up at that particular shop. Clarinda must have asked for her.

'Right, Grizel,' I said, a burly guardswoman behind me in the inter-rogation room. 'It's time you talked.'

'What about?'

'Oh, I don't know. Let's see. How about Clarinda Towart?'

'She's my friend.'

'Is that all?'

'None of your business,' she said defiantly. It looked like Lorna's feelings about Grizel were well based.

The guardswoman knew the procedure. She moved round the table and took up position behind the skinny citizen.

'You don't talk like that in here,' she said, putting her hands on Grizel's shoulders.

I don't like strong-arming citizens, especially female ones, but sometimes there's no choice. I could hear the star of *Spar/Tak/Us* laughing at me hollowly.

Perhaps threats would be enough. The spectral laughter went on.

'Here's how this works,' I said, smiling as warmly as I could. 'Whatever you say – or don't say – you're going to be out of circulation till we find Clarinda. So you won't be in danger from retaliation.'

'Clarinda isn't like that,' Grizel said scornfully.

Wasn't she? Were we chasing the sugar-plum fairy rather than a foul-mouthed, alcoholic prostitute linked to several murders? Could those links be spurious?

'What *is* she like?' I asked.

'She's . . . sweet . . . and tender . . .'

I showed her the picture in the missing woman's file. 'We are talking about the same person?'

Grizel nodded. 'It's the drink that changes her. Sometimes she's bad in the mornings. She's been better recently.'

'Where is she?'

The young woman met my gaze. 'I don't know, citizen. That's the truth.'

I suspected it was.

'And today was the first time you saw Christo Fleming in the shop?'

She nodded. 'He said he was a friend of Clarinda's. And he had the key.'

I thought about that. Christo's partner was Clarinda's friend, not him. She still hadn't been tracked down and he wasn't saying where she was. Was he acting on her instructions or had he taken over whatever Alice Lennox had been involved in?

I went to see how Davie was getting on with Fleming. The boxer was playing the defective memory and brain game so, after an hour of getting nowhere, we took a break.

My phone rang. It was James Michie.

'Not long till the Council meeting, citizen. Can you give me a briefing? I'll meet you in the command centre.'

'That was a short and one-sided conversation,' said Davie.

'Wait till you see the briefing the guardian gets.'

We went into what had been the Great Hall in the old days. Michie got up from his chair and led us to Davie's office. We brought him up to date.

'Disappointing,' was his response.

'At least Fleming's back in our hands,' I said, giving him the eye. 'Unfortunately Alice Lennox is still free as a bird, thanks to you.'

Davie nudged me.

'What about the girl, Lorna?' the guardian said.

I shook my head. 'Let's leave her for today. I don't think she's a major player. Can you put her somewhere comfortable with a guardswoman nearby?'

'There are secure rooms in my block,' he said, calling the duty watch officer.

Davie was looking at the files in his in-tray.

'Provisional report from Raeburn 297's team at the MacFarlane flat,' he said. 'It hasn't been occupied for weeks, maybe months. The place is tidy and there are no personal possessions.' Edinburgh citizens had very few of those until the regulations were relaxed. Even now, disposable income didn't run to much more than the odd special treat, usually in the form of food and/or drink.

'He also says there was nothing to suggest that what he calls "people of below average height" lived there.'

'So no clothes, adapted furniture and the like.'

'What does that mean?' asked the guardian.

'Search me,' I replied.

Davie had picked up another file. 'Door-to-door reports say that the MacFarlanes were known by sight, but nobody was friendly with them. They kept themselves to themselves.'

I made a call.

'Mary, it's Quint.'

The tourism guardian sighed. 'What now?'

'Magda MacFarlane.'

'What about her?'

'You tell me.'

'Dancer in tourist clubs and bars for years. Very popular.'

'And your use of her was in no way exploitative.'

'Careful, Quintilian. Magda was very enthusiastic.'

'As are all members of the Prostitution Services Department.'

'You're beginning to annoy me.'

'Is that right? Prepare to get even more annoyed. Why didn't you report her failure to show up for work months ago during the Council meeting?'

Silence brooded.

'Irritating man,' she said. 'All right, I'll tell you. I've known Magda since she joined the Directorate. Things got hard for them after Raoul retired – he had bad arthritis and was in constant pain. She came to see me and hinted they'd be leaving the city. I . . . I decided to give her as much time as she needed to get across the line.'

'Good of you,' I said, not sarcastically. The idea that Magda's bones were those in the morgue had struck me.

'I'd prefer you keep it to yourself.'

'I'll try, but there's also the question of her son, Cezar. Why didn't the Education Directorate report him to the Guard?'

'I'll take responsibility for that too, Quintilian. I asked Kate Revie to turn a blind eye. You're not to bring her into this, do you understand? If it comes to a head, I'll take the blame.'

'All right, but you're playing a dangerous game, Mary.'

She laughed drily. 'We all are. Why are you interested in the MacFarlanes anyway?'

'They came up in a case, not centrally.' I said the last words to put her mind at rest. My own was tossing like a storm-lashed sea.

If Magda was the female skeleton Sophia was putting back together, what had happened to her husband? And to their son, Cezar?

My participation in the Council meeting was brief, but long enough for Jack MacLean to turn his lip up at our failure to grab Clarinda at her shop – though he might well have been dissembling. I got a lift to the infirmary and went straight to Hector's room.

'Faaaaaaaail-uuuure,' he said, with a grin that displayed less than pristine teeth.

I looked at Fiona's stand-in, who raised her shoulders.

'Amazingly, he's better,' she said. 'The morphine's been reduced again. Don't get your hopes up though, citizen.'

I wasn't going to – the contrast with Fiona's unusual level of emotional intelligence was stark. Too stark.

'Hello, old man,' I said. 'You seem happy.'

'I'm stooooooooned.'

'Good for you. Seen any walruses?'

'The roof of heaven is oooooopen . . . I can see aaaaaangels dancing on the head of a nail.'

'Pin, I think.'

'Noooo, it's definitely a nail. Crucifiiiiixion nail.'

Je—

'The little birdies . . . are pink,' he continued.

'You did say the morphine dose had been cut?'

The nurse nodded. 'They sometimes get this way.'

I wanted to laugh, but to see the old man's great brain reduced to that of a dopehead was sad, not least because he hated narcotics.

I sat for a while and then headed to Peter Dobie's room. I wanted to ask him about the charms of Clarinda, after what Lorna had told me. No luck. He'd developed a fever and was unconscious. I considered talking to his wife, but that wouldn't have been fair. She was traumatized enough.

Eighteen

Davie and I had filled our bellies and were in his office, going through more files.

'You know what?' he said.

I didn't encourage him.

'Someone's playing silly bampots.'

'Bampot, i.e. an objectionable and/or foolish person, is not an Education Directorate-approved term, commander.'

'Still, it's true. First we get pygmy hippos blown up, then we come across a dwarf skeleton. Someone's into microphilia.'

'You looked that up.'

'I did.'

'Alternatively you could say that somebody's into microphobia.'

'Aye, right.' Davie scratched his head. 'Maybe it was Goliath.'

'You're suggesting big Dougie defleshed Magda MacFarlane, if it's her, and put Remtex in the zoo because he wasn't well disposed towards small creatures?'

He shook his head. 'Not the last bit. That's yours.'

Goliath had been in the city around the time the MacFarlanes disappeared, we'd established that. Perhaps he'd got out to the zoo as well. No proof, though. And nothing approaching a credible motive.

'What do you think?' Davie said, clearly having moved on. 'The citizens' pubs off Rose Street first and then the Lucky Strike?'

Debra Kilgour, the taxi driver's wayward daughter, would be in her place of work till late.

'The managers of the pubs are waiting for my call.'

I nodded and he made the arrangements. Twenty minutes later we were in the centre of tourist Edinburgh by night. It had an amazing propensity to get worse. In the fortnight since I'd last been in Rose Street, there had been a theme change. The current one was Regency Edinburgh, which meant that female auxiliaries were prancing around in high-waisted dresses that left little to the imagination and tartan bonnets; their male counterparts were in tailcoats and tight, tight breeches. Inside the nightclubs those garments would be removed. Tourists were being served mulled wine in fake silver cups and encouraged to try snuff. The results of the latter were gross.

Davie turned into a lane near Castle Street. There was a wire-mesh gate across the property at the end, a citizen in a brown corduroy jacket by the gate.

'Jackie Neil,' he said, nodding nervously. He had what looked like a spatchcocked hedgehog on his head. Some barber had got away with murder. 'Come in.' He let us through the fence and then unlocked the pub, which had the imaginative name 'Neil's'. Unlike the tourist establishments a few yards away, the bar, open only on Sundays, was poorly lit and painted in restrained colours. It was clear from the floors that no sawdust but gallons of spit had been applied.

Davie took out Duncan Denoon's photo.

'Aye,' the manager said, 'I know him. Not by name, but he's been coming here for a year or so. Not every weekend.'

'Who does he meet?'

'Ach, he's usually on his own. Likes his ale though.'

Davie looked dubiously at the plastic taps. 'Edinburgh Pale Ale? Thirty Shilling? Wouldn't get a wee boy drunk.'

'That's what we receive from the Supply Directorate,' said Neil piously.

'How about I drown you in EPA?' Davie said, grabbing the citizen and manoeuvring him till his mouth was under the tap. Then he turned it on.

I would have intervened, but the manager obviously wasn't being frank. Davie was quite rightly being earnest.

After beer sprayed around the place, he turned it off.

'So, Citizen Neil, you were saying?' Davie said.

The manager choked and spluttered, then managed to locate his voice. 'There was no . . . need for that,' he said, wiping his mouth.

Davie grabbed him again.

'No, no . . . that laddie . . . Duncan was his name. I heard her say it.'

'Her?' I asked, cocking an ear.

'The woman he met.'

My gut clenched. Clarinda was the obvious candidate.

'Describe her.'

'Tall, very tall – she looked down on most of the guys in here. And red-haired. Skinny, but still attractive.' He grinned. 'If ye like giraffes.'

This time I grabbed him, by the throat. 'What do you mean, giraffes?'

'Well . . . well, the laddie worked in the zoo, didn't he? I could smell the dung on him some nights.'

I sniffed. Jackie Neil must have bribed the last health inspector who visited.

'Anything else?' I demanded.

'Em, no . . . well, maybe one thing . . . he, he didn't talk much, but she was forever on at him. I heard her ask plenty of times, "Is it safe?".'

'What did he say?'

'He nodded his head and said it was safe, sure.'

I inclined my head at Davie and we headed out. We checked the citizen pub at the east end of Rose Street – that one was called the Black Ensign – and got nowhere. Duncan Denoon was a loyal regular at Neil's, it seemed.

We walked back to the Lucky Strike.

'Are you going to say it or am I?' Davie asked.

'Be my guest.'

'What was the education guardian doing in a citizen pub with a zookeeper?'

'Search me, and I don't mean literally.'

Kate Revie was a bit of a dark giraffe, having risen rapidly above several more experienced senior directorate officials after her predecessor self-combusted. I hadn't thought she was bent or demented, but female guardians weren't my field of expertise. I never understood my mother and every day with Sophia was a new adventure in tightrope-walking.

'We should call it in,' Davie said, looking at the framed photos outside the Lucky Strike.

'Call what in to whom?'

'Revie to Michie,' he said, turning his head as far to one side as he could.

'Yes, the dancer has no underwear,' I said, pulling him away. 'What, tell your boss that a fellow Council member likes a bit of citizen rough?'

'No, that she's interested in something being safe. What needs to be safe?'

I didn't reply.

'Remtex,' he said, in a low voice.

'You think Duncan Denoon blew up his beloved pygmy hippos?'

'Maybe by mistake.'

'Remtex isn't particularly unstable.'

'Depends on the detonators, but there's obviously something strange going on.'

'You're right. I'll need to access her file.' Guardians' records are hard to get into – unless you have a lover of that rank.

'Good,' Davie said. 'Can we go in now?'

'I can, as I'm not wearing a Guard uniform.'

His face fell. 'You look like a rubbish-man in that donkey jacket.'

'What makes you think the Lucky Strike doesn't generate an enormous amount of rubbish?'

'Why don't we just pick up Debra Kilgour and take her to the castle?'

I tapped the side of my nose. 'Because I want to see who she interacts with.'

'Interacts, is it?' Davie grinned. 'You're just a dirty old voyeur.'

'Go away, guardsman.'

'Don't you want me to wait?'

'No,' I said, heading for the girls in high-waisted dresses on the door. 'I may be some time.'

The Lucky Strike was one of the oldest casinos in Edinburgh, having been licensed in 2014, before the end of the drugs wars. Back then tourists were a hardy breed who got a kick out of being shot at on the airport road. The Council had recently set up the Prostitution Services Department and the waiters and waitresses were all members. That was no longer the case. I'd heard that one of the barmen was an ordinary auxiliary. There was progress Edinburgh-style.

My authorization got me as far as the main gaming area, where a bulky figure in a red tuxedo that would have fitted a bull stepped in front of me.

'I know who you are,' he said robotically.

I took in his badge. 'I know who you are too, Glen.'

His mouth split into a cavernous grin. 'Quint Dalrymple. How I loved your *Public Order in Practice* manual.'

'I wrote that a long time ago,' I said. I also regretted a lot of it.

'I wrote it five times,' said Glen.

'What?'

'I was shite at drill. They made me copy a chapter every time I put a foot wrong.' He guffawed. 'Happened almost every day.'

'I'm delighted for you,' I said. 'Now do you mind? I'm working.'

'Hush-hush, is it? Don't worry, I won't give you away.'

If you haven't already, I thought, brushing past him. The place was heaving, tourists round the roulette table, the numerous card games and the one-armed bandits. There was a floor show to the rear, canned music blasting out. As I got closer, I saw that Debra Kilgour was performing. If that was the right word.

'What *is* that?' I heard a fleshy man ask the curly-haired woman with him. They might have been from one of the Canadian states.

'Come on, Randy, can't you see? It's a—'

Her answer was lost in a blast of bass saxophone. By that time the chimpanzee had pulled off Debra's blouse. He was obviously enjoying himself. Surely they weren't going to go through with this? I'd never heard of bestiality being approved by the Tourism Directorate and couldn't imagine that Mary Parlane would stand for it.

Then I saw him, at a table below the stage, with three people I recognized only too well. On Billy Geddes's right were Glasgow's suave first minister, Andrew Duart, and his chief of police, Hel Hyslop, her curly hair with a different auburn tint. On his left were Angus MacDonald, the Lord of the Isles, in a kilt as usual, and a Chinese-looking man older than Chung Keng Quee. Another Malaysian? They were all avidly following Debra's embraces with her simian friend. I just had to go over and say hello.

Billy's crushed face registered the beginning of a scowl, but I got there before he could speak.

'My lord,' I said, bowing excessively to the white-haired old aristocrat. 'Your eminences.'

MacDonald nodded at my display of fealty as if it were the real thing, while Duart and Hyslop glared. Perhaps they thought I'd implied they were a pair of tits.

'Get lost, Quint,' Billy shouted, looking around for help.

'I take it this is the Malaysian consul.'

He stared at me.

'I know what you're doing in Edinburgh,' I said, in the Lord of the Isles' ear. 'Malaysia.'

He stiffened, which I took as a victory.

Then I turned to Duart. 'How are your dealings with Malaysia, first minister?'

Hel Hyslop couldn't have heard, but she stood up and showed the large pistol that was stuck through her belt.

'A Jarilo .45?' I shouted to her.

She covered it up immediately.

It was obvious none of them was going to talk so I went for the next best option — putting a dampener on their evening out. I moved quickly to the wall and activated the fire alarm. The sprinklers kicked in and everyone was soon soaked. The chimp ran squealing after Debra, understandably frustrated. He wasn't the only one. I kicked the manager, clearly identifiable by his gold tux and dung-flinging smile, between the legs.

'What . . .?' he croaked.

'Have you got a licence for that chimpanzee?'

'I . . . yes . . . I mean . . . no . . .'

'Then you're for the fucking castle.'

I looked at Billy and his company. They were gone, the bastards, but I'd seen the guilt written all over their faces.

I rang Davie and asked him to bring Mary Parlane down, after cancelling the fire brigade.

Debra Kilgour, sodden, had run to a dressing room at the rear of the venue. Fortunately one of the staff had got a harness round the chimpanzee and was dragging it to the exit.

'Stay here,' I ordered, showing him my authorization.

He complied.

I went in, waving away a couple of dancers with their mascara in ruins.

'Debra?'

'Who is it?' She didn't sound at all traumatized.

'Call me Quint,' I said.

'Dalrymple?' she said, screwing up her eyes. 'The one who questioned my dad?'

I nodded. 'Also the one who's about to hand you over to the tourism guardian if you don't start talking.' I looked at my watch. 'And I mean right now.'

'Talking? What about?' She was a pretty girl with a good body, but she already had the vacant look characteristic of PSD workers.

'That was a special show, wasn't it?'

'With Charlie?' She smiled. 'Don't tell me you're shocked. Anyway, I don't let him stick it in me.'

'What a relief.'

'He just comes on my tits.'

I shook my head in despair. 'Who arranged the show?'

She shrugged as she pulled on a good-quality purple woollen coat. 'Ask Max, the manager.'

'Smarmy guy in a gold tuxedo?'

'Aye.'

'He's currently experiencing extreme pain in his testicles.'
She laughed.
'Good for you. He's a cunt.'
'Uh-huh. Tell me about Clarinda Towart. Hurry. If the tourism guardian finds out what I saw here, you'll be on a city farm by morning.'
'Clarinda? What's she got to do with anything?'
'She was your mentor.'
'So?'
'Did she get you into bestiality?'
Debra laughed. 'It's no big deal. You think fucking fat tourists is better?'
'No, I think the PSD should be shut down.'
She stared at me, then looked away. 'Too late for that.'
I heard Davie's voice outside.
'I can get you out of this,' I said, 'but you need to tell me now.'
'Tell you what?'
'Where's Clarinda?'
Debra thought about that. 'Have you tried her flat?'
I raised my shoulders. 'You've had your chance.'
'No,' she said, grabbing my arm as I turned. 'You have to protect me.'
'I can do that.'
'Clarinda . . . she's fuckin' crazy.'
'Right. But where is she?'
Davie burst in. 'Quint?'
'Grab that piece of shit with the gold tux,' I said.
He left. Fortunately his place wasn't taken by Mary Parlane.
'Where is she?' I repeated.
There were tears in Debra's eyes. 'She uses a house in Blackhall. Her friend's parents live there.'
'The friend's name?'
She looked frightened. I assured her we'd look after her.
Eventually she spoke.
'Alice Lennox.'
I might have known. Another victory for the public order guardian, who'd let the nurse go.
'And the address?'
She hummed and hawed, but eventually I got what I wanted.

I told Mary Parlane what Max, her manager, had set up. She was suitably appalled and laid into him. As that happened, Davie escorted Debra out. He was taking her to the castle.

'Who ordered the display?' I asked the auxiliary, managing to slip the question in while Mary caught her breath.

'I can't tell—'

I applied my knee this time.

'Geddes,' he panted, after a deal of screaming. 'Billy . . . Geddes.'

I looked at the guardian. Her lips were set in a straight line but her eyelashes quivered.

'The finance guardian's SPADE tells you to put a chimpanzee with a PSD operative and you do what he says? Why wasn't I informed?'

'I . . . didn't want to . . . disturb . . .'

'That worked well,' I said. 'Have you seen Geddes's guests before?' I whispered to Mary Parlane who they were.

'Several times,' he said, desperate to please. 'They always tip generously.'

'When was the last time you saw the Lord of the Isles?' I asked.

'Two . . . no, three nights ago. The foreign gentleman was with him then too.'

'And the others?'

'A week ago.'

Mary told one of her bodyguards to handcuff him. I suspected she wouldn't have much of a voice by morning.

'I had no idea that outsiders have been – and are – in the city, Quintilian,' she said, when we were alone.

'Despite the fact that Council members are supposed to be informed.'

She nodded, then gave me a questioning look.

'You know more about this than you're saying, don't you?'

I turned for the exit. 'I know a tornado of excrement is about to hit this city. Set your house in order.'

I went through the gaming hall. There were chips and broken glass everywhere. Outside I watched as a van from the zoo took the chimp away. I hoped he got as caring a keeper as Duncan Denoon, without the end suffered by the pygmy hippos. The Asian gentleman in Billy's party was either the Malaysian consul or a businessman from that country, I suspected. Moving against him would be difficult, not least because Billy would be looking after him.

Meanwhile, we had to turn our attention to Alice Lennox; and, at the other end of the scale, Kate Revie.

I wanted Debra Kilgour in a safe place. Davie sent her to the castle with a sympathetic guardswoman. I didn't want her sharing accommodation with Lorna Dobie in the guardian's quarters.

'Alice Lennox,' I said.

'I've sent a team to Blackhall.'

'Tell them to stay in the shadows and wait for us.'

He relayed the message, then drummed up two more Guard 4×4s.

'Are there any lights showing in the house?' I asked.

Davie spoke to the squad leader. 'Apparently not,' he relayed.

'Go down there and call me when they turn up. I've got something else to do.'

Davie nodded. He had the good sense not to ask me what that was.

I could have gone to Sophia's residence and woken her up so I could use her computer, but I didn't want to. I'd need to wake her up to input the passwords and she needed her sleep as much as anyone. Besides, I was unhappy about involving her further in a case that now directly pointed at the Council, at least in part. Whatever my suspicions about MacLean and Calder, I now had a direct link to Kate Revie. The fact that Jackie Neil hadn't recognized her showed how little attention citizens paid to the ruling body these days. Or maybe he was playing dumb.

Alternatively, I could have gone to the education guardian's residence and forced my way in, but that would cause consternation among her staff – and perhaps she had a credible explanation for her meetings with Duncan Denoon. Besides, I knew very little about the woman and needed to see her file. There was another solution.

I hitched a lift from a Guard 4×4 and then walked up to James Michie's quarters in the former Governor's House. I had to show my authorization to get in, despite the fact that the guardsman on duty knew very well who I was. One of the guardian's keen young bureaucrats came down the stairs, adjusting his uniform.

'I need to see him,' I said.

'He's sleeping.'

'Fine. I need access to his office. You can do that, can't you?'

He froze and then hurried off to rouse his boss. I went up to the floor with the offices and waited outside the locked black door.

Michie arrived, rubbing his eyes. 'Has something happened, Quint?'

'Guardian ears only,' I whispered.

He sent his lackey away and let me in. The suite of rooms was spotless and smelled of lavender. I wondered if that was his choice.

'Tell me.'

So I did. He was horrified by the chimpanzee, but even more appalled by the outsiders' presence.

'What the hell is Geddes playing at? There's been no notification of Duart or the Lord of the Isles visiting.'

'Whatever Billy does, Jack MacLean's sure to know.'

That made him think. He was wary of the finance guardian and I didn't blame him. Then I told him about Kate Revie and the citizen bar.

He wasn't inclined to accept the identification. 'After all, you say the manager didn't recognize her.'

'She also failed to report the disappearance of her auxiliary Cezar MacFarlane to the Guard months ago. The tourism guardian said she asked the favour, but the education guardian went along with it. That gives us — you — a reason to haul her in.'

Michie nodded, still uncertain. Moving against other guardians always had a cost.

'What do you know about her?' I asked.

He rubbed his forehead. 'Not much, to be honest. We were appointed to the Council at the same time, but I hadn't met her before.'

'Let's check her file.'

He pulled back his shoulders, almost standing to attention like the guardsman he hadn't been for decades.

'*We* can't do that, man. Only guardians have that privilege.'

'You're a guardian.'

'Yes, so you'll have to rely on what I tell you.'

'No, thanks.' I executed a smart about-turn and headed for the door. I was almost out before he called me back.

'Very well, Dalrymple. I trust you.'

I grinned. 'The right decision. Otherwise I'd have told the Council about your refusal to comply.'

James Michie glowered at me, then moved to his computer.

I went behind him and looked upon Kate Revie's works and days.

Nineteen

It didn't take long to find the link.

'Kate Revie worked as a Finance Directorate controller at the zoo in 2023–4,' I said, pointing at James Michie's screen. I took out my notebook. 'And Duncan Denoon started in 2023.'

The guardian called up Revie's service report. We took in how reliable she'd been on the border and how highly regarded she'd been in the various directorates she'd served in.

'According to her superior at the zoo,' said Michie, 'her budgetary management was exemplary, her attitude admirable and her loyalty to the Enlightenment without question.'

'A lot can change in ten years,' I said, wondering where the public order guardian had been back then.

'Nothing's been proved against her,' Michie said sharply. 'Maybe she struck up a friendship with the unfortunate Denoon.'

'Which would have been against regulations. Anyway, why was she asking him, "Is it safe?"? Is what safe? You've got to admit, it sounds suspicious.'

'Not necessarily.'

I leaned forward and took the mouse from him, then scrolled down. 'How did she end up in the Education Directorate?'

'Transferred there in 2029,' the guardian read. 'Worked in the direct-orate's administrative department, quickly promoted to chief financial controller.'

'So she's good with money, or what passes for it in Edinburgh.' I clicked on the Courses Attended link. Over the years she'd attended twenty-three courses run by the Finance Directorate, twelve of them since 2031.

'Has she ever given you the impression of being in with Jack MacLean?' I asked.

'No. On the contrary, she stood up to him over her directorate's budget last month.'

That could have been for show, but what I got from Kate Revie's record was her independence, not a common characteristic in senior auxiliaries. She'd never stayed in a relationship – she was registered as bisexual – for more than a month; she'd worked as a volunteer in the city's most rundown areas when she was younger; and she ran – not a mile, not five, but fifty a week. Oh, and she'd written several discussion papers about Leo Tolstoy's social vision.

'I went to one of those,' Michie said, after I'd brought up the page. 'Fascinating, but she didn't like being contradicted. Not that I did so.'

I glanced at him. He was the city's chief enforcer, but he often came across as an overly well-mannered headwaiter. Then again, he was a consum-mate administrator like Kate Revie. Was this the way the Council was heading? Maybe that wouldn't be a bad thing – as long as all the members were clean.

'What are you going to do?' he asked. 'This thing with Denoon seems insignificant to me.'

'Does it? We'll see.'

My phone rang.

'A white van just turned on to Ravelston Dykes from Belford Road,' Davie said. 'Driver matching Alice Lennox's description.'

'Interesting. I'll join you. Wait till she's in the house. And for me.'

'I'm coming too,' said the guardian.

Oh joy.

We were on Queensferry Road, about five minutes from the house in Strachan Gardens, when Davie's voice came over the radio.

'Units to Ravelston Dykes, junction with Succoth Avenue! Guard vehicle attacked!'

I called Davie and asked what was going on.

'Alice fucking Lennox,' he said. 'She stopped the van and started shooting at my people. She's got a male sidekick.'

The guardian had already directed his driver to the long street that had once contained some of Edinburgh's finest houses and grounds. Now it was a citizen residential area, the properties split into flats. We arrived at a junction. To the left was a blazing 4×4. Michie called for a fire engine. By the time we got there another Guard vehicle had arrived.

I jumped down and ran over. The flames were raging and I couldn't get close.

'Any sign of the occupants?' I shouted to the guardswoman beside me.

She pointed down the asphalt. A guardsman was sprawled on his front beyond the reach of the flames, though I felt the skin on my face tighten. I grabbed him by his arm and dragged him away. I turned him over and jerked back as his melted features came into view. There were three large-calibre gunshot wounds to his chest.

'I saw him before he rolled over,' said the guardswoman, lifting me to my feet. 'Walk away, citizen.'

I did as I was told. The guardian was talking to a white-haired guardsman.

'No, sir,' he was saying, as I approached. 'Even if they'd hit the fuel tank, the 4×4 wouldn't have gone up like that.'

'What are you saying?' Michie demanded.

'Could have been a grenade.'

I called Davie. He'd heard what we'd found.

'No sign of the shooters,' he said. 'I've got all units and barracks looking for them.'

'So what do we do? Get into the house?'

'Wait for me.'

I went over to the guardian and we set off for Strachan Gardens, only a few minutes away. Guard vehicles were lined up on the main road on both sides of the turning.

Davie came to meet us.

'Guardian,' he said, nodding. He didn't bother acknowledging me. 'No movement in the house.'

Suddenly it came to me. We'd known there was Remtex in the city since the explosion at the zoo. It might have been the reason for the Guard 4×4 going up in fire and smoke.

'Evacuate the street,' I said. 'Now! The house Lennox and Towart have been using may be wired to blow.'

Michie stared at me. 'I thought you said Clarinda Towart might be there.'

'Not now. Someone warned her about the Guard presence – maybe Lennox. That's why they attacked the 4×4 and disappeared. Clarinda's also gone, you can be sure of that. Get the residents clear!'

There was a disciplined rush into Strachan Gardens, Davie to the fore. In a little over five minutes all the houses were cleared, the occupants led away up the main road.

'Well done, commander,' said the guardian.

'Well done, indeed,' I said. 'Did anyone come out of number 12?'

'No,' Davie replied. 'And a neighbour told me he hasn't seen the old folks for at least two weeks.'

'More disappearing citizens,' I said.

'The explosives technicians have arrived,' Davie said, wiping his face.

'What if Clarinda – or someone else – is watching and ready to detonate charges?'

They both looked at me.

'Stand down!' Davie called to a pretty guardswoman in padded grey overalls.

Michie wasn't impressed. 'We can't leave a potentially dangerous property unexamined, Dalrymple. And what about all those people? It's not a warm night.'

'It'll be more than warm if that house goes up.'

'It's only a supposition that the place is being watched,' the guardian said. 'If it's been booby-trapped, my people will spot that.'

I turned to Davie. 'You're the man with the experience.'

He shrugged. 'I go along with the guardian. The house might be full of evidence. It's worth the risk.'

He had a point, but I wasn't going to say so. Besides, this wasn't a democracy. What the guardian said went.

The technicians were told to get ready. I watched them pull on steel chest and leg plates, oversized helmets and heavy boots. Then they set off. We listened over the radio.

'At front gate.' Silence as they did their checks. 'Clear. Moving down path.'

My heart began the pound. Could Clarinda Towart be in the house, weapons at the ready? Did she have a Jarilo .45? Was she crazy enough to blow herself up?

'At front door. Checking.'

I tried to get my breathing under control. No good.

'More wires than necessary leading from the doorbell,' came the guardswoman's calm voice. 'Investigating.'

There was a long silence.

'Same at rear door,' came another voice.

'I'll proceed,' said the team leader. 'Explosive device behind the door, visible through letter box. Mercury switch motion-sensitive detonator. Investigating.'

Davie and the guardian exchanged looks.

'Are we far enough away?' I said. I wasn't thinking of myself, rather trying to exert indirect pressure on them to stop the techies. Direct pressure would have been a waste of time.

Michie glowered at me. 'Very well, ask her.'

Davie relayed the question to the techie.

'I've inserted an angled mirror. The quantity of Remtex is small, not more than three ounces. You're far enough away. Disabling.'

I opened my mouth, but nothing came out. The courage of the technicians was amazing.

After another long pause, the guardswoman came on the radio again. 'Disabled. No sign of additional devices on door. Opening.'

I had acid reflux, but I managed to keep it down.

'Opened. Proceeding into hall.'

There was another unbearable silence.

'No sign of other devices here,' came the level voice. 'Proceeding into living room.'

This was worse than any horror film. My fingernails were deep into my palms.

Amazingly, the guardswoman laughed. 'Framed kids' drawings all over the walls,' she said. 'They're swee—Oh my—'

I saw the leaping flame before I heard the blast and was able to cover my ears partially. It was still horrendously loud. I felt pieces of debris rain on to my head. The guardian was on the ground, his eyes screwed up, while Davie was standing open-mouthed, radio handset in his hand. His beret had been blown off his head.

Hostilities had commenced for real.

Guard personnel, trained for emergencies, rapidly got things under control. The evacuated citizens were led further away. A few had cuts and bruises from the explosion and paramedics looked after them. The surviving bomb technicians set about checking the neighbouring houses, following the firemen and women who dampened flames that had spread.

The guardian handled himself well, dispensing sensible instructions and encouraging his people. Buses were ordered to take the citizens to temporary accommodation in barracks. I watched them as they boarded. None bore any resemblance to Clarinda Towart.

'No sign of Lennox and her murderous pal's van,' Davie said. 'I've put an all-barracks alert out on it and warned the city-line posts.'

'They'll have dumped it and taken another one,' I said. Recently citizens had been able to buy or hire former directorate vehicles if they could show need – shopkeepers and the like. There was a thriving black market in fake permits as well as reconditioned vehicles.

After an hour the scene was secure. I saw Raeburn 297 and his team arrive.

'You're quite the comedian,' I said.

The auxiliary shrugged. 'I do my best.'

'Careful I don't do mine and tell the guardian what you've been up to.'

'Just a bit of harmless fun, citizen,' he said, his face straighter than Princes Street.

'Uh-huh. Good luck in there. The house we're interested in has been blown to pieces.'

Raeburn 297 smiled tightly. 'Pieces are my business.' He moved purposefully towards Strachan Gardens.

'Now what?' asked Davie.

'Back to the castle. We need to get a hold on everything that's going on.'

'Aye, I'm seriously confused.'

The guardian came up. 'I've just spoken to the senior guardian.'

'Oh yes?' I said neutrally.

'He's very concerned.'

'But not as concerned as he'd have been if the explosion had been in the tourist zone.'

'Well, no. He wants Lennox caught as soon as possible.'

I wondered about Fergus Calder. Did he really have no idea what was going on in his city? Had Jack MacLean and Billy Geddes kept him so substantially in the dark? Either that or he was going through the motions, something guardians are good at. Then again, Michie was the one who'd released Alice Lennox. Had that been his own idea?

My mobile rang.

'Quint?' Sophia sounded alarmed. 'Where are you?'

'Why? What's happened?'

'You'd better get over to the infirmary. I think . . . I think Hector's fading.'

My stomach somersaulted and for a few moments I couldn't speak.

'You . . . you think . . . or you know?'

'Just come. NOW!'

Davie gripped my arm. 'Hector?'

I nodded.

He pulled me to his 4×4 and got me into the passenger's seat. The drive passed in a blur. I ran across the infirmary yard, then up to the old man's room.

Sophia was standing at the open door. She gave me a sad smile.

'He's still with us.'

I went inside. Fiona was on the far side of the bed, manipulating tubes. She looked at me seriously.

'I've upped the morphine dose,' she said. 'The pain got to him about half an hour ago. He's holding on, but only just.'

I leaned over him, taking his skeletal hand. His eyes opened and he stared at me blankly.

'It's me, old man,' I said. 'It's Quintilian.'

No response.

I repeated my name.

His lips cracked into a pained smile.

'Failure . . . where . . . where have . . . you been?'

'Doing the city's dirty business. Never mind that.'

He frowned. 'Always . . . mind that.'

I blinked back tears. 'I'm minding you now.'

'Waste . . . of time,' he gasped. '*Mens non . . . sana in corpore . . . non sano.*'

Fiona raised an eyebrow when I swallowed a laugh.

'Can you not leave Juvenal alone, old man?' I said. 'There's nothing unhealthy about your mind.'

He laughed once, screwing his eyes up in pain. 'You . . . think?'

'Hold on. Fiona here's the best there is.'

He nodded. 'Aye . . . she's a good . . . lassie.' Then he took my arm in a surprisingly tight grip. 'The body . . . politic. It's even sicker . . . than me. Remember what . . . I told you . . . about Geddes and . . . the doctors. Sort them out. Promise?'

'Promise,' I said, drawing my sleeve across my eyes.

'None . . . none of that now . . . lad. I'm proud . . . of you . . . but don't waste . . . time with me . . . nail every corrupt . . . fucker . . .'

I nodded.

'Well . . . what are . . . you waiting for? Go!'

I looked at Fiona, and then Sophia.

'Go . . . failure. I'll be . . . here when . . . you come . . . back.' He pushed me feebly away.

I sat there exasperated, my heart breaking. Then I understood. He didn't want me to see him die. The old bugger wanted to spare me that.

'Go!' he said, his eyelids fluttering.

I got up and kissed him on the forehead.

Leaving the room was the hardest thing I'd ever done, but I couldn't deny him his last wish – even though, in typical guardian fashion, it was expressed as an order.

'Keep me advised,' I said to Sophia, unable to face her.

That was it. The case was now linked with Hector's passing. He was right. The city was dirty and I was going to cleanse it.

Davie was waiting for me, his face lined.

'Is he . . .?'

'Not yet. Get this. He's dying and he sent me away – told me to finish the case.'

'He's a rare man, your father. Still . . .'

'Still nothing. Back to the castle.'

By the time we got to the esplanade I had a grip on myself. The blood in my veins was ice and my mind had a clarity that had been lacking since the murder of Chung Keng Quee. I got my thoughts in order on the walk up to the command centre.

'Ah, Dalrymple,' said the guardian, from his seat on the dais.

'Come with us,' I said peremptorily.

In Davie's office, I closed the door.

'Right, gentlemen,' I said, 'the gloves are off. I want every lead followed up by dawn. I take it there have been no sightings of Alice Lennox or Clarinda Towart.'

'Correct,' said James Michie.

'What a surprise.'

'I don't follow.'

'Guardian, they're part of a sophisticated network. We have to put the squeeze on their protectors.' I watched his face carefully. He didn't seem to be guilty about Alice Lennox being on the streets. If anything, there were traces of shame.

'It'd help if we knew who they are,' Davie grumbled.

I laughed harshly. 'We do know. Jack MacLean and Billy Geddes – in cahoots with first minister of Glasgow and the Lord of the Isles.'

Michie suddenly looked bilious. 'I can't go up against the finance guardian. He's probably backed by the senior guardian. And then there are the outsiders. We have no jurisdiction over them.'

He was right about the latter. Andrew Duart and Angus MacDonald were honoured guests of the city.

'Don't worry about MacLean and Geddes,' I said. 'I'll handle them. You need to haul in Doctors Allison and Jones from the cancer centre . . .'

I hadn't finished, but Davie raised a hand.

'The surveillance team reported that there were nine truck deliveries at Pollock tonight.'

'Even more reason to raid the place.'

Michie nodded.

'And bring in Kate Revie. We need to question her about her ties with Duncan Denoon and Cezar MacFarlane.'

'Got it,' Davie said. 'I'll explain, guardian.'

My phone rang.

'Jimmy Taggart here, sir.' I'd forgotten about my old comrade in the Supply Directorate. 'Not woken you up, have I?'

'Hardly.'

'Aye, well, about Napier 311 – John Rollo.' The bent auxiliary shot by Goliath. 'I reckon I know who alerted his killer.'

This could be the lead we needed.

'There's a young lad in the Tourism Directorate, works for the guardian.'

My jaw dropped.

'Cramond 537.' Aka Ross Parlane, Guardian Mary's son. 'He was down here when Napier 311 left. Apparently they had a right rammy.'

I wouldn't have thought the youthful Ross was up to taking on an experienced auxiliary like Rollo.

'Any idea what about?'

'No, sorry. The witness I found said they were behind closed doors. But there was a lot of yelling, all right. Afterwards Napier 311 stormed out and

Cramond 537 made a call on his mobile. Unfortunately he turned away and my guy couldn't hear anything. Suspicious though, eh?'

'Definitely. Thanks, Jimmy. Let me know if anything else crops up.'

'Will do, sir.'

I cut the connection.

'What was that?' the guardian asked.

'A lead of sorts,' I replied. It wasn't what I'd been hoping for – that MacLean or Billy Geddes had made the fatal call – but it was interesting all the same. I wasn't going to share it with Michie, though. It led to the tourism guardian and I didn't want to set him up against her. At least not yet.

My phone rang again.

'You really must come now,' Sophia said hoarsely.

I headed to the door. 'Bring in Kate Revie and the doctors,' I said, then ran out.

All I could think of as I sprinted down to the esplanade was that Hector wouldn't be pleased to see me.

Twenty

'I'm so sorry, Quint,' Sophia said from behind me, after I'd been sitting by the old man for some minutes. She put a hand on my shoulder, but was sensitive enough not to do more.

'He just slipped away, citizen,' Fiona said. 'The morphine meant he didn't feel anything.'

I looked at my father's face. It was less lined now, his eyes closed and his mouth composed in a faint smile.

'He got . . . what he wanted,' I said, bending forward.

'What do you mean, darling?' Sophia said, her mouth close to my ear.

'He didn't . . . want me to see him go.' I let go of the old man's arm and held her close. 'He always got . . . what he wanted.'

'He was thinking of you, Quint,' Sophia said. 'Not of himself.'

I shook my head. 'He was thinking of the city. Fucking guardians. They put it first even on their deathbeds.'

She wasn't offended. 'I can assure you I won't.'

I breathed in her warm, familiar scent. Even though there was always an air of antiseptic, the underlying notes were hers.

Fiona was removing the intravenous tubes and cannulae, her hands moving gently.

'There he is,' she said. 'A fine old gentleman who's beyond pain now. My condolences, citizen.'

I nodded to her, attempting a smile.

'Come away now, Quint,' Sophia said. 'We should raise a glass to him.'

I let myself be led out, looking back once. But the remains on the bed were no longer Hector. He had already departed the prison-house of the body and Enlightenment Edinburgh. He was free.

But I wasn't. After Sophia had poured glasses of a decent malt and added a few drops of water, we raised them. I was suddenly lost for words, so she did the honours.

'I'll be better after the funeral,' I said. 'Can you keep him in the morgue until the case is solved?'

'Of course. Don't you want to take time off?'

'No,' I said, too brusquely. 'This is Hector's work I'm doing.'

'I understand,' she said softly.

I told her about the deliveries to the cancer centre.

'Right,' she said, 'tell Davie to keep me up to date on what they consist of.'

'Yes. I'll also let you know what Allison and Jones say under interrogation.'

Her eyes widened. 'Do you want me there?'

'I'll think about it. If they start playing hardball, I'm sure you can deal with it.'

'I certainly can.'

I had a thought.

'The Dobies.'

'The wife is completely out of it. I think the husband's fever has broken.' She made a call. 'Yes, he's conscious. Do you want to talk to him?'

I nodded. 'What about the skeleton?'

'We've finished the reconstruction. There are some bones missing and I still haven't been able to specify the cause of death.' She caught my eye. 'Do you want me to interview Peter Dobie with you?'

'No, thanks. I wouldn't want your gentle nature to be offended.'

'That bad?'

I shrugged, remembering the chimpanzee in the Lucky Strike. 'By the standards of this case . . .'

'Come round later, Quint. Please.'

'It's almost dawn. You need sleep now. So do I, but I'm running on adrenaline.'

'You know what'll happen when that dries up.'

'I do. Then again, it's hardly the first time.'

'That's what I'm worried about.'

I kissed her and left.

'Mr Dobie,' I said – loudly, in his ear.

The patient's limbs jerked, including the one in traction.

'Ah!'

'Sorry about that,' I lied.

'What do you want, citizen?' he said weakly.

'Clarinda Towart.'

I watched his reaction. The longer I waited, the more nervous he got.

'Lorna told me you fucked her.'

Dobie started puffing like a fish out of water.

'Nice,' I said. 'With your wife and daughter in the house.'

'I . . . I couldn't resist her. That woman . . . she's dynamite.'

Remtex, more like. 'Any idea why she'd waste her time with a middle-aged slob like you?'

'Here, what—'

'Here,' I said, grabbing one of the wires that held up his leg. 'What about answering the question?'

'She's a right nympho, that woman. Anything on legs.'

I tugged the wire.

'She wanted something from you – and I don't mean your pathetic cock.'

'I . . . she . . .'

'Spit it out!' I yelled.

His cheeks were red and his eyes blinking as if I'd thrown bleach in them. That would be my next move.

'She . . . she wanted to get in touch with Dougie.'

That rang true, not least because Peter Dobie's eyelids were no longer hyperactive.

'And you knew how to do that?'

He nodded.

'How did you do it?'

The blinking started again.

'I . . . I can't really say . . .'

'You can really say,' I said, tugging the traction wire hard. 'Or you won't really be able to walk again.'

Under a minute of that did the trick.

'I . . . my bus is the number 43. The south terminus is Firrhill. There's a . . . Christ, I shouldnae be telling you thi—aaah!'

'Go on,' I said, lowering the wire.

'There's a lad hangs about there, Kennie's his name.'

'Description?'

'About fifteen, skinny, shaved head, freckles all over his face. Oh, and a broken nose.'

'And you give him messages?'

Dobie nodded. 'Then he gives me replies a day or two later.'

Firrhill was about a mile from the city line and a likely place for couriers who crossed into the badlands to be based.

'There,' I said, smiling, 'that wasn't too difficult.'

'That's what you think.'

'Before I go, one more thing.'

Dobie groaned.

'Who told you about this Kennie?'

He blanched. 'Oh no, citi—Aaaaah!'

'Last chance,' I said, grabbing a second wire.

'No . . . no . . . ach, all right . . . it wus an auxiliary.'

That was no surprise. I tossed a coin mentally.

'Barracks number? And don't say you can't remember.'

'Napier,' he gasped, eyes locked on my hands. 'Napier 311.'

John Rollo. I'd guessed right.

Guess who was waiting for me outside the infirmary?

'Hello, Hamish,' I said to the young guardsman. 'Looking out for me again?'

'The commander's orders,' he replied, with a grin.

I directed him to the castle.

'Have you been out to Firrhill recently?'

'A couple of weeks ago. Why?'

I considered going there and grabbing Kennie with the freckles, but decided against it – he'd run a mile as soon as he saw the Guard vehicle. An undercover squad would have to pick him up.

'What's it like?'

'Headbanger Central. I was in a backup squad. A Guard vehicle had been attacked with a machine gun, would you believe? The bastards got away. One of our people was hit in the shoulder. Lucky. The arseholes must have been amateurs.'

'With a machinegun?'

That squared with what I'd heard. Firrhill and Colinton Mains beyond were established routes in and out of the city, no matter what the Guard did.

On the way up from the esplanade I called Davie.

'My people only found Dr Jones at the cancer centre. No sign of Allison.'

'Wonder if he was tipped off.'

'Who by?'

'Good question. What about the education guardian?'

'Aye, she's here. I've managed to keep Michie off her, but you'd better get a move on.'

I arrived at the interrogation cells five minutes later.

'There you are, Dalrymple,' the public order guardian said. 'I was about to start. It isn't done to keep a fellow guardian waiting.'

'You can listen on the wire, but you're not taking part in the interview, James.'

He didn't like it, but he acquiesced – having probably worked out that he'd be able to deny involvement if things went wrong.

I went in and gave Kate Revie my most shit-eating grin.

'What is this, citizen?' she asked, getting to her feet. 'I only agreed to come as a favour to James.'

'I'm sure he's very grateful,' I said, for the hidden microphone. 'Sit down, please.'

'Well?' she demanded, running her fingers through her red hair.

'Duncan Denoon.'

She didn't react – auxiliaries and guardians practised turning rapidly to marble.

'Whom you met on several occasions at Neil's citizen bar off Rose Street.'

A few cracks appeared in her facade.

'Oh, you mean the zookeeper,' she said lightly.

'The one you met in 2023 when you were financial controller there.'

'Em, yes.'

'Em?'

The guardian's cheeks reddened. 'I was unsure of the year.'

'Right,' I said, with a laugh. 'Is it safe?'

She froze.

'I said—'

'I heard you, citizen.'

'Well, is what safe?'

Silence.

'It couldn't be Remtex, could it? After all, Denoon's precious pygmy hippos were blown up by a Remtex charge.' My voice hardened. 'As were a Guard 4×4 and a citizen house in Blackhall.'

'I had nothing to do with either of those incidents.'

'Were you asking about Remtex?'

Kate Revie's head dropped. 'Yes,' she said, in a whisper.

'You were,' I confirmed loudly. 'You realize that undisclosed knowledge of explosives is enough to have you demoted and sent to a city farm?'

'Of course,' she replied, eyes flashing. 'You think you're so smart, Quintilian Dalrymple, but you know nothing of what's really going on in the city.'

I sat back in my chair. 'Enlighten me.'

The guardian got to her feet. 'I will not.'

'Shame. Have you met my friend Davie?'

'If you mean the commander in charge of serious crime, yes, I have.'

For a moment I wondered if she and Davie had been sexual partners, but I reckoned he'd have told me. He wasn't shy about his conquests.

'Then you'll know he's a dab hand with an auxiliary knife. Among other more delicate instruments of torture.'

I suspected Davie was holding James Michie to his seat. I hoped so as an intervention now would be catastrophic.

Kate Revie glared down at me. 'You can't threaten a guardian.'

'One who's as pure as St Margaret, no. You, on the other hand . . .'

She sat down rapidly, her head in her hands.

'You have one way out,' I said. 'Tell me everything.'

'I . . . I can't. You really must leave this issue alone.'

'No chance. Do you know Clarinda Towart?'

'I do not,' the guardian said, but her eyes gave her away.

'How do you know her?'

'I . . .' She looked at me desperately. 'I can't say.'

'You *won't* say,' I corrected. 'How about John Rollo, Napier 311?'

Kate Revie remained silent.

'I'll take that as a "yes", then.'

'Take it however you like,' she said, but there was no authority in her voice.

'Dougie Dobie, aka Goliath?'

More silence.

'You knew the killer of an auxiliary?'

'I . . .'

'Alice Lennox?'

'Who?' Now she seemed on firmer ground. 'You mentioned her in Council. A friend of Towart's? I don't know her.'

I believed her.

'George Allison?'

'He's the head of the cancer centre. I've spoken to him at Finance Directorate receptions.'

'Nothing else?'

'No.'

'What about Malaysia?'

'A sovereign state in south-east Asia.'

Prevarication is a dead giveaway. I let it go, partly because I didn't want to show all my cards and partly because her directorate wasn't on any of the contracts.

'This is going well,' I said, smiling ironically. 'How about Christo Fleming?'

'You mentioned him in Council too. He's a boxer. I've seen him in the ring.'

'And outside it?'

She shook her head.

'How about *Spar/Tak/Us*?'

Kate Revie was unable to control her eyes, which shot open. 'The citizen play?' she asked unconvincingly.

'You know very well, guardian. Did Billy Geddes take you?'

'Billy . . .' Her head dropped.

There was a rattling of keys and the door opened. Davie beckoned me out.

'She's cracking,' I said indignantly.

'Michie's climbing the walls. You're to stop.'

'Stay here,' I said, 'and make sure *she* does.' If the public order guardian had taken pity on his colleague, he might try to get her out.

I stormed into the room with the listening equipment.

'Citizen, this won't do,' James Michie said, standing up to face me. 'You can't treat a guardian in so cavalier a fashion.'

I laughed. If pressed, I'd have seen myself as a roundhead, minus the religious convictions.

'You know the terms of my authorization.'

'Yes, but—'

'Yes, but nothing. It's obvious she's involved. She knows Clarinda, she knew Goliath, she's scared shitless about Billy Geddes.'

The guardian raised a finger. 'About Geddes, you said you were going to deal with him and the finance guardian. I've seen no sign of that having happened.'

'I've been pushed for time.' I paused for effect. 'My father died.'

That made him blanch. He started to stutter condolences, then his mobile rang. He listened, unable or unwilling to get a word in. Eventually he put the phone down.

'That was the senior guardian,' I said. 'He's ordered that Kate Revie be released and forbidden that she be questioned again.'

'Among other things, yes.'

'What other things?'

He fiddled with his notebook and pen, the latter a black beauty that definitely didn't come from the Supply Directorate. Had he been got at by one or more of the outsiders? Or Jack MacLean? Had he told them that we knew about the Malaysian contracts? If so, why was I still in a job?

'You're to leave day-to-day handling of the case – or rather, cases – to the commander. I'm to supervise.'

My phone beeped. It was a text from Fergus Calder backing up what Michie had said. I was 'to provide strategic advice, staying off front-line investigations'.

To bloody hell with that.

Davie and I went to the canteen, where I strategically advised him not to eat three helpings of beef stew. He paid no attention.

'So what are we going to do?' he said, between mouthfuls.

I leaned forward. 'You report to me before the guardian. I'll tell you what to share with him.'

He frowned and then nodded. 'What do you want me to do?'

'Oh, nothing much.' I told him what Peter Dobie had said about the adolescent Kennie. 'Send an undercover team to Firrhill to pick him up. Then interrogate him yourself. Who are his contacts over the city line? Who's he brought into the city recently? That sort of thing.'

'Right,' he said, spraying bits of bread at me.

'Lovely. Next, Dr Jones. Let him go. If Michie asks, tell him I don't think the cancer centre's significant any more.'

'Meaning you're going to check it out.'

I grinned, and not just because the cheese in my roll was fresh.

An elderly, stooped guardsman shuffled towards us, a thick file in his hands.

'Brains,' Davie said. 'Looking for us?'

'Raeburn 37,' I said, making room for him on the bench.

'Citizen.' He turned his wrinkled face to Davie. 'Is that stew worth eating?'

'It's hearty,' came the reply.

'I thought they put hearts in the haggis,' I said.

Guffaws all round.

'I've got something for you,' said the old man. We'd used his code-breaking skills last summer. 'These newspaper cuttings.' He opened the file. 'An interesting collection. What's the owner's profession?'

'Bus driver,' I said. I'd forgotten about the articles and photos cut from the *Edinburgh Guardian* that we'd found in Peter Dobie's flat.

'That makes sense. There's a lot of pieces about the routes and vehicles over the years. The person who did the cutting is also interested in sport – originally rugby but now football – primarily women's teams.' He smiled. 'Plenty of photos, especially of players with their legs all over the place. Female athletes too. Very short shorts.'

'Could be a lesbian,' Davie said.

'Unlikely,' said Brains. 'This individual's also interested in car and bus modelling.'

'Does sound like a male,' I said. 'Peter Dobie's the name.'

'Though actually maybe there is an issue of sexuality. There are notices of almost every citizen play and show that's been licensed in the last two years. Your man – or woman – seems to have a real interest in the actors and performers. See, there are names underlined.'

I felt hairs rise on the back of my neck. Peter Dobie didn't strike me as a theatre-goer and Lorna was too young. That left Mavis. Perhaps the cuttings had been done by husband and wife separately. I rang Sophia and asked her about the patient. She called me back.

'She's come out of shock, but she's still pretty fragile, Quint.'

'Put a guard on her. I'll be over shortly.'

I turned to Raeburn 37. 'Can you give me all the theatre clippings?'

'Already collated,' he said, handing me a sheaf of newsprint held together by a large paper clip.

I went through them. Several names turned up frequently, and most frequently of all was Rory Campbell, the director and star of *Spar/Tak/Us*. I'd taken my eye off him – though there had been a surveillance team on him. Supposedly.

'Brilliant, Brains,' I said, getting up. 'Thanks.'

'Where are you going?' Davie asked.

I put a finger to my lips. 'Off the record, on the QT and very hush-hush – Edinburgh confidential.'

That shut him up; and also put a space between me and James Michie. From now on I was a private investigator, and I wasn't going near the Council meeting until I had enough evidence to burn whoever was pulling the strings in this city of tourism and bones.

Twenty-One

'How are you bearing up?' Sophia asked, taking my arm.

We were in her office, assistants banished. I told her what the senior guardian had ordered.

'Maybe it's for the best, Quint. You should sleep for a couple of days.'

'You're forgetting one thing – Hector bound me to this case.'

Sophia put her arm round me. 'He was dying, my love. He didn't know what he was saying.'

I looked into her eyes. 'Do you really believe that?'

She shook her head. 'That doesn't mean you should act against Fergus Calder.'

'I don't intend to. Think about it. He's kept me on the case, even at a distance from events. He wants me around.'

Furrows appeared on Sophia's forehead. 'Doesn't mean we can trust him.'

'No, it doesn't.' I told her about James Michie's intervention with Kate Revie. 'I'm not sure if we can trust him either. You'd better be careful. If he's told Fergus or Jack MacLean that we know about the Malaysian contracts, they may come for us.'

'I can look after myself,' she said, a bit too Ice Queen-like for comfort.

I knew she could, but there was also Maisie. I kept that thought to myself.

'Right, I'm going to talk to Mavis Dobie. Can you explain why I'm not at the Council meeting? I'm sure they'll all be falling over themselves to offer their condolences.'

'Most of them will,' she said stiffly. 'We're not all as crooked as a U-bend.'

I laughed. 'Did you invent that expression?'

'What?' she said. 'There have been plumbers around.'

'Ah.' I kissed her on the lips.

'Look after yourself,' she said.

'Ditto. Oh, by the way, have you heard anything more about that anti-alcoholism drug?'

'Alceteron? No, why?'

I shrugged. 'No reason.'

But, of course, there was a reason; one that I was keeping to myself.

* * *

Mavis Dobie was in the corner of an eight-bed ward, propped up on pillows. A guardsman was at the door. I checked with a nursing auxiliary, who told me the patient was eating again and had regained some strength.

I went over and drew the curtains around the bed.

'What's this?' she said, staring at me. 'I know you.'

'And I know you, Mavis. How are you?'

'Poorly,' she said. 'I keep seeing the bullets . . . hitting Dougie.' She sniffed and raised a tissue to her eyes.

I showed her the sheaf of newspaper clippings. 'These are yours, aren't they?' She looked at me uncertainly and then nodded. 'I love going to the shows. It's the best thing the Council's done, bringing them back.'

'Is that right?'

'Oh yes, all the colour and light, the costumes, the performers.'

'Like Rory Campbell?'

Mavis Dobie's eyes sprang open. 'Rory . . . oh, him. Aye, he's very good. I love *Spar/Tak/Us*.'

'Me too,' I said, smiling reassuringly. 'How about Alice Lennox and her man Christo Fleming?'

She tried and failed to control herself, but the quivering of her lips was traitorous.

I took her hand. 'Alice Lennox and a pal destroyed a Guard 4×4 last night and killed its crew. They also blew up a house in Blackhall. There were several fatalities.'

Mavis's face was very pale. 'No . . . she would never . . . never do that.'

'Out with it or it's the castle for you.'

She started to weep, but I wasn't having it. A few tight squeezes and steely glares put her right.

'They're . . . they were friends of Dougie's, she and Christo. We knew him from the boxing, of course.'

'When was this?'

'We first met them a year ago, maybe a bit more.'

So Dougie/Goliath had been in the city for longer than her husband and daughter had said. And had also known Clarinda's best friend.

'Did Dougie know Rory Campbell?' I was pretty sure Alice and Christo did.

'I don't think so.'

'And Clarinda Towart?'

Her cheeks reddened. 'That bitch. She took my daughter away from me and she turned my husband into her slave.'

That was more than I'd heard.

'Aye, he'd do anything for her,' she continued.

'Such as?'

'Find new recruits for the PSD.' She shook her head. 'Disgusting. The Council should be ashamed of itself.'

I nodded, then had another thought.

'You're a cleaner. Where do you work?'

Mavis Dobie tried to look unconcerned. 'All over the tourist zone. Depends on the rota.'

'No, it doesn't. According to your file, you're directorate-cleared. Which ones have you worked in?' Citizen files don't show the directorates where they work – that information is available only in the directorates' own archives.

'Em, I was in Labour for five years. Then Recreation . . .'

'And now?'

She gave me a reluctant look and I hardened my expression.

'Finance,' she said, in a low voice.

What a surprise.

'Did you do anything there except clean?'

She was terrified now, her face drenched in tears. 'Don't . . . don't make me . . . say . . .'

I showed her my authorization, which hadn't yet been removed or amended – no doubt that was a delight to come.

'Talk,' I said harshly, 'or I'll tell the finance guardian you held out on me. You notice that I'm empowered to question guardians too.'

She stared at me, then the tension went out of her body.

'Messages,' she said, her voice little more than a whisper. 'I was given messages . . . to deliver.'

'Who gave you them and who were they for?'

'The . . . the office of the guardian's special adviser . . . and they were to people all over the city. I had a taxi to take me.'

'Who was the driver?'

'Eddie's his name.'

That put Bruce Kilgour out of the picture.

'Who were the messages for?' I repeated.

'I cannae . . . I cannae remember . . .'

I stared at her and eventually she broke.

'The MacFarlanes?'

'No, I don't remember that name.'

'Rory Campbell?'

'No.'

'Clarinda Towart?'

'No!' she said shrilly. 'And I'd have torn it up if I'd been given one for her.'

'Napier 311 at the Supply Directorate?'

She nodded.

'Cramond 537 in Tourism?'

'Aye.'

'Any more?'

'The . . . the education guardian.'

So there it was. Billy Geddes and his boss Jack MacLean were illicitly linked to Kate Revie, John Rollo and Ross Parlane. Senior auxiliaries would never use a citizen courier unless they were avoiding official channels. The question was, why?

'Oh, and the Malaysian consulate,' Mavis added.

There was my answer.

'You won't tell anyone, citizen?'

'No,' I said, not entirely mendaciously. 'And I'll make sure Lorna doesn't go any further in the PSD.'

She gave me a grateful smile.

Sometimes my job was almost worth the hassle.

I called Davie and asked for an update.

'No sign of that Kennie lad in Firrhill. And Dr Jones has been released, order of the guardian.'

'Fuck,' I said, drawing a disapproving look from a nurse in the corridor. On the other hand, that showed how much power the cancer centre had – power that operated separately from Sophia. I knew she wouldn't have authorized his release.

'Who got to Michie?'

'Oddly, he didn't say. What are you up to?'

'Never mind. You know that guardsman Hamish?'

'Heriot 619? What about him?'

'Send him to the infirmary.'

'He's already there, not that I sent him, oh no.'

I laughed. 'He's mine now. Cover for him.'

'Yessir, yessir, three bags—'

'Shut up. No sign of Clarinda Towart or Alice Lennox?'

'Not a one. I'm going for a sleep.'

'Lucky you.'

I broke the connection and went into the yard. I'd considered telling

Sophia where I was going, but decided against it – she was better off not knowing.

Hamish was leaning against the Guard 4×4. 'Citizen Dalrymple,' he said.

'Call me Quint. We're going to be a team.'

'Brilliant!'

The young man's enthusiasm was encouraging, not least because I was about to risk our balls, asses and maybe lives. I didn't tell him that.

After we'd got in, Hamish asked where to. I directed him to the backstreets of Newington. When he'd found a quiet one, I climbed into the back and stretched out as best I could.

'Get some sleep,' I told him. 'It's going to be a long night.'

'I don't need sleep,' he said, with the bravado of the insufficiently experienced guardsman. The older ones knew that closing your eyes when you could was essential on operations. Then again, he didn't even know he was on an op.

I dropped into a deep sleep despite the uncomfortable plastic bench seat. Inevitably my father made an appearance, not as he'd been recently but when he was a guardian, wearing the tweed jacket with leather elbow patches that he'd had when I was a kid. He was speaking at a meeting of citizens, who applauded his every sentence and laughed at his carefully scripted jokes. He had the common touch, which was more than could be said for my mother. She also came to me, as she'd been in the early days of the Enlightenment – stern but fair, and dedicated to her duties at the Education Directorate. It was only later that the wielding of power corrupted her, though not many people knew how much. Her death in 2021 had drawn Hector and me closer, as had my attempts over the years to rein in the Council. The last thing I saw was him telling me to finish the case.

'It's 12.08,' Hamish said, when I stirred. 'Do you want some coffee?'

I took the flask he offered. The contents were still warm. The Supply Directorate must have got a delivery of new thermoses. From Malaysia?

'I have food as well.'

'Quite the organized guardsman. Have you brought bottles for us to piss in?'

'Shit. I mean, no.'

'Doesn't matter. There's a tree over there.'

The street lights in the suburb were faint. I made it to the sycamore and emptied my bladder. Back in the 4×4 I washed my hands from a bottle and then surveyed the food laid out on the passenger seat.

'Rolls with salmon paste, bananas and chocolate,' Hamish announced proudly.

'Are you expecting company?'

'I have a healthy appetite.'

'You weren't by any chance trained by Hume 253?'

'No, but I model myself on the commander.'

I suspected Davie knew that, whence Hamish's frequent appearances.

'What weapons are in this heap?'

'Heap? This is one of the Philippines' finest models, capable of—'

'Weapons.'

'Right. I have a Hyper-Stun, of course.'

I knew how unreliable they could be.

'And I have my combat knife and truncheon. I took the liberty – well, the commander suggested that I sign out another Hyper-Stun, a sub-machine gun, ten grenades and a Kelvingrove Micro-Crossbow.'

'A what?'

'It's a new Guard acquisition. I've trained on it. It has a 270lb draw weight and fires a bolt at 330 feet per second.'

'Why the hell do you need a crossbow?'

Hamish grinned. 'Silence is deadly.'

He had a point there, though I hoped we wouldn't have to use weapons.

'Only fire if you have to,' I said. 'And on my command.' Suddenly I was back in the tactical operations squad when I was in the Guard. That didn't make me feel particularly pleased.

'What now, Quint?'

'We're walking – to the cancer centre. And we'd better go armed.'

'Right,' the guardsman said, not in the least disconcerted.

We got out and went to the back of the vehicle. There was other gear in there: night-vision binoculars, a detailed map of Edinburgh and black waterproof capes. The night was cool with thin cloud cover. I didn't think it would rain, but the capes could be useful as camouflage. We kitted up. I took a Hyper-Stun, for all my distrust of them, a combat knife and an extendable truncheon, while Hamish filled a black haversack with grenades and the folded bow and its bolts.

'Apart from getting to the cancer centre,' Hamish said, 'is there a plan?'

'There have been a lot of deliveries recently. I want to find out what they are. Nine trailers have been left there today so we need to locate them.'

We looked at the map. It was Guard issue and showed all the buildings on the site.

'There's the main delivery area,' Hamish said, pointing to a space at the southern end of the compound. 'How are we going to get over the wall?' He reached for a coiled rope. 'With this?'

I shrugged. 'Maybe we'll be able to slip in behind a vehicle.'

He nodded. 'That would work.'

We set off. The suburban streets were quiet. The curfew had been relaxed but the local citizens stayed inside. Newington was one of the more secure areas but, no matter what the Council boasted, the streets weren't safe after dark. We didn't hear or see anyone, but Hamish's bulk and uniform would have put potential miscreants off.

Ten minutes later we were opposite the gate on the south-western wall of the cancer centre. It was closed, a guardsman in a sentry box to the left. I ran the night-vision bins around the wall and could see no cameras. We waited for half an hour but no vehicles went in or out.

'Stun?' Hamish said, inclining his head towards his colleague.

'Looks like you'll have—'

I broke off as the noise of heavy engines came from the south.

Hamish took the bins. 'Trucks, big ones. Three of them.'

They were coming from the opposite direction to the Supply Directorate depot.

I looked across the road. The gate had opened and the sentry had been joined by at least six other Guard personnel.

Then a large portion of hell broke loose. We stepped behind a garden wall as machine-gun fire rattled out, bullets striking the trucks. Then there were explosions, at least five of them. The front truck stopped, its cargo hold in flames. The Guard personnel at the gate ran forward, firing their Hyper-Stuns at shadowy figures in the smoke. Several of Hamish's comrades were shot down.

'We've got to help them,' he said, taking grenades from his pack and leaving it behind.

I went after him, Hyper-Stun set to the maximum charge that wouldn't result in death. There were shouts all around as we passed the first truck. I saw a guardswoman being rolled on the road by another to extinguish the flames that were consuming her tunic.

'Don't kill them!' I shouted to Hamish, as he stunned a man in dark clothes, who immediately dropped the sub-machine gun he was carrying.

Either he didn't hear me or the blood mist had come down over him. He threw a grenade at a group of people attacking the third truck. Two of them went flying through the air.

I saw a guardsman aim his Hyper-Stun at me and ducked. The prongs zipped over my head. Before I could react, he took several bullets to the chest and dropped to the asphalt.

I looked down the road. Hamish was at the head of a group of Guard personnel. They had fought off the attackers, who were dispersing to the south. One came towards me and I stunned him. He went down like a stone. Then I saw the person we'd been looking for – only for a couple of seconds, and her blonde hair was crushed under a cap, but I'd looked at her photo so often that I knew her features like my own. Running with a sub-machine gun in her right hand was Clarinda Towart. Then she was swallowed by the night.

The shooting stopped. The second truck was riddled with bullet holes, the driver bent over the wheel, while smoke was billowing from the third. A man jumped from the passenger door and ran towards me.

'Get down!' he shouted. 'LNG! Get down!'

There was a muffled explosion and then a much louder one. I found myself on the other side of a wall, my ears ringing. When I looked above the stonework, I saw bodies all over the road and pavements, several of them in pieces. All that was left of the trucks were their chassis, their payloads atomized.

Hamish came stumbling up the road, holding his head. I ran to him.

'Are you all right?' I shouted.

'Yes,' he said, putting his Hyper-Stun in its holster. 'Scrapes and bruises, and a sore head. There aren't many other survivors.'

'No, I can see that.' A couple of guardsmen were supporting each other. 'Come on, now's our chance.' His cape had been blown off and I dropped the remains of mine.

As we walked in the gate, more Guard personnel came running. Fire engines were arriving on the road. We slipped into the compound without attracting attention. I saw some large industrial waste bins and led Hamish behind them.

'What the fuck was that about?' he said, wiping his face. It was criss-crossed with cuts and scratches.

'Any idea who the attackers were?'

'No idea. I didn't hear them talking. They looked like they knew what they were doing, though.'

'The trucks were coming in here. I heard someone say "LNG". Do hospitals use that?'

'Search me. Shit, I left my haversack over there.'

'Not now. Did you see what was in the other trucks?'

He shook his head.

'Me neither.'

'Shouldn't we make a report?'

'Not yet. We haven't even started what we came here to do.'

Hamish nodded. 'Let's get to it then.'

'Anyone asks, you were in the firefight and you're waiting for your commander.'

'What about you?'

'I can look after myself,' I said, the bravado ringing hollow in my ears. Whatever was going on in Edinburgh, it was far too violent for comfort.

Twenty-Two

I'd my phone set to vibrate. It did so.

'Where are you?' Davie asked.

'That's restricted.'

'Because there have been explosions near the cancer centre—'

'And you thought of me? Sweet.'

'I'm on my way.'

'Make sure you take any of the surviving attackers in. At least one of them should come round from his stunning.'

'So you *are* there.'

'No comment. But you might want to remind patrols to look for Clarinda Towart.'

'You saw her?'

'I did, but don't tell Michie that. *Adios.*'

I terminated the call. It wouldn't do Davie any good to be linked to what I was about to do. Ditto Hamish, but it was too late for him.

'Right,' I said to the young guardsman, 'the delivery area.'

'It's on the other side of the compound.'

We set off, keeping to the shadows round the buildings. There were more lights than in the suburban streets, but not enough to hinder our progress. Five minutes later we reached the open space shown on the map. Except it wasn't open now – it was almost full of trucks and trailers. We slipped amongst them. It soon became clear that the vehicles didn't have Transport Department numbers and insignia. In fact, they didn't have any insignia at all.

'Outsiders,' Hamish said.

I nodded. 'What about the ones that were destroyed?'

'I didn't see any Edinburgh markings.'

'So where did they come from?'

'And how did they get across the border and the city line?'

Good questions. Another one was, 'What's inside them?' We went to the back of a trailer. There was a heavy padlock securing the doors.

'Shit,' I said, under my breath.

'No problem,' said Hamish, taking a small box from one of his tunic pockets.

'What's that?'

He grinned, then stuck the pointed end of a tube into the keyhole and squeezed. There was a click and the lock opened.

'We were issued with it a couple of months ago,' the guardsman said. 'Bolt acid, they call it. Melts the tumblers, apparently.'

Good of Davie not to have told me. Then again, I'd only have used it on my front door. I frequently locked myself out.

We pulled the doors apart and jumped into the cargo hold, flashing our torches on the contents.

'What language is that?' Hamish said, pointing at the pictographic characters.

'Chinese, I think.' I went round the crate. 'Here's some English. "Malaysia Company 329".' It appeared the contracts had been signed after all.

'Does it say what's inside?'

I shook my head. 'Got any crate acid?'

'No such thing as far as I know.' Hamish pulled out his combat knife and set to work. After a few seconds of silent struggle, he raised the lid. 'What the—'

'Hell would just about cover it,' I said, shining the beam on pointed green cylinders.

'Are they rockets?'

'Warheads, I'd say.'

'Why are they in the cancer centre?'

I looked closer. There were red markings on the sides of the cylinders, and the words BIOHAZARD Level 4.

'Is that bad?' Hamish asked.

'I'd hazard it is.'

Hamish rocked back on his heels. 'What did you say about LNG?'

I got a bad feeling.

'In weapons training they taught us about arms that outsiders might use on Edinburgh. Liquid natural gas can be used as rocket fuel.'

I said, 'Fuck,' and we heard a heavy footstep at the same time.

Hamish whipped out his Hyper-Stun and fired when a head came round the door. The guardsman fell like a sack of stones.

'We'd better get out of here,' I said.

We ran, crouching, to the nearest building. The sounds of the fire engines and rescue teams on Dalkeith Road reached us through the still night air. There were no other Guard personnel in our vicinity – presumably most were at the south-western gate. Which made me determined to find out more.

'Come on,' I said, running to the next building. A sign said it was the Cancer Research Institute, but I wasn't convinced that was all that went on. It was close to the delivery area.

There were two guards, one female and one male, at the glass doors. The latter was smoking, which would have got him demoted on the spot. I didn't think Dr Allison would be impressed either, though I'd begun to have major suspicions about the centre's chief.

'Which one do you want?' Hamish said, from the bush we'd crawled behind.

'I could never stun a woman.'

'Done.'

We got up and fired. The sentries' bodies thudded on to the concrete slabs.

'Don't you feel bad about nailing your comrades, Hamish?'

'No. This lot are obviously all Unguards.' That term was a recent addition to the local argot, though I'd been uncovering them for decades.

We pulled the unconscious sentries into the room that served as their mess, although it was as tidy as a normal Guard facility. Old habits die hard for the Unguard.

I looked at the board in the hall. There were room numbers and medical words I couldn't fathom. Then I saw two that made sense: Osteological Laboratory. Thanks to my old man's attempts to teach me Ancient Greek when I was a kid, I knew that osteology was the study of bones. I had also remembered the bones that had been found in the house with the dead Asian, the ones that Sophia had reconstructed into a female dwarf. Appropriately enough in this place, a tingle ran up my spine.

'Come on.' I led Hamish up to the third floor. There was an all-embracing chemical smell that made me want to sneeze, but it was cut with something more organic – something seriously rancid.

'Here it is,' Hamish said, pointing at a door. He immediately got to work with his combat knife. Five seconds later we were in.

And immediately wished we weren't.

Hamish put his hand over his nose. 'What's that stench?'

It had permeated my nose and mouth, almost provoking a total evacuation of my stomach. In front of us was a line of three stainless-steel boxes, taller, wider and deeper than coffins.

'You aren't going to open them, are you?' Hamish said, with more than a hint of desperation.

I walked down the lab. There were clip files on the side of each box and ventilation pipes leading from the tops to the roof. There must have been some loose joints. I looked at one of the files.

'Subject: male. Age: 24. Maceration Stage: 1,' I read.

'What's maceration?'

I wasn't sure, but I had a recollection that wasn't reassuring. There used to be a display in the Museum of Edinburgh about taxidermy before the Tourism Directorate decided it was too gruesome for visitors. It also showed how bones were treated; like the snake skeletons I'd seen the other day.

'I'm begging you, don't open it,' said Hamish.

I paid no attention and unlatched the shiny door.

'Fuuu—' Hamish stumbled away, his eyes wide.

Inside the box – a kind of incubator, judging by the warmth – lay the skinned and partially defleshed body of a man. His eyeballs and ears had gone, as had the internal organs. I slammed the door shut.

'. . . uck,' said Hamish, finally catching his breath.

I walked on past the other two boxes, which were labelled Maceration 2 and 3, the first a forty-three-year-old woman and the last a seventy-four-year-old man. I left them with what dignity they still possessed. I came to a door, but this one wasn't locked. I immediately had a feeling of déjà vu. Bones were laid out on steel tables like in the morgue. These were complete skeletons. I grabbed the clip file from the first table.

'Subject: male. Age: 66. Maceration Stage: complete.'

I saw unsightly growths on the right femur and tibia.

Then I noticed the initials at the bottom of the page.

G. A. – George Allison, director of the cancer centre. I remembered the display cases in the corridor leading to his office. This was where he got his kicks. He'd be getting several hard ones from me when I next saw him.

'Can we get out of here?' Hamish said, staring at the bones. 'Look, this one's perfect,' he said, pointing at the last tray. He was right. I could see no sign of damage on the bones. The man must have died of organ or soft-tissue disease; or wounding.

I raised a hand and we both listened.

Hamish ran to the far door, then waved to me. I joined him.

'Boots and voices on the ground floor. I think the stunned sentries have been discovered.' He looked around. 'We need to get out of here.'

We moved down the corridor, putting as much distance between us and the intruders. Or rather, between us, the intruders and the personnel legitimately in the cancer centre.

'Fire hose,' Hamish said, unwinding it. 'Open that window.'

I did as I was told.

'Remember how to abseil?'

'Don't I need straps and a friction hitch?'

'Take my gloves.' Hamish gave me them and then went down quickly but in full control.

It was a long time since I'd done it but I trusted my ancient auxiliary training. I dropped faster than I'd have liked, but Hamish grabbed me as I reached the asphalt.

'I want to check another delivery,' I said, leading him back to the trailer park.

We ducked behind a chassis as shouts rang out.

'Hurry,' Hamish said.

I moved down the line of trailers, choosing the last one. Hamish did his trick with the lock and we opened the doors. Well, well. Not a surprise. There were stacks of plastic boxes marked 'Alceteron' – the supposed cure for alcoholism. I used my combat knife to cut the seal on one and then removed a small bottle. Sophia could run tests on it.

'We need to go,' Hamish said. 'They're getting close.'

'Diversion, please,' I said, looking at the high wall ahead.

He grinned and detached a grenade from his belt.

'Don't throw that anywhere near the biohazard rockets.'

'Good point.' He pulled the pin, drew back his arm and launched the device towards the wall on our left.

When it exploded we headed straight on.

'Any idea how we're going to get over that?' I asked.

He removed three more grenades. One he threw in the same direction as the first and the other two he rolled towards the wall. The detonations came in quick succession. The wall in front of us didn't come down, but it sustained a lot of surface damage. Hamish managed to clamber up using the hand and footholds that had appeared. I almost fell, but he grabbed my arm and hauled me up. Then we both dropped to the other side. The darkness of the Enlightenment Park lay ahead and we were soon lost in it.

We stopped running when my lungs were about to pack in, taking refuge behind a low rise.

'Do you want me to go back for the 4×4?' Hamish asked.

'Do you think you can make it?'

'No problem. I'll go south and cut through the backstreets. I'll call you when I'm in the park.'

'Do not go back to pick up your rucksack.'

'But the crossbow . . .'

'Forget it.'

He didn't reply and I didn't realize he'd gone until I stuck a hand out to where he had been.

Amazingly enough I fell asleep. It was a balmy night.

My phone rang a couple of hours later. It was still dark. Hamish said that he was approaching from the south. I got up, stretching my arms and legs, and stood by the road.

'Good,' I said, after I'd got in. 'You went the long way round.'

'Yes, I did,' he said brightly. Too brightly.

'Liar. Out with it.'

'Well, I did drive up Dalkeith Road. No one saw me pick up my pack.'

I looked between the seats and saw the haversack, crossbow visible, in the footwell behind his seat.

'That wasn't very smart.'

'I'd have been on a charge if I didn't sign the bow back in.'

'What about the grenades?'

'Oh, they're always going missing. People keep them after ops.'

That wasn't hugely reassuring. I wondered how many Guard personnel were patrolling with explosive devices in their pockets.

'Where to?'

I'd been thinking about that. 'Go round Arthur's Seat and take us back into the centre via Willowbrae and Parson's Green.'

Hamish turned the 4×4 round and drove on without comment. We were on the eastern side of the hill, near Dunsapie Loch – now stocked with flamingos for the tourists – when a light started moving from side to side ahead of us.

'Shit,' I said. 'Gangbangers.'

Hamish nodded. 'Guard personnel would use more than one light. Run them down?'

'They might have put rocks on the road – it wouldn't be the first time.'

Hamish floored the brake pedal and turned off the lights. 'You go left, I'll go right,' he said, rummaging in his pack.

I slipped into the darkness, then proceeded on all fours as I went round the light. It was still being waved. I crawled through the dew-heavy grass as I got closer.

Then a boot landed on my neck.

'Keep still and dinnae say a wurd,' came a low male voice.

I complied.

'Over here,' my captor called.

The light approached.

'Who's this then?' said the man carrying it. 'Are youse on yer own?'

I made to speak, then decided nodding was the better part of valour.

'Fuckin' Guard cunt,' said the man with his boot on me. 'Let's gut him.'

I was still wearing the black cape. My arms were spread and I couldn't get to the combat knife in my belt. Where the hell was Hamish?

'Better see who he is furst,' said the man with the light. 'Roll him over.'

I was roughly turned on to my back, Boot Man now standing over me with a foot on each arm. His pal started going through my pockets, grinning when he saw the knife.

'Anither yin for ma collection,' he said, transferring it to his belt.

Then he found my authorization.

'Fuck me, Lez, it's that fucker Dalrymple.'

'The cunt who works for the Cooncil? He's definitely gettin' his guts oot.'

There was a dull crack from nearby and the two men fell backwards. Each choked and jerked for a few seconds, then lay still. I got to my feet, rubbing my arms, as Hamish came into the circle of light.

'Good shot, eh?' he said.

I couldn't argue with that. The crossbow bolt had gone through Boot Man's throat and carried on into the other man's.

'Shot of the century, more like. You took your time, though.'

'Not much accurate range on these things. I had to get close.' He looked around. 'Lucky there were only two of them.'

'Let's not wait for their mates to turn up.'

Hamish pulled the bolt from the neck of the second victim. We ran back to the 4×4, using the dead men's light. The morning Guard patrol would pick up the bodies. The fact that one of them had a combat knife would consign them to the 'Forget It' file.

Twenty minutes later we were at the Darnaway Street entrance to Moray Place.

'Go to the castle and get some sleep, Hamish.'

'Yes, sir. Do I make a report?'

'No. Try to avoid the commander and the guardian. I'll talk to them first thing.'

'Right.'

'And, guardsman? Good work. I owe you one.'

'Several, I'd say,' he said, smiling.

'Don't push your luck, son.' I laughed and walked to the checkpoint.

It was four thirty a.m. and the guardsman outside Sophia's residence wasn't happy about letting me in, but I still had my authorization.

I took off my sodden jacket and muddy boots, then went up to the mistress bedroom. Sophia woke the minute I opened the door and turned on the light.

'Quint? What's going on?'

'Nothing. My clothes are coming off, though.'

I had a quick shower and joined her in the bed.

'I've got a present for you,' I said, kissing her.

'I'm half asleep,' she said, with a groan.

I handed her the bottle of Alceteron. That woke her up fully.

'Get this tested, please,' I said. 'And be careful. There were rockets marked "BIOHAZARD" in the vicinity of the shipment.'

Then, against plentiful odds, I fell fast asleep.

Twenty-Three

'Well, well, look what the pygmy hippo, back from the dead, dragged in,' said Davie, arms akimbo.

I walked past him towards his office. Fortunately James Michie wasn't in the command centre. I had three texts from him asking where I was. I'd slept late and lunch would be standing in for breakfast.

'Coffee?' he said, not waiting for an answer and pouring me a cup from the flask on his desk.

I sat down, drank and quickly felt better.

'Know anything about two headbangers near Dunsapie Loch with what look like crossbow-bolt wounds in their necks?'

I shrugged. 'I don't even know how to work a crossbow.'

'No, but Heriot 619 does; plus, he signed one in this morning.'

'Leave the laddie alone. He's a real find.' I grinned. 'Reminds me of you when you were young.'

Davie grunted. 'Anything to report?'

'Well, you already know about the attack on the lorries outside the cancer centre.'

He nodded. 'All the drivers were killed, which leaves us without a clue about where they came from. Two of the attackers were picked up, both badly wounded. One of them died on the way to the infirmary and the other's in surgery.'

'They must have crossed the line. Someone's on the take there. On the border too.'

He scowled. 'Aye, as far as the techies can tell, there aren't any Edinburgh markings on what's left.'

'One of them was carrying liquid natural gas, whence the big bang.'

'I thought LNG wasn't explosive.'

'Search me. Maybe the tank was defective.'

'The other trucks were carrying small-arms ammunition and coils of steel sheeting respectively.' He looked up from the file he was reading. 'What the hell, Quint?'

I told him what we'd found in the trailers.

'Rocket heads marked BIOHAZARD? I can't keep that from the guardian.'

'I think you'd better. We can't be sure whose side he's on.'

Davie shook his head. 'I can't be sure how many sides there are in this case. Anyway, what's stuff like that doing in the cancer centre?'

'A very good question.'

'There were reports of small explosions in the cancer centre later in the night. You know anything about that?'

'Reports from whom?'

'The surveillance team – one of them stayed in the vehicle to monitor the north side.'

'Ah. We were causing a diversion.'

'Or two.'

'Yes.'

'You need to do some strategic advising if you want to stay alive, Quint.'

'I do.' The problem was, there were too many loose ends.

'Oh,' Davie said, 'we caught that kid Kennie out in Firrhill this morning.'

That perked me up. 'Is he here?'

'He is. He's already eaten two breakfasts.'

'Let's go and talk to him. Have you got his file?'

'He isn't an Edinburgh citizen.'

'How do you know that?'

'He told the team who grabbed him. He's been asking to see a Glasgow representative.'

'You haven't passed that on, I hope.' Most of the other Scottish states and regions have offices in the city. Edinburgh doesn't send the same to outsider states – the Council was too afraid of them being turned against the 'perfect' city.

'Do I look like a clown?'

I grinned. 'Not right now.'

'Piss off. I'll go and see if the guardian's around. If he isn't, I'll take you to the interrogation room.'

James Michie was still absent. That made me think. He usually spent much of the day in the command centre.

'Right, laddie,' Davie said, after we'd entered the grey-painted window-less room. The young man was handcuffed to the table, his broken nose and shaved head convincing statements of intent. 'Full name?'

'Fuck you.'

'Are you Chinese?' Davie asked.

'Awa' and bile yer heid, ya numpty!'

'That's OK,' I said, putting a hand on Davie's arm. 'Kenneth's fine.'

'Kennie, ya cunt.'

Davie raised his fist. 'Mind your tongue if you want to keep it.'

'Where's the Glesga guy, eh? Ye cannae keep me here.'

'Watch us,' said Davie.

'It's very simple,' I said, with a smile. 'The penalty for outsiders found in Edinburgh without papers is five years down the mines.'

The teenager tried to stay hard, but he was blinking too much.

'We can get you off that.'

'Whit dae Ah have tae dae?'

I shrugged. 'Talk.'

'Aw no, Ahm no clipin'.'

'No one's asking you rat on your pals,' I said. 'Just tell us what you're doing here.'

There was an interlude of shouting and swearing, none of it from our side of the table – remarkable restraint from Davie. Eventually Kennie dried up.

'I'll make it easier for you,' I said. 'Nod after each question.'

That got me a display of teeth-baring that would have gone down well in the zoo, but eventually he acquiesced.

'You used to meet the number 43 bus.'

Eventually he nodded.

'And take messages from the driver.'

Ditto.

'Which you gave to Dougie Dobie.'

'Who?'

His surprise seemed genuine. Had Peter Dobie misled me or had he been misled by Clarinda?

'Ronald Douglas Dobie.'

'Nivver heard ae him.'

'Goliath? Big guy?'

He raised his shoulders in ignorance.

'So who did you give the messages to?'

Kennie's grin was slack-mouthed.

'All right,' I said to Davie, 'break his fingers.'

'Now you're talking.' He grabbed Kennie's right hand and bent all the digits back.

'Naw, naw, Ah'll tell ye!'

'Last chance,' I warned.

'Aye, OK!'

Davie let go and scowled at the cringing youth.

'Who did you give the messages to?'

'How do Ah ken ye'll believe me?'

I smiled. 'You'll have to trust me to keep Thunder Boots here off your toes.'

'Aw right,' he said, hanging his head. 'Lachie.'

Davie and I exchanged glances.

'Lachie who?'

'Big Lachie.'

I glanced at Davie. He started looking for a photo of Goliath. Maybe he had yet another name.

Kennie shrugged. 'Nah, not him. Big Lachie's no' got any hair.'

Great. A big bald headbanger.

'What's his surname?'

'Whit?'

'Lachie who?'

'Dinnae ken.'

Davie applied main force.

'Ah tellt ye, Ah dinnae ken.'

I waved Davie away.

'So who tells Big Lachie what to do?' I asked. 'Hel Hyslop?'

'Fuck off. She's a fuckin' bitch.'

He was right there.

'What did she do to you?'

'Nuthin', but she's put plenty ae ma pals away.'

'So who's in charge?'

'Big Lachie.'

'What is he?' Davie said scathingly. 'A gang boss?'

'Naw!' Kennie was affronted. 'He's a freedom fighter. We all are.'

Davie burst out laughing, but I believed our prisoner.

'Who's he trying to free?' I asked.

Kennie gave me a broad grin. 'Everyone.'

'Do you know Clarinda Towart or Alice Lennox?' I asked.

'Naw,' he said emphatically.

Then he refused to say another word. I called Davie off before he did permanent damage.

Davie looked at me. 'Well, Mr Strategy, what does this mean?'

We were in the canteen, eating soup and filled rolls.

'There's no reference to any Lachie or Lachlan in the Guard database or in any of the files we're working,' I said.

'Must be an outsider,' Davie said, having emptied his third bowl. 'You saw Clarinda during the attack on the trucks. Maybe she's some kind of freedom fighter too.'

I nodded. 'I'll tell you what's weird. Kennie only—'

'Received messages, he didn't pass on replies. Or so he says.'

'Very good, commander. Meaning that this Lachie's got another way of communicating with his people in the city.'

'Clarinda, obviously.'

'Or Alice Lennox. He's got some balls, our Kennie.'

'We can't lay a finger on them, so that doesn't get us much further, Quint.'

'You think? Clarinda's running a group of rebels in the city. Alice is involved – maybe she took part in the attack on the cancer centre too.'

'So it was Clarinda who killed Chung Keng whatever his name is?'

'Quee.' I shrugged. 'Either her or one of her people.'

'Where does Goliath fit in?'

'He was working for the Lord of the Isles.'

'What's that scumbag aristo got to do with anything?'

'I think he's behind the Malaysian contracts. He's got oil money, remember.'

'And the Glaswegians – Andrew Duart and Hel Hyslop were in the Lucky Strike too.'

'They're all in bed together. MacLean's helping them take over Edinburgh, no doubt with a promise that he'll be the new boss.'

'So someone killed the Asian in Moredun to mess up the Malaysian contracts?'

I thought about that. 'Not sure. Remember the human bones you found? I'm wondering if they could be Magda MacFarlane's. Which points us to the cancer centre.' The horror of the maceration boxes came back to me. 'George Allison, the director, has got a thing about skeletons. He's also got a dwarf one on display.'

'And he's got a thing about biohazard rockets and other dubious cargoes.'

'He or someone else in the centre, yes.' I called Sophia.

'Quint, I was going to ring you.'

'Oh aye?'

'That sample of Alceteron you gave me. I'm glad you mentioned biohazard. My experts are still working on it, but it's definitely not an anti-alcoholism drug. It's a chemically engineered toxin and it's potentially lethal to humans and animals.'

I thought of the rocket heads again. 'Shit.'

'Indeed. What did you want from me?'

'Is there anyone else in your directorate with the initials "G.A."?'

She typed on her keyboard and then said, 'No, only George Allison.'

I thanked her and cut the connection. The initials 'G. A.' that I'd seen in the osteology research department were Allison's – confirmation but no surprise. I told Davie what I'd heard.

'So those Malaysian contracts include bio-weapons that could decimate the population of Edinburgh?'

'Or some other city.'

He stared at me. 'I'm losing track of this, Quint.'

I raised a hand. 'Clarinda Towart, who may have been working undercover as a rebel for years, finds out about the contracts from Chung Keng Quee's laptop – remember, it disappeared. She and her group go after the deliveries.'

'How did she find out where they were going?'

'Maybe that was in Chung's laptop too.'

'But why would official Finance Directorate orders be delivered to the cancer centre?'

'Because even though they're Finance Directorate orders, the Council doesn't know about them, so the Supply Directorate depot's out.' I had the feeling again that the senior guardian was out of that particular loop. 'So the Dobies were being used by both the Finance Directorate and Goliath.'

'Bit of a coincidence.'

'Unless Jack MacLean and Billy Geddes were trying to infiltrate Big Lachie's operation, using the least likely pair of couriers.' Then I thought of Clarinda Towart again. 'Or Clarinda was infiltrating the Finance Directorate. Her company was registered there.'

Unusually Davie was playing with a roll rather than eating it. 'Why did Goliath kill that Supply Directorate auxiliary?'

'John Rollo? Not sure, but I know how to find out. Oh fuck.'

Davie turned and gritted his teeth.

'There you two are,' said James Michie, arriving at our table. 'I've been looking all over for you. Why didn't you answer your phones?'

'Hello, guardian,' I said emolliently. 'We – I mean, Davie was undertaking an interrogation.'

'Sorry, guardian,' said Davie, playing along. 'I forgot to turn my phone back on.'

'Me too.' I shook my head. 'I need more sleep.'

Michie looked at us suspiciously, then sat down. 'Reports, please. You first, Dalrymple.'

So we were back to surnames. I couldn't really blame him, especially as I was about to give him another censored version of events. I still wasn't sure if we could trust him.

'Strategically,' I said, 'we're on the back foot.'

'I noticed,' he said drily. 'The senior guardian is pressing me about the attacks on the cancer centre.'

I glanced at Davie. 'I'm about to talk to the director, Dr Allison.'

'Rather late, aren't you?' Michie said.

Davie stepped in and told him about Kennie.

'Outsiders,' he said. 'I knew it. Speaking of which, where did those trucks come from?'

Good question, and one that would be a way of getting him off our backs.

'Guardian, could you put together a team to investigate the city line and border crossings?' I asked. 'You'll need to pick the most trustworthy people you have. I hate to say it, but Guard personnel are on the take.'

That fired him up and he left at speed. Fortunately he didn't order Davie to accompany him.

'He obviously doesn't think you're trustworthy,' I said.

'Screw you,' Davie said, with a grin.

I called Sophia again.

'I want to drag George Allison over the coals and I think it'll be more effective if you're there. Can you get him to the infirmary in an hour?'

'I can. Something to do with that attack outside the cancer centre?'

'That and the biohazard. Don't tell him anything though.'

'I'm not a complete idiot.'

'I'll take your word for it,' I said and hung up. 'Right, come on.'

Davie had finally polished off his roll. 'Where to?'

'So close we can walk – though we'll need transport afterwards, so let's not.'

As he drove off the esplanade, I said, 'The Tourism Directorate.'

He parked the 4×4 on the pavement in front of the steps, giving the guardsman on duty a steely look.

'Are you going to tell me what we're doing?' he said, as I led him up the stairs.

'Surprise.'

I was panting when we got to the sixth floor, but he wasn't.

Ross Parlane was at his desk outside his mother's office.

'Citizen,' he said. 'And commander. I'm afraid the guardian's in a meeting.'

I smiled. 'It's not her we want, it's you.'

The young auxiliary was immediately tense.

'Sit down, son,' Davie said.

After he'd done so, I stood over him across the desk, while Davie went behind him.

'Ross, you've been a bad boy,' I said.

'What do you mean?'

'Napier 311, a.k.a. John Rollo.'

The young auxiliary gulped – always a good sign.

'What about him?'

I clapped vigorously. 'Well done. You don't deny you knew him.'

'I knew him. What of it?'

I laughed and turned to Davie. '"What of it?" Been reading Walter Scott?' I leaned over the desk, all traces of good humour gone. 'What were you and he arguing about in the Supply Directorate depot shortly before he was murdered?'

A ghost couldn't have been paler. 'I . . . nothing . . .'

'You set him up, didn't you? You sent him to his death.'

Ross Parlane gaped at me. 'No . . .'

'Yes. Tell me why or I'll set the commander loose on you.'

The auxiliary looked down. He was shaking, his hands clasped tightly.

I decided to go for broke. 'Clarinda Towart. You're with her, aren't you?' I banged my hand on the desk and shouted, 'Aren't you?'

'Long . . . long live the revolution.'

'You little shit,' Davie said, grabbing Parlane and dragging him across the desk.

The door to the guardian's office opened.

'What on earth's going on?' demanded Mary Parlane. 'Quintilian?'

'Are you in on it too?' I asked quietly.

'Let go of my son!' she ordered.

Davie complied with alacrity. Ross's chin hit the desktop.

'You are, aren't you, Mary? You and Clarinda are mounting a rebellion.'

The tourism guardian stared at me. 'Don't be ridiculous.'

'That's why you covered up Magda MacFarlane's disappearance . . . Shit, Kate Revie's in on it too, isn't she?'

Mary Parlane was busy with Ross, settling him back into his seat and wiping his face.

'I think you'd better follow me, Quintilian,' she said, turning towards her office.

'No chance,' Davie said, taking command. 'We're all coming.' He beckoned to Ross, who stood up shakily.

I didn't think the guardian was dangerous, but Davie was right not to take any chances. There were bodies all over the city and I didn't know how connected Mary was.

'You were playing a double game, weren't you, Ross?' I said, looking at the miserable figure that Davie had pushed on to a chair. 'John Rollo was working for the Lord of the Isles. You wormed your way into his confidence and then tried to turn the screw on him. You wanted him to inform on his backer.'

'How do you know all this?' Mary said.

'I didn't,' I said, giving her a cold smile, 'until now. I thought Ross was part of Rollo's operation until he admitted to being with Clarinda.'

'Long live the revolution,' Ross said, this time more emphatically.

'Be quiet,' said his mother.

'And when Rollo wouldn't play ball,' I continued, 'you put Goliath on him, saying he was going to rat on their operation. But Goliath was working for the Lord of the Isles.'

'No comment,' said the guardian firmly.

Davie's hands tightened on Ross's shoulders.

'No comment,' the auxiliary said, his voice now weak.

'No comment, no freedom,' I said, first to Mary and then to Ross.

'You can't seriously be supporting the Council after what happened last night, Quintilian,' the guardian said. 'Who do you think the weapons in the cancer centre will be used against?'

That was the question. I gave it my best shot.

'Edinburgh citizens,' I said. 'MacLean and whoever else on the Council supports him are going along with the "yes" campaign, but they intend to take control of the city and stamp out any further movement towards democracy.'

Mary Parlane laughed bitterly. 'You don't know the half of it,' she said, shaking her head. 'MacLean and—'

She started to jerk about like a marionette, red blooms appearing on her white blouse. Then I heard the shots and watched from the floor as she collapsed over her desk. Bullets continued to thud into her back.

Ross's chair had gone backwards and Davie was under it, seemingly unharmed. The young auxiliary's grey suit jacket was a slew of blood, his head surrounded by a crimson mist.

The Parlanes' part in the revolution was well and truly over.

Twenty-Four

Eventually – though it was probably under thirty seconds – the shooting stopped. I'd taken refuge behind the steel file cabinet to the left of the guardian's desk, while Davie had miraculously been protected by Ross Parlane's riddled body. He rolled quickly to the far wall when the firing let up and squatted behind the mahogany dresser that displayed Mary's large collection of award shields and medals.

'What the fuck!' he yelled, fumbling with his phone. 'Shooting on top floor of Tourism Directorate, dispatch squads to buildings on north side of Lawnmarket now!'

I stayed where I was, thinking about what had happened. The Parlanes, obviously with Mary taking the lead, had moved against the Lord of the Isles' set-up in Edinburgh, even though they'd mistakenly believed Goliath was with them. That put them on the side of the angels. Those on Lucifer's team had taken them out in a way that replicated the killing of Goliath. Fergus Calder had been very eager for him to be disposed of. Did that mean he was behind this bloodbath too? Was MacLean with him? Mary hadn't mentioned the senior or the public order guardians, but she'd run out of time. I couldn't trust either of them.

'Let's get out of here,' Davie called. 'I'll go first.'

The room was full of dust and debris raised by the numerous rounds. I watched as he crawled quickly to the door, which was pocked by bullet holes.

'All right,' he said, from the other side.

I slithered like the fastest snake on the planet and got out of the line of fire.

'Lovely,' Davie said, shaking his head.

'Don't complain. You could have been perforated too.'

'You're even dumber than you look.'

'Meaning?' I was going through the papers on Ross's desk.

'Meaning the shooters were told not to hit us. Looked to me like they knew what they were doing.'

I filed that thought away – too much else was going on.

My phone rang.

'Where are you, Quint?'

'Sophia,' I said. 'We got . . . held up.'

'Well, don't bother coming if it's only for George Allison. He hasn't arrived and we can't locate him.'

'Interesting.'

'What?'

'Nothing. Leave it with me. See you later.'

There was a clatter of boots on the stairs and the door was shoved open. Hamish appeared at the front of a squad, Hyper-Stun in one hand. At least he hadn't brought the crossbow.

'You're in one piece,' he said, grinning at me.

'So am I, guardsman,' said Davie gruffly.

I couldn't help laughing. When it veered towards hysteria, I got a grip on myself. I'd known Mary Parlane since I joined the Enlightenment Party before the last election in 2003. She didn't deserve to die like that and neither did her son. There would be a reckoning.

Shortly afterwards, James Michie arrived. He took in the scene in Mary's office and emerged paler than a herring gull's chest. That was in his favour – or maybe he was just squeamish.

'Any sign of the shooter or shooters?' Davie said, on his phone. He listened and then groaned.

'What is it?' asked the guardian.

'Plenty of shell casings in the top room opposite but no fucking people. They're looking for witnesses.'

If Michie was taken aback by Davie's improper language, he didn't show it. He took me aside.

'This is a nightmare, Quint. A guardian killed in the middle of the tourist zone.'

'I'm sure you'll think of something to tell our esteemed visitors – a Guard exercise with blanks or the like.'

'Yes, but a guardian killed. That's only happened once before.'

It had and I was an eyewitness.

'A guardian and her son.'

'What?'

'The dead auxiliary's name is Ross Parlane.'

His surprise seemed genuine. 'That's . . . that's appalling. But how did he come to be working here?' Guardians were supposed to keep their children at arm's length, though since the regulations were loosened, there had been other examples of nepotism – though none at such a high level.

I shrugged. 'Shouldn't you be asking why they were killed?'

'Yes, of course.'

'Any ideas?' I said, pressing him.

He didn't like that. 'You're the man in charge of strategy in this investigation. What do you think?'

I was mulling over how much to tell him when my phone rang.

'Dalrymple, this is the senior guardian. Come to my office in the Supply Directorate immediately. Alone.'

'No.'

'I beg your pardon?'

'I'm bringing my sidekicks – two of them.'

There was silence on the line.

'Very well,' Fergus Calder said, then broke the connection.

'The senior guardian,' I said, to James Michie. 'My presence is required.'

'I'll come with you.'

'No, you won't.' I turned away. 'Davie, Hamish, let's move.'

'But . . .' said Michie.

'He hasn't asked you to come, has he?' I said. 'The trucks at the cancer centre – did you get anywhere on how they got through the border and the city line?'

His expression lightened. 'Yes. I've brought in everyone who was on duty yesterday afternoon and evening at the Soutra border post and the Sheriffhall tower on the city line.'

'Anyone talking?'

The guardian shook his head.

'Davie'll come back later with his thumbscrews.' I suspected the auxiliaries the Lord of the Isles had suborned would be difficult to break, even with Davie in Torquemada mode.

'What are you going to tell the senior guardian?' Michie said, grabbing my arm.

There was a question.

'I'll think of something,' I said, wondering how much to divulge.

As it turned out, the decision was easy.

The three of us took the stairs to the sixth and top floor of the dreary grey concrete and glass building next to what used to be Waverley Station. Hamish was easily first, Davie a creditable second and I a discreditable last. I bent over and sucked in air when we got there.

A guardsman in full combat gear stood at the near end of the corridor.

'Weapons?' he said, extending an arm.

'No,' said Davie and Hamish in unison.

The guardsman spoke into his comms unit and half a dozen comrades joined him.

'You out-Stun us,' I said. 'What's the problem?'

The guardsman spoke into his throat mike again, fiddling with his earpiece. 'Very well,' he said. 'The senior guardian will see you.'

We followed him down the corridor. It smelled of wood polish and air freshener, not that anything was going to cover the stink of corruption and treachery. The question was, how involved was Fergus Calder?

The door to his sanctum was opened by a guardswoman with dead eyes. We trooped in. To my surprise, none of the Guard personnel followed us. That wasn't the only shocker. Jack MacLean was standing to the left of the senior guardian's chair, while Billy Geddes's wheelchair was on his right.

'Sit down, gentlemen,' the senior guardian said.

'No, thanks,' I said, scowling at the trio. 'So you've all opened your legs to the Lord of the Isles. And let me guess – Andrew Duart too.'

Calder smiled. 'You're under a misapprehension, citizen. Oh, and my sincere condolences on the death of your father.'

Jack MacLean muttered something similar, while Billy opened his mouth.

'Fuck off,' I said to him, before he could speak. It wasn't just that the old man despised my former friend; I was guilty that I'd forgotten Hector so quickly.

'There's no need for animosity,' Calder said.

I gave a hollow laugh. 'Someone just displayed terminal animosity to the tourism guardian and her son in the city you're supposed to run.'

'Watch it,' said the finance guardian.

'And fuck you too,' I said. 'Have you sold the whole city to Malaysia yet?'

That caught the attention of all three behind the desk.

'Malaysia?' the senior guardian said. 'What do you mean?'

Jack MacLean whispered in his ear, while Billy gave me a look of superciliousness mixed with derision, his damaged face more macabre than ever.

'I know there are contracts with Malaysian companies, of course,' said Fergus Calder, 'but what have they to do with the tourism guardian's death?'

I wondered again about how much he knew. I needed to watch what I said.

'You remember how this case started?'

'Of course,' the senior guardian said, in irritation. 'With the murder of that Malaysian.'

'Chung Keng Quee. Can any of you tell me what he was doing in the city?'

'He represented several of the companies we're doing business with,' said Billy.

'Uh-huh – companies supplying the Finance Directorate with weapons, including rockets, propulsion gas and biohazardous material for the warheads.'

Fergus Calder's forehead looked like it had just been ploughed. MacLean bent to speak to him, but this time was brushed away.

'Is this true?' the senior guardian demanded.

I was right. MacLean and Geddes had been building their own fiefdom.

'Of course not,' the finance guardian said dismissively. 'Citizen Dalrymple's nothing but trouble. I've been saying for days that he should be dismissed.'

Calder ignored that, having turned to Billy. 'What have you done, you scheming little shit?'

'Nothing that isn't in the city's best interest,' MacLean's special adviser, executive said, holding the senior guardian's gaze.

'And how are biohazardous warheads to Edinburgh's benefit?' I demanded.

'You don't know what you're saying, Dalrymple,' MacLean said. 'You're out of your depth, man.'

'Is that right? Why does the city need main battle tanks?'

Fergus Calder looked like he'd been kicked in the balls. 'What?'

The finance guardian pursed his lips. 'That's only a provisional order. We haven't confirmed it.'

The senior guardian picked up his desk phone. 'Guard personnel in here immediately,' he said.

Billy grinned at me.

Four of the heavies we'd seen outside entered.

'Take the finance guardian and his lackey to the castle,' Calder ordered.

'Senior guardian,' said the squad leader.

In a few seconds MacLean and Geddes had gone, both without a word.

'I knew nothing of this, citizen,' said the senior guardian. 'What else have you discovered?'

I was in a spot. He seemed to be on the level, but long experience of guardians had taught me that they could never be fully trusted. Then again, I'd been kept on the case, obviously at his insistence, despite MacLean's attempts to have me ditched. I started with the Malaysian contracts. Fergus Calder had only heard about the one regarding tourists from that country.

'Is that why Mary was shot?' he asked.

I let that question go unanswered. 'The cancer centre – you heard about the attacks on the trucks there?'

'The public order guardian advised me, yes. Why were shipments being sent there?'

I kept my eyes on his. He didn't seem to be play-acting.

'That's one of the things I'm trying to find out. George Allison seems to have done a bunk.'

The guardian looked at me and then shook his head. 'I never liked that man.'

'How did he end up in the job, then? And don't tell me the medical guardian was keen on him.'

'No, she wasn't. He had good connections with the Finance Directorate even before he was appointed.'

'So Jinglin' Jack talked you into it?'

Calder nodded, grimacing as if his chair had just given him an enema.

'I presume the Guard squad that took MacLean and Geddes away is part of the team assigned to you,' I said. The Finance Directorate would have its own heavies.

'Get after them,' I said, to Davie and Hamish. 'There could be an attempt to free them.'

They exited at speed.

'Shit,' said Calder, head in his hands. 'What have I done?'

'I'd like an answer to that.'

He looked at me wearily. 'You've no idea how difficult it's become to run this city. The referendum has turned everything upside down.'

'The Council's actively encouraging a "yes" vote. Most citizens are pleased about that.'

'The citizens, in the main, are not the problem.'

'The outsider states.'

The guardian nodded. 'We've had to negotiate with them because otherwise we'd be a target. Last week Glasgow overthrew the feminist administration in Stirling.'

That made my heart miss a beat. My former lover Katharine Kirkwood had ended up there after she left Edinburgh a couple of years back.

'How bloody was it?'

'Not very, I heard. Some of the leadership escaped, probably towards the collectivist state of Dundee, though they won't stand much chance in Perthshire – it's more feudal than it was two hundred years ago.'

Great, but I had to let that go.

'Look, Fergus,' I said, still unsure how much I could trust him, 'we have to control this before more guardians are shot to pieces.' That got his attention. 'I don't know who took the risk of attacking Mary Parlane in her office, but she and her son were in contact with rebels.'

'Rebels,' he repeated hoarsely. 'The ones who blew up the house in Blackhall?'

'Alice Lennox is part of it and Clarinda Towart's involved too. I saw her outside the cancer centre last night.'

'What?' Calder spluttered. 'Why wasn't I informed?'

I shrugged. 'I'm still trying to work out what's going on. But it's pretty clear that the rebels – Mary's son, Ross, saw himself as a revolutionary – are aware of the Malaysian shipments, whence the attack. I'm guessing they found about them from Chung Keng Quee and/or the dead Asian in the house in Moredun.'

'We have to secure the cancer centre.'

I nodded. 'Do you trust James Michie?'

'Of course,' the guardian said pompously. 'I appointed him.'

I let out a sigh. 'Could he have gone over to MacLean?'

'I don't think so.'

'Then again,' I said, with a slack smile, 'I'm still not sure if I trust you. It isn't long since you and the finance guardian were gland in gland.'

Fergus Calder glared at me. 'I resent that. All I've ever done is my best for the city.' He paused. 'But recently I've got the feeling that Jack and Billy are following their own agenda. I haven't seen the Lord of the Isles or Andrew Duart for at least six weeks.'

'Even though they were in the city a couple of days ago – and may still be.'

'To be fair, I've kept my distance on the grounds of propriety. As head of state I have to retain a certain neutrality.'

'Unlike Duart and MacDonald?'

My phone rang.

'You were right, Quint,' Davie said. 'Two unmarked 4×4s intercepted the vehicle taking the finance guardian and fucking Geddes to the castle.'

'Where?'

'On the High Street, by St Giles.'

'Tell me they didn't get away.'

There was silence on the line.

'They were quick. The first one crashed through the checkpoint on George IV Bridge. The second took heavy fire but kept going. I've ordered a general alert.'

'I think they'll be heading for the cancer centre.'

'I've got road blocks on the main roads and patrols in the backstreets. They definitely won't make it to Pollock.'

'Casualties?'

'Two guardsmen killed and a guardswoman took a bullet in the thigh.'

'Are you telling the tourists it's another exercise?'

'Bit hard with blood and guts all over the place.'

'Is Hamish OK?'

'Aye.'

'Send him back here for me. I'll meet you in the command centre.'

'What about me?' the senior guardian said, almost plaintively.

I got to my feet. 'Stay here. Seal the building after I've gone.'

'Citizen, you're forgetting I'm in command.'

'Are you?' I said, turning on my heel.

The fact that he didn't call me back showed how little faith he had in his executive power.

Hamish, grinning vastly, was waiting for me outside the Supply Directorate.

'What are you so pleased about?'

'All this action. It's what I've been waiting for.'

'Guardsmen who get gung-ho are sent to the border.'

'I'm game.'

He drove up Jeffrey Street and on to the High Street. Further up, the road had been cordoned off but we were let through. I looked at the bullet-spattered carcass of a Guard 4×4. The bodies of the dead had been removed, but there was no shortage of blood. Davie must have given the order to clear the scene. I didn't have a problem with that. There was no need for Sophia or a scene-of-crime team. If the Old Town's main street wasn't back in operation for the tourists soon, there would be a panic.

As we headed for the esplanade, I realized that Clarinda Towart must have been working on revolution for a long time – long enough to convince Mary and Ross Parlane, let alone Kate Revie, of the need for change.

I wished I knew what she had planned next.

Twenty-Five

Davie and James Michie were in the command centre.

'Any sign of them?' I asked.

'No, citizen,' said the guardian, giving me a disapproving look. 'Why wasn't I informed that the finance guardian and his lapdog were being sent here?'

'Take that up with the senior guardian,' I said, uninterested in power games, especially now.

I called Sophia. 'Everything all right?'

'Why shouldn't it be?' she said, immediately suspicious.

'You heard about Mary Parlane and her son?'

'Yes. Awful.'

'And about MacLean and Geddes?'

'That they're enemies of the people? My, was I surprised.'

'Irony,' I said admiringly. 'I'm making progress at last.'

'Is there a reason for this call?' she said. I could tell she was smiling.

'That toxin – any update?'

'It's bad, in terms you can understand. One drop, aerated, could kill dozens of people in an enclosed space.'

'Great. And there are thousands of drops in the cancer centre. No sign of Allison, I suppose?'

'We can't get through to the place at all, by landline, mobile or any other way. It's like the centre's been shut off.'

'It very likely has. Have you increased the guard on the infirmary gate?'

'A message came from the command centre.'

'Is that a yes?'

'Of course, fool.'

'Love you too.' I cut the connection before she could reply. It didn't do to push Sophia too far.

Michie was on the phone, sitting in his chair on the dais, when I turned back.

'He's talking to the senior guardian,' Davie whispered. 'What's the plan, Mr Strategist?'

I was still thinking about that when the guardian re-joined us, holding his phone out. I took it.

'Dalrymple, I've told James that you have complete command.'

'Of what?'

'Of everything – the location and capture of Jack, I mean, MacLean and Geddes, the confiscation of all illicitly procured goods and putting down the so-called revolution.'

'Is that it? I'll be done by the Council meeting.'

'You aren't as funny as you think. And I'm cancelling the meeting. There's too much going on.'

'Also, of the guardians who haven't died or done a bunk, you don't know who you can trust.'

'Get the job done, man.'

'Jobs.'

He rang off.

'So,' said James Michie, 'you're senior to me.'

'No, I'm not, but I'm relying on you for support.'

'What do you need?'

'Let's talk about that.'

We only had one argument and I won it.

Half an hour later I left the castle with Hamish. Davie took four squads and turned right at the Tourism Directorate, heading for the cancer centre, while we continued down the High Street. After we got on to St Mary's Street, the 'yes' posters and banners increased in number. I'd almost forgotten about the referendum.

'Will this guy be armed?' Hamish asked.

'Did you just lick your lips? Yes, he might well be.'

'Ideally we should have backup.'

'Everyone else is busy, as you well know. And how many of your comrades we can trust is another issue.'

'I don't know anyone who's gone over to the finance guardian.'

'Guess what, Hamish. They've been keeping it secret.'

'I'd have spotted it. I've got an unusually high level of emotional intelligence. You can check my file.'

'That won't be necessary. Right, this is close enough.'

He parked under a tree. The blocks of flats in Dumbiedykes loomed in the late afternoon light.

'If we're lucky, he'll be asleep,' I said. 'Do *not* stun him, all right?'

'What if he comes at us with an axe?'

'Well, yes, obviously then.'

'Or a Jarilo .45?'

I'd forgotten about the Eastern European pistol that Goliath had used. I had a feeling we'd see more of those before this case was over.

'All right, put your Hyper-Stun on minimum.'

'Are you sure?'

By this time we were near the first block. Maybe I shouldn't have given James Michie a tongue-lashing when he told me he'd removed surveillance from Rory Campbell since the actor-director's movements had been regular and unsuspicious. Even an experienced Guard team would have eventually stuck out like fingers with no nails in this neck of citizen Edinburgh. But Campbell had been off my radar for some time and he was a strong lead to Clarinda Towart. People stared at Hamish's uniform with undisguised disgust, which he paid no attention to. In fact, he lapped it up.

'This is it,' I said. I led him in the open street door and up the stairs, which reeked of cleaning fluid and what it hadn't cleaned adequately.

'That one?' Hamish said, pointing his weapon at the half-open door to our right.

I went forward on the balls of my feet, entering the flat without touching the door. The lights were on and I could hear a tap dripping in the depths of the place.

'Someone had fun,' Hamish said, inclining his head to the living room.

It looked like an elephant had come to tea — the drapes had been torn down, furniture upended, crockery broken, and there were books all over the floor. The door ahead was also ajar, but this time the light was off. The sound of water dripping was louder now.

I moved forward.

'What the—?'

Hamish pushed past me.

'You're kidding,' he said.

'Not me.'

On the base of the shower lay a heap of white bones. On top of them sat a human skull, also pristine. They had to have come from the boxes in the Osteological Research unit in the cancer centre.

Hamish swallowed hard. So much for his bravado, though I couldn't blame him.

Someone had sent Rory Campbell a message that wasn't hard to decipher.

Was it the missing Dr Allison? And where was the actor-director? If I was him, I'd head straight for the border.

* * *

We went back to the 4×4, scaring off a group of small boys. It was nearly six p.m., too early for much to be going on at the Theatre of Life, but we had to check it out.

On the way I rang Davie.

'Anything to report?'

'Have I called you?' he said testily.

'So you're where you ought to be.'

'Yes.'

'This is like getting blood from a crag.'

'Nothing's happening. No sign of MacLean or Geddes. That's good, isn't it?'

'Maybe.'

'What about you?'

I told him about the bones.

'What the hell?'

'Someone – probably from the cancer centre – is trying to put the shits up Campbell.'

'That he'll end up as a skeleton?'

'Genius. I'll check in after we've been to the theatre.'

'If I'm still answering my phone.'

I froze. 'The biohazard?'

'And the other weapons that might be in the cancer centre.'

'Keep your distance.'

'Guess what? I am.'

He broke the connection.

Shortly afterwards Hamish pulled up outside the Theatre of Life. The doors were chained and there was no sign of life. Which was odd. Surely there would have been some people in evidence.

I got out and hammered on the glass. Nothing.

'Excuse me,' said Hamish, nudging me out of the way. He disposed of the chain with a bolt cutter. 'Standard Guard equipment,' he said, with a smile.

'Not in my day,' I muttered. We'd have used a hand grenade.

We went in. The foyer was clean, but silent as a stone. The place was festooned with posters and banners for *Spar/Tak/Us*. There were even swords and shields on the walls, cut and dented as if they'd been in countless battles.

I pushed open the door and walked into the auditorium. It had been cleaned as well, everything ready for the next horde of citizen spectators. I remembered the audience participation, actors mixing with the crowd, encouraging them to sing and cheer. The great crimson backcloth hung at the rear of the stage, reminding me of Edgar Allan Poe's *Masque of the Red Death*. Everyone died at the end of that story – 'And Darkness and Decay and the Red Death held illimitable dominion over all'. Was that the fate awaiting Edinburgh from the toxin and the rockets that would carry it?

'You look like you've seen a squad of ghosts.'

I turned to Hamish. 'More, many more. Come on.'

We climbed up on to the stage and went down the stairs on the left. The passage led to dressing rooms, prop stores and so on. I raised a hand.

'Did you hear that?' I whispered.

Hamish cocked his head, then nodded and drew his Hyper-Stun.

The sound – a series of light thuds – came from further down the corridor. I followed the guardsman. He stopped outside the room that I remembered being Campbell's. Someone had stuck a piece of paper on the closed door. It read '*STAR / Tak / Us*' – evidence of the actor-director's popularity.

I nodded to Hamish and he opened the door at speed, weapon raised.

'Clear,' he said.

I went in and looked around. Campbell's costumes were hung on a rail, his swords and helmets in a heap in the far corner. The large mirror was in the gloom, so I switched on the lights that surrounded it.

'Ew,' said Hamish.

'Ew indeed.'

A tongue had been fixed to the centre of the reflecting glass. It looked human and adult-sized.

'Is this telling your man not to talk?' Hamish said.

'You think? Where is he?'

'Here,' came a familiar voice.

I whipped my head round and took a heavy blow to my lower jaw.

Abyssal darkness.

I came to with a serious pain in my face and a bright light in my eyes. I blinked, then mumbled as I found that my hands were secured behind my back and my ankles bound.

'What?' said the man whose voice I'd recognized. 'I can't make you out, Citizen Dalrymple. In all sorts of ways.'

The light was moved and I saw a form in a dark jacket and trousers.

'George Allison,' I said, my voice sounding strange.

'Quintilian,' he said, squatting. 'You've been looking for me.' He smiled. 'I thought I'd make your job easier.'

'Very kind. Where's Hamish?'

'The guardsman? Don't worry about him.'

I stared at the doctor and got a blank look in return. 'If you've hurt him . . .'

'You'll what?' he said, grabbing my chin. 'Spit on me?'

I took a deep breath and prepared to reason with him. I wasn't in a position to do much else because he was holding a scalpel in his other hand.

'What do you want with Rory Campbell? Was it you who put the bones in his shower?'

'One of my people. He's been a pain in my colon.'

'What with him being a rebel and you being in with Jack MacLean?'

Allison stared at me and then laughed. 'You think you know it all, don't you?'

I tried to shrug. 'Fill me in.'

'Oh, I will. Once you're in the first maceration box.'

I shivered.

'I know you were in the lab, Dalrymple,' the doctor said, holding the scalpel against my nose. 'There are cameras.'

'Who are the people you process there?' I said, swallowing back bile.

'Citizens who meet my requirements.'

'What, you pick them off the streets?'

'Nothing as crude. They're relatives and friends of patients. When they arrive at the centre, my people gauge their potential and then they . . . disappear.'

'Ever heard of the Hippocratic oath?'

He smiled crookedly. 'Ever heard of *droit de seigneur?*'

'What, you screw them before killing them?'

'I was using the term metaphorically. I'm the master of the centre and I have the right to do as I like.' He rocked back on his heels, eyes on mine. 'Though that's a thought. I'm sure there are large men on my staff who would appreciate the chance to sodomize you.'

My mouth filled with foul-tasting liquid, but I swallowed it. I had to keep on questioning him. He was arrogant enough to gloat about his achievements. Then again, he'd probably cut my throat afterwards. Even more reason to stall him.

'Why have you been stockpiling weapons, including a lethal toxin, at the cancer centre?'

'Why do you think?'

'As I said, you're working with Jack MacLean. You were seen with his SPADE Billy Geddes.' I smiled sadly. 'That was my father's last contribution to intelligence-gathering.'

Allison laughed. 'A useless one, I'm afraid, though I mourn the former guardian's parting.'

I bit back an insult that would have led to my immediate death. 'Magda MacFarlane. You put her through the maceration boxes.'

'Magda . . .? Oh, the dwarf. Yes, I did.'

'So how did her bones end up in Mungo Rollo's house in Moredun?'

'Ah, Mungo. Drunks are so useful. Promise them a bottle and they'll do anything. It was a lure, of course.'

'So Mungo was working for you and MacLean.'

'If you say so.'

He was managing to gloat without owning up to much. I needed to get in his face.

'The tongue on the mirror. I suppose you took it from a patient.'

He nodded, his expression impassive. 'Where else? Inoperable cancer of the lower jaw. We put him out of his misery.'

'Good of you. The senior guardian knows about the weapon stocks. The clock's ticking.'

Allison shrugged. 'Anyone who goes near the toxin or the rockets will get a nasty surprise.'

'MacLean wants to take over the city after the referendum,' I said, speaking quickly as the scalpel came closer. 'I suppose you'll become medical guardian.'

'Instead of your girlfriend?' He caught my gaze. 'It's the maceration boxes for her. Maybe we'll put you together. That would be romantic.'

I saw a shadow to his rear.

'Please, Doctor,' I begged, 'I'll do anything . . .'

'Yes, you—'

Allison's face screwed up in agony as a spear point appeared to the right of his sternum. Then it was pulled out and he crashed back, clutching the wound and gasping for breath.

'Hello, citizen,' said Rory Campbell. He was dressed in combat fatigues that weren't Guard issue.

'Cut me free, will you?'

'Of course.' The actor-director used a *Spar/Tak/Us* sword on my bonds.

'Pretty sharp for a prop.'

'I have real ones for situations like this.' Campbell helped me to my feet. 'What do you want to do with him?'

I looked at him. 'You're in charge.'

'No, no, I'm just helping out.'

'Have you seen a young guardsman?'

He shook his head. 'Sorry. Allison had a couple of bodyguards. We dealt with them.'

'Right. Can I call the medical guardian?'

'Go ahead. I'll be out of here in seconds.'

I followed him up the stairs that led to the stage.

'Sophia, get paramedics to the Theatre of Life, star's dressing room. George Allison's there. His right lung's been pierced.'

'Quint? What about—'

I cut the connection. Sophia would be worried, but there was no time to lose. I caught up with Rory Campbell.

'Where are you going? To start the revolution?'

He turned to me. 'You *have* been busy, citizen.'

'Call me Quint. I can help.'

'By handing us over to the Guard? I don't think so.'

'The opposite – I can get you past the Guard.'

That stopped him in his tracks.

'Don't tell me you've suddenly changed sides, Quint. You've been the Council's lackey for years.'

I followed him across the empty auditorium, seeing my father's wrinkled face and hearing him tell me to clean up the city. He wouldn't have been able to stomach leaders prepared to use biohazardous weaponry on citizens.

'The city's going to go back to the Dark Ages after the referendum, Rory. And I know Mary Parlane and her son were with you.'

He stopped again. 'Were?'

Shit, he didn't know – news of their murders had been suppressed. I told him what happened.

'Those fucking bastards,' he said, breaking into a run.

A green van with a windowless cargo space was waiting at the kerb.

'Take me with you,' I said, as he opened the door.

'Why?'

'I've got friends in the Guard and the Medical Directorate.'

'The Guard's riddled with MacLean's supporters.'

The young woman at the wheel looked in the mirror. 'We need to go.'

'All right,' Rory said, taking me round to the other side and opening the door. 'But if I find out you're playing a double game, I'll gut you like a fish.'

A reply didn't seem advisable. He slammed the door and the young woman drove on.

'Who's this?' she asked, glancing at me.

'The famous Quintilian Dalrymple,' Rory said.

'That fucker?'

'He's one of us now, or so he says.'

'I want to keep loss of life to a minimum if it comes to violence.'

'It already has,' Rory said grimly.

'Why did your people blow up the Guard 4×4 on Ravelston Dykes and the Lennox house in Blackhall?'

He glanced at me. 'The former wasn't planned and the latter was a precaution. We knew you were getting close.'

'So it's my fault. Fuck you.'

Rory's face remained expressionless. 'Not your fault, apart from the fact that you've been working for the Council.'

'Several of whose members are, or were, with you – Mary Parlane, Kate Revie. Are there any more?'

'Possibly.'

We were heading down Minto Street, faster than was advisable at night. I wondered how much of my conversation with George Allison he'd heard.

'You do know that there's a stockpile of weapons in the cancer centre?'

'Of course,' Rory said. 'We've been attacking the shipments – small arms, ammunition, LNG . . .'

'I noticed. Are you aware there are rockets that can deliver a lethal toxin?'

'What?' they both said.

I explained.

'Jesus,' Rory said. 'That changes everything.'

'It does. Assuming Allison's got a team of specialists and that MacLean is pulling the strings, the danger to Edinburgh citizens is huge. Guard personnel I trust are watching the cancer-centre gates, but it's possible there are people already on the loose, ready to use the toxin.'

'Fucking MacLean and the shrivelled bastard who does his dirty work,' Rory said.

'Billy Geddes.' Now wasn't the time to tell them I'd been a friend of the SPADE. 'They were freed from a Guard vehicle on the High Street several hours ago. As far as I know, they aren't in the cancer centre.'

'Checkpoint ahead,' the driver said. 'Got our papers?'

'Let me do this,' I said. When we stopped, I held out my authorization. As I did, it struck me that the Guard personnel manning the post might be with MacLean.

'Right you are, citizen,' said the middle-aged guardsman with a nod.

'Keep this to yourself, please,' I said.

He tapped his nose as he raised the barrier.

'See?' I said. 'Aren't I useful?'

Rory looked at me and laughed. 'So far.'

'Where are we going?'

'Wait and see,' he said, turning round and clambering over the seat. I did as I was told. I could hear metallic noises from the rear.

'What's your name?' I asked the driver.

'Clarinda,' she said.

'Really?' I knew she wasn't Clarinda Towart. Then I got it. 'You're Spartacus,' I said to the actor-director.

'That's the idea,' Rory said, handing me a Guard-issue Hyper-Stun. 'All female revolutionaries are known as Clarinda and all males as—'

'Rory. How imaginative.'

'It's worked so far,' he said, coming back over with two large pistols.

'Jarilo .45s,' I said, recognizing them in the dashboard light.

'Correct.'

'Did you or one of your people kill an Asian in Moredun?'

'No comment.'

I sat back and considered my options. Rory seemed to trust me and he hadn't done anything to scare me – yet. But the thought that Allison's people might be out in the city with toxin in their pockets made me very nervous.

'We're going the wrong way,' I said, as we turned on to Gilmerton Road. 'The danger's in the centre. We need to find MacLean and get him to call his killers off, wherever they are.'

Rory turned to me. 'You're right,' he said. 'If you like, you can have a go at persuading the fucker.'

Then I got it. MacLean and Billy hadn't been rescued by their supporters. They'd been snatched by the rebels.

Twenty-Six

The young woman turned into the backstreets and I soon lost my bearings. She stopped outside a two-storey house that would have been built by the city council long before the Enlightenment Party came to power. There were no street lamps. Rory nudged me and I opened the door, then passed between the folds of a black-out curtain. Even in the inadequate lighting I was aware that dark-clothed figures were all around.

'It's all right, he's with me,' the actor-director said.

'It's that cunt Dalrymple,' I heard a male voice exclaim.

'I said, he's with me,' Rory said firmly.

No one else spoke. I was impressed. He pushed me further into the house. There was a thick curtain behind the door that blocked the lights inside. The sitting-room windows were covered by dark curtains. There was a foul smell in the air. The furniture was Supply Directorate basic, the yellow sofa well past its issue-by date. Then I realized who was crumpled up on it, facing away.

'Billy!'

Then my phone rang.

'Put it on speaker,' Rory said. 'Quiet, everyone.'

'Quint?' said Davie.

'Aye. What's going on?' There was a lot of crackle on the line.

'Can't you hear? War's broken out.'

I looked at Rory. He was nodding.

'Rebels?' I asked cautiously.

'Rebels or outsiders, I can't tell the difference, but there's a lot of them. They've blown up the cancer-centre gate on Dalkeith Road.'

'What are you doing?'

'Asking for orders.'

I raised my eyebrows at Rory. He shrugged and smiled.

'Don't fight them,' I said.

'What?'

'You heard me. Withdraw. I'll be in touch.'

'Are you all right? Where are you?'

'I'll be in touch,' I repeated and cut the connection.

'Sensible,' Rory said.

'Your people?'

'Yes.'

'Have you told them about the toxin?'

'Just before we got here.'

I remembered the call – I hadn't paid attention to it because I'd been thinking about MacLean and Billy.

'Let's hope they take charge before the lunatics in the cancer centre release the toxin.'

There was a cracked laugh from the sofa. Billy turned and I saw that he'd been beaten about the face.

'It's booby-trapped. Only Jack knows the password.'

'We're working on him,' Rory said, glancing up at the ceiling. 'Maybe you can have a chat to your friend here.' He left the room.

So he knew. There was more to Rory Campbell than I'd thought, which was a major cock-up in the way I'd handled the case. Maybe I could redeem myself, though to whom I wasn't sure. I sat down next to Billy. Before I could open my mouth there was a high-pitched scream from above that was rapidly cut off.

'Torture,' said Billy contemptuously.

'Is that worse than importing a biohazard?' I said.

'From my point of view, definitely.' Billy's self-interest was always to the fore.

'Want to come clean about what you've been up to?' I said, looking at the armed figures in the room. 'Or shall I hand you over to the nail-removers?'

'Fuck you, Quint!'

I wiped my cheek. 'All right, I'll tell *you*. Jinglin' Jack and you have been buying anything you can get your hands on to set yourselves up as city bosses after the referendum – primarily weapons, including the biohazardous toxin.'

'So?'

'So why did you kill Mary Parlane and her son this morning?'

'We didn't.'

'Right,' I said, not believing him. 'How about the Lord of the Isles and the Glaswegian high heid yins? You're in bed with them, aren't you?'

'Wish I could be in bed with Hel Hyslop,' he said lewdly.

'She'd eat you alive.'

'That's what I was hoping.'

'For fuck's sake, Billy! People are going to die. They're already dying.'

He raised his uneven shoulders. 'People always die.'

One of the men in fatigues moved towards him and raised his hand. I put up one of mine.

'Let's keep this civil,' I said, 'at least on our side.' That was a giveaway – I was identifying myself with the rebels. 'Billy, tell me the toxin's confined to the cancer centre.'

'All right,' he replied, with a twisted grin. 'The toxin's confined to the cancer centre.' I grabbed his arm. 'Honest,' he said, wincing. 'As far as I know.'

'Why should we believe him, Quint?' Rory said, having reappeared.

'There isn't much we can do if it's all over the city. At least we know to give it a wide berth.'

'He could be lying.'

'Do you want to take that risk?'

Rory shook his head. 'Our forces are on top anyway.'

'Who are they fighting?'

'Guard personnel, of course.'

I thought of Davie and hoped he'd pulled back. Then my phone rang.

'Quint?' said Sophia. 'Where are you?'

'What's happened?' I said, alarmed by the fear in her voice.

'It's Maisie. She's . . . she's been taken.'

'Who by?'

'Four guardsmen, according to my housekeeper. But that's not all. I was just called by a man whose voice I didn't recognize. He said that Maisie would be . . . would be cut to pieces if you don't call this number immediately.'

I keyed the digits she spoke into my phone. 'Don't worry,' I said. 'I'll sort this out.'

'Quint . . . I can't live without . . . without her.'

'I know. Trust me.'

Rory gave me a questioning look but let me make the call.

'This is Dalrymple.'

'No "call me Quint"?' said a man whose voice was muffled.

'What do I have to do?'

He laughed. 'What don't you have to do? Tell us where the rebels are, tell your sidekick Hume 253 to give himself up and turn yourself in too.'

'I don't know where Davie is,' I said desperately.

'Then the fingers from little Maisie's left hand come off.'

I heard high-pitched screams in the background.

'All right,' I said. 'Where do you want us?'

'Craigmillar Castle. In half an hour. And where are the rebels?'

'All over the place, but mainly at the cancer centre.'

'Not good enough.'

I looked at Rory and mouthed, 'Where are you?'

He nodded and whispered, 'The zoo.'

I relayed that.

There was a pause. 'Very well,' said the man. 'Go to Craigmillar Castle now.' Then he broke the connection.

'Fuck,' I said, then explained what had happened.

'You'd better call your Guard friend,' Rory said.

I did. Davie wasn't particularly perturbed except when I told him to leave his weapons behind. We arranged to meet at Cameron Toll, outside the Guard shooting range.

'How do you want to handle this?' said Rory, taking me into the kitchen. 'At least some of the bastards will go to the zoo. We've got friendly Guard personnel there.'

'And a load of Remtex. Is it safe?'

He gave me a tight smile. 'We've lost contact with Kate Revie. Who do you think's behind this latest move?'

'It's obvious, isn't it?'

'Aye. But what shall we do about it?'

We talked about that for a while, then I drove the green van with minimal skill to the rendezvous point.

'On your own?' Davie asked. He was leaning against a Guard 4×4 parked at the roadside.

'After a fashion.'

He gave me a probing look. 'Anything I should know?'

'Not really. We're going to have to play this by ear.'

'At least I've still got both mine.'

'Let's see how long for. Follow me.'

'Where did you find this wreck?'

'Never mind.'

I got back behind the wheel and started up. The engine had been reconditioned and provided plenty of power – just as well considering the load in the back.

About half a mile further on, I took the left turn that led to the ruined castle. When I was a kid it had been a tourist attraction, largely because Mary, Queen of Scots had spent some time there. Since the Council took power it'd had a chequered history. There was a Guard post quartered in it during the drugs wars, but more recently it had been deserted. It was on one of the main routes into the city, so it didn't surprise me that people involved in moving goods illicitly would have established themselves there.

I stopped fifty yards up the access road. It didn't look like we had company so I whispered, 'Go, go, go.' I heard the rear doors open then close quietly a minute later. Davie would have seen the figures who emerged and what they were carrying. I wanted him to know that we weren't going in with nothing but our bare hands.

Driving on, I saw a light waving across the road ahead. I remembered the headbangers who had ambushed Hamish and me on Arthur's Seat. These people were much more dangerous. I pulled up.

'Out, both of you!' shouted a burly guardsman holding a sub-machine gun.

Davie and I complied, and walked forward.

In the dark it was difficult to make out the castle. There was a crescent moon in the eastern sky and the ramparts rose up like the barrier between life and death.

'In the gate,' said a guardswoman, an Enlightenment tartan scarf over her mouth.

'What's a traitor doing wearing that?' said Davie.

We were surrounded and pushed into the outer court. Guard 4×4s were parked in lines three deep. Rory Campbell's people might have been many, but the person behind this rebellion had no shortage of supporters among the city's watch-keepers.

More Guard personnel were waiting at the gate to the inner court. Here there were some scattered lights. The walls of the ruined tower stood before us. Then the host of armed people parted and the public order guardian appeared.

'Shithead,' said Davie, under his breath.

'Gentlemen,' said James Michie.

'I wish I could apply that term to you,' I said.

'Careful, citizen. You wouldn't want Maisie to lose an arm, would you?'

'Let me be clear,' I said. 'If you or any other piece of excrement hurts that wee girl in any way, you'll die in agony.' I was aware that my eyes were bulging.

James Michie took a step back. 'You're hardly in a position to issue threats, Quint.'

'Don't call me Quint!' I was tempted to tell him that I'd recognized his voice on the phone, but that would be asking for even more trouble. 'Where's Maisie?' I said, now in pleading mode. 'Let her go, for pity's sake. She's only a kid.'

Michie's face slackened. I could see he didn't have the stomach for child mutilation or worse.

'Let her go,' I said again. 'Take me in her place.'

There was a long pause and then he bought it. He turned to his left. 'Bring out the hostage and drive her to the infirmary.'

I watched as Maisie emerged from an opening in the old walls, a female guardian by her side. Neither of them looked in my direction. After they'd gone, I relaxed. Mistake.

The guardian straightened his shoulders. 'Take them to the wall.'

We were grabbed and pushed against the stone surface.

'Going to face death like men,' said a heavily built guardsman, 'or do we have to tie you up?'

'You're mine,' growled Davie.

'In another life, commander,' the guardsman said, with a harsh laugh.

I looked to the front and saw the firing squad line up. My stomach clenched and my legs quivered. I got a grip. So it had finally come to this. We hadn't been able to delay the bastards enough.

Then Davie fell to his knees and started wailing. I was so surprised that I remained upright.

'Don't . . . don't do it . . .' he bawled. 'I'll tell you . . . everything you need to know . . . please . . . That cunt Dalrymple, he made me . . . he made me do it all . . .'

I stared at him, then realized he was playing the part I should have taken. There was no point in us both turning chicken, though.

'Get a grip, you coward,' I snarled.

'Hear that?' Davie cried. 'I'm just his poodle . . . Don't hurt me . . . please . . . please . . .'

I kicked him on the knee harder than I meant to. 'Bastard turncoat. After everything I've done for you.'

'Oh aye, everything,' he said scornfully. 'You ruined my career, you shithead. I could have been——' He broke off and extended his arms towards Michie. 'I'll serve under you, guardian . . . more loyal than anyone, I swear.'

'No, it won't do,' said James Michie, suddenly decisive. 'Besides, you've shown how you react under pressure.' He looked at the firing squad. 'Ready!'

Rifle bolts were pushed home and sub-machinegun slides racked. I thought back to the drugs wars, when I'd supervised summary executions. It was poetic justice that I was going to leave the world in the same way, even though I wasn't a crazed rapist or murderer.

'Aim!'

I thought of Sophia and then of my old man. She'd have to handle his funeral without me – if she survived the fighting.

As Michie opened his mouth, I stared into his eyes. He looked away, then his head exploded, the shot ringing out immediately afterwards.

Everyone dropped to their knees and looked around. Davie grabbed my arm and we ran to our left. Good move. Shooting broke out from behind the Guard personnel, many of whom fell screaming or silently to the ground.

'Keep your head down!' Davie shouted.

It wasn't the moment to praise his acting triumph, although the shooting quickly slackened as guardsmen and women who hadn't been hit dropped their weapons. More lights came through the gate and I saw Rory Campbell, blood on the arms of his fatigues. He ordered some of his people to collect weapons and others to supervise the Guard personnel.

'You cut that a bit fine,' I said. 'If Olivier here hadn't put in the performance of his life, we'd have been riddled.'

'Olivier? There were more sentries than we expected.'

'Have you got Maisie?'

'Aye. How did you know she was here?'

'I recognized Michie's voice on the phone.'

'Jesus, Quint,' said Davie, arriving at my side. 'You might have backed me up.'

'I did what I could. If I'd broken down or tried to negotiate, Michie would have given the order quicker.' I grinned. 'You should audition for *Spar/Tak/Us*.'

'I don't think there'll be many more performances of that,' he said. 'At least not in the theatre.'

I nodded, then relief dashed over me as a female rebel appeared with Maisie by her side. When the little girl saw me, she pulled her hand away and ran forward.

I kneeled down and took her in my arms, saying what I could to comfort her. I needn't have bothered.

'They were bad Guard personnel,' she said, trying to look at the bodies nearby. I signalled to Davie to stand in the way. 'I told them they were breaking regulations, I even gave them the numbers and sub-clauses of the relevant regulations, but they told me to shut up. I stamped my foot at them.' She pushed back and smiled at me. 'I've never done that before. I thought it only happened in Victorian novels.'

I stood up, shaking my head. 'Go with this lady,' I said, beckoning to the rebel. 'She'll look after you.'

The young woman nodded.

'But, Quint,' said Maisie, 'what about Mother?'

What about Sophia indeed? I rang her.

'We've got Maisie,' I said. 'She's fine. What about you?'

'I've closed the infirmary and posted our own guard personnel at all the entrances.'

My heart skipped a beat. 'Why?'

'There's a build-up of vehicles outside. I don't like the look of it.'

'You're right not to. If the worst happens, you know what to do.' I took a breath. 'My dearest darling.'

'Quint! That's the loveliest thing you've ever said to me.'

I muttered something and then rang off. She'd reminded me that we weren't out of the woods yet.

'What now?' Davie asked, having rearmed himself extravagantly.

'Do you really need an axe?'

'Yes.'

'Fair enough.' I turned to Rory. 'Have you got plans? Are you even in charge of this rebellion?'

He smiled. 'I don't trust you that much, Quint.' He handed me a Hyper-Stun. 'Not yet, at least.'

'What do I have to do to convince you?'

'It's not him you have to convince, citizen,' came a strong female voice from the gate.

I looked over my shoulder and there she was. Clarinda Towart's blonde hair was tied back and her fine cheekbones, though dirty, were prominent.

'Call me Quint,' I said.

'Call me Madam.'

We laughed in unison.

Twenty-Seven

'So we finally meet,' I said, following Clarinda through the inner gate. In the pale light of the moon I could see a lot of people in fatigues. Some were leading surviving Guard personnel away.

'No violence!' she called, then looked back at me. 'I've led you a merry chase, haven't I?'

'You have. Any chance of an explanation?'

She extended her hands to the scene ahead. 'The revolution's begun.'

'But you're a murderer, at least to the Council or guardians who aren't rebel sympathizers.'

'What about you?'

'I want to get rid of the current regime.'

She put a rough palm on my cheek. 'You're just saying that so I don't cut your balls off.'

'Correct.'

'Ha. I like you, Quint.'

'Can I call you Clarrie?'

She smiled. 'If you like.'

I could understand why the woman had been a success in the Prostitution Services Department. She looked on me favourably and I felt like I'd won the nearly fifties' hundred metres final. But there was more than a touch of steel beneath the surface.

Then she took out a Guard-issue combat knife. The steel was suddenly at surface level.

'Tell me what you know, Quint.'

'What's in it for me?'

'Fertility,' she said, running the point of the weapon down my flies.

That made me focus. 'Right. You found out about the Malaysian contracts from Chung Keng Quee.' I took my genitals in my hands, metaphorically. 'Wasn't too clever killing him in your flat, though.'

The knife-point scraped up my zip. 'I didn't.'

'Who did, then?'

'Never you mind.'

'So what happened? After taking him on a joyride to the theatre and round the suburbs, you led him to your bedroom, got what you needed out of him and left him there alive?'

'More or less correct.'

'Why did you take him to the theatre? Oh, Rory came with you and killed him.'

She shook her head, smiling mysteriously. 'Go on.'

I pulled my thoughts together. 'You got the Malaysian drunk, then took his laptop and phone. You squeezed his nuts for the passwords and so on.'

'Very good.'

'And you left him there because you had to make a call to your pals from a street phone.'

'Quite the wee smartarse, aren't you?'

'I try. So who did kill him? The old guy across the landing?' I remembered Charlie Dixon, who wasn't a fan of Clarinda – or of the cancer centre, for that matter.

'No.' That subject was clearly closed.

'There was another Asian out in Moredun. You didn't have anything to do with his death, did you?'

'I didn't kill him, no,' she said, leaning closer.

'Who did?'

The knife was brandished in front of my eyes. 'Keep going.'

I considered asking for something to drink, but decided against it. 'Your school friend Duncan Denoon stored Remtex at the zoo.'

'He did. Until someone got to it – the Guard, I presume.'

'So you weren't behind the explosion?'

'Certainly not. Some fucker was on to us.'

'What about Alice Lennox and Christo Fleming?'

'They're on our side. You'd better hope nothing happens to Christo.'

'I can get him released now the public order guardian's out of the way.'

She studied me. 'Rory trusts you but I'm not sure I do. You've been loyal to the Council for a long time.'

'Loyal in my own way,' I muttered, playing hurt. 'Things change.'

'You're right there.'

'You and the former tourism guardian – you were friends and allies.'

Lines appeared on Clarinda's forehead. 'Rory told me. The fuckers are going to pay for killing Mary and Ross.' To my surprise she started to cry violently, her breath coming in great gasps. 'Who . . . who was it?'

'Sniper or snipers from the other side of the Lawnmarket.' I paused. 'I was in Mary's office when it happened,' I added, unsure if that would improve my situation.

She glared at me. 'Go on.'

'You were keeping tabs on Goliath, aka Ronald Douglas Dobie.'

'We were. As that shithead the Lord of the Isles' man he unwittingly provided us with useful information. Then the Guard got to him. Was that you?'

I shook my head. 'You know who it was.'

'Yes. The question is, what are we going to do about it?'

'Keep rebelling?' I suggested.

Clarinda Towart laughed, putting her knife away as Rory Campbell arrived.

'Everything all right?' he said, with a concerned look.

'You sure Quintilian here's solid?'

'Not a hundred per cent, but it's in his interest to give us his best. The medical guardian's under siege at the infirmary.'

'Fuck!' I said. 'I've got to get over there.'

Rory put a hand on my arm. 'Our people are en route. You're no front-line fighter.'

'I can hold my own.'

Clarinda smiled weakly. 'Once that would have made me laugh, but that life's over.'

'You've been faking it for a long time,' I said. 'The drinking, the escort services.'

'I always faked the latter, Quint. The PSD teaches you how to do that before they send you out to do your duty.'

'Did you fake being in love with Lorna Dobie?'

Her eyes held mine. 'What's love?'

'You used her.'

'I did. We'd discovered that her father was a courier for the opposition.'

'The Lord of the Isles' people.'

'Primarily Goliath.'

'So you set wee Kennie up as an intermediary.'

'That got them running in circles.'

'Why didn't you get Mary Parlane to transfer you?'

'Because I've been collecting information to help the revolution for a couple of years now.' She frowned. 'Don't imagine that made screwing fat men and perverts any easier.'

'Mungo Rollo. You lured him to your office, didn't you?'

'We knew he was with the opposition. I tried to turn him.' Clarinda shrugged. 'Didn't work out.'

'So you killed him?'

'No. Change the subject.'

I looked at her sheathed knife and complied.

'C. T. Enterprises. You set it up to get yourself into the Finance Directorate.'

'Very good.' She spat on the ground suddenly. 'The things I had to do . . .'

'Jinglin' Jack? Geddes?'

'Among others.'

'The Glaswegian leaders? The Lord of the Isles?'

'They're all going to die.'

Her voice was so full of hatred that cold sweat ran down my arms. She was justified.

'What was Christo Fleming doing in your office with Lorna Dobie?'

'We didn't know Goliath had been killed at that point. We were going to use her to locate him. Then the Lord of the Isles pushed forward the deliveries. Things were coming to a head.' Clarinda smiled. 'Things have come to a head. We're going to lance the boil that's been festering in this city.'

I kept my mouth firmly shut. Davie came up, a rebel on each side of him.

'And this one?' Clarinda said to me. 'Do we trust him?'

'Are you up for a rebellion, big man?' I asked.

'I want to get the fuckers who killed Mary Parlane and her kid.' He eyed Clarinda. 'Are you the leader of this mob?'

She looked at Rory, then shook her head.

'It's Big Lachie, isn't it?' Davie said, looking more pleased with himself than I'd have advised.

'Who told you that?' Clarinda demanded.

'Wee Kennie,' said Davie. In the recent chaos I'd forgotten that.

'He's got a mouth on him. What else did he say?'

'Nothing,' said Davie, aware too late that he'd put his size-ten boot in it.

'Where is he?' Rory asked.

'In the castle,' I said.

'We'd better get over there,' Clarinda said.

'What about the cancer centre?' I said. 'The toxin could—'

'MacLean gave us the code to the booby trap,' Rory said. 'The consignment is secured, along with the rockets and everything else on site.'

'Let's move,' said Clarinda. Her phone rang and she moved away before answering it.

Rory stepped closer. 'How many of the Guard will fight against us?'

Davie glared at him. 'How many have already gone over to you?'

'Between a quarter and a third.'

'Bloody hell,' Davie said, shaking his head. 'How did that happen on my watch?'

'Judging by how quickly the personnel here surrendered,' Rory continued, 'a lot of the others haven't got the stomach for a fight.'

'It doesn't matter,' I said. 'Those who are still loyal to the Council will put their lives on the line. That's why I have to get to the infirmary.'

Clarinda returned. 'OK, we've got the green light.'

'To do what?' I asked. 'The centre's full of tourists.'

'A fact that won't have escaped the enemy,' she replied. 'But there are other ways of tying them down.'

'Such as?' said Davie.

She gave him a smile Rita Hayworth would have been proud of. 'Let's see, big boy.'

He was instantly spellbound.

Davie and I were in the back of an armoured personnel carrier that had been taken from the Guard. We were on Melville Drive, going past the tents on the Meadows that provided dance bands and beer to citizens at weekends. Rory was in the front, while Clarinda had taken a Land Rover to scout the area around the infirmary. The city was as quiet as it normally was after curfew, if you discounted the rumble of numerous vehicles to the rear. Some had already turned towards the local barracks. We'd heard that Hume, Davie's home turf, had surrendered without a shot being fired. The commander said that about fifty of his personnel were absent without leave, which suggested the enemy was concentrating forces. The question was, where?

Clarinda's voice came over the radio. 'On Forrest Road. Gunfire and explosions coming from infirmary. Waiting for support.'

Rory told the driver to turn on to the grass and head for the back of the hospital installations. No shooting was directed at us, which was a relief – the forces storming the place weren't sufficient to surround it. Within a few minutes several groups of heavily armed fighters had formed up on the grass.

'I know a way in,' I said to Rory. I gave Davie my Hyper-Stun. 'Can I have a gun?'

'You hate them,' the commander said.

'Not when Sophia's life is at stake,' I said, taking the Jarilo .45 I was handed. It was heavy and I held it in both hands. 'Come on then, Rory.'

He nodded and beckoned to one squad to follow. I went through a hole in the fence and reached the window to a storeroom. The bars had rusted away years ago and never been replaced, as I'd noticed once when Sophia and I used the place for a canoodle.

'Can you break the glass quietly?' I said to Davie.

Without hesitating, he put his elbow through the pane nearest the catch. To be fair, the noise wasn't much against the shooting from the front of the complex.

'We'll go in,' I said to Rory. 'Why don't you take your people along the side and flank the attackers?'

He gave me an appraising look and then nodded.

Davie had unlocked the window and pushed up the lower sash. He went in and I followed. There was a lot of screaming inside the building. The door was locked.

'Shit,' said Davie. 'I can't budge it.'

'Stand back.' I aimed the Jarilo at the lock and pulled the trigger. The recoil was so powerful that I ended up on the floor. The door swung open, though.

'Do you want to give me that?' Davie asked.

'I'm getting the hang of it. Come on, Sophia should be in the morgue.'

'What?'

'We arranged it a long time ago. If she's in danger, she gets into corpse drawer number thirteen.'

'Lucky for some.'

'Here's hoping.'

The corridors were empty. The staff had either done a bunk or were fighting at the other end of the complex.

Davie put his hand over his mouth and nose when we pushed the morgue doors apart. Two bodies had been abandoned in mid-autopsy, the skin of their chests pinned back and their innards on display.

I ran to the stainless-steel array of drawers and pulled open number thirteen. It was firmly closed, which was a bad sign. Sophia would have left it slightly open for air. She wasn't there.

'Let's get out of here,' I said.

'Not before time. Where to?'

'The front line, guardsman. Sophia will be leading her troops.'

We ran down the corridors, the gunfire and screaming getting louder. Then we ran into a mass of patients, some upright and others lying on the floor in their bandages and gowns. There were wards with north-facing windows and they had obviously been evacuated. I saw a nurse in the distance and fought my way through to her.

'Where's the guardian?'

'I don't know, citizen,' she said, her eyes wide. There was blood all over her tunic. 'She sent me back here half an hour ago. It's murder at the main entrance.'

'Was she hurt?'

'Not when I last saw her.'

'Come on, Davie.'

He went first and was a much more effective crowd-splitter. The further we progressed, the more wounded auxiliaries and Guard personnel we met. Then we made it to the rear of the entrance hall. It was mayhem. An APC had crashed through the doors. Bodies lay about the place, survivors were discharging Hyper-Stuns through the smashed windows and a small group of Guard personnel was firing the infirmary's minuscule stock of rifles.

Then I saw her.

'Sophia!' I screamed, diving across a slick of blood on the floor as a burst of machine-gun fire rattled above me.

She was sitting against a wall, a nurse tending a wound in her arm.

'Quint? What are you doing here?'

'Coming to your rescue. Why aren't you in the morgue?'

'I will be soon,' she said, looking despondently at the motionless bodies in the entrance hall.

'No . . . you won't,' I said, putting myself between her and the incoming fire. Looking over my shoulder, I saw Davie pick up a rifle from a dead guardswoman and run to a window.

Before I could open my mouth, there was a heavy volley of fire from the west. Immediately bullets stopped coming into the infirmary.

'Rory,' I said.

'Who?' Sophia asked. Her face was even paler than usual and I wondered how much blood she'd lost.

'An artery's been severed,' the nurse said, tightening the tourniquet at the top of Sophia's arm.

My stomach somersaulted. After all this, was Maisie going to be left motherless?

A few minutes later the firing began to die down. Then it stopped completely and was replaced by loud cheering. Rory climbed in a window and came over.

'They've surrendered, Quint,' he said, looking at Sophia. 'Is she going to be all right?'

I looked at the nurse. Her response was noncommittal.

'Surgeon!' I yelled, again and again.

After what seemed like an eternity, a thin man in bloodstained scrubs appeared.

'Deal with the guardian,' I said. 'Top priority.'

He got the message and helped the nurse get Sophia to her feet.

'You have feelings for her.'

I turned to find Clarinda at my side. Blood was running from a cut on her cheek, but she was otherwise unhurt.

'I do,' I said. 'Real and many.'

'I can't remember when I last had real feelings for anyone.'

A great sadness washed over me for the woman who had willingly let herself be abused. I hoped she'd she be able to enjoy the fruits of revolution.

'We have to press on,' she said, looking at Rory.

'Our forces got to the esplanade in time,' he said, 'so the enemy didn't make it to the castle. They're heading for the Supply Directorate depot.'

'We've got to stop them,' said Davie. 'There are weapons and explosives there.'

I found my phone and called Jimmy Taggart. There was gunfire in the background when he answered.

'Are you keeping them out?' I asked.

'So far, but we're being attacked from the rear.'

I turned to the rebel leaders. 'Have you got any forces near the depot?'

Rory nodded. 'A group's on its way from the Pleasance.'

'Hurry them up.' I glanced at Davie. 'We need to get down there.'

He nodded and led me to a window. Clarinda was on our heels.

Outside the infirmary there were dead and wounded everywhere. Rebels were collecting weapons and ammunition.

'Did it have to come to this?' I asked.

'Yes,' said Clarinda firmly. 'And you know it.'

She was right.

* * *

Davie drove me and Clarinda down the High Street. Rory and his troops were following in other vehicles. It was quiet, as usual at this time of night. At least tourists hadn't been caught up in the fighting, though that could change any minute.

'Engaging enemy on Jeffrey Street,' came a gruff voice over Clarinda's comms unit.

'We'll be there in a couple of minutes,' Davie said.

'The bastards will take refuge in the Supply Directorate if we don't stop them,' I said. 'That place is a warren.'

'Nothing a few pounds of Remtex can't fix,' Clarinda said, with a worryingly manic grin.

Her phone rang and she answered, listening intently.

'I strongly advise against that,' she said. 'The area isn't under our control.' There was a pause. 'Oh, all right,' she said angrily, then rang off.

'Big Lachie?' I said.

'What?' Her brow was furrowed.

'Your leader. I'm looking forward to meeting him.'

'You say that . . .'

My mouth went dry. It sounded like the senior rebel was even worse than Goliath.

Davie stopped at the World's End, the pub that once marked the last of Edinburgh before the old city walls and had more recently been done up as a tourist teashop. Gunfire and shouting came through the night air.

'Is there any way we can stop this?' I asked Clarinda.

Rory joined us. 'Want to let the fucker off, Quint?'

'I want to talk to him and find out what the hell he's up to.' I shrugged. 'Then you can do what you want.'

'Be our guest,' said Clarinda. 'Big Lachie's got the same idea.'

I looked around. 'Where is he?'

'He has his own way of moving about,' Rory said, grinning more widely than seemed appropriate given the proximity of the fighting.

'Come on, Davie,' I said.

By the time we got within fifty yards of the Supply Directorate, the shooting had died down.

'Get into the depot and see how Jimmy Taggart's getting on,' I said.

Davie shanghaied some rebels and hammered on the doors to the right, identifying himself. They opened and I caught a glimpse of the old guardsman. He looked to be fighting fit.

The rebels parted as Clarinda arrived, one of them approaching her.

'A few of them got into the directorate, Clarrie,' he said. 'They've barricaded the door.'

'Let me talk to him,' I said, taking out my phone.

'Go ahead,' Clarinda said, helping a female rebel to her feet. Several of the woman's fingers were missing and blood was spurting. That made the stump of my right forefinger twitch.

'This is Dalrymple,' I said, when the senior guardian answered.

'I can see you. What's to stop me ordering your death?'

'The fact that yours will soon follow. I can argue your case, Fergus.'

'Why would you do that?'

'To understand.'

'More like to undo everything I've worked for.'

'Yes,' I said, seeing no reason to dissemble. 'You live or you die. Choose.'

He laughed drily. 'That works both ways. I'll only negotiate with the rebels' leaders.'

I repeated that to Clarinda and Rory.

'That isn't going to happen,' she said.

'Why not?'

I looked down at the speaker. His bald head came up to my abdomen. That little bastard, Kennie . . . The dwarf's face was unlined and he wore a drooping moustache.

'Big Lachie, aka Cezar MacFarlane, I presume.'

'The same, Citizen Dalrymple.' His gaze was unwavering, the irises a dark shade of brown. He was wearing fatigues that had been cut to size and there was a Jarilo .45 in his belt.

'Dalrymple?' came Fergus Calder's voice from my phone. 'I want safe passage for me and ten 4×4s for my closest supporters.'

'Where to? You can't leave the city.'

'I wouldn't dream of deserting the state I lead, citizen.'

'You don't lead it any more.'

'Yes, I do,' he said, his voice shaking. 'I haven't been voted out by the full Council.'

'So what? Your allies will be caught and your enemies on the Council want to see the last of you.'

'You and the scum who've revolted have no jurisdiction over me. I'm entitled to safe passage. Then I'll negotiate.'

I relayed that to Cezar and the others.

'Rather depends where he wants to go,' said Rory.

Clarinda shook her head. 'Wherever it is will be a trap. We should blow up the directorate.'

'Enough lives have been lost,' I said. 'Besides, we don't know how many
Guard personnel are still with him.'

'I agree,' said Lachie. 'Find out where he wants to go, please.'

I asked the question.

'It isn't far. The New Tolbooth. Allow me to enter and I'll meet the rebel
leader, unaccompanied, on the second floor.'

'Unacceptable,' said Clarinda, when I passed the message on. 'A minimum
of two of us must go with Lachie.'

'Three on each side, unarmed,' I said to the guardian.

'Very well, but you must be one of them, Dalrymple.'

Clarinda and Rory were opposed to that, but Lachie wasn't concerned.

'Clarrie will come with us,' he said.

I told Calder.

'Very well. I'll leave here at seven thirty, not long after sunrise. Kindly
make the arrangements.'

I put my phone in my pocket and told the others.

Clarinda looked at her watch. 'That gives us two hours to check the place.'
She gave the order.

Davie appeared at the gate of the depot, his expression grim.

I went over to him quickly. 'What happened?'

'Situation stable, but old Jimmy took a bullet through the eye.'

That was a heavy blow, but there would be time to mourn him later,
along with Hector – they were the last of the old breed.

Right now I wanted to talk to Big Lachie.

Twenty-Eight

We drove in convoy to the Grassmarket, Rory staying behind to arrange
safe passage for the senior guardian when the time came. Davie cleared the
Guard personnel out of their mess in the New Tolbooth and took part in
the search of the large building with a group of rebels. He had already
struck up a conversation with a brunette who was carrying a snub-nosed
machine-pistol.

Lachie, Clarinda and I sat round the table and drank the coffee the
guardsmen and women had just brewed.

'So, Quintilian Dalrymple,' said the dwarf, 'you'll be wanting an
explanation.'

I smiled. 'There are a few points that need clarification. Like how you managed to infiltrate the Guard and auxiliary body to such an extent.'

'We've been at it for some time,' Lachie said.

'And you? What turned you into such a radical?'

'My father's illness was the last straw.'

'His arthritis?'

'No, he could live with that. He had colon cancer. He died in agony six months ago.'

'That isn't in his file.'

'Because I complained and everything went off the record.'

'Mary Parlane and Kate Revie didn't know?'

'They did, but I asked them not to tell anyone. Some things are private.'

I could understand that after Hector's final days. I wasn't going to ask what he'd done with the body.

'Then my mother disappeared,' Lachie continued. 'That fucker Allison took her, I'm sure of it.'

I decided against confirming that, at least now. He had enough to deal with.

'And don't forget, I'd been writing history textbooks for years. It became clear that Edinburgh was being run by ruthless people who cared nothing for the citizens.'

'Like I told you, everything kicked off before we'd finished planning,' Clarinda said, spitting on a cloth and cleaning the blood from her face. 'The deliveries to the cancer centre were the last straw.'

'You shouldn't have killed Chung Keng Quee,' was my riposte.

'She didn't,' said the dwarf. 'That was me. I put a cushion on his chest so my knees didn't leave separate marks.'

'Why did you use a ligature?'

'Experimentation.' If Clarinda was steel beneath the skin, this guy was diamond-hard.

'You were in the back of the taxi with him,' I said, understanding at last. 'That's why the driver went the long way round.'

Lachie nodded. 'I got in at Cameron Toll. The Malaysian thought I was part of the entertainment.'

'You got the files with the contracts. Why did you kill him?'

'Because he was a pig,' Clarinda said. 'If Lachie hadn't done it, I would have.'

I imagined the Malaysian had demanded sexual favours of a seriously distasteful nature. 'And the other Asian, the one in the house at Moredun?'

'That was me too,' Lachie said.

'He was no better,' Clarinda said. 'Besides, we wanted to put the shits up the fucking Lord of the Isles.'

'How come there weren't any—' I hesitated. 'Small footprints.'

'I was standing on a chair. Plus I was carried in and out. I don't leave traces.'

'And the bag of bones?'

'My mother,' he said, clenching his fists.

So he did know.

'Allison sent a message that they were there. So were some gunmen. We chased them off before the Guard arrived. I thought about resisting, but decided against it.'

'The remains have been treated with respect,' I said, putting my hand on his arm. 'They're in the morgue.'

'Thank you,' Lachie said solemnly.

'So it was you who killed Mungo Rollo,' I continued after a pause. 'Without a ligature.'

He raised his shoulders. 'The fool refused to come over to us. I have strong fingers and thumbs.'

That was disturbing, but understandable after what his father had suffered.

'And you changed your name because Cezar wouldn't cut it as a revolutionary leader in Scotland?'

He nodded, smiling. 'You know how often I was called Julius at school and work? The Romans were even worse than the Council.' He caught my gaze. 'Can we trust you?'

It was a reasonable question. Now that the action was over, I'd begun to question my position. I didn't give a shit about Calder, but armed insurrection was a big step. I'd done everything I could to stop one of those last summer. But this was different. And Davie had gone along with it. That helped a lot.

'Since I discovered Mary Parlane was with you, I realized your movement has a lot going for it.' I looked at Clarinda. 'You were playing with Goliath, the Lord of the Isles' man, weren't you?'

She shrugged. 'He was a killer but we strung him along – he was trying to find out what we were doing, of course – until he was shot to pieces. Didn't that make you wonder about the senior guardian?'

'I thought Jinglin' Jack MacLean and Billy Geddes were behind things, and maybe James Michie. It did occur to me that Calder was playing them, but he's very plausible. Now I see that he had Goliath killed to mess with MacLean's plans. And the same happened to Mary and Ross, to mess with yours. Michie was his man from the start, no doubt.'

Lachie nodded. 'We thought MacLean and his pet snake were the main men. It was only after Jinglin' Jack broke down under what I have to say wasn't very extreme torture that we realized he was only the fixer, not the strategist. Outsiders were pulling his strings.'

That reminded me of Fergus Calder moving me to a strategic role – which he knew I would ignore. He was cunning, using me to get after MacLean while he was aware of the contracts all along. What had he been intending to do with the toxin? I'd be asking him that.

'Did you have to involve those girls?' I asked Clarinda. 'Lorna Dobie and Debra Kilgour.'

She looked away. 'I discussed it with Mary. We decided that I had to keep my cover tight, whatever it took.'

I glanced at her boss. 'No more Prostitution Services Department.'

He nodded. 'Even though the city's income will take a hit, its humanity won't.'

I could see how he inspired the rebels.

'Why didn't you wait until after the referendum? The city's going to vote "yes".'

'That's what Calder wanted. Once democracy spoke, he'd have shut it down and turned Edinburgh into his personal fiefdom. Don't forget, he was senior guardian only until the referendum. That's why he was escalating his activities, as was his supposed ally MacLean.'

'Has the medical guardian's daughter been returned to her?'

Clarinda nodded. 'Apparently it was a happy scene.'

I took out my phone and called Sophia. She was unusually emotional, not that I blamed her. Her arm had been dealt with by the surgeon, though she'd needed a lot of local anaesthetic and the procedure hadn't been straightforward.

'When are you coming over?' she said, her voice faint.

'There is one more thing I have to do.' I paused. 'Sophia, did anyone approach you about joining the rebels?'

There was silence on the line.

'They did, didn't they? Who?'

'Never mind, Quint. I sat on the fence.' She laughed nervously. 'But I'm on board now.'

'Kate Revie?'

'Hold on, Maisie . . . Yes, it was Kate, about a month ago.'

'You didn't think of telling me?'

'Don't be angry,' she said, almost weeping. 'She swore me to secrecy. Here's Maisie.'

'I love you,' I said hastily.

'Hello, Quint man.'

'Hello, brave girl.'

'Do you know how to apply a tourniquet?'

'Yes.' It was part of auxiliary training, though I'd need a refresher course.

'Good. You can show me when next we meet. By the way, I'm going to call you Quilp from now on.' She rang off, Dickensian to the last.

The New Tolbooth was a recent addition to the city's tourist attractions. The original had been on the High Street, but there was more space in the Grassmarket. It was an ugly block with fake heads on poles along its front wall. Executions were held throughout the day – even hanging, drawing and quartering; the actors who did the cutting and so on had become adept in their use of animal parts and buckets of blood. The second floor was a museum of notorious Edinburgh criminals – wax and wood models of Burke and Hare, Deacon Brodie, John Kincaid, even the unfortunate Captain Porteous. They stood alongside the maroon carpet with their hands extended, like zombies about to tear you to bits. The room was a big hit with the city's visitors, of course.

Clarinda and I stood on either side of Lachie. We waited until Fergus Calder and two auxiliaries, one male and one female, neither of whom I recognized, arrived at the far end. They walked to the middle of the long room.

'Right,' said Clarinda.

'We haven't talked about what you're going to offer him,' I said, as we moved forward.

'Nothing,' said Lachie.

'Not even his life?'

'Not even.'

Fergus Calder was dressed in a well-cut suit and was smiling – never a good sign with senior guardians. He raised a hand and we stopped a couple of yards in front of them.

'We need to search each other,' he said, leering at Clarinda.

'On your knees,' said Lachie. He ran his hands over the senior guardian and then let him do the same in return. Clarinda was on the left and she checked the female auxiliary, who wasn't wearing a name or barracks panel. I was patted down by the middle-aged male auxiliary, who was sweating profusely. I wondered why. It wasn't particularly warm.

'Very well,' said Calder. 'Here are my demands.'

'You're not in a position to demand anything,' Lachie said.

'You think? One word – toxin.'

'We've disabled the booby trap on the consignment at the cancer centre,' Clarinda said, giving him a mocking smile.

He returned it. 'Can you be sure that's the only one?'

There was a pause.

'Go on,' said Lachie.

'Free passage for me and fifty of my people to Granton. A boat will pick us up.'

'Will it, now?' Clarinda said. 'Your friends from Glasgow?'

This time the senior guardian burst out laughing. 'Friends from Glasgow? You people haven't a clue.'

'Let's see about that,' I said. 'I've been thinking about why you kept me on the case. Obviously because you wanted MacLean and Geddes exposed.'

'You can do better than that, Quint. It wasn't long till I found out about the Malaysian contracts, even though you kept them from me.'

'James Michie.'

'Of course.'

'So why didn't you act?'

'It was to my benefit that Jack and his SPADE did the legwork. When I found out about the toxin – George Allison was with me even though they thought he was one of theirs – I took steps to secure my own stock.'

'Why?' Clarinda asked. 'Jinglin' Jack was going to use it against Edinburgh citizens anyway, wasn't he? Or at least threaten them with it.'

'If his paymasters, Glasgow and the Lord of the Isles, said so. Which I'm sure they would.'

'They were funding the deal,' I said.

Calder nodded.

'So what were you going to do with—' I broke off as the realization hit me. 'Your plan was to bombard Glasgow and the other population centres with the toxin.'

'At last you understand. I've been looking at ways of securing Edinburgh's position after the referendum for some time.' He looked at Lachie. 'And now, if you don't mind, that safe passage.'

'Screw you,' said Clarinda.

'Were you behind the bomb in the zoo?' I asked, seeking – ha – to defuse the situation.

'One of my people found out about the stock of Remtex. I thought it would be beneficial to raise the stakes by attacking a tourist attraction.' Calder grinned at me. 'That got your attention, didn't it?'

'It also led to the death of a citizen, as well as a couple of pygmy hippos.'

'A citizen who was in contact with an untrustworthy guardian.'

'Kate Revie – if you knew she was a potential opponent, why did you spring her from the castle? Is she alive?'

'Yes, unfortunately. I tried to talk her into acting as a double agent, but she escaped from some incompetent Guard personnel.' He laughed coarsely. 'You'll find their bodies behind Canongate Kirk.'

I stared at him but he didn't look away.

'And talking of bodies . . .' said Calder.

There was a sudden movement to our left. The bearded mannequin in a medieval leather smock brought a micro-crossbow from behind its back, raised it and fired. Clarinda dropped to her knees, clutching her throat, and then fell forwards.

'Hamish,' I said, dumbfounded. Then I remembered that standing motionless was a feature of advanced auxiliary combat training – as was using what was available for camouflage.

'Long live the senior guardian,' the young man said triumphantly. He put another bolt in the slide and pulled the mechanism back. 'Time's up, Quint. We need the wee man to call off his people, but you're superfluous.'

Before anyone could move, Lachie leapt over Clarinda's body and crashed into Hamish's upper thighs. The crossbow went flying and the medieval clothes constricted him. Lachie sat on the guardsman's chest and put his hands round his neck.

As the auxiliaries went to Hamish's aid, I dropped my shoulder and powered into Calder's midriff. Then I turned him so he was on top of me and locked my arm round his neck. He struggled but he wasn't in fighting condition.

'Let go of Big Lachie or Calder dies!' I said.

The man and woman held back. Then I called for Davie at the top of my voice.

It didn't take long for reinforcements to arrive. As I lay under the now former senior guardian I saw that skeletons were hanging from the hall's high ceiling. I hoped they were fake, but I couldn't be sure.

Davie took charge of Calder, while Rory knocked both auxiliaries out with single blows. Then he dropped to his knees and leant over Clarinda. A pool of blood had gathered around her head. He started talking in a low voice.

Lachie got off Hamish's motionless body, flexing his fingers. He had obviously perfected his way of killing larger people.

'Fucker,' he said. 'How was he not spotted?' He turned to Fergus Calder.

'I'm going to pull your fingernails out myself till you tell me where the toxin is.'

'No, no,' the guardian said feebly. 'It's in the depot at Stockbridge, the one that used to be Edinburgh Academy. The booby trap code is 24-52-98.'

'Thanks,' the rebel leader said. 'I'm still going to pull your nails out.'

Calder sagged in Davie's grip.

'But first we need to secure the city.' Lachie turned away and headed for the people in non-Guard fatigues who had gathered in the hall. Kate Revie was among them, as was Alice Lennox. Rory stayed bent over Clarinda, sobbing. Davie and I withdrew, holding the city's chief schemer between us.

I extracted a promise from Lachie that Calder wouldn't be punished without a public trial – new regime, new justice system. He took my point. I also managed to talk to Alice Lennox. The nurse was giving out orders with aplomb.

'You're obviously one of the leaders,' I said.

'And you obviously won't be,' she said, her brow furrowed. I could see she hadn't forgotten her time in the castle with me and Davie.

'Not my thing anyway. Tell me, why did you say Goliath was Eastern European?'

She smiled. 'Why do you think?'

'To confuse anyone and everyone. That's why you went after the under-cover guardswoman as well.'

'You're good, if rather late. Goliath was beginning to get in the way. We wanted him to be in your sights. I couldn't have dreamed Calder would get rid of him.'

'Wet dream, was it?' Davie asked, from the rear.

'Fuck off,' Alice said, turning her back on us.

'She'll come round,' Davie said, with a grin.

I doubted it.

The rest of the day passed in a blur. The revolution was well organized and most tourists didn't even realize what had happened. Guardians who weren't sympathetic to the end of the Council – only two – were imprisoned in the castle. Rebels were sent to each barracks and every directorate. Remarkably few auxiliaries and Guard personnel objected. In any case, it wasn't long till the referendum. Voting 'no' was still an option, not that there was any point in doing that. There was no doubt that the new regime was here to stay.

Davie and I grabbed a sandwich on the esplanade in the late afternoon. It was still a fine day, the blue sky completely clear.

'Why did you change sides so quickly, big man?'

'Apart from the Parlane killings? It was the toxin. I thought it was going to be used against citizens and I couldn't stand for that. Mind you, it's no worse than the madman using it against other states.'

'They'd have retaliated in a big way. They'll have the toxin too.'

'Aye. What do you think will happen to Calder?'

'I hope they'll be merciful.'

'Twenty years down the mines would do the job,' he said, grinning.

'That isn't an option for Billy,' I said. Jack MacLean and my former friend had been taken to the cells in the castle.

'He'll find a way to prove his usefulness to them.'

'Probably. What about you?'

'I thought I already had.' He scowled. 'It wasn't me who checked the meeting place in the Tolbooth.'

'I know. Anyone can make a mistake. Shame about Clarinda, but I don't think she had much left to give.'

Davie took another doorstop. 'I never thought a revolutionary heroine would come from the PSD.'

'No? They're heroes and heroines on a daily basis.'

'At least there'll be no more of that.'

'Until the tourists start going elsewhere.'

'Cynic.'

'I'm a sceptic, not a cynic. How many times have I told you?'

'Three thousand nine hundred and seventy-three.'

I thumped his arm.

'Anyway,' he continued, 'the new bosses might decide we're tarred by association with the old ones.'

I heard Lonnie Johnson singing 'Hard Times Ain't Gone Nowhere' and hoped it wasn't true. In the meantime, I had things to do.

Epilogue

On a fine day in early March we consigned Hector Dalrymple to the skies above Edinburgh. The smoke from the crematorium chimney was carried out over the Forth on the west wind. The old man would have liked that – his spirit would be hovering in the vicinity of the city. I kept his ashes, something the Council wouldn't have allowed, and I haven't yet decided what – if anything – to do with them. I appreciated that Lachie and Rory came to the service. They were busy setting up a government that would put citizens first, helped by Kate Revie and other high-ranking sympathizers. Many of my father's former colleagues and auxiliaries who remembered him from the early years of the Enlightenment came to pay their respects. Sophia, her arm in a sling, wanted to take Maisie away at the end but I insisted they stand next to me. I alone shook people's hands, but it was clear to all that we were a family.

There was a reception afterwards, at which Davie did his normal routine of eating and drinking too much, then leaving with a member of the other sex on his arm. Revolutions don't change everything.

Eventually, late in the afternoon, we went back to Sophia's residence. She'd been asked to stay on as chief medical officer, but it wasn't clear if she'd be keeping the house in Moray Place. Neither of us cared.

Soon it was Referendum Day. Many things had changed but the city's new leaders still supported a 'yes' vote. In terms of realpolitik, they were in a strong position, having in their possession the toxin paid for by the outsider states. Lachie made clear to Andrew Duart and the Lord of the Isles that the price of Edinburgh being part of a new Scotland was that the city have the means to defend itself. They didn't like it, I heard on the radio, but there wasn't much they could do. I wasn't keen on what had been known as mutually assured destruction when I was a kid, but it worked back then. Which was no guarantee that it would again.

Sophia and I went to vote at a centre that had been set up in Charlotte Square. The tented casino that was a feature for years had been closed down, the new government taking a hard line on gambling. Maisie tagged along as an unofficial exit poll. People were taken aback at first, then charmed by her ridiculously adult mien. It was obvious from early on that 'yes' votes were a huge majority. We walked back to Moray Place with Maisie swinging between us.

'O brave new city,' said Sophia.

'O brave new country,' I countered.

'That has such people in't,' said Maisie.

'Have you read all of Shakespeare?' I asked.

'Everything except *The Taming of the Shrew*,' she said. 'Its gender attitudes are insurmountable.'

Sophia and I exchanged glances and looked up at the cloudless sky.

It was after we'd finished tea that the bombshell was dropped.

'I've got something to tell the two of you,' Sophia said, with a soft smile.

'What now, Mother?' said Maisie. 'You aren't moving to a city that has better medical facilities?'

'There's a thought. But no.'

My heart was beating faster than was comfortable.

'Spit it out,' I said.

'Beautifully put. All right. I'm pregnant.'

There was silence, partly because I couldn't speak.

Maisie could, though. 'If it's a boy, can we call him Hector?'

I took Sophia's good hand and kissed it.

She felt my tears and smoothed them away.

'At last,' she said to her daughter. 'Something we agree on.'

I looked at the roughly cut wooden box on the kitchen floor. My father would never leave us, even if the child was a girl. Dalrymple and McIlvanney genes would live on. At a time of such change that was comforting.

'So,' I said, my voice unsteady. 'Where's the champagne?'

Maisie went off to root around in the cellar, with which she had a worrying familiarity – not that she ever sampled the goods.

'Are you happy about this?' Sophia said, leaning close.

'Happy? I'm over the castle, Arthur's Seat and the remains of the bridges.'

'Good. I love you, Quint.'

'Dearest darling, so do I.'

She hit me on the back of the hand with her teaspoon.

'That hurt.'

'Let me kiss it better.'

I did as I was told.